PRAISE FOR *Home Fires*

"Gene Wolfe delivers a strangely heartening dystopia."

—*The San Diego Union-Tribune*

"Elegant overall . . . There's a lot of pleasure in the way Wolfe paints his dystopia, offering up murky little snatches that cohere into an uneasily familiar world." —*Chicago Reader*

"Wolfe still has a few surprises up his sleeve, and *Home Fires* is one of them. . . . *Home Fires* is an adventure story, a love story, and the flip side of the standard 'going to the stars to fight aliens' story. The book is fast-paced and quite accessible, and shows that Gene Wolfe is as much at home writing adventure as he is writing epics." —*Analog*

"With complications involving spies, murderers, cyborgs, and pirates, Wolfe cross-examines his characters with a subtle, intelligent series of psychological and logical challenges. A somber, almost brooding tone permeates this compelling work from one of the genre's grandmasters."

—*Kirkus Reviews* (starred review)

"The action is interspersed with Skip's reflections on what's going on around him, and it's all rendered in a voice that might remind you of a more poignant Robert Heinlein from an alternate dimension. On one level, it's an adventure story and a romance—but this is Gene Wolfe, so expect it to set off some subtle but serious perturbations in your brain and soul, too." —*i09*

"[Readers] will be pleased by this latest display of all of the gifts of one of SF's authentic all-time masters, including original and balanced characterization, masterly world-building, and an ethical sensibility of the highest degree." —*Booklist*

"The purest SF novel from Wolfe in something like a decade . . . Amazingly, Wolfe's approach to SF themes that we thought we knew all about is as innovative and elegant as ever." —Gary K. Wolfe, *Locus*

"Wolfe excels at infusing seemingly everyday stories with a layer of complexity while never losing track of his characters' individual dramas. Part cyber-thriller, part love story, part SF adventure, Wolfe's latest novel should appeal to his many fans as well as to general readers."

—*Library Journal*

"*Home Fires* (A+/A++) is another winner for Gene Wolfe and mind-bending SF-without-gadgets/superscience at its best."

—*Fantasy Book Critic*

"Wolfe builds a romance and a mystery. . . . Red herrings and unknown, mistaken, or confused identities saturate the novel, making this well suited for readers, especially mystery readers, who don't often read science fiction."

—*Publishers Weekly*

"Gene Wolfe is the greatest living writer in the speculative field area. . . . His SF is always spot-on, and terribly, *terribly* engrossing. *Home Fires* promises the usual Wolfeisms—confusing identities, stories within stories, and weird romance. In a futuristic setting. What more can the heart desire?"

—*Roland's Codex*

"If every contemporary SF writer bar one were to be wiped out, it's a fair bet that Gene Wolfe would top many lists of who should be saved. . . . An essential addition to any SF library."

—*Interzone*

"*Home Fires* is a good read. . . . An impressive and interesting novel. It's worth a read, especially for those who like smart, subtle SF and are willing to pay close attention to what they are reading."

—*SF Revu*

"A terrific science fiction mystery . . . Red herrings abound in this exhilarating character-driven thriller."

—*The Midwest Book Review*

HOME FIRES

BY GENE WOLFE
FROM TOM DOHERTY ASSOCIATES

GENE WOLFE

HOME FIRES

A TOM DOHERTY ASSOCIATES BOOK   NEW YORK

TOR®

This is a work of fiction. All of the characters, organizations, and events portrayed in this novel are either products of the author's imagination or are used fictitiously.

HOME FIRES

A Tor Book
Published by Tom Doherty Associates, LLC
175 Fifth Avenue
New York, NY 10010

www.tor-forge.com

Tor® is a registered trademark of Tom Doherty Associates, LLC.

The Library of Congress has cataloged the hardcover edition as follows:

Wolfe, Gene.
    Home fires / Gene Wolfe.—1st ed.
        p. cm.
"A Tom Doherty Associates book."
ISBN 978-0-7653-2818-2
    1. Relativity (Physics)—Fiction. 2. Married people—Fiction. 3. Extraterrestrial beings—Fiction. 4. Human-alien encounters—Fiction. 5. Imaginary wars and battles—Fiction. I. Title.
    PS3573.O52 H66 2011
    813'.54—dc22

                                                                2010036106

ISBN 978-0-7653-2819-9 (trade paperback)

First Edition: January 2011
First Trade Paperback Edition: January 2012

Printed in the United States of America

0 9 8 7 6 5 4 3 2 1

Dedicated to my kind friend Nigel Price

ACKNOWLEDGMENTS

Here I should surely recognize the help provided, not only with this volume but with others, by David G. Hartwell and Stacy Hague-Hill of Tor Books and by Vaughne Lee Hansen and Christine Cohen of the Virginia Kidd Agency.

1

GREETINGS

"It won't be long," she promised.

"Not for you," Skip said. "A thousand years for me." Chelle smiled, and all heaven was in her smile.

Then he was looking down at his hands, and they were wrinkled and old. He stood before a mirror, but there was a mist between them that veiled his face from its own eyes. He raised his hand to push the mist away, knowing that his hand shook, knowing that horror waited beyond the mist.

He woke, sweating and trembling in his narrow bed, rose and went to the washbasin, poured water from the pitcher there into the bowl. The water smelled a little like sewage, but it felt cool and refreshing.

He soaked the cloth again, scrubbed his sweating face a second time. It was only a dream.

Only a dream.

In his dream he had gotten a yellow autoprint that had said she was back and he had been back too, back to the day she left. They had kissed . . .

That had been the dream. What had really happened?

He got a water bottle, filled his mug, and decanted this purer water into his teakettle. His striker lit the gas.

They had contracted. He remembered that, and it was no dream. Just before she had left, they had contracted. Together they had registered the contract. How romantic it had seemed!

"You'll have twenty years to devote to your career . . ." Chelle was lovely when she smiled. "We'll be rich when I get back, and you'll have a young contracta."

And he *was* rich, but she would (in all probability) never return to him. Now . . .

He looked at himself in the mirror, and saw that he needed to shave and that much of his stubble was white. His hair was gray at the temples, too, and through the doorway—what was that beside the screen?

Yellow paper, of course. He always used yellow for client copies. They were so frightened . . . He smiled to himself.

Always so frightened, though they tried (most of them) not to show it. Part of his job was to reassure them, and so there had been yellow paper in the printer.

Something seized him, and he stepped away from the mirror, trembling.

Five hundred. His watch, picked up from its place on the floor beneath his bed, read zero five zero six. His autocall would not come for more than an hour. He could go back to bed, go back to sleep.

He shuddered.

Shave. He would shave instead. Shave, clean up, get dressed, go out and get breakfast.

He went to the window. Magnificent! The view always inspired him. The window would not open, of course. Here, just below the penthouse, the wind would be savage.

Savage and cold.

For the first time it struck him that he could have it replaced with one that *would* open. He could have a floor-to-ceiling window that would open at the touch of a button. The cost would be trifling and tax-deductible. With a bit of creative accounting . . .

Trifling for him.

It would be foolish of course. No one would really want such a thing, and he would never do it. But he could.

Boswash, NAU, was waking. From horizon to horizon, lights sparked into being in the tiny windows of lofty structures that were, for the most part, less lofty than his.

That yellow page. The Weyer murder?

He shook his head.

Shaving occupied the next eight minutes. Preshave, shave, aftershave. Good! He had gotten everything done before the power began to flicker, although his shaver could be plugged into the backup if necessary.

He folded the yellow sheet without looking at it and slipped it into his jacket pocket. Breakfast first, he told himself. Business afterward.

And realized, almost with a start, that he had been lying to himself. He knew what was on the yellow paper.

No. He sipped fragrant tea. That had been the dream. His tea was supposed to smell like tea roses; the knowledge planted a garden in his mind: huge bushes with dark green foliage and cupped pink flowers. Or red. Or white. A fountain in the middle, one in which pure water flowed without letup. The subtropics. There would be places there with gardens like that.

Beyond another window, almost out of sight, wet and heavy snow was falling into the sea.

The penthouse had a private elevator that stopped for no other floor. He smiled to himself as he waited for wide bronze doors to slide back, remembering what the penthouse rented for. This elevator—his own elevator—served the upper fifty floors, but on this trip it would stop for none of them.

The street was cold and dark, as was to be expected. Filthy, too, like all streets, though the snow had arrived to cover its filth. Despite his firm rule against giving to beggars, he rubbed the hump of a pathetic hunchback and gave him five noras. There were only two others out so early. So early, in cold and falling snow. A flourish of his walking stick sent them scuttling back to their places.

A block and a half brought him to Carrera's. He sat, and waved a wait-ress over.

"The usual, Mr. Grison?"

He nodded, holding out the yellow paper. "I need a favor, Aleta. Will you read this to me? It's pretty short."

"Sure, Mr. Grison. Forget your glasses?"

"No. I've read it. I need to hear someone else read it." He nearly said, "I need to have it made real," but he did not.

"Okay." The waitress cleared her throat. "It says, 'Greetings. You have contracted with Mastergunner Chelle Sea Blue.' I didn't know you had contracted with anybody, Mr. Grison."

"The rest, please."

" 'In accordance with the law, you are hereby notified by Mustprint that Mastergunner Blue is being returned from outsystem. Mastergunner Blue will receive one year and forty-one days of accumulated leave after pro-cessing and debriefing.' Wow! She must have been gone quite a while."

Skip nodded. "By Earth-time she was."

" 'Mastergunner Blue is scheduled to arrive by shuttle at Canam Port day one-eighty.' " The waitress glanced at her watch. "That's this coming Saturday, Mr. Grison."

"Yes. It is. You don't have to read the rest."

"It says she may've been affected by her experiences—"

"I know what it says."

"And you'll have to make allowances for her." The waitress paused. When Skip did not speak, she said, "Would you like to see a menu?"

He was still smiling at her remark as he poured honey on his buck-wheat cakes. Yes, he would love to see a menu. Better yet, a psychological profile. . . .

Which might actually be possible.

It was oh seven thirty-five when he left Carrera's, and oh seven forty-seven when he entered the Union Day Building. The offices of Burton, Grison, and Ibarra were still empty and silent, lit by a single dim fixture.

Once seated in his office, he read headlines on his screen: ANOTHER SUI-CIDE RING UNCOVERED—NEW ENERGY CONTROLS—SHIPS SEIZED AS

CHAOS IN NORTHERN SAU WORSENS. The third made him grin; last week, the same news service had called the chaos total.

Still grinning, he posted a message to *All*: he would be gone for a week, and perhaps longer. If return by day one eighty-eight (or sooner) should prove impossible, he would notify them.

Next an order to Research: "Obtain psych. profile Mastergunner C. S. Blue; call me at once.—S.W.G."

After that, he assigned Mick Tooley to baby-sit the jewelry wholesaler case and the cyborg murder—the cases he had been handling personally. Tooley was to call him when necessary, but *only* when necessary.

What else?

Susan had tidied up his desk, and he had done little to disturb it. The wall safe yielded five thousand noras—more than sufficient, he decided, for emergencies requiring cash. A thousand for his wallet, and four thousand more for his briefcase.

From the doorway, Susan inquired, "Mr. Grison?"

He closed the safe.

"I just wanted to let you know I'm here if you need me. You beat me in this morning."

"I do. I was about to write you a note. I want a first-class compartment on a Bullet for Canam. Depart before twenty tonight."

"Yes, sir."

"I want a suite, one night, at the best hotel near the port. That's for the day after tomorrow."

"Yes, sir. Hypersuite?"

"If you can get one." He paused. "If you can't get a suite of any kind, then the best room you can get. Call me when you've got both, but not before. I'm leaving now. I want to get out before somebody ambushes me with something. Let Mick handle it, whatever it is."

"If there are several trains . . . ?"

"Nothing before noon—I've got to pack. The first one after that."

He was ready to go, but she whispered, "I'll miss you, Mr. Grison." Already feeling the pangs of treachery, he gave her a quick kiss.

Dianne, his secretary's assistant, greeted him with a bright smile and a cheerful hello as he left his office. Skip reflected that Susan would have work for her. As for him, he would have work for himself.

A doorman touched the bill of his cap. "Lester told me you were out early, Mr. Grison."

If he had made any reply at all, he had forgotten it by the time he reached his apartment.

ANSWERS might or might not be of help. He touched VOICE. "Gifts for returning servicewoman."

"Price?"

"Ten thousand and up."

"Age?"

Chelle's subjective age would have gone up by two years and what? A hundred-day or so. "Twenty-five."

"Designer dresses and suits, jewelry, small red car, total makeover."

"More."

"Cruise, private island, show horse . . ."

He telephoned Research. "Boris? What do returning servicewomen want most? Somebody must have done a survey, and there might be two or three. Let me know."

His gift met him at the station. "Are you Skip Grison?" Smile. "I'm Chelle's mother."

He studied her. She was shorter than Chelle and almost slender. Simply but stylishly dressed. "You're younger than I expected," he said.

She smiled again, a charming smile. "Thank you, Skip. You have my ticket?"

"Not yet. We can square it with the conductor."

"You'll be billed if I have to pay my own way. You understand that, I hope."

He nodded, trying to place her perfume. Apples in a garden? Sun-warmed apples? Something like that.

"There would be a surcharge of twenty percent."

"Certainly. I'll take care of it."

Another charming smile. "You look baffled, Skip."

"I am. I pride myself on my ability to think on my feet, and I was told to expect you. But I . . ."

"In a courtroom."

"Correct. I was going to say that even though I put in an order for you and knew you were coming, something about you took me by surprise. I need a moment to collect my thoughts. Where's your luggage?"

"A nice porter took it for me. I gave him the number of your compartment."

He raised his eyebrows. "You knew it?"

She nodded. "I found it out—it wasn't difficult. Thirty-two C."

"You're right," he said. And then, grateful for the opportunity to break off their conversation, "Let's go find it."

One side was Changeglass, switched off now for full transparency. His scuffed suitcases were on the lone chair, a red-fabric overnight bag on the lower bunk, a bed currently disguised as a couch. The door of the tiny private bath stood open; after a glance inside, Skip closed it. He stowed his briefcase under the lower bunk.

She was throwing switches. "Good reading lights," she said. "That makes all the difference."

He said, "It's only a day and a half."

"Thirty-four hours, if it's on schedule. So one day and ten hours, since these Bullet Trains always are."

"We need to talk." Removing his overnight bag, he took the chair.

"That's what I'm here for." She smiled, warm and friendly. "To talk with you and my darling Chelle."

"Can you play the part?"

"I don't play parts, Skip. Really, I don't." Now she attempted to look severe, but the smile kept getting in the way. "I am your Chelle's mother."

"You mean that she'll accept you, wholeheartedly, as her mother."

"She will, Skip, and she'll be right. You, thinking me a fraud, will be mistaken. Please try to understand. For thousands of years, we thought death the end, even though we knew of cases in which that had been untrue.

Until we could raise the dead ourselves, we refused to believe that death was not necessarily final."

Almost unnoticed, the train glided from the station.

"You call me Skip."

She smiled yet again. He felt that he should by now have come to detest that smile, but found that it enchanted him instead. "I do, Skip, and I shall continue to do so."

"Chelle calls you . . . ?"

"Mother." She sat down on the lower bunk.

"Then I'll call you Mother Blue."

Her eyes flashed. "Not without a quarrel. I have never used Charles's surname, and I most certainly don't intend to begin after going though a world of nonsense to terminate our contract. I am Vanessa Hennessey. You may call me that. Or Ms. Hennessey. Or Vanessa. But not Essy or Vanie or anything of that silly sort."

"Vanessa, then. I don't know where Chelle's mother is buried, but it should be easy to find out. Suppose that I do, and that I take Chelle there and show her the grave—her real mother's grave. What would you do then?"

Vanessa laughed. "Why should I do anything? Why should my daughter do anything, for that matter? I was dead, and now I'm alive. Pay close attention, Skip. You haven't been thinking."

"I'm listening," he said.

"Are you? We'll find out eventually. Every brain scan I ever had—and there were a good many of them—has been uploaded into the brain of a living woman whose own brain was scanned and wiped clean. Once it had been done, that living woman became me, the woman sitting across from you now."

"Ms. Vanessa Hennessey."

"Exactly. I'm so glad you understand."

This time it was he who smiled. "Who is legally dead."

"An error that could be corrected by any competent attorney. Surely you know that a person missing for seven years can be declared legally dead. You must also know that those people sometimes turn up, after which the record is set straight."

"I paid a small fortune to have you resurrected."

"A very small one. Yes."

He wanted to pace, as he had so often in court. "Thus it's against my interest not to accept you myself."

The delightful smile. "I'm glad you understand."

"Thus I shall venture one more question, and no more. None after this. Currently, I am paying the company by the hundred-day. I paid for the first in advance."

She nodded. "That's standard."

"Suppose I stop paying?"

She laughed. "As you will, eventually. I understand that. Let's say *when* you stop paying. We both know that you will. I'll be returned to Reanimation. My brain will be scanned and wiped, and the earlier scan uploaded."

"You'll be dead."

"I will. But I will die secure in the knowledge that death is not final— that if ever I'm wanted enough, I can be recalled to existence." Smiling, she turned to look at the factory buildings and city streets they passed. "I'd heard that these things were wonderfully fast, Skip. But hearing it and seeing it . . . How fast can it go?"

"Sixty-seven kilometers an hour. Or so they say. That's almost twice as fast as the fastest motor vehicles, so I wouldn't be surprised if they were stretching the facts a little."

"Marvelous!"

"It is. We're riding on a thin film of air, which is what makes the energy expenditure feasible. These cars are very light, of course. They say four men can lift one."

She laughed and clapped like a delighted child. "I'd love to see that done. To really see it, I mean, with my own eyes. They do all sorts of tricks on tele."

Later, in the dining car, she said, "You haven't asked me about Chelle. Not one thing. I've been waiting for it, Skip, but it hasn't happened. Want to tell me why?"

He shook his head.

"She divorced me, you're quite correct. She divorced her father, too, after she enlisted. Were you aware of that?"

"No." He studied the menu before touching several items.

"It doesn't mean she doesn't love me, and it certainly doesn't mean I don't love her. If you thought she didn't love me, why did you spend so much to bring me back?"

"I hope she'll like having you again. I wanted to get her something that would delight her, and you were the only gift I could find that seemed to have much chance." He hesitated. "I wanted to get you a separate compartment, a nice one near mine. We were too late with that, the train was full."

"We?"

"Susan. Susan's my secretary. She takes care of things like that for me. I asked if you'd mind sharing a compartment with me. They said they'd tell you that you had to."

"They did. I made no objection."

"Aren't you going to order?"

"I suppose. What's the green button?" The slight smile that twitched her lips made him suspect that she already knew.

"It means that you're ordering what the previous diner at the table ordered. Women—young girls for the most part—often want to do that. I don't know why."

"But you know about them."

"Yes, I do."

"I won't pry, Skip." The smile appeared in earnest. "Not now, because I know I wouldn't find out anything. Later, possibly. Some girls are terrified of ordering anything too costly. I was never one of those, but I knew some like that."

He nodded.

"Others are afraid they'll order something they don't know how to eat. Lobster or pigs' trotters, a dish that takes finesse. If they order what the man orders, he can't object to the price, and they can see how he eats it."

"So you ordered what I ordered, without knowing what it was."

"It seemed simpler like that. Either I'm not hungry at all, or I'm so hungry

I'll eat anything. I'll know when the food comes. Wouldn't you think they'd have a waiter to take our order? He could answer our questions then."

Skip nodded absently. "They do that in second class."

It evoked a throaty chuckle. "We privileged few needn't worry about keeping the proles employed. Perhaps that's what's wrong with the system."

"It may be."

"I was a wealthy woman, Skip."

He nodded.

"I've almost nothing now. Just a few noras that a woman gave me before she let me out at the station. I'm going to need more."

"You want more. I anticipated that."

"May I have it?"

"Not now. I have to have some way to control you."

"Surely there are others."

"There are, but I like this one."

She laughed. "You're rather too much fun to cross blades with. I could cut Charles to pieces in two minutes—it was part of the reason I opted out. Would you like to stay in our compartment while I shower and get ready for bed?"

He shook his head.

"No? I was hoping you would. I was going to charge you for it."

"No. I'll wait in the bar car."

A waiter arrived, trailed by an assistant who carried an identical meal. "Questions?" The waiter looked from one to the other. "Additional needs? Monsieur? Madame?"

"I've a thousand," Vanessa told him, "but you can't supply any of them."

As Skip sat in the bar car sipping Chablis-and-soda, the barmaid's assistant's helper muttered, "I wouldn't call you an enthusiastic drinker, sir."

"I'm not," Skip told her. "I'm just waiting for the dead woman in my compartment to go to bed."

REFLECTION 1

The Journey

We sleep, and believe we wake with the minds we carried into bed with us, bearing them as a bride borne in her groom's arms, the lifted, the treasured, the threshold flier; so we believe.

But we do not. That weary mind has been dispersed in sleep, its myriad parts left behind on the tracks, lying upon the infinite concrete ties between endless, gleaming steel rails.

We wake, and compose for ourselves a new mind (if some other does not compose it for us), a mind compounded of such parts of the old one as we can discover, and of dreams, and of odd snatches of memory—something read long, long ago, possibly something sprung into thought from a tele listing, the skewed description of a better presentation, the show as it existed in Platonic space. From such trifles as these and more we construct a new mind and call it our own.

And yet the personhood, the soul remains. A roommate I had one year woke each morning as a beast, woke roaring, shouting, and fighting. Fighting air, for the most part, for I soon learned to absent myself before his autocall, or to jump back if circumstance forced me to wake him myself; there is such a beast in all of us—no, several such beasts.

Chelle told me once that she woke each morning as a child, though strictly speaking it was untrue. It was most often true, I think, when she

had been drinking and she was awakened an hour or two later, still somewhat drunk. She was small and guilty then, weeping for misbehavior she
knew not of, a child like so many accustomed to being blamed and punished, quite often severely, for an act done or a word spoken in purest in-
nocence. Thus I, who had met her at the university, came to know the child
she had once been, and in truth to love and dread that child.

For me, on the morning of the yellow notice, things were otherwise—or
perhaps the same: I thought myself young and thought Chelle with me in bed,
or (when at last I accepted her absence from our bed) in the lavatory. She
had reentered my life, and so my hungry brain embraced and swallowed her,
gulping down Chelle whole, Chelle here and now. And since she *was* here, *was*
now, I myself must be twenty-seven. Twenty-seven and awakening in the
studio apartment I shared with Chelle before she enlisted and shared with her
afterward only when she got leave. All this when the present Chelle, my new
Chelle, was nothing more than a single sheet of yellow paper fallen from my
printer.

Then I knew myself old; and for a moment, only for a moment, before I
pushed back sheet and blankets, I thought I heard the light steps of Susan's
departure. She would leave me now, I thought, leave me to sleep and
go down to her three rooms to wash and eat and dress and prepare for the
day's work. I had heard her, I thought; yet the door had neither opened nor
closed.

I rose, and knew that I had not known the pleasure of her company during the night and had not wanted it. We are never quite so alone as we are
in the company of others; a paradox, but a paradox in a world so filled with
them that one more can make no difference—or only a small and trifling
difference, though that difference may mean the world to some unfortu-
nate individual.

As this one to me. I live by defending others from a law that is grown
monstrous, devoid not only of justice but of the very thought and ideal of
justice. I defend others, yet no one is more alone than I. In centuries long
past, the accused was defended by a champion, a knight (paid, unless the
accused was of the highest rank) who engaged the accuser's champion in the
court of justice, confident that God would defend the right. The time-wind

rises, the mist disperses, and we see that nothing has changed. I have my squire and my pages, my body servants and men-at-arms, now called secretaries, clerks, researchers, and detectives; figuratively it might be said that I ride into court with Susan's scarf bound about my helm. Yet who is more alone than I?

May God defend the right!

I look out over the city like an eagle from a spire of rock, and it is not my kingdom but my hunting ground. Nor am I the only hunter; others hunt there, and some may hunt me. The common man, so celebrated a century ago by those who were even then plotting to bring him down, has in this age been driven to the wall. Every elective office is held for life, and those who hold those offices may rule by whim if it be their whim to rule so. Hated, they glory in it, and know not how weak they are.

I know how weak I am, or I think I do; my imitation Vanessa does not, or so I believe, but she surely knows how weak she herself is, and she is far weaker than I, weaker than Susan, and no doubt far weaker than her daughter, the strapping lacrosse player, the glory of the women's track team. It is not Vanessa's weakness that attracts me, for I, possessing a superabundance of weakness myself, am never attracted to it; rather it is her defiance of her weakness, for there is no human quality more attractive than the courage of the weak.

Even in a dead woman.

2

WHEN JANIE COMES MARCHING HOME

The sky seemed oddly threatening. Patches of clearest blue separated cloud towers the color of city faces. Like all the rest, Skip studied the sky and watched for the shuttle, buffeted by the crowd and striving to shelter Vanessa from similar shoving and elbowing. "I thought they'd be about my age," he whispered. "I wasn't ready for these kids."

"They are waiting for their fathers and mothers, for parents they've been told about but can't remember." She seemed cool and collected, small and splendid in the black wool coat he had bought her and a black pillbox hat whose scarlet feather matched her earrings.

"There are some as old as we are." It sounded more defensive than he had intended.

"Some. Not many."

Then there were cheers, and the young man on Skip's right pointed and shouted. Very far away, a shining dot had emerged from one of the gray-faced clouds. The crowd surged against the fence, which bowed but held. Military Police—big men with polished white helmets above tired, brutal faces—were clearing a path with white batons, shoving people aside and whacking the shoulders of those who refused to move.

Half a dozen uniformed women unrolled a red carpet; somewhere nearby a band struck up "El Continente de los Héroes."

"Catchy, isn't it?" Vanessa whispered.

There seemed to be no point in answering her, and Skip did not. To the north, the shining dot had sprouted stubby wings.

"It looks too small to hold many people." Vanessa was shading her eyes with her hand and squinting; there were tiny lines at the corners of her eyes.

Skip said, "I think it must be the size of a bus."

It was far larger, swooping down toward the end of a runway as long as many highways, a runway so long that its end was well beyond their sight. The thunder of rockets—just the little braking rockets, Skip reminded himself—was like a storm at sea.

"Her name," he said.

Vanessa turned to him quizzically.

"Chelle Sea Blue. Her eyes are as blue as the sea down around Tobago."

Perhaps Vanessa replied; if so, Skip did not hear her. He was watching the shuttle bringing Chelle. It looked as large as a ship without masts—a ship in drydock, with no part hidden by the sea. Stopping, it turned and rolled toward them, moving slowly and ponderously on landing gear with so many wheels that Skip, who often counted things by reflex, lost count of them—huge rubber wheels, some of which (and perhaps all of which) were clearly powered.

A man standing behind him said, "Imagine how big the mother ship is!"

Skip nodded, though he knew he had not been addressed.

A stunned silence had settled over the crowd; the band was heard distinctly once more, a band that seemed much too small for the occasion, a little band of children welcoming a stainless-steel archangel. "The Union Anthem" had always sounded as though it had been composed by a machine, but never more than now.

A silver gangplank unrolled from an airlock a hundred feet in the air, a gangplank that stiffened as it came and brought its own spidery railing of slender posts and still more slender black cords.

Someone shouted, "Here they come!" But they did not come.

Vanessa was sniffling. After a moment, Skip gave her his handkerchief, a man's handkerchief, white with a dark gray border, a handkerchief so large that it might easily have been knotted about her slender throat like a bandana. "My baby!" It was gasped, not said. "My baby!"

He put his arm around her shoulders.

"I only had one. I never wanted more. But . . . But . . ."

"I understand."

An officer with a bullhorn had appeared, tiny at the top of the gangplank. ". . . WHO TOUCHES ANY SOLDIER WILL BE TAKEN INTO CUSTODY. ANYONE WHO BREAKS THE MILITARY POLICE LINES WILL LIKEWISE BE TAKEN INTO CUSTODY."

The crowd growled in response, one vast beast with a thousand savage heads.

The officer disappeared into the shuttle. For thirty seconds, a minute, two minutes and more, nothing happened.

The band struck up a march, a bass drum thumping the cadence while two trap drums pranced around it, the whole punctuated by trumpets that for once sounded like trumpets on a battlefield.

And they came, a single file of women and men in blue garrison caps and dress cloaks, booted feet drumming the long silver gangplank and arms swinging. Someone shouted, "Oh, don't they look fine!"

In reply Vanessa whispered, "They don't tell anyone when the dead and wounded come back."

The first marching soldier stepped off the end of the gangplank, and the crowd surged toward her—toward her and toward those who came behind her. The white-helmeted MPs shouted. Their white batons rose briefly above the heads of the crowd and fell upon them.

More soldiers came, and more, an endless stream; and the crowd parted for white-helmeted MPs dragging a gray-haired woman in handcuffs.

"There she is!" Vanessa was shouting and pointing. "Chelle! Chelle, darling! Over here!"

With Vanessa in his wake, Skip fought through the crowd and pushed past a white-helmeted MP to seize Chelle and kiss her. The shock of a white baton on his shoulder was less painful than Chelle's startled stare. Goaded to savagery by pain and stare, Skip whirled, grabbed the coat of the MP who had struck him, butted him in the face, kneed him in the groin, and let him fall.

When he turned again, Chelle was gone, the crowd was rioting, and soldiers were no longer marching out of the ship. Grinning as she was forced tightly against him by the rioters, Vanessa asked, "Where the devil did you learn that?"

"Law school," he told her.

He had nearly unpacked when Vanessa knocked at the door of his hotel room. "I can't speak for you, Skip, but I'm starved. There's nothing like stoning the police to give one an appetite." She sniffed. "You still have that dreadful gas on your clothing. You must change—shower and change."

"I will," he said, and returned to his shirts.

"You brought so many clothes!"

He nodded absently.

"I brought everything I have, but it isn't much." When he said nothing, Vanessa added, "That's a hint."

"I thought so."

"Two dresses and a pants suit. A few cosmetics. I ask you."

"Ample. Now get out of here. I have to change, as you suggested. I have to shower. I'll get you when I'm ready to eat."

Vanessa leveled a long, crimson-tipped finger. "I am starving, I've scarcely a nora, and I'm not leaving 'til I am fed. If you try to throw me out bodily, I'll scream my glamorous little head off. I bite, too."

"I'm going to strip—"

"Shut up! Do you think I've never seen a naked man?"

"Keep your voice down."

"One must shout at idiots when kindness doesn't work. You have a robe, I see it in your closet. Take your robe and go into the bathroom. Take off those clothes and have a nice shower. Put on the robe and I will bring you fresh clothes piece by piece. Why did you bring so much anyway?"

Skip sat down on the bed. "Chelle has a year's leave coming. I was hoping—I don't know that it will happen—that we could go off together right away."

"The EU?"

His shoulders rose and fell. "Wherever she wanted. Paris or Antarctica or around the world."

"Without me."

"Correct."

"You will stop paying, and I will die again. Is that right?"

"Only if you turn yourself in."

"I'll be broke and friendless. Starving on the streets, and they'll be counting on that."

He sighed. "I specialize in criminal law, Vanessa. Maybe you knew that."

"It must be interesting. Serial killers, hijackers, burglars, and counterfeiters. The woman who drove me to the station told me."

"Then let me tell you something. Nearly everything is against the law on this continent. Cockfighting. Using a few watts over your energy allotment. Signing with someone too young to contract. Picking your nose in a public park. On and on and on. As a result there are at least seventy million fugitives, and there could be more. Nobody really knows."

"Most of whom nobody gives a hoot about."

He sighed. "You're right."

"Reanimation would care a great deal about me. More than enough to offer a reward. Enough to have its private security run me down, a friendless woman without money."

The telephone on Skip's nightstand caroled; the screen lit to show Chelle's anxious face.

While they waited for a room-service dinner, Skip said, "If they won't let anybody off base, what are you doing here?"

Chelle grinned. "I hopped over the fence. Went AWOL. Bad, bad Chelle!"

"Won't you be punished?"

She shook her head. "I could be—court-martialed and reduced in grade. All that shit. I won't be. There are too many of us, and we're just back from the smokehouse and in line for uppity-ump awards and citations. I'll go back tomorrow morning, get a chewing-out and a lecture, and keep processing. I'm going to sleep here, right? With you?"

Skip nodded. "I certainly hope so."

"But you deserted to see me," Vanessa protested. "You didn't even know who Skip was."

"Yeah." Chelle paused, looking from one to the other. "Except that I didn't desert. I went away without leave. You don't desert unless you put on civvies, and you have to have been missing for more than a week."

She yawned and smiled at Skip. "Hey, listen to me—I've turned into a guardhouse lawyer. You probably know all this already."

He shook his head. "Military law's a different field. I should have boned up on it while you were away. I'll do it, now that you've come back."

Vanessa said, "You're getting out, aren't you, Chelle? Getting a discharge?"

"No, sir! Not 'til I use up my paid leave."

Their food arrived, and Skip signed for it.

"I've got a ton of pay coming, too," Chelle remarked as the waiter left. "How long was I gone?"

"Twenty-two years, one hundred and six days." Skip cleared his throat. "I didn't count the hours. I was . . ."

"Speechless, Counselor?"

"Looking for the best word. Devastated. Knocked off my feet. Half dead. *Veritas nihil veretur nisi abscondi.* None of those I've found are quite right, and I'm still groping for it."

Chelle uncovered her plate. "This smells heavenly. Army food's not really as bad as everybody thinks, but I'm starved and this is going to be better. So I'm going to ask questions now, and you two are going to have to answer while I liberate the best chow." Abruptly her voice grew serious. "This one's driving me nuts. Why don't you look old, Mom?"

Vanessa snapped, "Please don't call me that. You know I hate it."

"Last time, I swear. Why don't you?"

"I've been away."

"In space? Sure! You had to be." Chelle's strong, white teeth tore the breast of a chicken.

"I shall not say more, darling."

Through the chicken, Chelle managed, "Where's Charlie?"

"I neither know nor care. I voided our contract—unilaterally, which is quite difficult. It was after you divorced us, thus you were not notified."

"Uh huh."

"Charles grew boring as he aged. Perhaps Skip has as well. You'll have to tell me."

"I haven't *grown* boring," Skip declared, "because I was boring already. Chelle found me restful after combat training."

"Atter lif wi' you." Chelle swallowed. "You're a breakdown trying to happen to somebody else, Mother dear."

"Why, Chelle! That's the nicest thing you've ever said to me."

"Absence makes the heart horny, or whatever it is. Why won't— I've got it! You were a spy! I'll bet you were good at it, too."

Skip said, "I can't imagine how a human being could spy on the Os."

"Electronically." Chelle was mining her baked potato.

"We spy on the EU, and they upon us," Vanessa told him. "Everybody spies on Greater Eastasia."

"I know, but it doesn't involve interstellar travel."

Chelle said, "Right. We're all allies together out there, arm in arm as we march through thick and thin and all that shit. One of the best noncoms we had turned out to be an EU spy, Master Sergeant Pununto. I killed him. Do you know that as soon as I finish my dinner—yours, too—I'm going to rape you? I just decided on it. Anybody want wine?"

Vanessa held out her glass, and Chelle poured. "While he was in that goddamned bathroom getting dressed I damned near broke down the door. What kind of underwear does he wear?"

Before Vanessa could reply, Skip said, "Not relevant."

"I'll find out. Probably those cool silk loincloths—they're big right now."

"Chelle, really!"

"Now listen up, Skip, 'cause this is serious. I could be stuck here for weeks. I don't know, but I could be." She took a pencil and a small notebook from a pocket of her uniform. "I'm going to give you my service number, and the number of the base commander's office. Phone tomorrow and ask where I am—what part of the processing. They'll say they can't find out without my number. It's a damned lie, but give it to them and ask when I'm getting out. That's important. They might tell you, but they won't tell me. Go all legal on them and you'll probably get it."

Skip said, "I understand. What I don't understand is why they may hold on to you for weeks."

"They think we're crazy, that combat's shoved us over the edge." Chelle fluffed her blond curls. "Those pricks call themselves soldiers, but there's not a fucking one of them—"

"Chelle!"

"Not a fucking one of them who's been shot at. I've put 'Base' beside the base number. The one with 'Chelle' is my phone. When you've got the info, call up and tell me. We can take it from there."

Vanessa said, "Choose the world cruise, Chelle. He wants to decamp with you, and there's nothing like a world cruise. Get a first-class stateroom. Veranda and sauna."

Chelle raised an eyebrow. "Do you really have that kind of money now, Skip?"

"For you, yes. We're not rich, you understand, but we're not badly off. May I ask a few questions? There's something I want very much to find out."

"Fire when ready." She laid aside her pencil and notebook.

"You didn't recognize me when you saw me in the crowd. You recognized your mother immediately, but not me."

"Right. She looks the same way she did when I left, or just about. You're older. It took me a while tonight to see you through the changes."

"Yet you called this room."

"Oh, that. Simple. I started calling hotels asking for Mother. This was the second one, and they said she was registered, but—"

"As I was," Vanessa confirmed, "and as I am. Vanessa Hennessey. I have my own room."

"I didn't think you two were sleeping together. But you weren't in there. Want the rest of it?"

Vanessa nodded.

"There was the man who kissed me. I didn't think that was Skip—I thought it was probably a mistake. Skip might be here just the same, so while I had this hotel I asked if Skip Grison was there. They said he was and connected me. Are you through eating, Mother?"

"Yes, I am. I'm a light eater, darling. Surely you remember." Vanessa turned to Skip. "I want to thank you for a very pleasant dinner. By the way, Chelle darling, we did sleep together. It was on the train coming up."

"No shit?" Chelle looked startled.

"We shared a compartment," Skip explained. "We had to, because the train was full by the time Vanessa tried to book. We did not do what Vanessa implied."

She smiled prettily. "I suggested it, but he said my berth was too small. To spare my feelings, I'm sure. Most men relish a tight berth."

"I believe him," Chelle said. "There's no way I could ever believe you, Mother dear. Not about anything."

"Never credit men about sex," Vanessa told her. "To hear your father talk . . . Well, they cannot be believed, and I ought to have taught you that."

"The Army did. Since you've finished your food, how about going back to your room?"

"How rude you are!"

Absently at first, then with fascination, Skip noticed that Chelle's left hand held her pencil and was writing in her notebook with it.

"I remember you," Chelle told Vanessa. "I know you forward and backward, and you haven't changed a hair. I need to get to know Skip all over again."

"I'm sure it will be fascinating exploration for you both—provided that one of you has brought the requisite medications."

"We're still contracted, aren't we, Skip?" For a moment Chelle looked stricken. "You wouldn't be here if you'd backed out some way."

He nodded. "You're not sorry?"

"Hell, no! Want to check that for yourself?"

"Yes. As soon as possible."

"Then please tell my dear momma to get the fuck out of our room."

Vanessa rose. "You won't forget my predicament, will you, Skip?"

He shook his head.

When she had gone, Chelle said, "So Mother's got a problem, or says she does. Want to tell me about it?"

"No. Ethically, I can't. But even if I could, I would prefer not to."

"Why's that?"

"Because I'd be betraying someone I enlisted to help me, that's all. If she wants to tell you, fine. But she's asked my assistance, and I like to think I'm an honest man and not just an honest lawyer."

Chelle had a charming grin; he wondered whether she knew it. "Lawyers are all crooks. Ask anybody."

"Right. And all soldiers are thugs. May I kiss a thug? Again?"

Her nod seemed strangely shy.

When they parted she said, "We've a lot of catching up to do. Are you good at cross-examination?"

"I am. Very."

"Just like that?" She smiled.

"Let me enlarge on it. I've made a lot of mistakes in cross-examination, and I know it. But when I listen to others trying to do it, I understand why so many tell me I'm good."

"Then I'm not going to let you ask me questions. I won't ask you any either. You answered the big question I had when you came here." Chelle sat down on the bed.

He sat beside her. "You answered mine when you asked the hotel about me when you couldn't find your mother."

"Thanks. She's changed somehow. You probably don't remember how she used to be."

"Did I . . . ?" He paused. "Yes, I saw her once. We ran into her in some restaurant."

"Simone's. You saw her twice. At least twice. The other time was when she went on base and tried to get the Army to turn me loose. We were in the Enlisted Personnel Club watching a couple of my friends play Ping-Pong."

"Yes, I remember."

"Mother'd gotten through to the base commander—she knows politicians—and he asked me to come to his office and explain that I didn't want a discharge. You came with me."

"You're right. She was vehement."

"She threw a fit. She's good at it." Chelle paused. "I expected her to throw one when I told her to leave, but she didn't. Was that because she's so worried about her problem?"

"That's a question."

"Yeah, I guess it is. Can I take it back, Counselor?"

"Certainly. You may withdraw it without prejudice if you so choose."

"Then I do."

"That's good." His arm found her waist. "Because I didn't know the answer."

"She's changed. That's not a question. It's fact."

"If you say so, I'll accept it. I'm sure I never saw her after you left."

"I'm glad you're not wearing a tie."

"In that case, I'm glad I'm not."

She toyed with one of his shirt buttons. "I'll bet you'd like to undress me."

"You'd win."

"And I'd like to undress you, but . . . Those earrings. Maybe you noticed Mother's earrings."

He shrugged. "I thought them pretty."

"They are. But they're just red feathers. No stones. Her dress looks nice on her because she's still got a good figure and knows how to wear clothes, but I looked it over pretty carefully, and it's off-the-rack. She's poor now."

He nodded.

"You said the compartments were gone when she tried to book. On the train."

"I did. Yes."

"Okay. I don't think she was going to pay for a compartment. You got her to come, and I think you were going to pay for it. You're probably tired of talking about her. Undressing is better."

He smiled. "More interesting, certainly."

"You know, I'm glad you said that." Chelle's hand tightened on his. "It makes it a little easier to say what I've been too chicken to say. You'd like us to undress right now. You'd like to go to bed, and so would I. I've been— well, you know."

"There's something you feel you ought to tell me first."

"Yeah, and ask a favor, too. Asking a favor isn't a question. Doesn't count."

"Correct."

"Please don't get all upset, Skip."

"I won't."

"Just like that? Try hard not to."

"I won't get upset. You have my word."

"Here's the favor. I'd like us to undress each other with the lights out."

He rose. "I understand." A switch near the door extinguished every light in the room.

Her voice reached him through the darkness. "I don't think you do. I don't see how you could."

"You're a young woman. Biologically, you're twenty-five. I am a middle-aged man. Biologically and in every other way I'm forty-nine. I'm not overweight—but I'm not twenty-seven, either."

"That isn't it at all. Will you please sit back down? I want you to kiss me, and I want you to call me Seashell, the way you used to."

It should have been funny, but he felt his eyes fill with tears.

"Here it is. I was blown all to hell, Skip. The doctors put me back together as well as they could, but there are scars."

Unable to speak, he nodded. His hand had found her shoulder in the dark; bowing before her, he kissed her.

"I took my own shirt off. I guess you found that out when you put your arms around me."

It was difficult, but he said, "I did, Seashell."

"Want to do the rest for me? If you don't, just say so and I'll go."

. . .

Much later, while she was in the bathroom doing the things that women did at such a time, he thought back on all that he had heard and seen that evening.

The line of light beneath the bathroom door vanished with a click. He heard the door open and her soft barefoot step before she said, "Your turn."

He rose. As he passed the table at which the three of them had eaten, he picked up the little notebook beside her plate. In the bathroom he read:

Mastergunner Chelle Sea Blue.
Sv #66797-9053-0169101
Base telephone 8897 4434-83622
Chelle 7990 7374-17840
I am Jane Sims   Jane Sims   I am Jane Sims

REFLECTION 2

———————— ❧ ————————

Seashell

"God is love."

"Love is blind."

If these be true, then God is blind: simple logic that would appear to have escaped the theologians. *Res ipsa loquitur*, love is not blind, neither God's love nor man's, though we all wish at times to escape God's eye, and though it must at times appear that the lover cannot see what we see—unless, of course, we ourselves are that lover.

Like God, the lover sees but forgives. Chelle is hard and violent, but that is scarcely a fault; she could never have returned to me if she had not been both. She is self-centered; how could a woman so tall, so strong, and so lovely not be? She seems blind to my faults, but without that blindness I could not have had her love; I am a mass of faults, held together as it were by a little skin and the law, *mortalium rerum misera beatitudo*.

These arms—my arms—held her. That is the sole great and significant point, the pivotal thing and the unforgettable thing. We had made love: I clumsily and without spontaneity, she a tigress and a nymph. (Indeed, I ought to have been Zeus, since none but Zeus could have matched her.) Nothing that we did in bed, nothing that we could ever do there, could match that first embrace, when I held her in my arms beneath an overcast sky, with the cold wind whipping dust from between a thousand parked cars and the crowd jostling us without courtesy, mercy, or effect.

The Army thinks her mad and so do I, a woman so young and fine cleaving to a balding middle-aged lawyer? Yes, Chelle is mad, and I am mad to love so much something that I cannot, finally, possess—as mad as an astronomer who loves the stars. Bedlamites wandered naked once, begging, with traces of the straw they slept in still in their hair, or so we read, those few of us who still read anything at all. Did they love at times, the naked madman and the naked madwoman? Surely. Oh, surely. Chelle and I were naked, Caliban and Miranda, and how we loved! Let the Army think her mad and let her go with me. The Army itself is mad, as are all bureaucracies.

And yet Chelle loves it.

The resurrected Vanessa is sane, and as a sane woman must surely see that I see through her every stratagem, though she does not desist from them and in fact doubles and redoubles her efforts. How can I resist her? I have had brain scans, too; will I not find myself in similar straits at some far-off date, a resurrected defense lawyer restored to life's shallow shadow to defend the indefensible? Then how I shall struggle to prolong the case! Struggle, knowing that I will live no longer than the cause I champion in that future court. "Ladies, gentlemen, visiting Os, and self-aware mechanisms of the jury, surely you realize that your verdict, whenever you may reach it, must . . ."

Jarndyce and Jarndyce.

Who is Jane Sims? Well, quite obviously, Chelle is. Multiple personality disorder is by no means unknown, though I would think it must be uncommon. Can it be cured? If so, how? I should ask Boris.

What if I wake beside Jane Sims? What will she be like, and what will I be like in her company? How long will she persist, and what will she want to do? Want me to do?

So many questions.

Where's Charlie? We did the show in high school and had a most wonderful time pretending to be English and Victorian, inserting lovely little digs at the EU. Now I find the question with me still.

Where is Charlie? Chelle and Vanessa hardly speak of him. Hey, kids! One of our cast is missing.

He visited Chelle when we were in college, as to the best of my knowledge her mother never did—a tall blond man who had run to fat. He wore sunglasses indoors and out; when I asked him about it, he told me quite frankly that he did it so others couldn't tell what he was looking at.

That frankness is the quality I remember best. Women delight (or so they say) in men who are brave and strong, yet vulnerable—in men who will feel the lash, in other words. Charles C. Blue, I feel quite certain, would never feel any woman's lash.

Once, in an old stone restaurant not far from the campus, we talked about firings; and now, when I have to fire someone I can sense the ivy on the walls outside and feel that if I were to look down hard enough at the surface of my desk I would see the clams casino that Chelle's father insisted upon ordering as an appetizer.

He had spoken casually of firing his secretary. I said that it must have been a trying interview, and he laughed. "I said you've been doing a lousy job for the past year so clean out your desk, and she started bawling. I told her to shut the hell up or I'd say she stole office supplies. Which she did, by the way. I told her I wanted her out in an hour, and she almost made it."

Chelle said, "Charlie!"

"Look, honey. She could have done a good job if she'd wanted to. She'll be two or three years on unemployment, and when she finally gets a job she'll try to hang on to it." Charlie laughed again. "I'd phoned NEO, so she had to fight her way through the applicants. Don't you think she loved that?"

"She thought you'd never fire her."

"Because I'd been balling her? It was grow-up time, honey."

I would never fire Susan. Nor will she ever give me reason to. There never was a better secretary, nor a more loyal one; although she believes that Dianne will replace her (as Dianne herself believes) Susan will remain with me for as long as I practice my profession.

"I got a secretary and two assistants for as much as I'd been paying Marcia," Chelle's father told us. "They know what happened to her, so they won't sit around doing their nails and wondering about a five-letter word for jaguar."

3

GETTING AWAY

The executive smiled the smile of a gambler who knows that he can only win. "I told you I'd give you fifteen minutes, Mr. Grison. You've used only six. I'll try to be equally concise."

Skip waited.

"You say that Vanessa Hennessey is a human being, and that reverting her will result in her death. For that death you threaten Reanimation with the law, both criminal and civil. We can prove by public records that Vanessa Hennessey died some years ago. Fingerprints and retinal patterns will prove that the woman to whom you refer is in fact an employee of ours, and not Vanessa Hennessey. Let me add that I have no intention of divulging our employee's identity to you here. It will be divulged in court—if necessary. Comment?"

"None at this time."

"Good." The executive offered Skip a cigar, which he declined. "Mr. Grison, you're in an odd position. I won't say an unethical one, but it's pretty odd. You're Vanessa Hennessey's sponsor as well as her attorney. Pro bono?"

Skip nodded.

"Odd, to say the least." The executive rolled his cigar between his palms. "If you succeed, you'll be saving your own money."

"I would also be freeing Ms. Hennessey. As things stand I can stop pay-ing. That would be tantamount to a death sentence, so I hold the power of life and death over her. I don't want it."

"You signed a contract with us. I assume you read it thoroughly. An attorney would."

Skip nodded.

"In that case . . . ," the executive studied his cigar, "you may have no-ticed that although we have no right to increase the payments agreed upon, we have the right to refuse your payment and reclaim our employee." He sighed. "That, you see, is what we do in such cases as this. Your most re-cent payment has been refused, Mr. Grison. Check your account, and you'll find that your money has returned to it."

"I was afraid of this."

"You should've been more afraid of it." The executive closed large, yel-low teeth upon his cigar and lit it with a gold Florentine lighter.

"My client will not willingly come back to you."

"Here we differ, Mr. Grison. Our security people will contact her, and she'll come. They're very persuasive."

Skip stood up. "You asked for my comments, which I withheld. I'll offer them now. You're not an attorney, Mr. Feuer. I'm certain your company must have some on retainer, and I suggest you consult them. Your case is much weaker than you suppose."

"You are about to rush out to warn your client." The executive's gentle smile was worse than a smirk. "You'll be too late, and the case you boast will be moot."

Skip left, followed by a puff of reeking smoke.

A card that would open Apartment 733 was in his hand, but there was no need for it; the lock had been broken out of the doorframe. Grimacing, Skip pushed aside the door and went in. A tele, a telephone, and a sofa—period. The black tele looked old; presumably she had bought it used, as he had suggested. The pink sofa had been more than a trifle worn; it was ruined now, its disemboweled cushions scattered across the floor, their springs exposed, their stuffing shredded. In the bedroom, blankets and sheets had been torn from the bed. The pillow had been cut open. The drawers of a battered bureau had been pulled out and thrown aside. Skip examined them, bending and peering to scrutinize their interiors without touching them.

He was about to go when his right foot sent a small, brown object skittering across the bare concrete floor. He picked it up, opened it, and tested the edge.

From his own apartment he called Michael Tooley. "You won't have forgotten the woman we talked about, Mick. Have you heard from her?"

"No, sir. Nothing."

"Have you been in contact?"

"No, sir. You gave me her number, but I haven't used it and she hasn't called me. Should I call her?"

"No. I was just in there. There's no one there."

"Am I to take it that there should've been, sir?"

"Not necessarily. Do you still eat lunch where you did this summer?"

"Yes, sir."

"I'll be there. If I can't come I'll call you. Wait half an hour. If I still haven't come or called, talk to the police."

"Like that, sir?"

Skip paused, took out the slender brown object, and touched its edge to the rosewood of his telephone stand. "I'm afraid so," he said.

The old man's resale shop was on Avenue AA, not quite too far to walk. Selecting a platform rocker, Skip waited for the old man to deal with his customer.

"Good morning, Mr. Grison." The old man smiled as his customer left. "Something I can do for you?"

"I hope so. I sent Vanessa Hennessey to you. Did she come?"

The old man rubbed the side of his nose, with his forefinger. "Good-looking. Younger than I expected. Spent . . ." He paused. "Four hundred and ninety-eight. About that. Pretty much all of it for furniture. I got Acacio to deliver it for her. He's cheap, and as good as anybody. Is she going to sue me?"

"I wish she would." Skip took the brown object from his pocket. "Did she buy this here?"

The old man studied it for a long moment. "You know, she did. I asked her what she wanted it for, and she said she just liked it. I think I had it priced at two noras, but since she was buying so much I threw it in."

"Good of you. What's it for?"

"It's an old-time shaver." The old man demonstrated, holding handle and blade at an obtuse angle and not quite touching the edge to his cheek. "They had to be careful, though."

"It looks more like a knife," Skip said.

"No point." The old man demonstrated, tapping the blunt end of the blade with his finger.

The park was too far to walk, but Skip walked anyway, edgy and eager to spend his energy on something. There was a chill in the air; the sky, gray and lowering, veiled the upper two-thirds of the towering buildings.

Mick Tooley was sitting on the bench farthest from the silent fountain, sipping coffee from the same cracked mug he used at the office and frowning at two gray pigeons. He rose. "Glad you made it, sir."

"So am I." Skip sat. "That number I gave you was for her apartment in my building. She doesn't have a mobile phone as far as I know."

Tooley resumed his seat.

Skip sat, too. "You can probably forget the number."

"This is Reanimation, sir?"

"Probably. I talked to them this morning."

Tooley nodded. "How'd it go?"

"Badly. I told them we had a good case, which we do. They—his name is Feuer, he's a vice president—indicated that their security boys would make our case moot." Skip paused to turn his coat collar up. "When I got away from him I tried to call her. That may have been a mistake."

"So you were careful with me."

"I tried to be, yes. After that I went straight back to my building. I thought they didn't know where she was, and that Feuer had spoken as he did so they could follow me to her. I also thought they'd think I was going to my own appartment to get something, and they'd wait to follow me when I came out."

"Sounds good."

"I went straight to her apartment instead. It had already been broken into and searched. Searched pretty thoroughly. She wasn't there."

Tooley said, "Then they didn't get her, sir."

Skip studied him. "You think not? Why?"

"Because they searched. They want her, not something she's got."

Skip nodded.

"So they were looking for something that might tell them where she went. Did she have luggage?"

"You're good. You're very good. I wish I'd had you with me."

"Thank you, sir."

"Yes, she had an overnight bag. It wasn't there." Skip paused to think. "Chelle hasn't gotten her leave yet. Tomorrow, she says. She sounded confident."

"That's good, sir."

"My point is that Vanessa can't have joined her. She can't have walked into Camp Martinez and announced that she was staying with her daughter."

"A hotel room?"

Skip shook his head. "She'd need a credit card at the very least. Identification, too, very likely. She hasn't got either one."

"You said she was a clever woman, sir."

"You're right, she is and she may have gotten some somehow."

"I'll get the Z man on it. It's his kind of problem. Okay if I pass along your description?"

"Yes. Of course. Give him everything you've got. Chelle and I plan to book a cruise. We'll do it and board as soon as she gets leave. If Zygmunt finds out anything—or if she contacts you, which I'd think more likely—call me right away. Otherwise, you're in charge as long as I'm not there."

"You don't have a picture, do you, sir?"

"I'm afraid not. I wish I did." He handed Tooley the brown object. "Ever see anything like this? Be careful if you open it. It's sharper than broken glass."

"A pocketknife? No, I've never seen any quite like this one." Tooley handed it back.

"It's probably two hundred years old, or so I was told by somebody who knows about such things, and it was meant for shaving. The brown handle is bone—he thought it had been dyed that color. Vanessa got it from him, and I found it in her bedroom. She'd bought furniture from him. He'd probably had it in stock for years with no takers, so he gave it to her. When I came in it was on the floor."

"So they didn't want it."

"Correct." Skip opened the blade. "The thing that interests me is that it seems pointless in two senses. Why did she want it?"

Skip had been relaxing on the veranda outside their stateroom for an hour or more when Chelle dropped into the chair next to his. "I have the most amazing news! You won't like it. Want to hear it?"

He turned to look at her. "You're so beautiful that my spirit would soar if you'd come to announce the end of everything."

"That wouldn't be amazing, just the Os. This really is amazing. I hope you won't be angry."

"With you? I couldn't be."

"With her." Chelle took his hand, holding it between both of hers; he noticed yet again that her right hand was noticeably larger than her left. "Mother's on the ship."

He straightened up. "You're not joking? Are you sure? You didn't just glimpse someone who looked like her?"

"I—I hugged her." For a moment Chelle was silent. "That was after we'd talked for a minute or two. She . . . She said to call her Virginia. Virginia Healy. That's what they call her here, she said."

"Which worries you, as it should."

"I want a drink." Chelle rose, posing. "I was hours and hours in the spa. Don't you think I look pretty?"

"Lovely. You glow."

"That means sweat, and I did. I want a cold drink and something to eat. Do we have to go to the dining salon?"

"No, and it would be better not to." Skip took out his phone. "I'll call food service, and that will give you time to think over what you want to say."

"I know what I want to say. I'm trying to decide how I feel. You brought— not now. I want something tall and tropical, icy cold, with fruit juices and rum."

"How about the umbrella?"

"Tell them they can keep it." Chelle sat again. "I want a club sandwich, too. A big one."

"Anything else?"

"A teddy bear. Never mind, you're my teddy bear. I hold you and feel comforted. And safe. Pretty soon I'll stop hitting the dirt when I hear a loud noise."

Skip smiled and ordered.

"Let me start like this. I didn't hate her today."

"I never thought you did."

"Sorry, but you're wrong. Furthermore I told you about it that time in the restaurant."

"I didn't believe you."

"You should have, because it was true. Before I went into the Army, Vanessa was a bitch with stardrive. God knows my father had his faults, he drank too much and he cheated on her, but he never molested me and he was semi-nice. Vanessa should've been a Halloween costume. Nothing was ever right unless she did it. Nobody was good enough for me, and Charlie certainly wasn't good enough for her—she had married beneath her, and let that be a lesson to me. Didn't you notice that I never brought you home to meet my folks?"

Staring out at the rolling green Atlantic, Skip said, "Actually, I didn't. I should have."

"Why doesn't the food come?"

"I suppose because it's not ready. How's the spa?"

"Small but good. The masseur's a big black lady they call Trinity. It's where she was born, she says. They ought to be Swedes, but she's good and she's got arms like a weight lifter. I liked her, and I think she liked me. Her brother's a soldier."

"What about the rest?"

"You haven't said a word about my hair. Is it me?"

"Not quite, but it will be."

She fluffed her golden curls with both hands. "Could our children be blonds, Skip? Any of them?"

"I didn't know we were going to have any."

"We are. That's not negotiable. If you don't like them, we can put them up for adoption." Chelle paused. "Only I think I'd rather keep them. I'll be a bad mother, though."

"You'll be a wonderful mother."

"Because I had a bad role model." Her voice fell. "Only I couldn't hate her today. I—well, I just don't know. I tried."

"You shouldn't."

"Shouldn't hate or shouldn't try?"

"Both. We've got to hate when we can't help hating. It's legitimate then, because we can't help it. The other thing is the essence of evil."

She grinned, happy with the change of subject. "Isn't it supposed to be the love of money? Charlie used to say that."

"Nine times out of ten, the love of money makes people work harder and do a better job."

"Yeah. I guess so. Or fear does. Like when we were digging in. People worked until—you wouldn't believe it. Fear made me clean up my room when I was a kid. Fear of what Mother was going to say and keep on saying. Saying over and over again, with no forgiveness. Not ever. I was afraid of how she'd look and how she'd scream and keep on screaming. I couldn't help hating her. Can you understand that?"

Picturing the scene, Skip nodded. "Yes. Easily."

"You brought her up to Canam because you thought I'd want to see her." It was an accusation.

"You're right. I did."

"I didn't! I hate the sight of her, hate the sound of her voice."

"You didn't recognize me, Chelle, but you struggled through that crowd to get to her."

"Yeah. I suppose I did." So softly that he could barely hear it, she asked, "Do you understand yourself?"

"Mostly, yes."

"I don't. I mean, I don't understand me. When I met her here, just a few minutes ago. I was glad to see her, but I didn't want to be."

He waited.

"Why did you bring her here? It was supposed to be just you and me."

"I didn't."

"Really?" Chelle stared.

"Yes. I'm going to tell you some things she wouldn't like you to hear. In a way, I shouldn't. But I haven't promised not to, and they're things I think you ought to know."

"I won't tell her you told me."

"Thanks. You know she doesn't have much money now. You commented on her feather earrings once."

"I remember."

"She has one other pair. They're attractive and look like gold, but they're plastic. She needed a place to stay, and I found an apartment for her in my building. It was on the seventh floor, and everything below the twenty-fifth is—well, you know."

"Cheap. Did she pay her own rent?"

"No." Skip shrugged. "It wasn't big and it didn't rent for much, but she was happy to have it. She furnished it with used things. Used furniture— still serviceable, but used—is very reasonable."

"She must have hated that."

"I don't know. I—"

A knock at the door of their stateroom announced the arrival of their lunches. When they were settled at the table, Skip sipped his gin-and-tonic and wondered how best to restart the conversation.

"We should have asked Mother," Chelle said.

"Asked her what?"

"Asked her to lunch. Can she afford to eat?"

"If she could afford passage on this ship, even in tourist class, she certainly can. Food's included in the ticket. Tourist-class passengers eat in the tourist-class dining salon. It's not fancy, but if you don't mind a lot of canned and dried stuff, there's nothing wrong with the food."

"Have you ever been there?"

He shook his head.

"Then how do you know?"

"I checked things out before I booked, that's all. The information on their site covered all three classes. What the rooms looked like, where they were on the ship, what the food was like, and so on. What deck were you on when you met your mother?"

"This one. The spa's on this deck, too. Why are you looking like that?"

"Because tourist-class passengers—and second-class passengers—aren't permitted on this deck. Now eat your sandwich."

Obediently, Chelle did. "Maybe they're not, but if they have guards to keep them out, I never saw any. We could call her up and ask her. How could we get hold of her?"

"Wait. We need to talk, so let's finish lunch."

"I didn't hate her. I met her and I was surprised to see her. Flubbergassed. And I hugged her, and she hugged me. I'm bigger and stronger than she is now. . . ."

Skip nodded.

"That didn't seem right, but she didn't seem to mind. You paid the rent on her apartment? Isn't that what you said?"

"I took care of it, yes."

"But you didn't buy her a ticket on this boat?"

"Ship. No, I didn't."

"Have you gone up to watch them work the sails?"

"No." Skip turned on the fan. "If you'll stop asking me questions, I'll tell you what I've been trying to tell you for the last five minutes."

"What is it?"

He sighed. "Someone's after her. Let me back up and explain. Mick Tooley's a bright young guy in our firm. I told him about your mother and gave him her number. I told her about Mick, too, and gave her his number. She was to contact him if she needed anything."

"But if someone is after her . . . ?"

"This was before I knew that." Skip sighed again. "Here I'm guessing, but I don't believe she knew anybody was after her then either."

"I see. Go on."

"I went there the day before we left. It had been broken into and searched fairly thoroughly. She wasn't there."

Chelle's eyes were wide. "You must have thought they'd gotten her."

"No. It seemed clear they hadn't. For one thing, her overnight bag was gone. Her clothes were missing, too—all her personal possessions. For another, the break-in had to be quite recent. If it hadn't been some of the other tenants would've reported it—you could hardly walk past the apartment without noticing that the door was broken, and it was near the elevator. I talked to the doormen, and they hadn't seen her for at least two days."

"You—you should've canceled our trip!" Chelle's glass slammed the table. "You should have told me. You bastard!"

"Naturally you're angry. What would you have done if I had?"

"I'd have tried to help her! What the fuck do you think I'd do!"

"Keep your voice down, please." For a moment Skip was silent, biting his lower lip and feeling terribly, terribly old. "Your mother has your number. If she had needed your help, wouldn't she have called you?"

"If she could. Only if she could." Clearly, Chelle was struggling to keep her anger under control.

"You met her just a few minutes ago. You hugged her. Did she ask your help?"

"You smart-ass bastard!"

"As you like." Skip sipped his drink. "She did not. She had my number, too. She did not call me. She may have called Mick Tooley—as I said, I gave her his number. If she did, which I doubt, he thought it better not to tell me. I've found him a young man of sound judgment."

"You didn't tell me! You didn't tell me one damned thing!"

"You're right, I didn't. At least not until now, when it seemed to me it might do some good. We may be watched, Chelle. Both of us."

She stared at him, her face flushed, her mismatched hands trembling.

"She and I traveled to Canam together to meet you. Later I found her an apartment and gave her money for furniture. Anyone who traced her recent movements would certainly have concluded that she was associated with me. You see that, don't you?"

"I hate to think of Mother being mixed up with a slick bastard lawyer like you."

"But she is. And with you, a heroic soldier. Anyone who looked into her history would quickly learn that she had one child, a daughter, and that child's identity. The simplest search would reveal that her daughter was in the Army and had recently returned to Earth."

Chelle rose, trembling; she had never looked lovelier. "My mother has been risking her life for this planet. You knew that, and you left her high and dry so you could run off to screw me, a woman young enough to be your kid."

"Chelle! Please listen."

"I'm through listening. You listen to me. There's a deadbolt on that door." She pointed. "If you're the first one in here tonight, you bolt it to let me know. I'll find someplace else to sleep. If I'm first in, I'll bolt it and you can jump in the goddamn ocean for all I care."

After finishing his drink and sandwich, Skip switched off the fan, carried their tray into the passageway, and left too, going up on the Main Deck to watch the working of the sails.

And think.

REFLECTION 3

Old Things

I have forgotten the old man's name; I remember everything else: his tousled gray hair and the old white shirts he always wore, threadbare shirts sometimes patched and darned but always clean, the jeans and the blue rubber-soled shoes from Eastasia.

His shop was always clean, too. I would have expected dust, but the old lamp with the peeling bronze finish was immaculate and every chipped Dresden plate shone. He spent the hours between customers scrubbing and dusting, he told me, and thus fled depression.

Vanessa fled as well, and it is possible (though not, I think, probable) that she too fled inner demons. Could she not have searched her tiny apartment herself, slashing her faded pink cushions with the bone-handled shaver? She would have hated the cramped rooms I gave her and the old furniture. Could she not have avenged herself on both?

Yes, but that is the point, or so it seems to me. When tenants vacate a place they hate, hate because of the money it snatches from their account each hundred-day, perhaps, or because their neighbors make noise or cook cabbage . . .

When they truly hate the place they are leaving, they vandalize it, smearing obscenities on its walls, stealing its electrical outlets, and so on and so forth—all the rest of that long, sad catalogue; I know it only too well. Nothing of that kind had occurred. The search had been a search, and not vandalism. Vanessa had (they had thought she had) some small item, a paper or something of the sort, a thing that might have been hidden almost anywhere. What it was, I could not guess, and it may have been something that did not in fact exist.

If it did not exist, what was it they thought she had? What made them think she had it? If it did exist, what was it and where did she get it?

Chelle thought her mother had been a spy. She had said so in my hotel room. The walls of such rooms are notoriously thin; she may well have been overheard. Or a surveillance device may have been planted in the room. Or Chelle may have expressed the same thought on some other occasion, most probably a debriefing.

Suppose that Chelle had brought home something she should not have, and that she had given that forbidden object to her mother. Or that someone suspected she had. That, too, was possible. In that case, Chelle herself held the answer to all the riddles—assuming that she knew what it was she had.

Have I lost her? If I have, I am well rid of her. It should be possible to imagine a less suitable mate for a middle-aged attorney, but it might take an hour's thinking. If I have lost her, I will be miserable—and fortunate in my misery.

I have not. No, not yet. Or if I have, I will strain every faculty to win her back. What would be the point of boasting my advantages—the contract we signed, my wealth and position, her college memories, and the rest? All of them together will weigh less with her than my lined face and receding hairline.

There is another: Vanessa.

And one more: Chelle's own good sense. She rejected my logic, but rejected it in a storm of emotion. Whatever else Chelle may be, she is no fool. Storms are powerful, but storms (like men) do not endure.

Vanessa . . . What age is she? Biologically between thirty-five and forty, I would say. The woman into whom Vanessa's every thought was uploaded was thirty-five at youngest, forty at oldest. Or so I (a poor judge) would imagine; but how old was Vanessa? How old at death, how old when she had her last scan?

Scans can be loaded into a mainframe. How are they loaded into the brain? If her case goes to trial, I'll need to know that.

If she died in a hospital, she may well have been scanned just before death. Those things will be a matter of record. Boris can find them out for me.

Vanessa wants me, and who can blame her? She needs a hold to counter the hold I have on her. She will not get that one.

How old? She was alive when Chelle was twenty-three; I know, because I saw her then. Such a woman would not have married before twenty, or so I think.

I wish Susan were here. She is always a better judge of women. I could send for her, perhaps.

No. Not if I judge Chelle correctly. Susan must stay where she is.

Say that Vanessa was twenty-three when she contracted with Charles C. Blue. Forty-six when I saw her? Perhaps. If she had lived, she would be what? Sixty-six, sixty-eight, seventy. Charles was older, certainly, and is most probably dead. If not, seventy-five at least. Can I make use of a wealthy and ruthless man of that age?

Very possibly; and if he makes use of me, he will be billed. Zygmunt could find him, certainly. Houses, cars, and all the rest.

A new woman? That, too, is possible.

These men on the ladder lifts, how hard they work and how desperate they must be to take such work and cling to it. How long can an athletic man do such work? I wish I had binoculars.

4

JUST ONE OF THE GUYS

A seat alone would have suited his mood better, but the only unoccupied seat that offered a good view of the sails was next to a lean old man whose beard and long white hair danced in the wind; Skip took it.

The sails interested him—the complexity of their rigging, and their sheer size, great sheets of some white synthetic that seemed to fill the sky. The sailors who worked them were brawny men, many of them big, yet when they lay aloft to take in sail (as they did when he had been on deck for an hour or so) they seemed hardly larger than ants. The seven fiberglass masts were taller than many office towers.

"We've a blow coming," the old man next to Skip said; he indicated the sails with a wave of his blackthorn stick. "That's why they're doing that."

Skip nodded absently, wondering where he had seen the old man before.

"Your first cruise?"

"No. My third."

"My ex and I used to try to take a cruise every year." The white-bearded man had begun packing tobacco into the bowl of a corncob pipe. "Some years we'd make it and some years we didn't. I don't mean just this cruise, there's a hundred plus. You can never run out."

"I see."

"If you want to learn more about working the ship, there's a class. Call the social director. She'll sign you up."

"Perhaps I will."

"Quite a few go on these because they're getting set to die." The old man paused to light his pipe, but Skip did not speak.

"It comforts 'em. The sea's eternal. If Earth were to die, if the Os were to blow up the whole thing, there'd still be seas like this on other worlds. I think about it sometimes." As he spoke the old man watched Skip, bright blue eyes just visible above his dark sunglasses.

"They won't," Skip said. "We're fighting for control of habitable planets, and habitable planets are rare. The Os want them, and so do we."

The old man's mouth smiled, but there was no smile in his eyes. "Suppose they could get control of all the rest by blowing up this one?"

Skip shrugged, leaned back, and shut his eyes. When he opened them again, the old man had gone. Skip had not heard him leave.

He thought—as he had so often thought through all the lonely years—of Chelle fighting on whatever godforsaken world they had sent her to. "One of the best noncoms we had turned out to be an EU spy. I killed him." She had said that not long ago. "If you love Earth you leave it." She had said that just before she left, and he felt he understood it a bit better now. The Os would never destroy a habitable world; there would be a negotiated settlement (however unfavorable) long before it came to that. But if millions of people believed they might . . .

No doubt the government encouraged it; there would be more soldiers, more Marines.

He used his mobile phone to call the office of the ship's social director. "I understand there are lectures on the operation of the ship. I'd like to attend one."

"Certainly." The speaker looked young and bright, and sounded the same way. *"We'll be starting tomorrow at ten. One hour, so you'll have ample time for lunch. What's your name, sir?"*

He gave it.

There was a lengthy silence. Then, *"There seems to be a bit of trouble about your record, Mr. Grison. Could you come to our office? We're on I Deck, in Compartment Three Thirty-eight.*"

"Could you—" But she had hung up.

The elevators were long-lift only, as they were in most buildings ashore. Fortunately, Main Deck to I Deck qualified, and the long walk through stifling corridors to Compartment 338 gave him ample time to wonder about the problem with his records—why it had not been discovered earlier, for example.

"The social director would like to speak to you in person, Mr. Grison." The girl behind the desk was indeed young and looked bright; she gestured toward the door on her left. "She'll see you right away."

Vanessa smiled pertly as he came in. "You don't look surprised, Mr. Grison. Are you?"

"Not very, Ms. Healy. Surprised to see that I was right, if you like. Can we talk here?"

"We could, but—come with me."

She led him down a passageway, around a corner to a companionway, and up to G Deck. Down more passageways to a room she unlocked; it was dark save for the watery light admitted by portholes that were scarcely higher than the tossing waves of the Atlantic.

"We're going to use this for lectures and classes." She shut and bolted the door. "To be honest, I don't think my office is bugged either. This is more exciting, though. Don't you agree?"

Skip said, "We're less liable to be interrupted, at least."

"And I get to sit with you in the dark. If I were to switch on the lights, it would be recorded and I'd have to make up a story. It's the energy thingy."

"I understand."

"They work the sailors like slaves. Maybe you've seen it?"

"Certainly I saw them working hard at times."

"I keep thinking, give them electric what-you-call-ums to wind up their ropes, and send some of them into space to fight, the way they sent Chelle. You agree, don't you?"

Skip shrugged. "It costs a great deal to train and equip a soldier, and much more to get one to a contested world. Few of those men would repay the expense—or so I'd guess. Is this coincidence? Your being on our ship?"

Vanessa tittered. "You can't be as silly as that. I know you're not. I checked the passenger lists."

"I didn't know they were public."

"They're not. Do you want the whole story?"

"I do." He noticed that the ship's roll seemed more pronounced. "Very much."

"All right. At a dinner years and years ago, I sat next to a nice young man who worked for this line. We chatted and I was oh so charming. I can be charming when I want to."

"I know."

"Well, I knew you and Chelle were going on a cruise, so I looked up this gentleman and told him what Chelle thought. I'm sure you remember. She thought I'd been out in space, too, and that was why I wasn't an old lady now. So I said I'd been out in space for the government and I couldn't say anything about it." Vanessa paused. "He let me see the passenger lists and took me to dinner. I didn't have much money, so that was very nice. I liked him, and Charlie's history. I told you, didn't I?"

Skip said, "I'd think he'd be too old for you."

"You're right. He was, a bit. Still he was terribly nice. Do you know who's not too old for me? Who's exactly the right age?"

"I understand why you left the apartment. Still, I wish you'd told me you were going." When Vanessa said nothing, he added, "I suppose you were afraid I'd have tried to stop you, and you're probably correct."

"It wasn't that at all. They tried . . . I was afraid to tell anybody. Terrified! Put your arm around me. I'm serious. Do it. I need a man's arm around me, and you're just right for me and—oh, damn! I'm g-going to c-c-cry."

He hugged her.

"I was so t-terribly frightened. Horribly, horribly frightened. I—I talked it down for a few days, but now I'm frightened again. They tried to k-kill me, Skip. They did! I was going to a few places I remembered, just to see what they were like now and who was there. Oh, Lord!"

"What was it?"

"It seemed so funny at the time. I kept a straight face until I got away, but then I laughed until the people around me must have thought I was crazy. I laughed, and I had almost forgotten that part."

"Tell me."

"I went to Simone's and there was a woman there eating with some man. I didn't recognize her, but she must have been much younger. Anyway, she recognized me. Her mouth dropped open. Do you know what I mean? And she positively gawked! So I pretended I hadn't seen her and scooted, but after that I had to laugh. And—and . . ."

Vanessa had begun to tremble again. Skip tightened his grip.

"He stabbed me. Just stabbed me in the back while I was walking down Seventy-second with hundreds of people around us. He did! I know you won't believe me, but it's the truth."

He gave her his handkerchief.

"Women were screaming and I was on the sidewalk trying to get up, only I had this thing in my back that hurt and hurt, and nobody would pull it out, and there were police all around and people saying, 'I didn't see it. I didn't see it.' Over and over."

"You're not making this up?"

Vanessa had begun unbuttoning her sleeves. "I'm going to take off my blouse. I don't want you to pull off the bandage, and it's too dark for you to see the place anyway. But you can feel the bandage—it's a little bit above my bra strap. Go right ahead and feel it. Be gentle."

As well as he could judge, there was pad of gauze somewhat smaller than the palm of his hand, held in place by tape. It was, or might have been, stiff with blood.

"We've a doctor on board—an official doctor, I mean. Dr. Prescott. He changed the bandage for me yesterday, and he says my body will absorb the stitches as the wound heals. Do you want to hear more about Tim? That's the nice man who got me this job. He's president of the cruise line now. I told him which ship, and I'd take any job to get on it and be there for Chelle and all that nonsense, and he said could you be a social director, we haven't got one for the *Rani*? The mandate's five to four, you see, and every little bit helps."

Skip nodded.

"Well, of course I could and I said so, so here I am."

When Skip did not speak, Vanessa added, "I could take off my bra so you could feel it better. Wouldn't you like that?"

"No. I'll leave if you do."

"All right." She sat. "Only I'm going to leave my blouse off for now. We've got huge fans and vents that catch the wind when there is any, but it's so dreadfully hot all over the ship."

"First I should tell you that Chelle's angry with me. I'll answer—"

"Of course she is. If she hadn't been, I wouldn't have stripped."

Although Vanessa could not have seen them, Skip's eyebrows went up. "She told you?"

"No, indeed. Your face did. When I spoke with her, she was deeply in love with you. Or that's what she said."

"I see." He took a deep breath. "I was about to say that I'd answer your questions, but you must answer mine first—my questions about the attempt on your life. I'm going to do my best to protect you, and these are things I'll need to know. Did you see your attacker?"

"You defend criminals, don't you? Isn't that your business?"

He chuckled, surprising himself. "That's what people think it is, and they may be half right. I defend persons accused of crime, Vanessa. They're criminals, of course—but that's because everyone is. Did you see your attacker? Don't stall."

"No. No, I didn't. It was somebody behind me, and then I fell down."

"Was it a man or a woman?"

"I don't know! I just told you so."

"You've been wearing ten-centimeter heels every time I've seen you, so I assume you were wearing them then. In those heels you must be as tall as quite a few men."

"Not as tall as you are, Skip. You've a good two fingers on me."

"Did you see the knife? After they pulled it out, I mean."

"No. They never showed it to me. I suppose the police have it. What difference does it make?"

Skip shrugged. "It's something we know your attacker had, and it might tell us something about him. Was it a dagger?"

"Isn't that just a knife you stab people with?"

"A dagger is double-edged. It's made for stabbing. Knives are made for cutting, for the most part. When people are stabbed, it's usually a kitchen knife. Often it's part of a set, a set that will be one knife short. It was the stabbing that made you give up the apartment I gave you?"

"That's right. Because I was in the hospital the first night. After I got out, I thought, they'll be looking for me and by this time they may have found my apartment. You're not checking out my breasts."

"Sorry. I didn't know you wanted me to."

"Well, I wouldn't want you to stare, but it would be nice if you noticed them."

"I have. Who is 'they'?"

"People from the company that brought me back, from the Reanimation Corporation."

"Do they have a good reason to want you dead? What is it?"

"You haven't been making the payments. You told me you haven't. Why are you looking at me like that?"

"Lots of reasons." Skip wanted to pace and did, only slightly impeded by the roll of the ship. "In the first place, I didn't tell you I hadn't been making the payments. I said I was going to stop."

He pressed a button to light the dial of his watch. "Today is Tuesday. When were you stabbed?"

"It was a Wednesday, I think."

"A week ago? This is important. Wednesday of last week?"

"Don't be silly, we sailed the next day. It was two weeks ago."

"You spent Wednesday night in the hospital. What about Thursday?"

"That," Vanessa said primly, "is none of your affair."

"Friday? Will you tell me that?"

"Certainly. In my cabin on this ship. The social director doesn't wait until the passengers come to get on board. There were all sorts of things I had to do to get ready. My assistant had never done this before. Neither had I, but I told her I had and that gave her confidence. Confidence is very important."

"Go on."

"After that I taught her all about dances and balls and dress codes, and we talked about shuffleboard and badminton tournaments. She's a good diver, so we decided to have diving contests, too, and a putting tournament. You need things for people of all ages, but especially for older people because there are more of them. Then there's dress-up night every Friday. We've a man who takes your picture, and dress-up night is good for his business. He pays, naturally, and he's got to—"

Skip said, "I understand, and I won't ask any more questions about your sleeping arrangements."

"Well, I wish you would. Because after we made our plans my assistant's Girl Friday came and we had to start all over with her. And I wanted to say that two of the officers are very nice, but they are—you know—taken. My little cabin isn't as comfortable as yours, but it's not too bad. Would you like to see it?"

"No."

"Well, it's ten ninety-one J. I know you think you and Chelle will make it up, and I hope you're right. But until you do?"

"No," Skip repeated.

"Besides, a little variety can be quite nice. You'll see. You know, I thought of taking you there straightaway when we left my office. I ought to have, but you'd have worried about people listening, and this is more romantic anyway."

"You didn't think your office had been bugged."

Vanessa shook her head. "Why should they? They'd just try to kill me, wouldn't they?"

"I don't know." Skip paused, considering. "In the first place, the time line is all wrong. On Friday, two days after you were stabbed, I called Reanimation and told them I might take them to court. It got me an appointment just before lunch with a vice president named Feuer. I went straight back to the building, and your apartment had been thoroughly searched."

"How did they know I lived there?"

"That's just it. Suppose they had begun to act when they got my call—which they did, come to think of it. Feuer told me my payment had been refused. Even so, they would have had to learn your address, get one or two security agents into my building, and search. A search like that would take one person at least an hour. Probably more."

"What were they looking for?"

"I'd love to know. I don't. Let's get back to what we do know, which is that it wasn't Reanimation's security goons who stabbed you, and it wasn't their security who searched your apartment. The timing is wrong for both."

"I liked it better when you had your arm around me," Vanessa said.

"Besides all that, Reanimation's a business. It's got to act sensibly for the most part, or go under. They want that pretty body of yours back alive."

"Well, they don't act like it!"

"We don't know how they act. Listen to me. The mind of a Reanimation employee has been wiped and your own mind uploaded into her brain— the brain that you call yours for the time being. It means they had a nice-looking woman of thirty-five or forty in their database who resembled you and would consent to being used like this. She must be very valuable to them. Injuring her or killing her would be the last thing they'd want to do. Kidnap you, wipe the brain and reinsert her mind, and they'd have a strong case. 'There she stands, ladies and gentlemen of the jury. That is her body, the body she was born with. And as you have heard, she consents to everything we've done.'"

"I see."

"Kill you, and it's murder. Not some two-bit hate-speech charge but real murder. This country has far too many people, or thinks it does. The result is that the government kills as many as the politicians can justify. Murder means execution, and quickly. The murderer dies; so does everybody they can convict as an accessory."

Vanessa said, "Well, somebody wanted to kill me."

"I agree, and we need to find out who and why. What were they looking for in your apartment?"

"I haven't the least idea."

"Think!"

"Skip . . ."

"Yes?"

"Do you remember when we met at the railroad station?"

He nodded.

"It was one of the very first things since I've been back. I don't remember dying. I know I must have, but I don't remember it."

"Of course not. You can't be scanned after death."

"The last thing I remember is going to Saint Andrew Kim's for a transplant. After that, I was lying on a gurney in a different room. I got up and a woman helped me dress and drove me to the station. She told me a lot about you on the way and gave me a little money. Well, of course I wanted to see Chelle, so I did what she'd said to. I had nothing then. A few clothes in a little bag."

"I remember."

"Everything I had after that, I bought with money you gave me. I don't steal, Skip. It's so, well, déclassé."

He had stopped pacing to stare out a porthole.

"I never hid anything there. Not a thing. Tim gave me a little money. For these shipboard clothes, you know." Vanessa held up the white blouse. "If they were looking for some sort of treasure that would be very funny."

"I've been trying to convince myself that they were looking for something that would tell them where you'd gone."

She shook her head vigorously. "After I was stabbed, I went back there to pack, but I had no idea where I was going afterward, and I was in and out in ten minutes."

"They cut open sofa cushions, so they were looking for something you would've hidden." Skip paused, and snapped his fingers.

"You've thought of something. What is it?"

"Your face, basically. It's a very pretty face. Delicate features, sharp chin, perfect nose."

Vanessa's smile flashed in the dim light. "Why, thank you!"

"Big eyes, with a tiny upward tilt. Most of all the vivacity. Chelle didn't recognize me at Canam, but she knew you at once."

"Well, naturally she would."

Skip shook his head. "Not naturally at all, because that's not really Chelle's mother's face. It's the face of the Reanimation employee, an attractive woman about thirty-five whose name we don't know."

"It's mine now!"

"You're right, it is. And because it's animated by your personality, it exhibits your characteristic facial expressions." Skip paused, scanning the empty chairs as though gauging the reactions of a jury. "But suppose the woman you saw at that restaurant—the woman you didn't recognize—didn't recognize you at all, never having seen you. Suppose she recognized the face, a face she had seen on another woman last hundred-day or last year, a woman whom she and her male friend had been searching for." He returned to his seat.

"You mean they didn't know that I'm me?"

"No, I mean they don't care. Do you think it would make any difference to them?"

"Why, I have no idea!"

"I don't think it would. They'd have to assume that Reanimation will reclaim you eventually, wipe you, and replace you with the employee's scan. When it does, the person they fear will be back. I say 'they' because I think it was the man who stabbed you. The woman must have told him who you were. My guess is that he jumped up to follow you. You didn't see his face?"

Vanessa shook her head. "His back was toward me. The woman was facing him."

"He will have followed you, I think, and stabbed you when he felt he had a chance to get away afterward. Your wound's at the shoulder blade. That indicates a tall man holding his knife under his hand and stabbing down. It can't have been a big knife, or he'd have done more damage, but presumably it was all he had. That means he wasn't a pro. Can you describe the woman?"

Vanessa pursed her lips.

"Think back."

"I only saw her for a second or two. Wait. Round face, not bad-looking, thirtyish. Brown-blond hair over her forehead. Heavy, I think."

"She was sitting down when you saw her?"

"Yes, that's why I can't be sure how tall she was. But she was eating something white, and it was probably mashed potatoes. So heavy. Besides, girls with round faces are usually fat."

Skip nodded. "Or vanilla ice cream, but I suppose that would be the same thing."

"I should be getting back to my office. Goodness only knows what's been going on there."

"One last question." Skip held out the slim brown shaver. "Why did you have this?"

Vanessa screamed.

Back on deck, in a yellow deck chair flanked by empty chairs, Skip spoke into his mobile phone. "I want the Z man to check something out for me. A woman was stabbed on Seventy-second Street two weeks ago. She was taken to a hospital. Her name may be Vanessa Hennessey or Virginia Healy. It could also be something else. I want him to find which hospital and what address she gave, assuming she gave one. Have him talk to the investigating officer and find out as much as he can. If he can't get a look at the weapon, tell him to get the officer to describe it."

Tooley said, *"They'll think we're going to defend the offender, sir. Are we?"*

"No. Absolutely not. Tell him we want the offender caught as much as the police do, but we can't reveal our connection yet. Soap him."

"Got it. Anything else?"

"Not now," Skip told him, and hung up.

The prow was supposed to be off limits to passengers, but he went there anyway, finding a spot where few of those on deck could see him. A warm breeze toyed with the straw hat he had brought to ward off the sun, whispering in his ears and ruffling his shirt. Below him, the sharp prow split the self-healing sea. Beyond him, the tapered steel bowsprit, up-tilted and longer than many a street, pointed south. High overhead, two-score sailors labored, their cries no louder than the mewing of the gulls. Behind him, before him, and above him, the sails did their work in silence, urging the immense square-rigger *Rani* south.

Ever south.

. . .

He tried the door at 23C, which opened to his cabin card. Opening the bedroom door as well gave him the briefest glimpse of a naked man who sprang from the bed, scooped a bulky bundle off the floor, dashed out onto the veranda, and vaulted over the rail. Like late applause, something fell with a crash, knocked over by his swift passage.

Skip shut the outer door and bolted it, then closed the veranda door and bolted that, too.

"Sorry." Chelle sounded sleepy. "I was supposed to lock you out. I forgot."

"That's good. I need a place to sleep."

He had switched his mobile phone to VIBRATE, and it did. The tiny phone-pic showed Vanessa with shoulders bare and the end of a strip of tape barely visible. *"Have you been looking for me? I'm in ten ninety-one J. I thought you might have forgotten."*

"No," Skip said, "but thank you for the offer. I do appreciate it."

"It would give me a chance to apologize."

"That's hardly necessary," he said, and hung up.

Chelle yawned. "Who was that?"

"Just a friend." He sat down and took off his shoes.

"I already know."

"In which case there's no need to cross-examine me, and no need for me to lie."

"Aren't you going to ask who I was sleeping with?"

Skip unbuttoned his shirt. "If you want me to, yes. Not otherwise."

"You should be concerned. We're contracted."

"I am concerned, but it doesn't follow that I have to ask. *Non sequitur.*"

"That's good, because I'm not sure I can tell you. There was a party for us vets. Mother cooked it up for my benefit, I think. She must have pull with somebody."

"She doesn't need it. She's the social director."

"Really? She peeked in for a minute."

"Just doing her duty."

Chelle yawned again. "Anyway, I met a lot of people, and he was one of them. Just one of the guys."

"I see."

"I wasn't looking for a reason to lock you out, if that's what you think. If I had been, I wouldn't have forgotten to bolt the door."

"That's not what I think."

"Good. There's booze in our little refrigerator. Can I get you to fix me a drink?"

"Certainly." Skip was taking off his trousers. "What would you like?"

"Anything and soda. Anything and water, if there's no soda."

There were three bottles of club soda. After striving vainly to recall her preferences of twenty-odd years earlier, he mixed club soda with the rum in a miniature bottle.

"This is good. What is it?"

He told her.

"I know I'll be hung over in the morning, but I'd rather not be tonight. Rum because of where we're going, right?"

"Right."

She finished it, set the glass on the floor beside the bed, and lay down again. "That was either Jim or Jerry, I'm pretty sure, only I'm not sure which. They looked a lot alike, and I kept getting them mixed up."

"Natural enough."

"You mean I was hammered. I wasn't. I'd had two or three drinks, but I wasn't even close to it. I remembered our cabin number, didn't I?"

"Obviously." Skip slid between the sheets.

"Do you remember what we were fighting about?"

He shook his head. "Not at the moment."

"Me neither." Chelle snuggled closer. "I'll remember in the morning, but it's gone now."

Much later, when she was sleeping, he heard her say, "Don? Don? . . . Kiss me, Don."

Then, "Where's Don?"

REFLECTION 4

Winds

The wind has risen and the ship rolls. I don't want to think of Chelle stumbling down that carpeted, cream-colored corridor with him, but the image returns each time I wipe it away. The roll throws them against one wall, then the other. Chelle giggles, and I know a deep despair.

Some of his clothes may still be here. If they are, his passport may be in them, in a jacket pocket, if he wore a jacket. Certainly his wallet will be in a hip pocket. It will have forms of identification, possibly a driver's license. The Army must give its soldiers a picture ID, or so I would think. I shall know his name and face, but what good will that do? He fought bravely for us—for me and all humanity—and found a beautiful, willing comrade on this ship. Of what is he guilty? Were he guilty as sin, I would forgive him.

And did I really believe that a man of forty-nine could satisfy a girl of twenty-five? In daydreams, yes. Dreams have value, but they are not to be believed.

Could Tim satisfy Vanessa? For one night, perhaps. Perhaps if she really wanted love, and perhaps she did. Wanted it, and wanted a protector. Women must have a reason, men only want a place.

Chelle's reason was . . . ?

Anger might do it. She was angry at me and wanted to hurt me, as she did. That fits with the unbolted door. Or she longed to cling to the familiar, to men who were dirty of tongue and clean of heart—to the soldier's world. She was drunk. How drunk? And forgot to bolt the door.

What does sex matter when you may be killed tomorrow?

Vanessa wants me, or perhaps only wants to free her daughter from me. Or both. Who are those officers? Two were attractive, she said, but taken. Am I not taken? I know nothing of this ship's officers. Do they really work their seamen like slaves, those officers?

Wage slaves. What is any employee but a slave? When we contacted the agencies to get a flunky for Dianne, we got . . . What was the number? A thousand applicants? Two thousand? Susan told me.

One child per family in Greater Eastasia. One per family, and a male generation so that foreign women must be bribed or stolen.

Should we do that, too? Women from where, or would we abort boys? Another law, and decent men and women dragged into court for the second child they concealed and the lies they told on paper to make that forbidden child someone else's, the legacy of a dead cousin, the child of a soldier fighting the Os.

Fighting as Chelle did.

How happy I would be to defend them! But what would the law do? Kill the second child? Surely not. Upload another's mind into it, perhaps. Replace a legal child who had died. . . . We meddle and meddle, and wonder why it does not make us happy.

What of the woman whose body Vanessa wears? Who was she? Boris couldn't get it, but the Z man might; and if Vanessa's attackers were really after that nameless woman it could be important.

Suppose a woman wanted to hide? To disappear? Not as so many have, a new apartment and a new name, a new search for a new job they'll never get.

A search for any job, brain surgery or blues singing because they'll never get it, will never have to prove they can do it or even that they know something about it. No, not just that, but to vanish in such a way that the most dedicated searcher could never find her.

How many such people come to Reanimation?

Why did this one want to hide?

5

DAY TRIP

Vanessa's voice filled the ship, at once authoritative and chatty. "...*finally, let me say that no one is required to go ashore. It's strictly voluntary. If you remain aboard, please check the* Bulletin *for today's activities before calling the social director's office.*

"*Now permit me to recap . . .*"

"Okay, I'm ready," Chelle said.

"We don't have to." Skip had watched her preparations morosely.

"*You require no special papers. Show your cabin card if you're asked for ID. You don't have to change money. Noras are accepted everywhere. Food in restaurants should be safe, but do not buy food from street vendors unless . . .*"

"You don't." She got into her backpack. "I'm going to do some shopping. If you want to stay here on the ship, that's okay."

"*Take sunscreen. If your pocket is picked or your purse stolen, report it to the local police. We can't help you. . . .*"

"I'm going if you're going." He rose.

"*Do not give to beggars.*"

She turned to face him. "To tell you the truth, I wish you wouldn't."

"I'm going with you." It had hardened his resolve.

"*All staterooms, and cabins with two-digit numbers, can board now. Go to Main Deck, port-side . . .*"

Chelle hurried away, with Skip in her wake. The door of their stateroom closed silently behind them.

By the time they reached the Main Deck, the line was already long; a steward was going along it checking cabin cards.

"I've got a question," Chelle said. "Please don't tell me you don't have an answer."

"I may have to."

"Why do you feel you have to go with me?"

Skip shrugged. "Because you may need my help."

"In other words, you've got more money."

"I hadn't thought of that, but I suppose I do." He was silent for a moment; then he said, "You're young and very brave. It can be a bad combination."

"You don't want to see what there is to see ashore?"

He shook his head.

"Okay, you don't. But I'm going to see it just the same, and I'm going to make you see it."

The line shuffled forward. A young man in a brilliant Hawaiian shirt came to stand beside Chelle. "Hey, that was some party last night, wasn't it? I'm glad you came."

"Me, too," Chelle said. "I had a blast." Her smile vanished. "Skip, this is my buddy *(mumble)*. This is my contracto, Skip Grison."

"Pleased to meet you, sir." The young man offered his hand.

"I'm honored," Skip said. "You fought the Os?"

"Yes, sir. Forty-second Combat Elites."

"Doubly honored, in that case." The sharp stench of the harbor had crept through the opening ahead, a smell of salt sea, dead fish, and wood smoke. "I didn't quite catch your name."

"It's Al Alamar, sir. Albano Alamar, really, but call me Al."

"Want to come with us, Al? Do a little sightseeing and have some lunch?"

"I can't, sir. I'm in one ninety-seven. But I'll be going ashore on the next launch, sir."

"Perhaps we'll see you then. You'll be welcome to join us."

When he had gone, Chelle said, "That wasn't Jerry. Did you think it was?"

Skip nodded. "Or Jim. Yes, I thought it might be."

"Jerry. It was Jerry. I'm almost sure."

"I see."

"I'll know as soon as I talk to either one." There was something bitter in Chelle's smile.

"Really? How?"

"He'll smirk."

"I see." Skip sighed. "Did I, Chelle?"

She stared at him.

"That morning in the Northwestern Inn at Canam? You stayed the night. We got dressed in the morning, collected Vanessa, and went down for breakfast. Did I smirk?"

A steward rescued her by asking to see their cabin cards.

The launch was crowded but comfortable, topped with a wide awning of restful green; brawny rowers, seated along its sides fifty centimeters below them, sent it skittering across the blue water like a bug.

"Look at the ship!" Chelle had turned in her seat to see it. "My God! Just look at it!"

"Polymer hull and fiberglass masts," the man seated on her left told her. "The old-time ships never got half as big. The sailing ships I mean. They were wood, except for iron right at the end."

Chelle turned away from him. "The *Rani*. Isn't that what they call it?"

Skip nodded. "The SQ *Rani*. It means it's square-rigged."

"It must be the biggest ship in the world."

Skip doubted it but said nothing. This small port, certainly, held nothing of comparable size: another launch, and eight small craft that were presumably fishing boats. The drying nets draped everywhere made him think of theater curtains. Fishing nets had been made of synthetics once, he reminded himself. (This from the caption on a picture in a travel brochure.) There had been no need to dry them. Now they were cotton or hemp, and would rot if they were not dried. Vendors were gathered at the pier, awaiting their arrival. How much money had Chelle brought? And what was it she planned to buy with it?

They filed out with the rest. The launch's crew was pushing aside vendors for them. Seventeen little horse-drawn vehicles—buggies? chariots?—lined the broad street beyond the pier, each drawn by a lean and far from attractive horse. Chelle shook her head when Skip asked whether she wanted to ride, striding imperiously along as if on parade.

He paused to give a nora to a beggar. She stopped and looked back frowning, then smiled. "Poor man!"

The beggar bowed his head and held up the hooks that had replaced his hands.

"He can't work," Chelle said.

"I know. That's why I gave him something."

Other beggars were gathering. Skip flourished his walking stick and glared.

Chelle said, "I'm going to buy him something to eat. If you don't like it, you don't have to come."

Skip pointed. "There's a place over there, the Sea and Shore."

Sadly, the beggar shook his head. "They not let me go in, mon."

"You must eat somewhere," Chelle said.

"Park? We go park, lady?"

"You can eat there?"

The beggar nodded. "My name Achille."

Achille led them down several wide and quiet streets flanked by buildings with badly fitted doors and flaking paint. The park boasted palm trees, shade trees, huge green bushes with big pink roses, and a small fountain, a fountain that, amazingly, still played. They chose a shady stone bench not far from the fountain, Chelle with Skip to her left and Achille to her right. One vendor sold them spiced meat and boiled corn wrapped in corn husks, another cool water mixed with papaya juice.

"I suppose we'll get typhoid," Skip said, "but they can cure that pretty quickly."

"Could he stay in business if it made people sick?"

"Perhaps not."

"Then it won't make us sick, either. Achille's really hungry. Did you notice? I thought I was 'til I saw him."

"I take it the Army fed you well enough."

Chelle nodded. "We worked twelve or fourteen hours a day, ate like wolves, and slept like babies. This was on Johanna, which was where I was."

"It was habitable."

"Sure, real Earth-type. That's why both sides want it so bad." Chelle turned to Achille. "That enough?"

He nodded.

"Good. The gentleman here gave you a nora?"

Slowly Achille nodded again.

"I'm not going to take it away from you." Chelle held out a bill, displaying it between mismatched hands. "This is a hundred noras. See the numbers in the corners? I'm going to give you a chance to earn that much. If you can do what I ask, you get a hundred noras. If you can't—or won't—you don't."

Achille nodded.

"I want to buy a pistol, a good one. You take me to somebody who'll sell me one right now, with a little ammo, no questions asked. Do it, and I'll pay you a hundred noras."

Skip said, "Are you sure this is wise?"

"Hell, no. But somebody's tried to kill my mother. You ever try to buy a gun back home?"

He shook his head.

"Neither have I, but people used to tell me how tough it was if you couldn't get a license. One guy I knew—this was before we went up—stole an Army gun, got it out, and sold it. He got three thousand and said the guy he sold it to was going to offer it for six. So I could buy one, maybe, but it would take a hundred-day or more."

"I could—"

Chelle interrupted. "I know. You could steer me to somebody back home. If we got caught they wouldn't do a lot to me. I'm tail and a vet and all that shit, but you'd lose your law license. This is better."

"You'll have to go through customs when we leave the ship."

"Sure. I'll cross that bridge when I get there." She turned to the beggar. "What about it, Achille? Can you do it?"

"Other side mountain? You go?"

Chelle nodded.

"I find good mon. Good driver. You wait." Achille trotted away.

Chelle stretched. "How do you suppose he lost his hands?"

"Cut off for stealing."

"Yeah, that's what I thought, which is why I grabbed on to him. He must have been in the EU."

Skip shook his head. "I doubt it."

"Well, it's sharia law, and that's only in the EU."

"Not now," Skip told her.

Achille returned, riding in the front seat of a battered taxi brown with dirt and rust. "This Hervé. Hervé drive us."

Hervé looked as old as his taxi, and lugubrious. "Go north side mountain?"

Skip said, "Correct."

"Come back?"

"Yes."

"Hundred nora."

Achille began to argue frantically, an argument that lasted five minutes or more. At last he said, "Ten nora."

The driver spoke to Skip. "Thirty for each."

Another argument.

When it was over Hervé held out his hand. "You pay now."

Achille whispered something to Hervé, who got out and opened the door for Chelle. Skip walked around the taxi and got in on the other side.

Winking over the back of the front seat, Achille whispered, "I say we go Tante Élise."

"She must be a good woman," Chelle remarked.

"Strong, this woman. Mos' strong!"

. . .

There were goats in the road during the long drive up the spine of the island, and once a pig. Once, too, they passed a young woman, graceful, brown, and barefoot, who was carrying a huge bunch of green bananas on her head. From time to time they stopped briefly at remarkable views; and when at length they reached the highest point on the island, the *Rani* appeared no bigger than a toy boat in a bathtub.

"I want to get out and stretch my legs," Chelle announced. "Can I do that, Achille?"

"Better we come not so late."

"Just for a minute." Chelle got out.

Skip asked, "Are you afraid the store will close?"

"Start cer'mony. You go temple?"

"Would you come, too, if we do?"

Achille nodded.

"Then I will. It might be interesting."

"You got dance, mon. Unter Boy lash you proper if no dance." Achille laughed aloud. "Sharp spur got old horse cut caper. You dance?"

"I dance," Skip affirmed.

"We go temple. I say, good mon, good lady. See pray. Buy after. Give hundred nora?"

"Chelle will," Skip told him. "I won't."

The moon was up by the time they arrived. When the ancient taxi rattled to a stop, they heard chanting and the feverish thumping, rumbling, and tapping of drums. Skip paid. "Wait here. We'll hire you again for the ride back, and give you a ten-nora tip. Will you wait?"

"I wait," the driver said, and sprawled across the front seats. When Skip turned to look at him a moment later, he saw the flare of a match; it was followed by a puff of cigar smoke.

The temple was walled with rough masonry, although open to the night sky. A gate of weathered slats wound with barbed wire swung wide to

admit them. Inside, a throng of ragged men and women danced in an intri-
cate pattern around a score of flickering candles. Achille joined their dance
at once.

"What's this?" Chelle whispered.

"Church," Skip told her. "Let's dance." He took her arm, but she hung
back.

A boy of twelve or so ran toward them, yelling and flourishing a rattan.

"What's he saying?" Chelle's eyes were wide.

"Dance or he'll—" The rattan flashed down. Skip tried to block the
blow with his arm, with only partial success, and noticed that Chelle did not
wince. "Hit us," he finished. "There are no spectators, only participants.
Would you care to dance?"

They did, following the chant as well as they could, stepping this way
and that, clapping, gesturing in time with the drums. The dance went on
for a time that seemed very long indeed.

As though at some secret signal, it stopped. The tall woman who had led
the dance sprang onto the seat of a chair with astounding agility and began
to shout to the night sky—almost, to howl.

Achille insinuated himself between Skip and Chelle. "She Tante Élise.
Sell gun."

Mopping his face with his handkerchief, Skip said, "We'll see."

"What's she saying?" Chelle asked.

"Call dead," Achille whispered.

"Ghosts?"

Skip said, "Don't tell me you're afraid of ghosts."

"Hell, no. There aren't any."

The other dancers were resting now, some squatting, some sitting on the
grimy stone floor. Skip and Chelle sat, with Achille squatting behind them.

The shouting continued, and the deepest-mouthed drum took it up, not
beaten but scraped by the callused fingers of its owner.

After a time that might have been five minutes or ten, another drum
joined it, beaten, but beaten so slowly that the woman on the chair might
have shouted a hundred words, or twice a hundred, between its chthonic
thuddings.

"That's not a regular drum, is it?" Chelle, already sitting as close as possible, whispered her question into his ear.

Skip shook his head. "A hollow log. The ends are plugged, and there's a cut down the middle to let the sound out."

"Can you see it from here? I can't."

"I noticed it while we were dancing."

"They were all looking at us. Did you notice that, too?"

Skip nodded.

A new woman seated not far from them began to howl, a wordless, animal sound.

Chelle leaned forward. "Will the dead come, Achille?"

"Many come, lady. Many dead."

A third drum joined in with an excited tapping; and Skip, following the gaze of others, saw the wire-wrapped gate swing open.

The woman who entered walked stiffly. Her unblinking stare focused nowhere, on nothing.

The woman on the chair ceased shouting to issue an abrupt command.

The newcomer's mouth closed.

"We used to hold the whole of Johanna," Chelle said. "The Os drove us off most of it. Then our Navy shot up their fleet, and we started driving them back. That was when I got there. Reinforcements, you know." Chelle's tone was almost conversational.

A woman on the farther side of the enclosure screamed, "Ottilie!"

Slowly, the newcomer turned toward her.

"We kept driving them back and driving them back," Chelle continued. "We retook a lot of positions that had been lost the year before."

A man had shuffled through the open gate, a man whose empty face seemed little more than skin stretched across a skull.

"Our people tried to take our dead with them when they pulled out, but a lot got left. They were buried, mostly, when their trenches and blockhouses were knocked down. I didn't have to help dig the fucking corpses up, thank God, but I was around when it was done."

"I see," Skip said.

"So I saw them, and they smelled like—"

"There you are!" Vanessa had stepped through the gate. She smiled and waved. "What in the world are you two doing here?"

Chelle gaped.

Skip motioned to Vanessa, and the crowd parted for her like water, people scrambling to their feet or scuttling across the stone floor.

Smiling, she crouched before them. "I've been looking everywhere for you two."

Skip said, "How did you find us?"

"I met a local woman, that's all. She told me to go to the other side of the mountain and follow the sound of the drums, so I did. The gate was open and I came right in."

When the ceremony was over, Achille led them to a small, dark house. "Mambo come soon," he promised.

"We're going to miss the launch," Vanessa remarked. She did not sound unhappy about it.

"We already have." Skip glanced at his watch. "It's one fifteen."

"Then there's no point in hurrying."

Chelle said, "They were dead. Those people you came in with."

"Were they, darling? I didn't notice."

Skip shook his head. "I know they looked dead, and they smelled dead, too. But I won't believe anybody can make the dead walk again."

"Mambo make dead rise, mon. She wants, they come. Kill you, mon. Anything she say."

Chelle looked around nervously. "You called her Tante Élise before."

"Is her name. She Mambo."

"Like I'm a mastergunner?"

Skip said, "More or less, I believe. My guess is that is means Reverend."

The door of the dark house opened behind him as he spoke. The tall woman who led the dance gestured, and Achille trotted inside. Vanessa followed him quite nonchalantly.

"Are you going in?" Chelle sounded resolute.

"We've come all this way to see her—and missed the *Rani*, I'm afraid."

Vanessa glanced back at them. "No, no! They won't actually sail until high tide."

"And that is . . . ?"

"About eight o'clock. It's just that the launches don't run after midnight. We can find a boat and hire it."

Chelle muttered something, and Vanessa added, "Trust your mother."

A candle, short but very thick, kindled in the middle of the room. It was followed by two more on a tiny mantel. Nothing and no one had lit them, so far as Skip could tell. The large woman Achille called Tante Élise held out her hand.

"You give money," Achille instructed them. "You no give, she no speak."

Chelle opened her purse. "How much?"

"Money, lady!" He sounded angry. "You know money? Give money! Some you got."

"She must be a lawyer." Chelle dropped five noras into the outstretched hand.

The tall woman closed it without glancing at the bills. "What is it you wish?"

"I've come to buy a handgun. This man says you sell them. I want one, and I'll pay you well for a good one."

"Will you carry it?"

Chelle nodded.

"Where?"

"That will depend on the gun."

For a moment, it seemed that the tall woman might smile. "You can shoot?"

"Hell, yes."

"I didn't have to pay her at all," Vanessa whispered. "She just came up to me."

Skip pretended he had not heard.

"You buy for this man."

Chelle shook her head. "For me."

"I will show you three. You may choose. If you do not choose, three more. If you do not choose, you must go."

"I understand."

The tall woman turned and left, moving as soundlessly as any cat.

Vanessa said, "She's really quite kind."

Skip chuckled. "Let's hope you're a good judge of character."

Chelle said, "I trust her. I don't like her, but I trust her. That's odd, isn't it?"

"Not really. She has dignity, and people who have it keep their word for the most part."

"Like you."

He shook his head. "Hardly."

The tall woman returned and handed Chelle a gun. It was of bright metal. One grip was pearl, the other of some dark wood.

Chelle shook it, pulled back the slide, and handed it back. "This was a good one once, but it's fired a hell of a lot of rounds. I'd like to see it rebuilt, but I can't rebuild it with what I've got here."

The tall woman nodded. "This is not so dear."

It was a revolver. Chelle cocked the hammer and tried to move the cylinder. "It's good," she said, "but only six shots. Let me see something else."

The tall woman nodded approvingly. "We are seven here." The third gun was dark and dull, and almost impossibly narrow; Skip saw Chelle's eyes widen.

"It is this that you wish," the tall woman said.

"You're right. All right if I call you Tante Élise?"

The tall woman nodded again.

"I'll buy it if I have enough money, Tante Élise. How much?"

"And a hundred rounds of ammunition?"

Chelle nodded.

"We must see." The tall woman beckoned to Achille. "Take that candle. We go out. Light our way."

Achille did, grasping the thick candle by digging the points of his hooks into the wax; he looked more frightened than ever.

"Is that loaded?" Skip asked.

Chelle said, "The chamber indicator says so."

"Stop here," the tall woman told them. She pointed to Achille. "Walk forward until another prevents you."

Chelle said, "You can speak your language to him if you want. I'm sure he'll understand you better."

The tall woman did not reply.

Skip watched Achille's advance. He moved cautiously, clearly hoping he would be told to halt. The flame of his candle flickered and twice seemed ready to go out, though Skip felt no breath of wind.

Suddenly the candlelight showed a dark figure with arms outstretched to bar Achille's way.

"Give him the candle," the tall woman said. "Turn to look at us. Stand straight. Stand still. Will you move?"

Achille shook his head violently.

"Do not move your head. Do not speak."

The dark figure behind him placed the short, thick candle upon Achille's head and held it there.

"If you wish the gun you hold," the tall woman told Chelle, "you must shoot out the flame."

Almost casually, the gun came up. Chelle's grip tightened and she fired—long before Skip had expected it.

The candle winked out and the tall woman said, "This gun is my gift to both of you."

"Thank you!" Chelle was smiling broadly. "Thank you very much! Now we have to buy a gun for my mother."

REFLECTION 5

The Ride Back

The goats and sheep and hogs are still abroad, though the maiden and her bananas are no longer to be seen. Was she at the temple? I doubt it, but it is certainly possible. There were a great many people there shouting and jumping, forever standing up and sitting down. She may have been among them. She may have danced with us. Or not.

The man who barred Achille's way was dead. So Achille says, and I believe him—or at least, I believe that he believes he's telling the truth. The dead man stood behind him, taller than he, to make him stand still. What fear had the dead man of Chelle's bullet? He was already dead.

Or at least, believed he was.

Our headlights show us animals, first a dog in the road, then a goat. There is something Satanic about goats, and there was something very Satanic about this one, with its beard and S-shaped horns. How easy it would be to think the ceremony Satanic, though there was no invocation of Satan. Only strange but unforgotten African gods. There were holy cards in Tante Élise's house.

Can God hate people so cheerful in their poverty?

Chelle, her head upon my lap, snores softly, stirs, and sleeps again. Achille is asleep in the front seat. From the jump seat, Vanessa stares out at the night in silence. Neither of us wish to wake Chelle. Certainly I do not.

. . .

Don, she whispers. *Don* . . . Then something else; I catch the word *dead*, but nothing more. Is Don dead? I hope so.

She bought Vanessa a little automatic, a thing like a piece of jewelry. Silver-plated, I think, though it might be chrome. If I were to see it in sunlight I might be able to tell, or so I think. She said it was old but could not have fired more than two hundred rounds in all its many years. Vanessa fired it at a tree—seven shots.

Seven of us were present, Tante Élise said. Chelle, Vanessa, Achille, Tante Élise herself, the dead man, and me. She must have counted our driver as well though he was asleep in his taxi, so far away that the shooting did not wake him.

I will stop the driver when we reach the summit, but only if Chelle is awake.

Vanessa went to this side of the mountain and followed the sound of the drums. Went how? Followed how? I would have assumed that the social director would remain aboard, as perhaps she did until Tante Élise came for her.

Achille has his hundred noras. He will attach himself to us, if he can. And I will scrape him off, unless I find him useful.

Of what use he might be once we leave this island, I cannot imagine.

Vanessa leans back. Her eyes are closed. Does she sleep? I would be wise to sleep, perhaps, if I can. Will I drop Chelle . . . if I do?

Drums in my dreams. Drums and dancers? Was the ceremony a dream, too? The blood and the dying, gasping animals? Does Chelle have a gun, and Vanessa? Chelle's will be in her purse, surely. It has fallen to the floor. When I try to reach it, she stirs. Do her eyelids flutter? It is too dark to see.

At the summit, I will tell her I want to get out. My legs must rest from her weight for a while.

And I want to look at the stars.

6

STATEROOM ONE

The *Rani* was gone. Fog or no fog, there could be no doubt of it. A smaller vessel might still have been in port, invisible behind the goblin curtains that had become its atmosphere; no fog could have hidden the *Rani*'s long white hull and towering masts in so small a harbor.

Skip glanced at his watch. "You said they wouldn't sail before eight. It's seven thirty-five."

"They weren't supposed to." Vanessa was scanning the fishing boats.

Chelle said, "They told you that, Mother?"

"Yes. Absolutely. I was worried about the passengers who might be left behind. Captain Kain told me there'd be boatmen hanging around the docks offering to ferry people back, and he wouldn't up anchor until high tide. So I wanted to know when that was, and he said eight o'clock."

Achille asked, "What you do, mon?"

"Give chase," Skip said. "They can't have been gone long. If it weren't for this mist, we might be able to see them. There are men working on that boat." He pointed with his walking stick.

"Yes, mon. I see."

"Run over there. Tell them we'll pay them if they can get us to the *Rani*."

Achille dashed away.

The boat was small, and smelled of fish twice as much as was to be expected. Chelle sprang aboard it without assistance; Skip climbed in more cautiously, and together they helped Vanessa aboard. Their crew of three raised worn brown sails spread wide by gaffs, after which the younger men manned sweeps while the owner took the tiller.

Chelle's hand found Skip's. "What if we can't catch them?"

"We go to Hispaniola. There should be an airport there, and if we're as lucky as five people can be, we may be able to charter a plane to fly us to the next port on the tour."

"Someone who can get that much fuel. . . ."

"Exactly. Which is why we'll need wonderful luck. It will cost a great deal, if we can do it at all. This boat won't, so it's worth a try."

Vanessa joined them. "There are only four of us, and the beggar won't be boarding the *Rani* with us."

Chelle said, "Tante Élise said there were seven people there. Remember, Mother? I think she thought any gun—"

Skip had his finger to his lips.

"Well, you know. Anyway I thought about that, about seven, and the man who stopped Achille made six. We four, Tante Élise, and him. So there was somebody else."

Vanessa said, "Skip?"

"I simply meant that we would need more luck than four could have."

The rowers shipped their sweeps as the sails filled. The owner shouted at them, and one climbed the foremast with an agility Skip could only envy.

Vanessa was taking off her shoes. "They make it hard to balance," she told Chelle.

"You think he's hiding something, don't you?"

"Surely not, darling." Vanessa's smile was angelic.

The man at the masthead shouted and pointed, then slid down.

"We catch," Achille said. "Catch today, mon."

Chelle asked, "Will we, Skip?"

"I think so. There isn't a lot of wind, and it takes a pretty good wind to move a ship like the *Rani* fast."

From his place at the tiller, the owner nodded and grinned. "You sleep beeg boat."

Chelle went to the bow, where Skip soon joined her. "Am I intruding?"

"I was hoping you'd come." She put her arm through his. "I wanted to talk to you in private."

"What about?"

"Lots of things. Can I start with the Army?"

"Certainly," Skip said.

"I'm not going back."

He shrugged. "That's your decision."

"I used to think so." Chelle sighed. "When you wanted to go on the cruise I thought I could use the time to think things over."

Skip had seen what the lookout had seen: sails not yet over the horizon. He stared at them, saying nothing.

"Last night—do you realize we haven't slept?"

"You dozed in the cab coming back," Skip said. "So did I."

"That's right, so you got a little sleep. Enough?"

He shook his head.

"I hardly got any. Mother slept, and Achille slept before either of you, and woke up last. Only I didn't mean that when I said last night. I meant the night when we screwed and slept together in our cabin."

"The screwing was Jerry. Not me."

"Yeah, right. I'm sorry. I forgot."

"Was he good?"

"Not very. But before that, at the party. Do you remember me telling you that Mother had peeked in?"

Skip nodded.

"That wasn't really it. Not quite. She came in and handed me a gram. I asked what it said, and she said she hadn't read it. That was a lie but it was what she said, and she beat it before I could read it myself. It was from Camp Martinez and said I was being discharged. I told you I was taking psych tests."

He nodded again.

"Well, I flunked them. I'm mentally and emotionally impaired. So discharge, and disability pay for the rest of my life."

When Skip did not speak, Chelle added, "It's pretty good, too."

He put his arm around her. "I can imagine how you must feel."

"It isn't that. I can handle my feelings. Now I can. I just wanted to tell you that was why I took Jerry to our cabin. I'd been planning to leave early and lock you out. That's the truth."

"I believe you."

"But I got hammered instead. I grabbed the guy I had been talking to because he had a hand on my—up here. You know."

"I grasp the concept."

"You do now. Yes. It's yours. Only then . . ."

"It wasn't," Skip said.

"Whatever. I wanted to explain, and I wanted to let you know I'm not right. Did you guess?"

"My guesses don't matter." He took a deep breath. "I love you, Chelle. That's what matters, and if you love me, that's all that matters."

"I do. I really do. I know you don't believe me, but it's the truth. That's the first thing I wanted to talk about."

He kissed her; and it lasted for a long, long time and ended too soon.

"Now we're going to fight again," she said when they parted.

"You may fight me, but I won't fight you."

"Okay. Deal. Have you made it with Mother?"

It took him by surprise. "Certainly not. Why do you ask?"

"Because she wants you to. I can tell, Skip, and I think you can tell, too. What's the number of her cabin?"

He tried to recall it. "I don't remember. J Deck, but not the rest of it."

"She told you, though?"

"Yes. Yes, she did."

"All you'd have to do is crook your finger."

"At first, yes. After that, I'd have to keep her entertained. Charlie Blue couldn't, and I doubt that I'd last as long as he did."

"Would you try?"

Skip considered, counseled by the gentle roll of the fishing boat. "If she were all I had? Yes, I suppose I would, in a feeble, middle-aged way. I wouldn't succeed, and I know it. But I'd try to postpone failure."

"She's my mother. What if I take after her?"

"I answered that already."

"Fair enough. Did you notice the corpse in the water? No, I can see you didn't. It was close to the wharf. You had to look almost straight down."

"Perhaps we should have reported it," Skip said.

"I thought of that, but we didn't have much time and we couldn't have helped him. He was floating facedown, and part of his head was gone."

"Don't cry. Please." He embraced her.

"It's just . . . Thanks for the hug."

"Anytime." Skip held her a little more tightly.

"I couldn't think of his name, but nobody could forget that shirt. He came to stand with us when we were waiting to get off the ship. He was at the party."

"Albano Alamar."

"Yeah. Him." Chelle wept.

Not knowing what else to say, Skip said, "I imagine that could be a rough town at night."

It did not seem to help. When Vanessa joined them a few minutes later, that did not help either.

Ten or twelve hours later, their captain shouted up at the ship, making a trumpet of his hands. After what seemed a long wait, a dark-faced man with a thin mustache looked over the side. "You desire to come on board?"

"Yes!" Skip called. "Two passengers and an employee! We were left behind!"

The dark face vanished. Vanessa said, "What's the matter with them?"

Skip was getting out his wallet. "I imagine they're debating how to get us on board without stopping the ship."

He had paid the owner when the dark face reappeared. "You, señor. You first. Then the other man. Then the women."

"Whatever became of women and children first?" Vanessa muttered.

Chelle said, "They don't want to be accused of feeling us up afterward. Do we want Achille, Skip?"

He shook his head. "I'll tell them when I get on board."

A rope was thrown into the fishing boat and tied to a mast. After fifteen minutes or more it became the monorail of a canvas contrivance resembling a pair of trousers.

Vanessa raised her eyebrows. "I thought they'd lower a boat for us."

Without replying, Skip stepped over the broad ring that formed the waistband, and pulled it up. A moment later, ring and trousers pulled him up, moving him almost horizontally at first, then higher and higher until two swarthy men grabbed him and heaved him across the Main Deck railing.

The man with the thin mustache was leaning against a bulkhead; his arms cradled a submachine gun. "Your cabin number, señor?"

"Twenty-three C."

"Ah! You are rich. We will discuss your ransom tomorrow, I think. Sit down." The man with the mustache gestured with the barrel of his submachine gun. "Over there."

Skip sat, and watched as the canvas contrivance was sent down its rope again. "You're hijackers, aren't you?"

The man with the submachine gun pointed it at him. *"¡Silencio!"*

Achille was next up. He put the point of a hook through the cheek of one of the men who had pulled him up, and was knocked down and kicked repeatedly.

Vanessa followed; she seemed to grasp the situation immediately, and explained that she had very little money. "Technically, I'm just a petty officer. I'm Virginia Healy, the social director, and a citizen of the North American Union."

The man with the thin mustache made her a mock salute with his submachine gun. "As I, señora, am not."

"May I go to my cabin? I'll stay there, if that's what you want."

"No, señora. Sit beside that man."

"Him?" Vanessa hesitated, looking at Skip. "I was on the boat with him, Señor . . . ?"

"Del Valle, señora. *Su servidor.*"

"He's really quite unpleasant, Del. I would prefer—"

"*¡Abajo!*"

Vanessa sat, and Skip watched the canvas contrivance go over the rail once more. "Do me a favor," he whispered.

"I apologize for being so nasty, I only wanted him to think—"

"Put both hands behind your back. Like mine."

"We weren't in cahoots." Vanessa's hands moved as she spoke.

"Good," Skip whispered.

The contrivance returned bearing Chelle. She cleared the railing, and the ring supporting the canvas trousers fell at her feet.

The man with the submachine gun smiled slyly. "I fear, señora, that—"

He staggered backward, dropping his submachine gun. There were more shots, two or three coming so quickly that Skip could not count them, although afterward it seemed to him that everything had taken place in slow motion: Chelle drawing from inside her loose blue blouse; blood oozing from a hole in a man's face to soak his thin mustache; two men falling toward each other, so that their dying bodies nearly collided; Skip himself struggling to get to his feet, hampered by air far thicker than water.

He stumbled across the deck to the submachine gun and scooped it up.

The deck thundered, pounded by running feet. He felt, rather than heard, another shot and saw the first man fall, saw the dead man's look of surprise and the dark off-center dot on the dead man's forehead.

Awkwardly, he braced the steel butt-plate of the submachine gun against his shoulder, so intent upon haste that he did not recall that he had never fired such a gun before, had never fired any gun. Pulling the trigger made the gun jump and rattle in his hand, surprising him so much that he let go of the trigger. There were half a dozen dead men on the deck now, and behind and to his right another gun reported in swift and measured words: *Dead! Dead! Dead!*

Eight or nine or ten now.

Skip's finger found the trigger and he fired again, a five (or six) round burst. A carpet of the dead and the dying stretched toward the bow. Beyond it other men had turned to flee.

Chelle grasped his sleeve. "We'd better get inside before they get on top of us."

He followed her. Vanessa had gone already, or so it appeared. Achille was searching the body of the man with the thin mustache, searching clumsily but swiftly, tearing at the dead man's clothing with his hooks. Skip motioned to him.

Then ran, sprinting to keep up. A perforated metal guard kept his left hand away from the hot barrel of the submachine gun. As he ran, he tried to guess how many cartridges were left. His first burst had been . . . Ten or twelve? More? The second about five. How many shots did these things hold?

Chelle had stopped to look back at him. He slowed and managed to gasp, "Where we going?"

"To Stateroom One!" She pointed up. "Run!" At once, she was dashing away, easily outdistancing him.

"Mon! Mon!"

He stopped and turned.

"They after us!" Achille waved a hook.

"Get down," Skip told him, and raised the submachine gun.

The veranda had seemed safest, so that was where he was. If they came, there would be no chance for him to run out into the corridor. But if they looked only through the Changeglass veranda doors, they would not see him sitting on weathered teak on the far side of the farthest chair.

This was B Deck, he decided. This veranda was larger than their own, so B Deck or A Deck. And the sun was—oh, blessedly! blessedly!—sinking into the western sea.

Idly, he explored his empty submachine gun. Push this little switch down, and the trigger would not move. Push it up and it would. This button held the sheet-metal box that should (but did not) contain cartridges.

"Here, ladies and gentlemen of the jury, is the very weapon employed by the defendant—that is to say, by me. My esteemed colleague the prosecutor will try to draw your attention from it. I must draw your attention to it. The weapons employed by criminals—"

His mobile phone vibrated. Laying aside the empty submachine gun, he found the tiny, shaking instrument and flipped it open.

His first whisper was so soft that he could not hear it himself. He tried again: "Hello?"

"This you, sir? You're in shadow."

"Yes, Mick, it's me. I'm outside and the sun's almost down. Ask questions if you want to establish my identity."

"Okay. Who're we defending in the cyborg case?"

"John J. Weyer."

"Who's Virginia Healy?"

"That's a name that a certain woman may have used when she went into the hospital."

"Fine, it's you. I've got the Z man's report. The name she gave at the hospital was the first one you gave me when you called, Vanessa Hennessey. The hospital was South Side Community. She checked herself out the next day. Do you—?"

"Wait," Skip said. "Early or late?"

"Eight fifteen. My guess is that's as early as she could do it."

"I concur." Skip paused to think, shading his eyes as he stared out at the Caribbean. "What else?"

"Nothing much except the knife. The Z man got a look at it, but they wouldn't let him take a picture. It was a steak knife, he said. Thermosetting handle, ten-centimeter blade, slightly curved. Serrated. Sharp point."

"Ah!"

Tooley chuckled. *"Glad we pushed your button."*

"Anything else?"

"Mixed descriptions of the stabber. The cop—his name is Burgos—found three people who said they'd seen him. He was average height, tall, well dressed, white, and Latino. He was or wasn't carrying something in his other hand, a newspaper or an attaché case. Helpful?"

"No."

"Aren't you going to ask whether we've found Vanessa Hennessey, sir?"

"I never told you to find her. I asked you to try to trace her movements."

"Meaning that you know where she is."

"Correct."

"Still alive?"

Skip sighed. "I hope so. She's Chelle's mother. I told you that."

"Yes, sir. How is she? Ms. Blue, I mean."

"Mastergunner Blue. She's not out yet, although she will be soon. Technically, she's on leave."

"I've never seen her, sir, and I've been trying to get a description. I know you're contracted."

"Correct." Skip sighed again. "We are."

"Beautiful?"

"Depends. How do you feel about tall, rangy blondes with one hand bigger than the other?"

Tooley chuckled. *"That would depend on which hand, sir."*

"The right hand."

"Love them. I may try to move in on you."

"You'd probably succeed. I haven't told you about the clear blue eyes or the glowing smile. You may never see them, but they're there."

"Going to keep her under wraps, sir?"

"I wish I could."

"There's something—well, I hesitate to mention it, sir. But . . ."

"You feel you should. I've got something like that, too. You first."

"All right." Tooley took an audible breath. *"Your secretary's resigned. That was day-before-yesterday. I talked to her."*

Skip said nothing.

"I didn't learn a lot, sir."

"Susan? Susan quit?"

"Yes, sir. I asked her to stay 'til Friday to brief Dianne. And me. Next week Dianne will have to hold the fort. With you away, there can't be much for her to do. She'll have a half a year to get the feel of it."

"Uh huh."

"I'm the one who told her, sir. I said she was your acting secretary until you

came back, that she'd have to ask all her questions fast, and that you'd decide whether to make it permanent when you got back."

The sun was almost down; Skip peeped at it, a segment of burning red gold. "I may not come back," he told Tooley. "I'll explain that in a moment. Did Susan give any reason for resigning?"

There was a silence. Skip waited.

At length: *"I think you know the reason, sir."*

"Of course I do, Mick. That wasn't what I asked you. I want to know what she said, if anything."

"She said she would never be thirty again, sir."

"Nor will I. Did you tell her that?"

"No, sir."

The sun had gone; high in the west, Skip saw the first star. "I doubt that she will want to come back, but if she does give her back her old job. No loss of seniority. Say she's been on unpaid leave."

"Got it, sir."

"This ship's been taken, Mick. Hijacked."

Tooley's whistle was audible.

"They spoke of ransom." Skip wanted to sigh, but did not. "Chelle killed the man who spoke of it, and that was my fault. I wasn't thinking clearly, just worrying about what they would do to her." He paused, wanting to pace up and down.

"I'd say you had every right to worry."

"Yes, I suppose. If I had it to do over . . . Well, maybe I'd do the same thing. At any rate he's dead now."

"They're holding you, sir?"

"No. I'm hiding. I have good reason to believe they'll kill me if they find me. And—"

Tooley interrupted. *"What did you do?"*

"That doesn't matter. The thing is that I don't want you to notify the Coast Guard."

"I had just decided to do that as soon as we hung up."

"Don't. It seems certain that the captain or one of the other officers got a message out, to say nothing of the passengers. We may have hijackers—hell, we do—but this isn't the seventeenth century. So they probably know already. Unless there's someone a lot more important than I am on board . . ."

"I've got it. What if I could organize a private rescue?"

"Then do it. I'm not certain the Coast Guard would rescue us, to tell you the truth. I've been involved with a couple of hijacking cases—"

"I know, sir. The City of Port Arthur. International Law of the Sea Tribunal. All that nonsense."

"In one of those cases, the ship sunk. The hijackers scuttled it—or that's the official line. Do hijackers take ships in order to sink them?"

"I wouldn't if I were a hijacker."

"Nor would I. Do you think you can really organize a rescue?"

"Yes, sir. It'll take money, but I believe it might be done."

"See Ibarra. You'll have to sell him on it. You don't have to sell me. I just hope you can pull it off."

"You can count on me." Tooley cleared his throat. *"I've told you what I called to tell you, sir. All right if I ask a question?"*

"Of course. What is it?"

"What are you going to do now? You said you were hiding."

"I'm going to try to get into Stateroom One. That was what we tried to do when we got loose—get to Stateroom One. There were hijackers, and I don't know whether they got Chelle and her mother. I heard gunfire, and when I got there I fired and ran. A cabin door was open and I ducked inside."

"And hid?"

"No. I'd seen a young man—this was yesterday—who jumped from veranda to veranda. I didn't actually see him do it, but it was what he must have done. He was about your age, I'd say. I'm quite a bit older than he was, but I did the best I could, balancing on the railing with a hand on a partition and grabbing a railing post of the veranda above and so on. Scrambling up. Those partitions are between the verandas horizontally, but you can swing around them if you try. I stopped here when I was too tired to go farther."

"I hope you're rested now, sir. What's in Stateroom One?"

"I don't know," Skip said.

REFLECTION 6

The Best Course

The moon is high—clearly I slept. They'll sleep, too. Most of them and perhaps all of them. What have they done with the passengers? There's no one behind these glass doors, no one in the bedroom behind this veranda. Luggage, yes, and a rumpled bed; but no people. We would have seen bodies in the water, surely. Not a great many perhaps, in proportion to the passengers and crew; but ten or twenty, certainly. We saw none, except for poor Al Alamar. He returned to the ship, found the hijackers in control, and tried to fight them. He was a soldier, and a brave one.

Did the other soldiers fight? Some of them at least? There were a good many on the ship, apparently, most of them in second class. There were enough for Vanessa to hold a meet-greet-and-hook-up party for them.

Chelle went, and I ought to have gone with her. She was angry, but would she have made a scene if I had come in later? Very possibly she would, if she were drunk by then. Certainly she was drunk later—or so I'd like to believe. Was our seventh person drunk too? Was Jane Sims drunk? Did she think Jim or Jerry might be Don? Was Don a soldier? I'd like to think that he was, and that she did.

If the soldiers fought, Jim and Jerry may be dead, for which I now owe them even more. As much as I owe poor Al Alamar.

I'm no soldier nor am I brave, only a killer with an empty gun. Vanessa thought I was brave because I fought that military cop. That wasn't courage, only rage. Rage because he had struck me, and frustration because Chelle hadn't recognized me. We killers, we murderers, how often we do it because we're angry or frustrated or both. That man who kicked a little child to death. His girlfriend's child, and perhaps he was its father. He or some other man she had met in the same bar or another bar. . . .

Chelle may be pregnant; but if she is, the infant she carries will not be mine. Will I ever have a child?

Have a son? Will I, someday, kick him to death?

How many murder cases have I defended? Eight I can think of offhand. Even a murderer deserves to have someone to speak for him, someone who will explain to the jury why he did what he did and show him where his best interests lie. I did what I could for them, even for the woman who killed her own children.

I'll do my best to defend Vanessa, if I ever get the chance. Who will defend the man who tried to kill her? And will he do his best for him, his best for the faceless man, tall and well dressed, with the steak knife?

Who'll do his best for me? Men with machetes dashing down the corridor, into the fire of my submachine gun . . . Into the fire of this gun I hold, dashing to their deaths.

When I'm killed tonight, it will be one more. We all have to die, and I've had my dream. Chelle returned to me, still as young and fresh as she had been twenty years ago. That was what I wanted. I got it, and the rest has been anticlimax.

Would I live for her if I could? No. My living will do her no good and may do her a great deal of harm, but I will live for myself if I can.

What's in Stateroom One? And how did Vanessa learn that it was there?

Did they reach it? She and Chelle? Is Chelle still alive? I must find out if I can, must help her if I can. Would she do the same for me? Certainly, and without a moment's thought.

These glass doors are locked. I might climb up or down, but it will be easier to try another veranda forward. As tired as I am—tired, stiff, thirsty, and hungry—that will be the best course. There ought to be a refrigerator inside a first-class stateroom, mixers and snacks. If I put my left arm and my head through this strap or whatever they call it, I can carry the submachine gun slantwise across my back.

And now up on the railing and step across—carefully, carefully—and the veranda door here is already open.

How easy it was!

7

IT'S MY SHIP

Whether the hijackers would keep the ship's wind-powered generators in operation had been the question; clearly the answer was yes. The corridors were still well lit, and the elevators still ran, though none would carry a man from B Deck to A Deck. Skip thought it likely that Stateroom One would be on A Deck, and looked.

It was not. The lowest number on A Deck was ten, and the companionway he had used reached no higher. He was sweating by the time he found another companionway (marked CREW ONLY) that led to the deck above. There a neat bronze plaque announced: SIGNAL DECK.

The bridge—so marked by a small brass sign—was a dozen paces to his right and up a short stair; voices murmured in Spanish behind its closed door. Nearer was a door bearing a single digit: 1. It was, of course, locked.

Another door, this at the aft end of the corridor, was not. Skip opened it and stepped out into the night. As his eyes adjusted to the gloom he saw that the signal deck was surrounded on three sides by weather decking, the roof of the A Deck staterooms. There were chairs there and a few tables, round tables whose pale white tops were trumped by a full moon. With his empty submachine gun slung across his back, he might pass for a hijacker here.

As he had expected, a sliding glass door not quite below the port bridge wing promised entry into Stateroom One. As he had also expected, it was locked—or latched, at least. Though it was difficult to judge by moonlight, it did not appear that the security bar was in place. He had defended burglars; but real burglars (he reminded himself wearily) carried burglar tools. He had keys and a few coins, his penknife, and the gun.

The latch was guarded on the outside by a polished metal molding, probably brass. To the best of his memory, the veranda door of 23C had been latched with a simple hook, raised and lowered by a handle on the inside. He tugged at the molding, without result.

He could smash the glass with the submachine gun's steel butt-plate, presumably; but the noise would surely alert the men on the bridge. Glass could be broken with a minimum of noise by taping it first. Unfortunately, he had no tape.

He dropped into one of the chairs. If only he had a tool—a claw hammer, for example—he could probably bend back the metal molding. That done, a screwdriver or almost any other tool might have served to lift the latch. Would he have to go below again to look (God alone knew where) for tools?

Half a minute's thought suggested that it might be possible to bend back the molding with the butt-plate, if he could get it off. Informed by moonlight, his fingertips told him it was fastened by two large screws, and that the screws had wide slots; a coin might serve as a screwdriver.

He was trying it when his coin discovered a narrow depression in the butt-plate, a depression long enough for him to get the nails of three fingers into it. A firm pull flipped up a lid, and turning the gun muzzle-up dropped objects into his lap. The first was round, presumably a vial of oil; the second proved to be a slotted metal tip trailing a strong cord. The third was a multi-tool that included a coarse screwdriver blade about eight centimeters long.

It bent the molding easily. Lifting the latch was almost as easy. The glass door slid silently back, and Skip stepped silently in. The stateroom seemed twice the size of the one he had shared with Chelle, although its smaller bed might have been responsible for part of the apparent increase. After drawing the drapes he switched on a desk light.

The paneled walls held two pictures, both of the *Rani*. The desk a third—a long-faced, bearded, smiling man in uniform; a pretty woman ten years past youth, also smiling; and three smiling children.

Files in the desk, and a keyboard and screen front and center. Pencils, pens, paper clips, and paper. Telephone on a nightstand. Printer in the corner. Uniforms and a dinner jacket in the closet; two pairs of shoes, both black and highly polished, on the closet floor. Starched white shirts, underwear, socks, and pajamas in drawers. A tele in a cabinet, books on the shelves beneath it. Could this be all?

The bathroom door was not quite closed. Skip pushed it open and for a long second saw only the muzzle of a pistol; during that second, its bore seemed the size of a railway tunnel. He raised both hands.

"Volver," said the bearded man holding the gun. A circular gesture of his left hand illustrated his meaning.

"I'm not a hijacker." Skip turned around. "I'm a passenger, Captain."

"A passenger with a submachine gun."

"An empty submachine gun. Correct."

"Sit down. Right there on the floor."

Skip did.

"Name and cabin number? Class?"

"Skip Webster Grison, and yes, my first name really is Skip. Stateroom Twenty-three, C Deck. First class—but you know that. B and C are all first-class. A is—"

"I know what A is. Did you say your gun's empty?"

Skip nodded.

"You killed hijackers with it?" The captain strode past Skip and turned to face him.

He shrugged. "I tried, Captain, and eight or ten went down. They can't all have been dead."

"Where did you get the gun?"

"I took it from a dead man."

"A dead hijacker? You killed him?"

"No. Chelle did. I just took his gun."

"Chelle is a friend of yours, I take it."

"She's my contracta, Captain. Why don't I just explain? It will go faster."

"Go ahead. Let's hear it."

"Chelle knew somebody had tried to kill her mother. Her mother's your social director."

"You mean Virginia?"

"Correct. Chelle's an expert shot and wanted a gun so she could protect her. We went ashore and got one, but we had to go to the other side of the island. By the time we returned you'd put out."

"I didn't. The hijackers did. I thought they might run her aground, but they were lucky. Go on."

"I hired a fishing boat to take us out to the *Rani*. It took most of the day to catch up, but we did. When—"

"By 'we' you mean this woman Chelle and yourself?"

"Yes, plus Chelle's mother and a beggar who had been interpreting for us. We took him on the boat because we couldn't talk to the men who sailed it without him."

"I understand."

"The hijackers took me on board first, then him, then Virginia, and then Chelle. Chelle had her gun by then, and she knows how to use guns. She killed the man who had this gun, and I grabbed it."

"And shot some more?"

"Yes. So did Chelle. Three or four others, I'd say. After that she ran. I didn't realize at first that she was running after her mother, but now I think she was. Chelle can run like a deer, and I couldn't keep up. I managed to get close enough to ask where we were going, and she said Stateroom One and pointed up."

The captain nodded. "Go on."

"She got ahead of me again, and I heard shots. All this was on the Main Deck—perhaps I should say that. There was a transverse corridor, and Chelle had turned off it toward the middle of the ship."

"She was heading for the elevators, I imagine."

"I suppose. All I know is that when I went around the corner myself, I didn't see either of them, just three hijackers with guns. I shot them, and I was still pulling the trigger when my gun stopped firing."

"You didn't know why those women were coming here?"

"No. The men I shot seemed to be dead or dying. All of them had guns, and if I'd any sense I'd have picked them up. I stared at the men instead. Then the elevator doors opened, and I ran. Do you want to hear the rest?"

The captain nodded.

"I found a card room with an unlocked door and ducked inside. After ten minutes I felt trapped in there, so I went out on deck, climbed on top of a little table, grabbed the rail of the veranda above, and pulled myself up to C Deck. For a while I tried to get to our cabin, but there wasn't anything in there I wanted. Not really."

"Go on, Mr. Grison."

"I'm ashamed to. There wasn't anything, and I was afraid they'd look for me there. If they had Chelle or her mother, they might know our cabin number. So I climbed up to B Deck instead. I hid there until it got dark."

"Then you came up here."

"Correct." Skip drew a deep breath. "I hoped Chelle and her mother would be here. They weren't, as well as I could judge, but I decided to try to get in myself. They'd wanted to go here, and I thought there had to be a reason. Perhaps they just wanted to see if you were still alive."

"Hardly. I know what they wanted—or what Virginia wanted, anyway. I'll show you in a minute. Where are these bastards holding their prisoners? Have you got any idea?"

"None. But I'm certain they have prisoners. The man who had this gun told me that he was going to hold me for ransom."

The captain nodded. "That's where the money is, ransom for the passengers and the ship. The ship is insured, of course. But when an insurer can get a ship back and return it to its owner, he doesn't have to pay. Ransoming the ship's cheaper than paying off."

"What happens to passengers who aren't ransomed?"

The captain's smile was grim. "What do you think happens, Mr. Grison?"

"The crew, too?"

"If the company won't pay to get them back, yes, they die. It's the threat of death that brings the ransoms, so the bastards have to keep the threat credible. I'll be ransomed, or I think I will. So will you and Chelle, or so I'd imagine. Virginia?"

"Yes. I'll call a man who works with me."

"Good. But the steward who's been taking care of your stateroom will die. So will the seamen who've been working the ship and a good many more. The actors who put on our live shows, for example, and all our cooks and barmen and croupiers. We carry five crew to every four passengers, Mr. Grison. The Union Employment Administration requires it. Some of our crew were ashore when the ship was taken, but only a few. The hijackers jumped us just before sunrise."

"I see."

"So did Virginia. She saw what I'm going to show you. She's a charming woman, isn't she?"

"Very."

"That's why I let her see the arms chest. She had no real need to know, but I was showing off. What caliber is that gun of yours?"

"Nine millimeter parabellum. It's stamped on it."

"Good! That's what we've got—all that we've got, in fact. You must know something about guns."

"Not much." Skip sighed. "I'm an attorney, Captain. I've defended cases in which guns were involved. That's all they ever were to me, the prosecution's Exhibit A. Now I wish I knew as much as Chelle."

"Your contracta?"

"Correct. She was a soldier. Technically she still is, although she'll be discharged next year. Can I see the arms chest?"

"Of course. We'll reload that gun of yours, too." The captain stepped past Skip. "We'll have to move the tele. I'll show you."

"May I stand up?"

"Yes, of course." The captain offered his hand. Skip took it and stood.

"It's fastened down," the captain said. "Everything is, even my chair. You can't have furniture sliding around in a storm." He reached behind the tele cabinet and pulled. "There's a self-aligning catch, very clever. Now I can push this to one side."

He demonstrated, revealing a steel lid with a combination lock. "I'll bet you were expecting something bigger."

"I was," Skip said.

"A pistol for each officer. That's all the company will provide." The captain was turning the dial. "Three hundred years ago, ships still carried a weapon for every man in the crew, a cutlass or a boarding ax in most cases. Now—well, I shouldn't talk against management."

"You had no chance to issue what you had."

"You're right, I didn't. I didn't even have time to arm myself. They caught me right here in my pajamas and held me on the bridge for most of the day. Two of them were taking me somewhere below when they saw a chance to loot and got busy with that. I slipped away and hid. When it seemed that things had quieted down, I came back here. I almost never lock my door. I doubt that a lawyer would believe that."

"A lawyer would certainly want to know why."

"Because the officer of the watch is under orders to call me anytime anything unexpected turns up, day or night. The bridge is right next door."

Skip nodded.

"I run up there in pajamas and slippers. A robe, too, now and then, but not often. That's why my door is never locked." The captain pulled up the steel lid of the arms chest, revealing a row of semiautomatic pistols held in a padded rack. "I locked it behind me when I came in, of course. I got this gun and a spare magazine and locked the chest back up. Then I thought that since I was here I might as well get dressed. That's what I was doing when you came in."

The telephone on the captain's desk chimed. Both men stared at it, then at each other.

It chimed again.

"I think I'd better answer it," the captain muttered. He seemed to wait for Skip to object; when Skip did not, he added, "It might be important."

Skip nodded, and the captain picked up the receiver. The young woman who appeared on the screen was neatly and nautically uniformed. The captain said, "Yes. Speaking."

The young woman spoke at length; and the captain said, "As a matter of fact, he's right here." He turned to Skip. "It's for you."

Skip accepted the receiver.

"Mr. Grison? Are you S. W. Grison the attorney, sir?"

Skip nodded.

"Of Burton, Grison, and Ibarra?"

"Correct."

"This is the Judge Advocate's Department, sir. I'm in South Boswash, and I represent the Coast Guard. My name is Lieutenant Fabre. A young woman from your office called to notify the Coast Guard that your ship, the Rani . . . *I think she said the* Rani . . . *"*

"Correct," Skip said again.

"That it had been attacked by hijackers."

"It's Captain Kain's ship," Skip said, "but you're correct. It has been."

"I felt that it might save a great deal of legal wrangling, and expense, if I spoke to you, sir, and clarified our position. The Coast Guard has jurisdiction in NAU territorial waters only, sir. Outside those waters, the UN has jurisdiction. Were you attacked in NAU territorial waters, sir?"

"No. The Antillian Union."

"I see. And are you in NAU territorial waters at present?"

"I can't say, although I think it likely. Hold on a moment, please, Lieutenant." Skip turned to the captain. "We're headed toward Yucatán, aren't we?"

The captain nodded.

Lieutenant Fabre said, *"That was a leading question, sir."*

"I suppose. We're not in court at present."

The captain said, "If we're not in NAU waters now, we soon will be."

Lieutenant Fabre smiled. *"You'll have to establish that in court, sir. I'm sure you understand."*

"If we enter NAU territorial waters and are not rescued, there may well be a legal action," Skip told her. "The Coast Guard could render the entire question moot by rescuing us, however."

"I feel sure we're tracking your position." Lieutenant Fabre did not sound sure.

Skip said, "If you don't mind, Lieutenant, we're busy here."

"I'll have to check." Lieutenant Fabre hung up.

So did Skip.

"They won't do it," the captain told him.

"You're probably right, and there's a chance they may sink us and claim the hijackers did it."

"I've heard the rumors."

"Now then. If you can give me ammunition, I want it. I want a pistol, too. You might consider carrying a couple more yourself."

"What for?"

"To give to anyone who might be able—and willing—to use them. That's what Virginia had in mind, I'm sure. She had a gun already, and so did Chelle. Most of the passengers will want to sit it out, figuring they'll be ransomed, but a few will fight. The crew will fight, knowing they'll be killed."

"I see what you mean." The captain massaged his jaw. "I going to ask you a very personal question, Mr. Grison. If you want ammunition and a handgun, you're going to have to answer it. That's not polite, I realize."

Skip nodded. "This isn't the time for courtesy."

"Exactly. You had a first-class stateroom, and from what you say, you're a wealthy man. You'll be ransomed, and you'll ransom your contracta and her mother. Why are you willing to fight?"

"Not to save your life or the lives of your crew. It's hard to admit this even to myself."

"As long as you're ready to help me get the ship back, you don't have to answer," the captain said.

"I will anyway, because I want to get it out in the open. First, because the hijackers will kill me if they catch me. I've shot—I don't know . . . I was going to say eight or ten, but it could be more. Some will have lived, and they'll be able to identify me."

"Maybe not."

Skip shrugged. "Second—this is the hard part."

"Go on."

"Second because I need to prove myself to Chelle. To myself, too. Perhaps to myself most of all. Chelle went to some godforsaken planet and fought like a lioness. I stayed here, kept the home fires burning, and won a few cases. Have I told you about our hands?"

The captain shook his head.

"Her mother and I were already on board, already captured when Chelle got there. The offenders had a life preserver with pants. You got into them and held on, and they pulled you up."

"A breeches buoy."

"Thank you. I put my hands behind me as if I were in handcuffs, and I got Chelle's mother to do it, too. I wanted Chelle to know what was going on."

"I understand."

"She did. She had her gun out in an instant and shot the man who had this machine gun I've been carrying around. She's a very good shot."

"But she was doing the fighting, and not you? Is that what you're telling me?"

"Correct. More offenders were coming—I suppose they'd heard the shot. I got this gun, pointed it like you'd point a garden hose, and held the trigger back. Chelle fired, too. You know the rest."

"Perhaps we'd better go."

Skip nodded. "Will you give me that handgun?"

"I'll give you two, and couple of spare magazines. Can Virginia shoot?"

"I don't know. I doubt it, but Chelle bought her a gun."

"We'll have to find people who can, and are willing to fight. I'm taking two myself. One of us may not make it home."

"Neither of us," Skip said.

"If I don't and you do, I want you to tell my wife I fought bravely."

"I will. You've got my word on it."

"Even if I didn't."

Later, outside the bridge, Skip said, "Why are you fighting, Captain? The cruise line would ransom you."

"You told that girl on the phone," the captain said. "It's my ship."

REFLECTION 7

Guns

The little man with the big mustache had killed his wife. I remember the pain in his eyes and the hands that twisted each other's fingers. "You have all these things," the little man had said. "People and things you think will help you . . ."

He had said that over and over and every time he said it I nodded.

"Our family doctor. We'd gone to him for years. We thought he was our friend. It was psychiatric he said, and he didn't do that. He wouldn't treat psychiatric cases. So we went to the government. Everybody's supposed to get medical care. Everybody, and it's free." He had battered his wife into submission and strangled her with a lamp cord.

"Supposed to." I think that's what I said.

The little man seemed not to have heard me. "They assigned us a psychiatrist. We never even spoke to him. He had all these patients, his girl said, hundreds and hundreds of patients. He'd get to Janice when he could, but it would probably be five years."

I felt embarrassed then, as though it were my fault, and in a way I suppose it was.

"Our minister wouldn't talk to her. She had to come to him—that was what he said. She had to come to the rectory willingly, asking his help. She wouldn't go out of the house, Mr. Grison, and she said nothing was wrong with her. Every time we talked, it ended the same way. She'd say I thought she was crazy, but she wasn't. She'd say I told everybody she was crazy, but it was a lie. I'd told her mother she was crazy, and her mother had called her up and told her all about it, but she wasn't crazy, no, she wasn't crazy, I was crazy, and I'd better stop lying about her or I'd be sorry. Her mother was dead."

I nodded and said, "I see," trying to make it sound as if it did some good, as if I'd helped him in some fashion.

"Our children wouldn't help me. Jewel tried, but she brought her back after two days. The others wouldn't even try. They've got their own families to take care of. I understand that. I know how it is, but they could have done something. I'd worked hard so they could eat well, so they could have nice clothes for school. That—it should have counted for something."

To which I had agreed.

"She had friends. Three of the women got together and came over. They played some card game with her, and they all laughed a lot, and whispered among themselves, and told about their children. It lasted about four hours, and when it was over they came to me in a group, all three of them came, and they said there wasn't anything the matter with Janice, she was perfectly fine and maybe she had been upset or something. As soon as they left, it was just like it had been before. Nothing had changed."

The little man had leaned forward, suddenly intense. "She could turn it on and turn it off. She was only crazy when she wanted to be. Try to understand!"

And I had told him, "They can be very deceptive, I know."

The little man had slumped as if exhausted. "She tried to set fire to the house three times, Mr. Grison. She'd wait until I was asleep, then get up and try to set fire to the house, and there was nobody but me to take care of her. I was in there with her, there in the house alone with her. I was all alone."

It's what we do when we're all alone. We kill.

Here are the guns the captain gave me, right here in my belt. Guns are for that time. The police will protect us—but not when we need their protection. Our government will protect us, until we need its protection. The

UN will protect us, so long as it doesn't violate the UN's great unwritten rule: *In disputes between the third world and the NAU, always side with the third world.*

How much help is the third world giving the human race against the Os? The Europeans are fighting, even though we spy on them and they on us. The Greater Eastasians are fighting, too, while spying on the NAU and the EU—perhaps because the NAU and the EU spy on them. The SAU's fighting itself, and so is bound to win, and lose.

As for the rest . . . We think of their people as poor and hungry, and so they are. The governments that have robbed them of everything are waiting now to despoil us. Those governments are poor and hungry, too. As poor, and as hungry, as so many vultures.

The captain and I, alone and frightened here on this ship, are humanity in the same way that the word represents the thing. Or if not humanity, then Western civilization. Here, I am the law and the ideal of justice, the ideal our masters have forgotten—the ideal they would spit upon if they recalled it. I am justice, law, and civilization; and I am going to fight like a rat in a corner.

A cornered rat with two pistols and a submachine gun.

8

GOING DOWN

"You come down!"

The shouter was on the Main Deck, clearly visible in the moonlight. *"Come down quick or we shoot!"* One of his companions clarified that statement by shooting, his rifle pointed almost vertically up.

The shot was answered by what sounded like a string of obscenities from the topgallant yard of Number 5 Mast.

"Missed 'em," the captain whispered. "Nobody fell."

Skip nodded. They were watching from the dubious shelter of a veranda overlooking the stern.

"Four of them are bunched up there. Do you think you can get them with that machine gun?"

Before Skip could shake his head, there was a shot from the fantail, aft of Number 6 Mast. The flash, a pinprick of yellow flame smaller than a spark, was gone in an instant; the report, half lost in the immensity of the silent sea, small and weak.

Yet the hijacker with the rifle lurched forward, his steps awkward and uneven. He bent, crumpled, and fell on his face. The remaining three opened fire, joined by three others some distance away.

Skip vaulted the railing without a moment's thought.

He landed, perhaps fortunately, on a seventh who had been running onto the open deck. Afterward, he could not recall how he had gotten to his feet or how his submachine gun had gotten from his back to his bruised hands, only stumbling toward the men he felt certain must be shooting at Chelle, hearing the captain's shots behind him, and dropping to one knee before firing a short burst—the submachine gun leaping and shaking in his grip, although it seemed then that he heard no shots, neither his own nor the shot fired by the lone man at the base of the mast, who turned and fired before he fell.

He stood, no longer shooting; and the captain shouted up to the men on the topgallant yard: *"Get down here! See those weapons? They're yours. Come down and claim them."*

After that, he was in Chelle's arms, and she in his, although he did not relax his grip on his submachine gun.

"They'll come," he said. "They must have heard us."

"Out of that door there." She pointed. "One at time, with the light behind them. Want to bet I can't go five for five?"

They held their meeting in the first-class tearoom, a place of polished wood, old framed prints, and fine china. All four of them were tired and more than a little baffled.

"If they scuttle," Chelle said, "they'll drown first. I don't think they'll do it."

"They will or they won't," Vanessa told her. "Nothing in this world is less predictable than a frightened man."

The captain chuckled.

"It's the truth! Women are criers, screamers, or fighters. If I know the woman, I can tell you exactly what she'll do. Men . . . Well, it depends on thousand things."

Chelle said, "Skip wasn't frightened. He jumped that rail like a tiger. I saw him and you didn't."

"If he wasn't frightened, he doesn't count. Were you, Skip? I was hiding behind a ventilator and so was Chelle."

"Afterward," Skip told her. "Only afterward. They were trying to kill Chelle, half a dozen of them."

Chelle made a rude noise. "I was firing from cover, not hiding, and those dumbfucks couldn't hit a bull in the ass with a bass fiddle."

The captain said, "We can argue about that later. The hijackers in the hold are our present problem. What can we do about them?"

"Rush 'em," Chelle said. "Keep them waiting for two or three days, then rush 'em."

Mildly, Skip said, "What if they scuttle?"

"We escape in the boats and they drown."

Vanessa asked, "Would we have time to launch the lifeboats, Richard?"

"Yes, but we'd lose the ship, and we might die in the boats. Or some of us might."

Skip said, "We're not as strong as they think we are. I tried to fool them at the parley, and I succeeded. Don't question that, please—it will just waste time. I fooled them, but they may not stay fooled. If they don't, they may rush us."

Chelle said, "Cool! Let 'em try it."

"They may." Skip leaned forward.

The captain laid a notebook on the table. "Let's list our options. We can rush them, or we can wait for them to rush us. Anything else?"

Vanessa said, "How well can you steer without the rudders? Well enough to get us back to the NAU?"

"I don't know. That's what Mr. Reuben is trying to find out, steering with the sails. If you mean mainland North America, I think you can forget it. It's too far, and we'd be tacking. How do you tack without a rudder?"

"I have no idea."

"Neither do I, and I doubt that it could be done. A fore-and-aft rig *might* manage something, but we're square-rigged."

Chelle said, "Aren't there a lot of islands?"

"Yes, and we were going to visit a few of them. But they're well east of our position, and the prevailing winds have been driving us southwest. We can counter that to some extent. Maybe we could even counter it enough to slip between Grenada and Tobago and round the shoulder of South America. That would buy us time, and we might be rescued."

Skip asked, "What if we can't? You said we *might* be able to do that. Suppose we don't make it?"

Vanessa shrugged. "Then we hit Tobago, I suppose. Richard?"

"Or Trinidad. Most likely of all, we ground somewhere on the north coast of the South American Union. I'm not going to write that down, because it's almost the worst thing that could happen, in my opinion. Not quite as bad as sinking, but close. It's what *will* happen if nothing we try works."

Chelle's hand found Skip's. "What if we rush them and win? Could you repair the rudders?"

"The steering gear. They haven't done anything to the rudders themselves. The steering gear's electric, and all they had to do was pull a couple of wires, or cut them. It should be easy to fix."

"Then that's what we do, damn it!"

Vanessa's voice was almost a whisper. "With you out in front, darling?"

"Damn fucking right, Mother!"

"In that case, I vote against it, Richard."

Skip said, "So do I."

The captain laid down his pencil. "We're not voting yet."

Vanessa edged her chair nearer his. "You've got an idea, and I'll vote for it. Whatever it is."

Skip nodded. "What is it, Captain?"

"Let me lay a little groundwork first. For years now, northern South America has been a disaster. Revolution and banditry, crime and corruption, every kind of hell. We've steered clear of it, and so have the other cruise lines. The Caribbean islands have been relatively safe up until now. If that weren't true, we wouldn't have put in at La Glaise."

Skip said, "Where you were blindsided. I understand."

"Grenada has been another regular stop. It's EU, not SAU."

"EU?" Chelle said. "Over here?"

"That's right. There are a few EU islands. Jamaica's the biggest. Grenada's the nicest, in our opinion. We've never had trouble there, and it's in their interest to have as many cruise ships stop off there as possible. Tourism's the main industry. I want to try it."

Chelle said, "If we can get there, sure. Maybe they can front us a little tear gas."

Skip nodded. "I agree, Captain, but I have a question."

"So do I," Vanessa said, "and I think it's the same one. You're the captain, Richard, so why ask us? Why don't you just do it?"

The captain drew a deep breath. "Because I need your cooperation—all three of you. Lieutenant Brice is in the infirmary, and some of the best people I had are dead. I don't want another fight with the hijackers before we make port there. It would be a fight we might lose."

He paused, then spoke to Chelle. "You're headstrong, Ms. Blue. I don't want you to organize an attack on your own, and after what I've seen you do, I'm afraid you might do it. You're a soldier? That's what Mr. Grison told me."

Chelle made him a mock salute. "Mastergunner Blue at your service, sir."

"I certainly hope so. We've quite a few vets among the passengers, and Mr. Gorman tells me that they—and you—were our best fighters. Would they follow you if you tried to surprise the hijackers?"

"Absolutely. Every one of them."

"I want you to give me your word you won't do it, at least until we reach Grenada—or fail to reach it. Will you?"

"You've got it, Captain," Chelle said.

"Thank you. I'm deeply indebted to you." He turned to Vanessa. "You're Ms. Blue's mother, Virginia? That's what Mr. Grison told me, although you seem much too young."

Vanessa's smile would have charmed a man far less susceptible. "I was a mere infant of twenty-three when Chelle was born."

"But if Ms. Blue here fought . . . ?"

Chelle said, "You're right. I was gone over twenty years, Earth-time. My mother'd be pushing seventy now if she hadn't been up in space herself. She won't talk about it, damn her. Not to me and probably not to you."

Vanessa smiled again. "My lips are sealed."

"I understand," the captain told her. "You were a civilian employee of the government. We'll leave it at that."

"As I said, Richard, my lips are sealed."

"Not where your daughter is concerned, I hope. You're bound to have a good deal of influence with her. I'd like you to exert it to prevent a premature attack. That's why you're here."

"I'd do it even if you hadn't asked, Richard. I'd rather die myself than see Chelle killed."

No one spoke until Skip said, "What about me, Captain? Why was I invited?"

The captain seemed to hesitate. "You're an attorney, Mr. Grison? I believe you told me so."

Skip nodded. "Burton, Grison, and Ibarra. Chet Burton's our senior partner, but he's retired."

"You do the senior partner's work without the senior partner's pay."

"If you want to put it that way. I'm doing all right financially."

"I imagine you are." The captain cleared his throat. "You and Ms. Blue are an extraordinary couple. We're very lucky to have you two on board."

Chelle said, "Thanks."

"I feel blessed in all three of you." The captain studied their faces before he spoke again. "Something was said earlier about Mr. Grison's jumping the railing. Like a tiger was the way you put it, Mastergunner Blue. I was nearer than you were, and I confirm it. He realized—he's told me this since—that they were shooting at you."

Vanessa said, "You must have gone over that railing too, Richard. You were on deck with two empty pistols when I got there."

The captain nodded. "Thank you. That brings me to my point, and I didn't know how I was going to get there. I'd never have gone over that railing if Mr. Grison hadn't done it first. As it was, I followed him without thought and without hesitation. Are you—"

As the captain spoke, the door opened. Achille looked in and made an odd, urgent gesture.

Skip said, "We'll be through in a moment."

When the door had shut, the captain said, "I was about to ask whether you were the leader of the passengers."

"No. I don't think they have a leader."

Chelle said, "He is, Captain."

"That is my impression as well. Whether you're their leader or not, Mr. Grison, I know you have influence and I want you to use it."

Soon after that, the meeting ended. The captain and Vanessa left together, going up the stairs to the signal deck. While Skip and Chelle made their way forward, she asked, "What do you think Achille wanted?"

"I have no idea. Something was wrong with him. Did you notice?"

"Sure. One side of his face was swollen."

"You're right. He'd put a hook through the face of one of the hijackers, and they beat him for it. That's not what I was getting at, though. I lost track of him when the shooting started, and he looks different now. It took me a moment to put my finger on it."

"Maybe he took a bath."

Skip was silent.

When they had passed a dozen weary doors, Chelle asked, "Where are you going?"

"To our stateroom. I thought Achille would be waiting outside. He wasn't and I'd like to be where he can find me, at least for the next hour or two. I'll probably go out on the veranda and read. What about you?"

"Going down to the second-class bar. I just decided." Grinning, Chelle raised her larger hand. "I swear I won't have more than a couple of beers, and I won't cheat on you. Trust me?"

Skip nodded. "I love you too much not to."

"Okay. I need to talk to the guys and tell them to lay off the rough stuff until we get to that island he's heading for."

"Grenada."

"Yeah, that was it. I'll circulate and pass the word. Then I'll come in and make you drop your book."

As he walked down the corridor to their cabin, Skip decided that he would read for no longer than one hour. If Chelle had not returned by then, he too would look in on the second-class bar.

Achille was waiting outside the door. "We talk, mon. Mus' talk. I got big news. Bad news."

Skip slipped his key card into the lock. "Come in. I've got a question, but I may not need to ask it after I hear your news."

Hesitantly, Achille followed him in. "Is good, I come in this place?"

"You're worried about Chelle. She isn't here, and you'll be gone before she comes back. You said you had news. What is it?"

"They take me, *los picaróns*. Take my hooks."

Skip nodded. "I should have noticed that when you opened the door and waved to me. I knew something was wrong with the way you looked, but I didn't know what it was. How did you open the door?"

Achille grinned. "Roll him between arms, mon." He demonstrated, one brawny forearm on top of an imaginary doorknob and the other below it. "This how I do him all days."

"I see. How did you get away from the hijackers?"

"They let me go, mon. Take my hooks, I no fight then. Give paper and let go. I say I take to you. In pocket my shirt." Lifting one shoulder and bending his head, Achille caught the top of a soiled note between his teeth.

Skip took it. It proved to be a list of names, some printed, some cursive: David Arthur Pechter, Gregorio I. Lo Casale, Joe Bonham, Donald Miles, Gerald Kent-Jermyn, and Angel Mendoza.

Achille pointed to the last. "Is gone, mon. He give slip before let me go. Him, him, him, him, him they still got. Rope on hands, feet, so they not give slip, too."

"These five men are their prisoners?"

"Is so, mon. They give paper, make every mon write his name. They give me paper, say you come talk or they—" Achille made a throat-cutting gesture with the end of his right stump. "You come talk?"

"Yes. Yes, certainly."

"No gun. No knife."

Skip nodded. "Chelle doesn't have a laptop. I ought to have gotten her one." A short search uncovered paper with the ship's name and image blazoned on top, and a pen.

> *Chelle, darling,*
> *The hijackers are holding some of our people, and Achille and I have*
> *gone to talk to them about it. Should they hold us, too, don't try to*
> *free us before Grenada. I, who love you so desperately, will love you*
> *all the more for that.*
>
> *Skip*

A freight elevator in the stern carried them down to the hold, where two hijackers watched its doors. Skip displayed his empty hands, identified himself, and stepped out into what seemed a rocking warehouse filled with boxes and more stainless-steel drums—filled, too, with stale air and foggy yellow light.

The hijacker who held an assault rifle told the one with a machete to tie Skip's hands.

"No!" He held up his hands again. "I've come to negotiate, not to surrender. There will be no negotiations as long as I'm bound."

"*¡Puras vainas!*" snapped the hijacker with the assault rifle, and Skip's hands were bound. The hijacker with the machete marched him off between dark and beetling cliffs of barrels, crates, and boxes to a small, windowless office where an older hijacker took his feet off the desk and picked up a large knife. "You are no *el capitán*." His English was accented but understandable.

"Correct," Skip said.

"*¿El jefe?*"

"I am the captain's attorney."

The older hijacker grunted. "I will speak *el capitán*. No you."

"Untie me and send me back to him, and I will tell him so."

"One *millón* noras, we wish. One *millón*, and to be put *a tierra*."

"You want me to bargain with you, señor. I won't do it until you untie me."

"You agree? You agree, I cut *la cuerda*."

"Cut the ropes, and we'll talk about it."

For an instant, Skip thought that the older hijacker intended to stab him. The blow came, and for a time that might have been anything he thought absolutely nothing.

When consciousness returned, he was being dragged by the feet into a dark place. There he lay, head aching and hands numb, for hours that seemed very long.

REFLECTION 8

Negotiations

Although I have often racked my brain for some means of softening up my opposite number, I never hit on this one. I will agree to anything, if only they will cut the ropes and let me go. They will do it, then start negotiating with the captain from a position of strength, insisting loudly and truthfully that I have already acceded to their demands.

They will also have a fine opportunity to gauge my importance as a hostage; if an immediate rescue is mounted, my value is high. And so on.

There may be such an attempt, ordered by Captain Kain. Or an unofficial attempt, headed by Chelle. Or no attempt at all.

If I were the man I would like to be, I would hope for the last. I am not.

The captain asked Vanessa to the meeting because of her assumed influence with Chelle. When I asked him why he had asked me, I expected him to say that I was Chelle's contracto, and so on and so forth. That I too would have influence with her.

He said nothing of the sort; thus he has sensed what I have: that we are drifting apart, despite all my efforts. She screwed Jerry—that's how she would say it—not so much to strike at me (Chelle does not strike like that) as from simple boredom.

Or the desire for a younger partner. She must find me as repellent as I find her attractive. Was Jerry the fifth man on Achille's list? If I were made to bet, yes.

What can I do?

Tied up here, lying helpless in the dark, nothing; but if she comes, if she rescues me, she is certain to value me more as the (aging) lover she saved.

If.

What will I do when she casts me aside? Vanessa would be far too costly. Too costly, and utterly, dangerously, unpredictable.

Poor Susan will be out of the question. Someone who resembles Chelle? If I could find someone—which I doubt—it would be sure to end in disappointment.

Reviewing my conversation with the man behind the desk . . . Just what went on when Achille was released? The man behind the desk protested that I was not the captain, as though he had expected the captain to come in person. Could he have been as naive as that? Absolutely not. He was a man of middle years, and the hijackers presumably chose him as their leader. Certainly they accept him as leader.

Achille did not say he had been asked to fetch the captain. He said, in fact, that he had been told to take his paper to me. It was me they wanted. Me, specifically. The leader's complaint must have been meant to disguise that; he had gotten the man he wanted, and did not want that man to know it.

Why?

All my life I have feared death; I think I could die now, gladly. I was afraid that the man behind the desk was about to stab me. Now I wish he had. Nothing. No more pain and no more sorrow. Oblivion.

Unless there is indeed some existence for us when the bodies we have worn are carrion. Who would not like to believe that? Does my mother's ghost hover around me? What does she think of the man I have become?

She would forgive me everything. She always did. Why was it I never forgave her?

The man behind the desk wanted me. For myself? That is at least possible. If it is true, I wish that he would begin to make use of me. Or that I would die, and deprive him of the pleasure.

Everyone at the office assumes that I want Chet Burton to die. How I would despise myself if it were true! Chet, who took on an unproven young attorney? Chet, who taught me more than law school ever did?

Would-be attorneys used to sit in court, hour after hour, day after day, and so learned the law. We could use an infusion of that, I think. A big one. Let each student of the law attend court for two years before taking the bar exam. Those who failed it then would fail because they knew more than their examiners.

Boris knows more law than I do. He could pass the bar easily—if only they would let him take it. He knows more law, but he does not know courts, does not know the tricks of prosecutors, does not know the sympathies of juries, does not know the judges. He would have to learn those things. But he could.

Would Boris try to get me out if he were here? Yes. I doubt that he would succeed, but I know him and he would try. What about Luis? Perhaps.

What about Chelle? Chelle is here. Chelle counts. We are contracted, and I am rich. Chelle will be single, beautiful, and rich.

She will not come. Why don't I die?

9

ACHILLE'S MIRACLE

Skip was never sure afterward how long he lay in darkness. Perhaps he slept. Certainly he worried, and toward the end he prayed for death.

Perhaps there had been furtive steps; if so, he had not heard them. Something was moving his arms, ever so slightly. Rats? Rats might be gnawing at his fingers; he would, most probably, feel nothing.

There was a new odor, too—the stink of sour sweat? A new sound, soft grunts widely separated. And then the unmistakable sound of someone spitting.

He turned his head, not far but as far as he could. The darkness was unbroken, and at last he said, "Who is it? Who is that, and what are you doing?"

"My—" The speaker had been interrupted by the sound of gunfire, distant but unmistakable, echoing through the hold.

Skip said, "Who's shooting? Do you know?"

(One more shot, alone, followed at once by a faint scream.)

"I chew rope, mon. My name Achille."

"Thank God. There's a penknife, fairly sharp, in my left-hand trouser pocket."

"I can no reach in, mon. For this they cut my hands."

Skip sighed. "And you couldn't open it if you had it. I understand."

"I talk, no more chew."

Seeing the wisdom in that, Skip ventured no further questions. When the rope parted at last, he pulled his hands apart, rolled onto his back, and managed to sit up. His feet were still tied.

"I rest mouth," Achille said. "No more chew."

Skip nodded absently—a nod Achille could not have seen—and beat his hands against each other, hoping to restore them to life.

Two shots, then a third.

"You lady, mon. This I think."

"Chelle?"

"Is so, mon. One mon give slip? He tell lady."

Somewhere nearby, an automatic weapon fired three short bursts.

Skip was fumbling in his pocket with a hand whose pain was just short of excruciating. He found his knife, and managed to open it with his teeth. Some minutes afterward, he and Achille crept away, hiding in shadows from men who were too busy fighting to notice them.

Skip scarcely heard the captain; his mind was occupied with the captain's audience, which he had counted. It was a motley group, a hundred and sixty-two crew members and seventy-four passengers—two hundred and thirty-six in all. The crew members were young and muscular for the most part, mostly male, brown, black, and white. Four fat men in snowy tunics were chefs; they looked resolute, but Skip wondered whether they would fight.

"We were determined," the captain said, "to avoid any showdown before we reached Grenada and had a chance to send the children and old people ashore. Then too, we hoped the Grenadan police . . ."

The big woman in the middle of the room was a masseur; the captain had whispered it earlier. Skip tried to recall her name. Trinidad? Something like that.

"This changes everything. Mr. Grison broke free with the help of this man, whom Mr. Grison had hired earlier as an interpreter."

The captain's gesture indicated Achille, who raised an arm ending in a hooked and pointed device that might almost have been the head of a medieval weapon.

"They had taken his prosthetics, by the way, but we've had a machinist fit him with substitutes that should enable him to fight."

Vanessa was fidgeting in the front row. The sleek little pistol Chelle had insisted on buying for her suited her perfectly, Skip decided: small and bright, with shiny pearl grips. She turned it over and over in her hands.

"As many of you have heard, Mr. Grison succeeded in finding and freeing three of the men who had gone into the hold without authorization."

As he watched, Vanessa pushed back one of her long sleeves, revealing the spring holster he had nearly forgotten strapped over what seemed to be livid welts.

"Two were too badly hurt to escape. The other three are with us here. Would you like to hear from them?"

There was a chorus of nods and assents.

"Then you shall. Sergeant Kent-Jermyn. Why don't you go first?"

The sergeant stood, a rangy man of thirty or so with high cheekbones and cropped brown hair. He clasped his hands behind him. "The captain's putting me on the spot. That's okay, I've got it coming. It was my show. I lined up the others, good soldiers who wanted to fight. Some are dead, or we think they are. Dave and Greg are going to die unless they get to a medic soon. We all had guns, and the enemy got them. That hurts worse than anything they did to me. I can't speak for Joe and Don, but if you're willing to go down there, I'll go with you. With a gun if I can get one, with whatever I can find if I can't."

Skip applauded as he sat down; within a second or two, everyone in the room was clapping and cheering.

The captain raised his hands as soon as one or two people had stopped. "Private Bonham?"

A stocky young man with a wide, cheerful face stood. "I'm no hero. I wanna say that first. Sure, I went down there and shot, and I think I got three. One for sure and two probables. Only when the sarge said we had to give up, I just thought my God I might get out of this alive yet."

He sat—and stood up at once. "What he said about fighting again, that goes for me, too. You're going to need us. We know how to skirmish and you don't, and now they've got Mastergunner Blue and how many more?"

Skip said, "Seven ex-soldiers, men and women, went down with her. The hijackers say she's still alive, and that four others are. We don't have the other names."

"I got it, sir." Bonham's cheerful face was anything but cheerful. "They'll rape her. Shit, they've raped her already, only there's guys that don't just wanna fuck. They wanna beat up on the girl. Biting—all that shit." He paused to swallow. "I came on this boat hopin' to get laid, sir, and I got it, too. Three times so far. Only I—well, I try to leave the girl happy, you know?"

Skip nodded. "I understand perfectly."

Bonham sat again, and the captain said, "Have you anything to add, Corporal Miles?"

He rose, taller than Bonham and serious-looking. His short, dark hair was beginning to thin at the temples. "Yes, sir. Quite a bit, I'm afraid. I'll make it as quick as I can."

"Go ahead."

"When I heard that Mastergunner Blue had come down trying to get us out . . . Sir, I wanted to go down right then. Just me, and I didn't even have a gun. Sarge grabbed me and Joe helped hold me, or I would've done it. It was crazy, and they made me see that. But Mr. Grison here went down alone—"

"Under a flag of truce," Skip told him. "I went down hoping to negotiate their surrender."

"So maybe I could've done something. I don't know. Most likely I'd just have gotten killed."

He coughed. "Nobody's talked about tactics, so I'm going to. There's three freight elevators go down there. There's a couple ladders, too. I saw one when I was down there, and I talked to this lieutenant about an hour ago, Mr. Reuben. He said there are two, one forward and one aft so anybody down there can get out if the elevators lose power. There's elevators forward, aft, and in the middle—amidships is how they say it. You can get maybe ten guys onto each elevator. Not much more than that."

He glanced at Kent-Jermyn. "Am I running on too long, Sarge?"

Skip (who had been staring at Achille) said loudly, "Keep talking, Corporal."

"Thank you, sir. Okay, they've got barricades set up in front of the elevators. Only one or two guys at each barricade, but you've got to get over the barricades first, and that was where we lost men. The ones who were watching our barricade started shooting, and the rest came on the run. They don't watch the ladders much, but anybody who tried to go down those would be a sitting duck. So what I say is that if we're going to rush them, we've got to have at least thirty men with guns. Put ten on each elevator and send all three down at the same time. Give me a gun, and I'll take one elevator." He sat down.

The captain said, "Thank you. Anyone else?"

A sailor raised his hand. "Most people would take a hour getting down those ladders, sir. Not me and my mates. You've seen us on the ratlifts, and I've been down there working a hell of a lot. We'd have fifty topmen at the bottom of one of them ladders faster 'n you'd believe."

Half a dozen others assented.

"Thank you." The captain's gaze roved the room. "Does anyone else want to propose a plan?"

No one spoke.

"All right, then. I'm going to meet with Mr. Grison to discuss one. I want you to stay here. Mr. Valentine has been working on the weapons problem. He'll share out what he has and talk to the rest of you about arming yourselves now, and after the fighting starts."

It was the tearoom, the room in which Skip and Chelle had conferred with the captain and Vanessa earlier. "I can get us coffee if you like," the captain said.

Achille nodded with enthusiasm.

Seeing it, Skip said, "Please. And something to eat, if you can manage that."

The captain made a call. When he had hung up, he eyed Achille frostily. "You don't need an interpreter when you talk to me. Why did you bring him?"

"Because I realized during the meeting that he had done something that seemed close to impossible. When you sent me down to negotiate with the hijackers, he came with me. He was the one they had sent to tell us about their prisoners, and I thought he might be useful. As he proved to be much later."

"He freed your hands? I know you said that."

"Correct. Chelle was attacking while I was trying to get loose, and he told me that one of Kent-Jermyn's men—Angel Mendoza—had escaped and told Chelle about the rest. Just now it struck me that he must have gone back up here while I was lying in the hold in the dark. He hadn't known that Mendoza had talked to Chelle when he showed me his list of names—he would surely have mentioned it. But he knew it when he freed me. Obviously, he hadn't been hiding in the hold all that time, which was what I had assumed."

Skip turned to Achille. "You were in the freight elevator with me. I went out with my hands up, and that was the last I saw of you. Where did you go?"

"Up here, mon. Is big drum in elevator."

"A big stainless beverage drum. Yes, I remember."

"I hide back of him. When they take you away, I go back up. Talk lady."

The captain said, "How did you get back down there?"

"I slide in air pipe, mon."

Skip said, "You would have had one hell of a fall if the hold had been empty."

Achille shrugged, and the captain said, "It isn't. We've supplies enough to get us to Melbourne even if we run into a good deal of bad weather."

"I was hoping," Skip said slowly, "to get something we could use. As it is . . ."

The captain said, "We send ten fighters down in each elevator, and send the topmen down the ladders at the same time. Or we wait until we reach Grenada—and pray to God we don't run into storms. You want to do the first, and I want the second. That's what we have to thrash out."

Gloomily, Skip nodded. "Thirty armed men and women in the elevators, plus the topmen on the ladders. Say thirty down each ladder. How many guns have we got?"

"Twenty-one, plus your pistol and your machine gun. So twenty-three altogether." The captain's face looked longer than ever. "You'll be on one of the elevators?"

"Certainly. You're counting Chelle's mother's little pistol?"

"I'm counting everything, including my own gun. We gained thirty-one in the initial fighting—I'm including your machine gun. I had six in the arms chest in my cabin, making thirty-seven. Your Chelle and Virginia had two more, making thirty-nine. We lost eight when that sergeant and his men went into the hold without authorization, leaving thirty-one. We lost eight more when your Chelle went down as well, leaving twenty-three."

"Chelle had her own gun," Skip said wearily.

"I'm counting that. She took seven other soldiers and former soldiers with her, giving the hijackers another eight guns."

When Skip said nothing, the captain added, "So twenty-three people who can shoot will have guns, if we follow your plan. That's what Valentine is telling the group right now. The rest will have knives and clubs, and they will be told to try to pick up guns as the fighting progresses. You may like that picture—"

"I don't."

"Nor do I. We could turn out their lights down there. That might help. I don't know."

"It might hurt more than it helped," Skip said. "I think it would."

"We could block their ventilators, too. That would at least make them uncomfortable."

"After which they would threaten to kill Chelle if we didn't—"

There was a knock at the door.

"That'll be our coffee," the captain said, and added loudly, "Come in!"

The young officer who opened the door had no coffee. "There's a boatload of Mexicans alongside, sir," he said. "They say they've come to rescue us."

REFLECTION 9

A New Plan

That was the wrong meeting. Nothing of importance was decided. Nothing happened. The one that mattered was the meeting we held after Mick and Soriano came aboard with their men—with their men and one woman. That was the meeting that mattered, but I was so exhausted by that time that I can't remember who said what or even just what part I played in the discussions.

I know we shaped our plan in that meeting—my plan. I suggested it first and Soriano seized it, adding details. We'd need the best fighters, and a few good-looking women who would fight. We would not have to have me, Soriano said. I could remain on the deck above, I could wait for them on M Deck in safety.

I knew I had to go. My guts melted to slush while I argued with them, and it was all I could do to keep my voice steady and meet their eyes. I spoke just the same, knowing how bad I looked and how bad I sounded. "I've got to go." I repeated that over and over. "I've been down there and I escaped from them. You're going to need me. You've got to bring me along, dammit. Got to!"

It brought out the angels. Angel Mendoza was first. When I admitted I knew no Spanish, he said he'd go with me, tied up just like I would be, and interpret for me. Mick was standing beside me before Angel had finished.

He was going to go, too, he said, leading the anglos he'd enlisted in the scant hours before his plane left Boswash.

I said we'd take only those who volunteered. A dozen of Soriano's men volunteered at once; he said he'd make thirteen, an unlucky number, and in the end we took only ten. We'd need more, I said, more prisoners, and Soriano agreed. Don and Joe volunteered at once, with Sergeant Kent-Jermyn. After that, it was like pulling teeth. It was after we had gotten a few more men, all of them crew, that Soriano said we ought to have women, a few good-looking women that the hijackers would ache for. Vanessa's hand shot up. There were tears in her eyes; one caught the light, and I'll never forget it. The poor woman! The poor, poor woman!

We made her stand up and come up front with us so the rest could see her; and Soriano, who cannot have known her, hugged her.

A tall man's hand was up then. He was one of Mick's anglos, a lanky man with a handsome, pale face. He smiles easily, as I have seen since that meeting; but he was not smiling then. Mick said, "That's the way! Come up here, Rick."

It wasn't until Rick Johnson had left his seat that I saw Susan behind him. I've never been more stunned. Owen Speidel told me quite casually that he had been guilty an hour after I'd gotten him acquitted, and this was like that, like being hit with a ball bat. I saw how frightened Susan was, and felt sure she'd seen how frightened I was. I'd loved her for years; but I'd never loved her half as much as I did then, when Chelle had returned to me and I no longer wanted Susan.

I never loved her half as much as I did when her hand went up and she came up to stand next to Vanessa. She had a short-barreled revolver holstered on the belt of her jeans. All Mick's people had guns, handguns or long guns, and so did Mick. Later I learned that Mick had paid for them with money that Luis Ibarra had authorized, and that Soriano had introduced Mick to the people who had sold them. Luis had recommended Soriano to Mick, and Luis had been right. Luis had also told Soriano that Mick was on the way, and could be trusted.

But Susan with a revolver on her belt!

We think that we know a man or a woman, when so much of what we know is actually that man's or that woman's situation, his or her place on the board of life. Move the pawn to the last row and see her rise in armor, sword in hand.

10

RESCUE

Angel Mendoza, his hands wrapped with rope, stood beside Skip to interpret; Skip's hands were wrapped as well.

"He says they've got many more prisoners," Mendoza whispered. "We are the most important, but just a sample. He's got to exhibit us to the boss of all hijackers. Then the boss will understand what he's come to say, and there will be an agreement and no shooting. If there's shooting, he says, they will win. They will kill all the hijackers and keep all the money, but to join forces is better. There are beautiful women topside, and they throw the stick whenever they wish. If no partnership, they have gas. They'll use it to kill everybody down here."

Skip whispered, "Do they believe him?"

Mendoza shrugged. "They don't shoot."

Crates were moved aside, the barricade demolished. Skip hung back as though frightened, and was prodded (as he expected) with the barrel of a riot gun. A well-remembered passage, scarcely wider than a hand truck, ran down the center of the hull. For a short time that seemed long, they trudged between bulging cliffs restrained by cargo nets, with armed hijackers before and behind them and Soriano (whose Spanish Mendoza had been interpreting) swaggering in the lead. A long machete dangled from Soriano's belt, a belt into which two stag-gripped pistols had been thrust.

To Skip, who kept his head down as he stumbled along, they seemed very like Chelle's—the new pistol, she had told him, recently adopted by the Army but in such short supply that almost nobody below the rank of colonel had one.

The little office near the freight elevator had not changed; they crowded into it: Soriano, Llanes, and Garcia; Skip and Mendoza; Mick Tooley; and the handsome, worried-looking man Tooley had introduced as Rick Johnson. All the rest—more than a dozen "prisoners" including Vanessa and Susan, and the rest of Soriano's *mercenarios*—had to wait in the dimly lit passage with eight hijackers. There were introductions and handshakings.

Soriano addressed the older hijacker who had struck Skip, and Mendoza interpreted: "You see this man? Now he is the leader of those who defeated you and locked you up down here. Their captain fights us to his death, but this man surrenders and lives. These others we bring you, too. This man, he is your prisoner before we came?"

"Yes, he is an eel."

"I give him to you again, Señor Ortiz, if you wish him." Soriano twisted the tip of his black mustache. "This I do to show I am an honest friend. You desire to beat him? Do it! He is yours."

"You have taken the ship?"

"We have. We shall return it to its owners, and for that they must pay very much."

"Then you have no need of me, Señor Soriano. Nor of my men. Set us ashore, us and our prisoners. We will not fight you."

"I could do this, but I will do more. Join us and you will be one with us. You tried to take this ship. You may have it and share our joy."

"You are a man of much heart. It is not pleasant that I take advantage of you. No! Set us ashore, shake my hand in parting and wish us well, and when next we meet it shall be as friends."

"Alas, señor, you shame me. I must confess that I—even I, whom men call the victorious and the crippler of his foes—require your assistance. I have the ship, and this you comprehend, but I have not mariners sufficient to work it as I would wish. Join us—"

Grunting, the older man pointed to Skip and Mendoza. He rose, left his desk, and cocked his fist. When he was almost near enough to strike, Skip let the rope that had looped his hands fall and Soriano's arm hooked the older man's throat from behind. The older man gasped.

Skip's pistol joined Mendoza's, thrust into the older man's face. "We've twenty-one here already, and a hundred more on M Deck waiting for the sound of a shot. Tell your men to lay down their guns."

Skip and Vanessa found Chelle bruised, bloodstained, and half naked, and freed her. Her first words were, "I think I need to see a dentist."

Skip was on his knees beside her. "There may be one on the ship, Seashell."

"And a psychiatrist." Her voice was weak. "I'll tell you about that later. Have you got my gun?"

He shook his head.

"You have to help me look for it."

Vanessa smiled, "Do you know, I've never given you two anything? Not even a toaster. Do either of you know about weddings? It's like contracting, only in church and not legally binding." The ship heeled and seemed for a moment to tremble, and she added, "What was that?"

"We're going about." Skip rose as he spoke. "Heading for home. With control of the rudders, there's no reason not to."

"Lovely! You and Chelle can have a proper wedding. Do you want one?"

"I certainly do." He helped Chelle stand; her right arm hung limp.

"One gives gifts." Vanessa opened her purse. "There should be contract gifts, too. Don't you agree? I haven't any birdseed to throw, but I have a gift. Perhaps I should save it for the wedding." Her eyes sparkled as she drew a corner out: mottled polymer.

"My gun!" Chelle held out her left hand; her right still dangled at her side.

"Well, certainly. Skip caught that horrible Ortiz and marched him off without a word. Only there was a man with Skip who made me uncomfortable. Possibly it was because of his tweed jacket. Who could stand tweed in this heat? So I stayed behind and went through the horrible man's desk, looking for papers and so forth. I didn't find any but I found this, and I knew you'd want it back."

"You . . ." Chelle hesitated. "You came down to rescue me, Mother? To try to?"

"I don't think I understand this gun at all. The bottle-shaped bullets and everything. I wanted to try it, but it didn't seem safe. What's that funny thing on the trigger? Don't hold your hand out like that, Chelle darling, it's not polite and I'm not going to give it back to you until you ask nicely."

"*¡A la puñeta!*"

Vanessa smiled. "That was a favorite expression of Charles's, and I never understood it. Now you can explain it to me."

Chelle gave Skip a painful smile as he lifted her right arm into the sling he had knotted from his shirt. "Please kick the shit out of my goddamn mother, so I can hug her—that's if she really came down here for me."

Skip said, "She did."

"Yeah, she must have if she went through that desk. Why did you let her do it?"

"Various reasons." He adjusted the sling. "For one thing we wanted people who looked like harmless captives but could and would fight, if fighting were needed. For another—"

"And you thought Mother would?"

"No. I knew she would. As long as the hijackers had you, she'd fight like a tigress to get you back. I haven't known her long, but—"

Mick Tooley had come in. "You found her, sir."

"Indeed he did." Vanessa looked demure. "Guided by a mother's love, he could scarcely fail." She spoke to Skip. "Perhaps you should introduce us?"

Swaying, Chelle said, "Give me my goddamn gun before I knock you down." Skip tried to steady her.

"Please, Chelle darling. Not in front of strangers."

Tooley stepped back. "If you'd rather I'd leave . . ."

"Stay," Skip told him. "Your presence may prevent a murder."

"Mine." Vanessa's eyes were bright with tears.

"Virginia," Skip said, "this is Michael Tooley. You may remember that I gave you his number when Chelle and I were planning our cruise. Chelle, this is Mick Tooley. He's the sort of young lawyer I was when you left Earth."

Chelle offered her left hand. "It's a pleasure, Mick. I'm your boss's contracta. From this point on, a part of your job will be to convince him he's not too o-old for me. Think you can do it?"

"I'll try," Tooley promised, "and I believe I have a clean handkerchief big enough to go around your head."

Susan was waiting in the sitting room of Stateroom 23C when Skip opened the door. She rose, smiling. "It's good to see you. To see you in private, I mean. I've been seeing a lot of you in public."

"I understand. Why don't you try the big leather chair? It's a bit more comfortable."

Susan remained standing. The smile remained as well. "Aren't you going to ask me how I got in here?"

"You bribed the steward, I imagine."

"Not at all. I found your Ms. Blue in the infirmary, explained that I was your secretary and needed to speak to you privately, and promised to return her cabin card. She let me have it."

Skip removed Tucker's *Guide to Modern Military Law* from the seat of his reading chair and sat. "I hope you'll excuse me. It's been a long day, and I'm tired."

"That's what I've come to say, really. That I excuse you."

He nodded and thanked her.

"A long day for me, too. I was seasick on the boat that brought us from Boca. Did Mr. Tooley tell you?"

"That you were seasick? No."

Susan sat down on the couch. "I thought you'd have a thousand questions, and I'm prepared to answer every one I could dream up. Don't you have any?"

"I'm exhausted, as I said." Skip hesitated. "There are two reasons for not quizzing you. May I explain?"

"I wish you would."

"The first is that I'm not entitled to. You came with Mick—"

"I joined him in Boca."

"I stand corrected. I thank you for that. I'm deeply indebted to you, just as I am to Mick and the rest of his party. I'm further indebted to you because you volunteered for the hold. We wanted women—attractive women who would fight, if fighting were necessary. You and Vanessa stepped forward, and I was stunned. I still am."

"What's the second?"

"I haven't finished with the first, but as you wish. I don't want to question you because I anticipate that any questions of mine would evoke tears and recriminations. I deserve both and more, I know. But I'm not looking forward to them."

"There are women who can cry whenever they want to," Susan said. "I'm not one of them. There have been a lot of times recently when I wanted to cry. Sometimes I did, and felt better afterward. Sometimes I couldn't. It's like wanting to breathe when you're under the water."

"You're asking my permission to cry."

"Yes. I suppose I am." She rose and wandered into the bedroom. "We had a nice cabin, but it wasn't as nice as this."

"That was a different ship."

If she had heard him, she gave no sign of it. A few seconds later, she slid back one of the veranda doors and stepped outside. "It's cooler out here."

He followed her. "It is, now that the sun's low. Chelle and I opened them— this was the first night out—after we came back from dinner, but we were afraid to leave them open when we went to bed. That seems rather comic after everything that's happened."

"After the hijackers."

He nodded. "Then Chelle went to bed with a guy she met at a party, and they left them open. I know that, because he jumped out of bed and ran out here when I came in. His name was Jerry, Chelle said. Jerry ran out here, knocking over a lamp, and jumped the railing. He may have hurt himself, I suppose, but I don't really know."

"She cheats on you."

Skip shrugged. "I wouldn't call it that. I cheated on her while she was gone."

"With me."

He nodded. "So I can't complain. And I don't. What was it you wanted to talk to me about?"

"Maybe that's the best way."

He waited.

"Here's what I was going to say. I was going to say that you had told me—once—what would happen when your Chelle came back. You had told me, but I hadn't believed you. When I got you the train tickets to Canam, I still didn't know."

He nodded.

"When I found out why you'd gone up there, it knocked the props out from under me. That's when I quit. I went into Mr. Ibarra's office and cried my eyes out. He shut the door and let me cry as long as I wanted. Then he said he understood, and the firm would tell anybody who asked that I could walk on water."

Skip said, "Luis is a good man."

"Yes, he is. It stuck in my mind for some reason, that business about walking on water. And then somebody—I won't tell you who—called and told me you were in trouble and Mr. Tooley had gone to Tamaulipas with a dozen men to help you, and they were going to hire mercenaries and buy a boat. So I went too. I met them there, about an hour before they sailed."

Skip nodded. "I owe you a great deal. I believe I've said that already, but I'll repeat it."

"You don't owe me one damned thing, Mr. Grison. I couldn't help doing what I did." Susan's hands writhed in her lap. "I love you. It's something I can't control. Would you rather I stayed away?"

"It might be better if you did."

"I . . . understand. Can I tell you what I was going to tell you? I was going to say I love you, and I'm sorry I got all upset and quit. But I did and that's that. Only if you ever want me, I won't be hard to find. I was going to say you could stay with your contracta, but sometime you might remember the cruise or the skiing vacations. If you did—I'm not saying this, it's just what I planned—all you'd have to do is call me." Her laugh held no merriment at all.

He said, "I'm glad you're not saying that."

"So am I. I'm getting a little of my pride back, or that's how it seems to me. I've had some time now, and I've been terribly seasick. Being seasick puts everything in perspective. I'm still an attractive woman, or think I am."

"You are."

"So I'm going to try to find somebody. Somebody nice who wants to contract."

Skip nodded.

"Somebody who'll love me, poor dowdy little Susan, the way you love your Chelle." Susan took a deep breath, held it, released it, and took another. "So this is what I'm really saying, Mr. Grison—it doesn't bother you that I'm not calling you Skip?"

He shook his head. "Call me whatever you like."

"What we had for nine years and eighty-seven days is over and done with. I'm not going to try to restart it. If you try to, it won't work. Mr. Ibarra promised he'd give me good references."

Skip said, "So will I."

"I'm sure, but I don't want them. There are a million women out there trying to land secretarial jobs, women working as waitresses and maids who have business degrees. A lot of them have wonderful references. I know some who are posted on every website in the world and have spammed out résumés by the thousand. Women who offer to go to the north coast at their own expense for one interview. I've got thirteen years with Burton, Grison, and Ibarra. May I come back? Please?"

Skip nodded. "With no loss in seniority. I'll see to it."

"Thank you. Thank you, Mr. Grison." The words were scarcely audible.

"You won't have to come back as my secretary, Susan. I realize that—"

146 ~ GENE WOLFE

"I want to! That's exactly what I want. It will be all business, I promise, and I'll be the best secretary anybody ever saw."

"You always were. Do you really want your old job back?"

"Yes! You—you said you needed women who'd fight if necessary. I've still got the gun Mr. Tooley gave me in Boca. Look!" Susan's hand went to her holster. "Tell me to shoot a couple of those hijackers, and they're dead. Order me to do anything you want done, Mr. Grison except—except what . . ."

"I won't," Skip said quickly. "Now take your hand off your gun."

Susan did, and sat down on the bed.

He went to her. "You've become what you told Chelle you were. It's a business relationship, a permanent one, and that's how it's going to stay. Let's shake hands."

Susan's hand seemed damp, weak and a trifle too small, and he realized with a start that he had already grown used to Chelle's. Feeling awkward, he cleared his throat. "Now that you're my confidential secretary again, I want to ask you a question. It's a delicate matter, so don't tell anyone I asked."

"Of course not."

"If you know anything, if you have even the smallest scrap of information, I want it. No matter how trivial it seems."

Susan nodded. "Yes, sir."

"Have you ever heard of a woman named Jane Sims?"

For a fraction of a second, it seemed him that Susan had recognized the name; there had been, he felt, a flicker in her eyes, a slight tightening of her mouth. Then she said, "No, sir. Who is she?"

"She's a woman Chelle mentioned. I don't want to pry, but it's something I may need to know. So I'm trying to find out."

"What about Boris?"

"I've got him looking already. Are you sure you didn't recognize the name?"

"Yes, sir. Unless you mean Jane Simmons. I used to know a Jane Simmons."

"You're no longer in touch with her?"

Susan shook her head. "Not for years, sir. We were never really close.

She contracted with a woman in the rapeseed oil business, and they went off to someplace in Asia."

"I doubt that she's my Jane Sims."

"So do I. You said you were tired, sir. If you'd like to lie down . . . ?"

"I'd like to, but I can't afford it. I was going to take a long, cold shower, then go back to the infirmary to see Chelle. Since you'll be going there, we might as well go together."

It was on J Deck, aft. The middle-aged nurse at the reception desk said, "You want to see Chelle Blue? Both of you?"

Skip nodded. "I'm Chelle's contracto, and this is my secretary, Susan Clerkin. We need to talk to her together. It won't take long."

"Ms. Clerkin was here . . ." The nurse pressed buttons and studied her screen. "At fourteen thirty-five. Weren't you one of the people who brought Ms. Blue in?"

Skip nodded again.

"Well, I can't let both of you in together."

"Yes, you can. Ask Dr. Prescott."

The nurse frowned. "He's not here."

"In that case, I'll have him paged."

"Are you going to be long?"

In the end they were admitted, and found Chelle in bed with her head swathed in bandages and her right arm in a cast. She tried to sit up, and did when the nurse cranked up her bed. "This is great! Got my cabin card?" Her grin made Skip want to turn away.

Susan held out the card. "Here it is. I'm glad we didn't wake you up."

"Not a bit! I was just staring at the ceiling and trying to figure out how I'd like to die. Fighting, sure. But would I want to know it's coming, so I could get ready? How much time? Stuff like that."

Skip said, "That doesn't sound healthy."

"Sure it is—takes my mind off my troubles. I got blown all to hell up on Johanna, maybe I told you."

Skip nodded.

"That was one hell of a lot worse than this. This is kid stuff. The dentist says not to eat anything tough for a while and my teeth should root again, or whatever you call it. Not come out. I got a scalp wound and they're bleeding bastards, but it's been sewed up good and they gave me a transfusion. I'll be back on the field in the third quarter."

Skip said, "What about your arm?"

"It's busted, that's all—simple fracture of the humerus, so there's a titanium plate and a bunch of screws in there now. One of those bastards hit me with a crowbar. See this black dingbat in my cast? High-frequency sound, with all the best undertones and overtones. It'll heal fast, and it's been splinted and pinned already."

Susan said, "Is there anything that we can do for you?"

"Yeah. Yeah, there is. That white box in the corner? My stuff's supposed to be in there, only I'm not supposed to get out of bed. Look inside, and see if you can find my gun. The nurse says it's in there, but who the fuck knows? I'd like to check on her."

Skip opened the cabinet and pointed.

Susan said, "Yes, it's right here."

"Hold it up, okay? Don't touch the trigger."

Susan did.

"Great. Bring it over here. I just want to hold it for a minute."

Susan hesitated, then looked her question at Skip.

He nodded.

"I'm not going to shoot anybody. I just want to feel it."

Skip took the gun from Susan and put it into Chelle's right hand.

"That's great." Chelle's smile warmed him.

"What is it?" Susan asked. "I don't know much about them."

"A Springfield MIL 31-3. It's got everything you need and nothing you don't—high capacity, a comp that hides flash and doesn't knock your ears off, ambi safeties, flat trajectory, lots of knockdown, and a jewel of a trigger. Was that old lady magic, Skip? Or was I?"

"Tante Élise? Both of you, I think."

Chelle turned back to Susan. "You went down into the hold to get me, didn't you? Somebody said that."

She nodded.

"You had a gun? Do you still have it?"

"I . . . Yes. It makes Mr. Grison nervous, but I do." After a moment she repeated, "I don't know very much about them."

"So you think people like me, people who love their guns, are nuts. I've used a gun to save my life. That's the difference. They'd sent us some new 'bots, and they were good but it was desert camo. They might as well have been bright yellow, and they got picked off pretty fast. We were supposed to come in behind them—"

The middle-aged nurse in the office outside had raised her voice, "You can't! Don't you listen?"

The words of the reply were indistinct but its tone was unmistakable. A moment later, the door opened and a lean man in a tweed jacket stepped through. He shut the door firmly behind him and held it shut with his heel. "Bureaucrats!"

Skip said, "Chelle, this is Rick Johnson. He came with Mick Tooley and was one of your rescuers."

Susan added, "Came prepared to fight. He has a gun like yours."

"Not quite," Johnson said, "but it's a good one. You're Mastergunner Blue, ma'am?"

"Sure." Chelle grinned. "But I'm not really holding a gun on these folks. I just wanted to see it and make sure it was safe."

"I understand." Johnson was studying Chelle's gun. "There's no reason for you to trust me to keep it for you, but I will if you want me to."

"So will I," Skip said.

"Thanks." Chelle moved the gun from her right hand to her left and gave it to him butt-first. "With three of you here, I've got a great chance to ask about the other guys who went into the hold." She paused. "Not your bunch. Sergeant Kent-Jermyn's and mine. Some didn't come out alive. I know that. Does anybody know which ones made it out?"

No one spoke.

"From my bunch or the earlier bunch?" Chelle looked from face to face.

"I can't tell you," Skip said. "I know we freed some, but I'm not sure how many."

"When I was down there," Johnson said slowly, "we got out four, I believe. Four alive, not counting you. Three had to be carried."

"I saw them," Susan said.

"I took down seven," Chelle's voice had sunk to a whisper. "Somebody said there were eight in the first bunch."

Skip nodded. "That's what I was told, too."

"What about Don?" To hear her, Skip had to bend until his ear was almost at her lips "Don Miles? Does anybody know about Don?"

Outside, a shrill new voice argued with the nurse: *"But she's my daughter!"*

An explosion shook the ship.

REFLECTION 10

Susan Clerkin

When did I see her first? I really have no idea. There's the secretarial pool, normally of five girls. The juniors have secretaries only when they require them, drawing a girl from the pool at need. Someone—was it Hal Hutchins?—drew Susan, and she straightened out a mess that ought to have taken a week in half a day.

I marked her then, serious, short and a little plump, blond and attractive. Mrs. Rosso got pneumonia, and I got Susan to fill in for her; by the time Mrs. Rosso came back, Susan was better than Mrs. Rosso had ever been. The UEA had been after us to hire more people, so I kept her on as Mrs. Rosso's assistant.

She has a mind for detail, which is what I've always needed, and is (or was) loyal to a fault. I took her out to lunch at first, a reward for good work—then out to dinner. She must have sensed that I was attracted to her; I've never known whether she was attracted to me.

Apparently she was. Just now, I saw how she looked at Rick Johnson; and I wondered whether she had ever looked at me like that. There was a time . . .

I remember it now. I'd been writing something. I sent it, and saw Susan watching me from the doorway, her face expressionless and her eyes full of dreams. It frightened me a little, but it took me years to understand why.

. . .

All the women knew before I did. Una Quin's secretary told Una, and Una told me. I can still see her, grinning over her coffee cup. "You must like blondes."

I said I did, and that she must have seen the picture on my desk.

"Well, blondes like you." She winked. "That ought to be a lot more fun."

I knew who she meant at once, said I didn't believe it, and as soon as I had said it wondered whether I could be wrong. On one hand, it seemed impossible that any woman could be attracted to me, an attorney nearing—no, let's be honest. Just a middle-aged lawyer, not quite tall, with little enough to offer any woman beyond a quick mind.

Yet I had learned in court to speak directly to the female members of the jury. (How many men must have died at the end of a rope when juries were all male!) Look them in the eye, move from one to the next, and linger longest with the least attractive.

Passion and conviction will win the case. They always do.

Chet and I sitting in the courtroom with the accused between us. Chet looking at his watch and winking. "We'll adjourn at five." I nodding and grinning, knowing that at five, when our client had caught a cab, Chet and I would go to the Front Office and he'd buy me a vodka-and-tonic.

Knowing too that when I had finished my summing-up, two jurors had looked back at me. Knowing that the smiles had been friendly. Middle-aged women, both of them; women I had talked to like a lover as I paced back and forth in front of the jury box. Telling them about the flaws in the prosecution's case, warning them that the police, too, want a conviction and describing the kinds of things the police do to get one.

The longer the jury stays out, the better the chance for an acquittal. It's an old rule; but like so many of the old rules, it still holds.

How many times have I paced my office, trying out this line of argument and that on Susan? Groping and listening, waiting for her to say, "Then she's really innocent after all! I wasn't sure."

There has always been something tragic about Susan, and I believe I've come to understand what it is. It's the tragedy of the second-rate, the helper, the sidekick, the supporting actor, the horse nearest the door. Susan is a superb secretary, but she would fail as the employer of a secretary.

We slept together twice a week for years. How many times all told? Not a thousand. No, not so many as that. Eight hundred perhaps. Eight hundred, and so I ought to know. She was a fine partner, tender and eager. Yet time after time I found myself imagining that I was with someone else.

Usually, Chelle. When I've been with Chelle I have never imagined another; nor do I think I ever will. But what of her? Whom does she picture now, in order that she may achieve orgasm? Is it Don or Jerry or Mick? Or all three?

Susan, I know, thought only of me. There was no Don with Susan. Only Skip. Or more likely, only Mr. Grison; Susan was always ill at ease when I made her call me Skip.

11

⌒〰⌒

RIGHT AND LEFT

"Oh, my God! Oh, my God!"

Vanessa was sobbing in Skip's arms, and Rick Johnson was cursing, his voice low and savage. Skip was not sure who had spoken. Possibly it had been Susan, but quite possibly it had been Skip himself.

Three sailors arrived with fire extinguishers and began to spray the smoking ruins with foam. Almost idly, as one sees things in a dream, Skip saw a wristless hand in the wreckage. *That's a woman's hand,* he thought; there was crimson polish on the nails.

"What was it?" Johnson coughed and backed away. When no one answered, he added, "What did they blow up? I'm new here."

Skip only shrugged, his arm around the weeping Vanessa.

"That woman went into the hold with us. She and this other woman here."

Susan said, "Yes, we did. They asked for volunteers, for women particularly. Skip and the captain did."

"I was there," Johnson told her. "I volunteered too."

"A black woman volunteered, but they didn't take her. They took this woman, though. And they took me."

Skip said, "I want Mick Tooley, Susan. Find him for me. Try your phone to start with. There's a classroom on G Deck. I'm not talking about the big meeting room on E Deck—a smaller room on G Deck. It could be Room Twelve. Tell Mick to meet us there as soon as he can."

He turned to Johnson. "I know your name, but who are you?"

"I can tell you, but you'll have to do a lot of snooping around to verify it." Johnson had taken out his wallet. "Here my driver's license, with my picture on it, if that interests you."

Skip shook his head.

"Right. Come to think of it, I've got something better—a little better, anyhow. My gun license." He slipped it out of his wallet and handed it over. "Look under training, and you'll see ex-military."

Skip did, nodded, and handed the license back.

"I was West Point, and after graduation I got stuck in Military Intelligence. They sent me off—I can't tell you where—and by the time I got home to Earth I'd put in over twenty years. You know how that works, I'm sure."

Skip smiled. He had relaxed a trifle.

Susan said, "Lieutenant Colonel, right? You look it."

"Don't I wish!" Johnson grinned. "I was a captain, Ms. Clerkin, but a captain with twenty years' service. I took my leave. I assume Mastergunner Blue's doing that."

Skip said, "She is."

"After that I tried a desk job here. That lasted . . ." Johnson paused to think. "Two hundred-days or so, about half a year. It bored the shit out of me, so I applied for a discharge and got it. I've been knocking around trying to find something worth doing ever since. Mick Tooley works for you, Mr. Grison?"

"He's a junior member of my firm, yes."

"Well, Tooley put out a call on one of the mercenary sites. I thought it sounded interesting, and the money was good. So—"

Susan coughed. "I texted Mr. Tooley, asking him to meet us on G Deck, and I hate looking at this. Can't we please go up there now?"

Skip nodded, and led Vanessa away. The air of the corridor seemed clear, but there was enough smoke in it to sting his eyes. Feeling foolish, he blinked back tears. Johnson was asking Susan what had been blown up, and Susan was saying she had no idea.

Vanessa murmured, "Polly's dead. So is Amelia. I know they are."

Skip wanted to say that one or the other might have survived; but he knew it would sound as false as he felt it to be, and kept silent.

"I killed them." Vanessa stepped in front of him and clutched his shirt. "I killed them when I volunteered, but I didn't mean to."

He said, "I doubt that the hijackers did this," and managed to get her to the stairs. The stairwell, closed off as it was by massive watertight doors, had purer air, and G Deck, when they reached it, better air still. The door to the conference room was not locked; Skip and Susan opened the portholes, welcoming a warm breeze from the sea.

"You want to have a conference?" Johnson was not sweating, Skip noticed, despite the climb and his tweed jacket. "Are you sure you want to include me?"

Skip nodded and flipped open his mobile phone. "Give me the second-class bar, please. I don't know the number." After a second or two, he said, "Thank you."

Susan asked, "Collecting more people, Mr. Grison?"

"Trying to. Yes."

"I might be able to help."

"I know, and I may have to call on you." Skip dropped into the nearest chair and spoke into his phone. "My name is Skip Grison. Could I have yours?"

Susan gave Vanessa a package of facial tissues.

"There are soldiers on this ship, Marlon. Men on leave or recently discharged. I'm sure you know them."

Skip listened intently.

"Correct. I'm trying to find Corporal Donald Miles. Do you know him?"

Johnson said, "He was in that first group they talk about."

Skip nodded, and spoke into the mobile phone. "If you see him within the next hour or so, please ask him to come to Compartment Twelve on G Deck. Tell him I'm anxious to speak with him." He snapped his phone shut.

Susan said, "I could get coffee. Probably some sweet rolls or something. Would you like me to do it?"

Mick Tooley came in, tired and worried. "There's been an explosion on I Deck. Do you know about that?"

Skip nodded. "We were there. Sit down, please."

The chairs were large and black, and reluctant when it came to moving across the soft Lincoln-green carpet.

"You already know Chelle's mother. I may not have told you that she's the ship's social director."

"No one did," Tooley said. "I had assumed she was a passenger."

"This is pro forma," Skip said. "Susan, did you know that this lady, on this ship her name is Virginia Healy, is the ship's social director?"

"No, sir. I didn't know who Virginia Healy was, sir. Just that the bomb— can we stop calling it the explosion?"

Skip nodded. "You're right, it was almost certainly a bomb."

"Just that the bomb killed two of her friends, or she thinks it did."

Skip turned to Rick Johnson. "What about you? Did someone tell you that Virginia was our social director?"

"No. No one told *me*."

"But you heard someone tell someone else. Please tell us everything you can. It's important."

"I can see that, but I don't have a lot of information to give you. It was in that meeting when you and Mick here, and Soriano, were recruiting people to go down into the hold with you."

Skip nodded. "Go on."

"She volunteered, and somebody behind me whispered, 'Who's that?' Somebody else whispered, 'She's the social director.'"

Tooley said, "Did you recognize their voices? Either one of them?"

Johnson shook his head.

"You don't know who they were?"

"I have no idea. I—to tell you the truth I was trying to decide whether I would volunteer. I raised my hand just after they spoke, I think. I heard the question and the answer, but I paid very little attention to them."

Skip said, "Yours wasn't one of the first hands to go up, as I remember."

"You're right. It wasn't. If there had been more hands raised, I wouldn't have raised mine at all. You had said it was going to be very dangerous, and I felt sure you were right—that it was something just short of a suicide mission. Off Earth . . ."

Vanessa went to him. "If you know anything, anything at all that might help, please, please tell us! You didn't know Amelia or Polly. I understand that. But they worked for me, they were nice girls, and they tried to do a good job, both of them. Amelia had been a champion diver, and—and . . ."

Skip had risen. He put his arm around her.

Johnson cleared his throat. "I didn't want you to think I was bragging, that's all. I told you I was in intelligence, and I was. Maybe you thought it meant I had a desk job, and if that's what you thought I wanted to leave it right there."

"I did," Skip said. "I take it I was wrong."

"I went into some very tight places, Mr. Grison. I did it because it was my duty. It didn't seem to me that it was my duty to volunteer, and I had to think things over. I did, and went into another tight place, this time with you, and I'd like to know what's going on."

"So would I." Skip cleared his throat. "I need to fill in some details. Virginia will already know much of what I'm going to say—perhaps all of it. I apologize for boring her, and for boring Mick, at least a little bit. But everyone here needs to understand where we stand in this."

He paused, and Susan said, "Go on, sir."

"Virginia is Chelle's mother, as I said a moment ago. That's why—"

Vanessa said, "A bad mother. You know my name and I know you went down into that dreadful warehouse place with me, but I don't remember yours. Will you forgive me? I've had a terrible shock. I lost . . . l-lost—"

Skip intervened. "This is Susan Clerkin, Virginia. She's my confidential secretary, and she joined Mick Tooley here after Mick set out to rescue us. We're indebted to her, and to Rick, too."

Johnson said, "I probably know less than anybody about what's been happening on this ship. I know Susan pretty well and know the ship was hijacked, but that's as far as I go."

"Virginia's had some memories wiped," Skip told him. "You were in Military Intelligence, so you probably know more about that than anyone here."

Johnson shrugged. "We don't like to do it and don't do it unless we have to. If you're asking whether I've done it myself—"

"I'm not."

"The answer is that I was never authorized. Medical personnel only. If you're asking whether I myself have been wiped, the answer is no. There are no blanks in my memory."

Susan said, "How is it done?"

"You should ask a doctor, not me. Roughly, then. You can record a person's memories and personality by picking up minute electronic impulses in the brain and recording them. You stimulate all the parts of the brain until you have everything in digital form. When you've got it, you wipe the forebrain by countering its impulses. After that you edit the record you made, generally by searching out words and images. Maybe you look for *Operation Grief*, for example, then for mental images of an armed drone. When you find things you want forgotten, you delete."

Susan said, "And then you upload the data back into the brain?"

"Exactly." Johnson paused, looking troubled. "It's not perfect, you understand, and it's highly dependent on the skill of the operator. Sometimes this bit or that bit escapes, so to speak."

Skip said, "I didn't know that."

Johnson shrugged. "Most people don't, but it happens. I know you're an attorney. Susan and I talked a lot on the boat, and she told me quite a bit about you. Let's say we've got you and we want to wipe everything related to a conference you had three years ago with a Ms. Smith. We know more or less what Ms. Smith must have told you, and what you must have told her. We search for that stuff in your record and delete it. We look for mental images of her and delete those, too."

Skip nodded.

"Swell, but suppose that while she was with you, she asked to use your private restroom. You said yes, and thought over what she'd been saying while she was gone. When you thought about it, you felt certain emotions. Okay, after you were uploaded and released as wiped, you might have a memory you couldn't quite place, a memory of sitting alone in your office and feeling certain emotions while hearing a toilet flush."

Tooley asked, "Are you saying that something like that could be dangerous? A serious failure?"

Johnson nodded. "Suppose there were things on your desk then, a picture of an old man and a clock showing date and time."

Tooley nodded. "I've got it."

"When I signed with you, I told you about the patrols—that we were sent out to take prisoners."

"Right."

"I made arrests, too, and questioned the people I'd arrested. That was the main thing I did, keep tabs on suspects, sweat them after they'd been arrested, and report what I'd learned. Let's leave the Os out of this. They don't think the way we do, and they don't do any wiping. Greater Eastasia does a lot of it. They send in spies who've forgotten they're spies, people who do certain things when the time comes without knowing why they do them. We looked for indications of that. Once you suspect somebody, you can download his mind and run searches. Swell, but the equipment's costly and delicate—we had two setups and one was usually out of service—and the whole thing can take a day or longer. So guys like me look for subjects whose minds might be worth searching, and try to find out enough to give the people who would do it some direction."

"We need to do some searching ourselves now," Skip said. He took out his pistol and laid it on a small table at the front of the room. "I think everybody here is armed. I know most of you are. Get out your guns, please, put them on this table with mine, and go back to your chairs. I ask it as a gesture of good faith."

Johnson said, "What if we won't comply?"

"Then you'll be asked to leave."

Johnson nodded, took out a pistol that looked very much like Chelle's, and laid it on the table beside Skip's.

Skip said, "Susan?"

She nodded, rose, and laid her snub revolver there; her hand shook a little. Susan's revolver was followed by Mick Tooley's big, dark green semiautomatic.

Vanessa was pushing up her sleeve. Skip said, "Do me a favor, Virginia. Just take off that wrist holster and put the whole affair on the table."

Vanessa did.

"Most of you will have observed Virginia's arm. It's badly scarred, and the scars are fresh."

Vanessa had pulled her sleeve back down. "I try to keep them covered up. I mean, at dinner people wouldn't . . . You understand, I'm sure."

"I do." Skip smiled, making it reassuring. "How did you get them?"

"I have no idea."

He nodded.

Johnson said, "You didn't do that business with our guns just so we could see this poor lady's arm."

"No. I wanted to watch your faces as you handled your guns. Someone tried to kill Virginia before she boarded. Mick knows about it. A man with a steak knife came up behind her and stabbed her in the back."

Johnson gave a low whistle.

"I have reason to believe—reasons I won't go into now—that she had seen her attacker from behind. She saw him only briefly as he sat eating in a restaurant."

"Eating steak," Johnson said.

"She didn't see what he was eating, but you're probably right. Whatever it was, a third person saw her and told her attacker. He got up—I don't know this, but it seems very probable—and followed her, having filched the steak knife from the restaurant. He may have hidden it in a newspaper. Some of the witnesses to the stabbing say her attacker had one."

"Do you have a good description?"

"No," Skip said. "Mick?"

Tooley shrugged. "Everything, sir?"

"Yes. What you told me, and anything else you may not have said. Empty the bag."

"Okay. Two described him as tall and thin. One said he was average height. Two said white and one Latino. Good clothes—they all agreed on that. One thought he was carrying a newspaper, one thought it was an attaché case, and one didn't notice that he was carrying anything."

Johnson said, "Go on."

"That's it, except for the knife. The police have it, but a man who works for us got to see it. It was a steak knife, he said, just as Mr. Grison told you. Slightly curved blade, serrated edge, sharp point. A black handle of some kind of synthetic." Tooley turned to Skip. "I had our friend check restaurants within walking distance of the attack. He found two that used knives like the one the cops showed him. Do you want them?"

Skip shook his head. "After she was stabbed, Virginia was taken to a hospital. She left it in the morning, went to her apartment, packed in a hurry, and fled. She was afraid, obviously, that the man who had stabbed her would track her down and try again."

Tooley and Johnson nodded.

"I went to her apartment soon after she left, as I told Mick earlier. I found an object on the floor there, an object that's in my pocket now. I don't want to take it out and hold it up because it terrified Virginia when I showed it to her earlier. I'll pass it to anyone who wants to see it, asking that you hold it so that she can't see it."

Susan moved her chair nearer Vanessa's. "Is that all right? What he said? Do you mind if he does it?"

"I don't." Vanessa took a deep breath, and let it out in an audible sigh. "I don't have to see it. He showed it to me, and I know what it is. I'll shut my eyes."

Meanwhile, Johnson had put out his hand; Skip put the brown object into it.

"Sharp!" Johnson had opened the blade.

"It is," Skip said.

Johnson closed it and passed it to Tooley, who offered it to Susan. When she shook her head, he returned it to Skip.

"I'd known Virginia before her daughter and I boarded this ship. She'd worn long sleeves then, but so what? It was cold, so everybody wore long sleeves. It's warm here, and nobody wore them except Virginia."

Johnson said, "Her gun. She had to hide it."

"I was with her when she got it, and she wore long sleeves before that. That may have been why the woman who sold it to her suggested it.

Perhaps I should have seen those scars then, but the room was dark—just a couple of candles. Later I saw them in one of our meetings, when she put her gun away: long scars on her left forearm."

Skip waited for questions, but there were none. "Earlier I had showed her the brown object, the knife or shaver or whatever you call it, that I just showed Rick. She screamed when she saw it, but she couldn't explain why it frightened her so much."

Johnson said, "It had made the scars?"

"No. It couldn't have. They're recent but not as recent as that. I know when and where she got it, and it wasn't long before she came aboard. I think those scars were made by something similar, a folding knife with a brown handle or another old shaver. When she saw this one in a shop, it woke some memory. She wanted to buy it, but she had been a good customer and the shopkeeper gave it to her. She left it behind when she fled the apartment I had given her. Seeing it unexpectedly in my hand, she was terrified."

Skip paused, looking from face to face. "The way she got her scars is pretty obvious, I'd say. Not more than a year ago she tried to kill herself, holding the knife in her right hand—she's clearly right-handed—and cutting her left wrist and forearm."

Tooley said, "She failed."

"Correct. She didn't cut deeply enough or she cut in the wrong places. Or she was saved by someone who came in before she'd lost too much blood. Her suicide attempt was edited out, as Rick would say, but traces clearly remained. It was a traumatic event, and her memories of it must have run deep."

Susan asked, "What are you getting at, sir?"

"A suicide ring. We were defending a case involving one before Chelle and I left the city."

"You're right, sir. David D. Boon."

Vanessa rose. "You—you're going to say I belonged to one. I don't know a thing about them. I— There was something on the news. . . ."

Skip nodded. "Those memories have been taken from you, and it's good that they were. Quickly, then. They're very much against the law because they make a fine cover for murder. If someone—"

Johnson interrupted. "I don't know a lot about them either, but I know the members don't kill themselves. They kill each other."

"Correct. The people who join them have tried to kill themselves in almost every case. They haven't been able to do it. They lose their nerve or realize at the last moment that their life insurance will be voided by suicide. When they join, they pledge themselves to kill the member who's been in the ring longer than anyone else. That member may insist he's changed his mind, or run, or do whatever he chooses to try to cheat death. It doesn't matter. The other members have sworn to track him down."

"Him or her."

"Exactly. I think Virginia joined a ring. The people who edited her memories took that one as well as the memory of her suicide attempt. When Virginia went into a certain restaurant, one of the diners—a female member of the ring—recognized her. This woman told the man she had been eating with, another member. He followed her with a steak knife and stabbed her in the street. I don't know all that, but it accounts for the facts I have, and it's the only scenario I've been able to put together that does."

Susan said, "This is horrible, just horrible! Why are we talking about it?"

Johnson turned to look at her. "The bomb, of course."

Tooley said, "You're saying we brought the person who planted the bomb, Soriano and me. Only it would almost have to be one of mine."

"You're right," Skip told him. "I'd like you to list the names of the people you got from the mercenary website. Will you do that and give it to me?"

Tooley nodded. "I haven't got my notebook here, but I'll make the list and get it to you as quickly as I can. Full names and service numbers."

"Two of us are here right now," Johnson told Skip. "Susan and I came with Mick."

"I know." Skip went the table and glanced at the guns. "It seems obvious to me that members of the ring traced Virginia's movements after she left her apartment. They found out she was on this ship, but the ship had already sailed. Mick posted his announcement on a mercenary website—"

"It was a help-wanted ad." Tooley grinned. "And I put it on all the sites I could find, sir. There were seven of them."

"It gave the name of the ship? I've been assuming that."

"The ship's name and your name, sir. Not Virginia's. I didn't know she was on board when I entered it."

"In that case they must have traced her movements. Either that, or they were confident enough that she was associated with me that my name sufficed. They signed with you. I've been saying 'they,' but it's probably a single individual. He signed with you, and once he was on board he quickly learned that Virginia was the ship's social director. He had brought a bomb. I have no idea how he managed to plant it in her office, and the women who might have told us are presumably dead."

Johnson raised his hand. "I've been thinking about the people behind me—what they said and how they said it. I think they were women, both of them. I think I told you the first one said, 'Who's that?' and the second one said, 'She's the social director.'"

"You did. Do you want to correct that or enlarge on it?"

"Yes, sir. I do. I believe the first one said, 'Who is that who raised her hand?' and the second said, 'She's the social director.'"

"Both were women? That's the important point."

Johnson shrugged. "I can't swear to it, but that's my impression."

"I see." For a moment, Skip fingered his lower lip. "It may not be significant, of course. Others may have asked the same question or the women behind you may have been overheard."

"They were," Johnson said. "By me."

Susan rose. "I'd like my gun back, Mr. Grison."

"Certainly." Skip picked her revolver up and handed it to her. "Do you have to leave?"

"No." Still holding it, she remained at the front of the room. "This is going to be a lynching—or . . . or that's what I think. That man's trying to put the rope around my neck."

"I'm not," Johnson declared.

"Look me in the eye and say that! When we were on the boat I thought we were in it together, and now you want to k-kill m-m-me."

Skip put his arm about her shoulders. "Nobody's going to hurt you, Susie. Nobody!"

Johnson said, "I wasn't trying to. I didn't know it was you."

"I was sitting right behind you! Mr. Grison, will you listen to me for just a minute, please?"

He nodded. "Of course I will."

"You were asking for women. You said you needed women who'd pretend to be prisoners to back up Soriano's claim that there were good-looking women who'd be at the mercy of the hijackers if they'd throw in with him."

"Correct."

"And afterward the women might have to fight. That—I'm not your Chelle Blue."

Skip smiled. "I was surprised when you volunteered. Surprised and very pleased."

"I was going to wait until you asked me. I thought that when nobody would, you'd call on me. You know, what about you, Susan? And then I'd stand up and say something brave, only Virginia put her hand up. There was this big muscular woman sitting with me, and she hadn't volunteered but Virginia had. Is her name really Virginia?"

"On this ship, as I said."

Susan hesitated, fingered her revolver, and returned it to its holster. "She said Virginia was the social director. Then I put my hand up and she did too—the woman beside me. When you came in here you asked me whether I knew this lady was the social director, and I lied. I lied to you! I lied because I didn't want you to think I'd done it."

"I understand, and nobody's going to lynch you. You may leave if you like."

Susan shook her head and sat down.

Skip walked the length of the room, turned, and spoke. "A moment ago Rick said that two of the people who had come with Mick were here now. In a sense, three were—the third being Mick himself." He paused.

"I don't suspect any of you, and I need to make that clear. Mick and Susan are people I've worked with for years, three years plus in Mick's case and even longer for Susan. Rick himself looked a little more suspicious. For one thing, he's tall. Some of the witnesses to Virginia's stabbing said her attacker was tall."

Tooley added, "Two out of three, actually."

"For another, he was eager to get in to see Chelle. By that time he could easily have learned that Virginia was Chelle's mother. If his bomb failed, something he learned from Chelle might be quite useful."

Johnson grinned. "I'd never realized that I was such a Machiavellian character."

"It didn't take long for me to see how unlikely he was. He not only had a gun—all of us have guns now—but he had a license for it. The steak knife strongly suggests that Virginia's attacker was unarmed when he sat eating in the restaurant. Rick's gun suggested another reason."

Returning to the front of the room, Skip held it up. "Look carefully. Chelle's, which is probably a later model, has ambidextrous safeties. This one doesn't. The safety is on the right side, where it would be operated by the thumb of the left hand. Here, compare it to mine."

"They're reversible," Johnson told him. "I had the battalion armorer change mine."

Tooley said, "I take it that Virginia's wound is on the right side. I should have checked that."

"I've seen it, and it is. On the right side, high up. She wears heels, as you may have noticed. The man who stabbed her need not have been freakishly tall, but he was certainly above average height."

"You've got a gun in your hand," Tooley remarked, "and nobody else has one except Susan. I take it you're about to name the bomber."

Skip returned his gun to the table. "I'm not. I wish I were. I got you together—Chelle would be here too if she weren't so badly hurt—so I could tell you what I know and ask your help. You brought eleven people south with you, Mick?"

Tooley cleared his throat. "That's right. Eleven including Susan and Rick."

"Leaving nine. One of those nine almost certainly planted the bomb. Susan, you and Rick were with them before Soriano sailed, and afterward on the boat. Who do you think is most likely? I realize that—"

"Skip!" Vanessa interrupted him. "I must talk to you, darling."

There was a knock at the door.

REFLECTION 11

The Ring

Thought and speech come easily to me. Action is hard. That's a new realization; for so many years I thought myself a man of action. Yes, I filed appeals and sent others—always others—scurrying around in search of witnesses. I did those things and thought that I acted. More than once, I simply asked Susan or Mrs. Rosso to do them.

Our seamen are men of action. So are Soriano and his mercenaries. What of the men from Boswash whom Mick will list for me?

I think of them as men because Mick says they're all men. Susan was the only woman. Can they all be men of action? The man we seek is a man of action surely. He learned very quickly that Vanessa was the social director and planted his bomb as soon as he could get away from the rest.

Although he may have learned it when he learned that Vanessa was on this ship. Why not? NB: Call Zygmunt. Who asked questions at the offices of the cruise line? Name and description.

I was a man of action while I carried my submachine gun. When I think back on what I did then I know it's the truth. This pistol doesn't have the same effect, perhaps because I've never shot anyone with it. Will I shoot the bomber when I find him?

Only if I must. I will shoot him and he will die, which was what he wanted when he joined the ring. They won't try me for machine-gunning hijackers; they'd be laughed out of court. But if I shoot him? Say that it's Rick. . . .

And it may well be Rick; a left-handed man could have stabbed her from one side; we'd have to know the direction of the wound.

Rick's a veteran, and honorably discharged. He would have to have an honorable discharge to get that license. They'll certainly want to try me for that, nor can I fault them for it.

The submachine gun is under my bed. I would never have believed that I would sleep with a submachine gun under the bed.

What else?

The suicide ring, of course, although it will be difficult. We lack the name of a single member.

We lack that, but Reanimation has it, Reanimation has one name at least, though Reanimation will not surrender it easily. Find the name of the employee they're looking for—surely they're looking for her by now—and trace her associates. One or more are on this ship. Two would seem more likely, and there could easily be three. Ask Mick. Did two or three enlist together? Did any of the men he enlisted appear to know each other? We must learn those things.

There's more. The police will suspect certain persons of belonging to suicide rings. With luck, Zygmunt may be able to learn their names, or some of them. Mick said he could give me the service numbers of his men as well as their names. That suggests that none used aliases, though it doesn't prove it. Have the numbers checked; the Public Service Administration will provide names.

When I shut my eyes I see the ruin blocking the corridor. I smell the smoke. There were no screams save Vanessa's. She was on her way to her office, she said, when she stopped at the infirmary to talk to Chelle.

I see the dead hand, the nail polish and the ring with the big watery stone. Did the young woman I spoke to there have a ring like that?

I wish I could remember.

How pretty she was!

12

JANE SIMS

"Sit down, Don." Skip indicated a chair. "Would you like something to eat? Or a drink? The first-class kitchen's supposed to be a bit better than second class. It may not be true, but that's what they say. I'd think the bars are probably about the same."

"Dos Equis, sir, if it's not too much trouble."

"Of course not. I'll have one, too." Skip picked up the telephone and ordered.

Miles waited expectantly.

"You're wondering why I wanted to talk to you."

"Yes, sir."

"I need your help, or think I do. You've probably guessed that already."

"I'll be happy to help you any way I can, sir."

"I know. I feel sure of that, but I'm going to have to ask you some personal questions. It wouldn't be fair for me to do that without briefing you, without giving you some idea of why I'm prying into your private life. You went down into the hold with Sergeant Kent-Jermyn to fight the hijackers."

"Yes, sir. It was a damned fool thing to do. I know that now."

"It was a very brave thing to do. I admire you for it. Everybody admires you." Skip paused, collecting his thoughts. "Some of you were killed.

Others were captured. When you were, Mastergunner Chelle Blue led a party down there to rescue you."

"Yes, sir."

"Mastergunner Blue and I are contracted. Did you know that?"

"Yes, sir. Lieutenant Brice told me. He's one of the ship's officers, sir."

"He is, Captain Kain has mentioned him. There's a Captain Johnson on board, too. A captain in the Army, I mean. Do you know him?"

"No, sir."

"He was in that meeting room when you came in. I should have introduced you to everyone, but I was so anxious to talk to you that it was all I could think of. Do you know Virginia Healy?"

"No, sir. Wait a minute—wasn't that the woman who volunteered to go down as a prisoner? The first woman who raised her hand?"

"Correct. She's Mastergunner Blue's mother." Skip sighed. "She's Chelle's mother, and someone's trying to kill her. That's one reason I'm poking and prying—a peripheral reason, or I think it is. Sometime peripheral reasons turn out to be not so peripheral later."

Miles nodded. "Yes, sir."

There was a diffident knock.

Skip opened the door, and signed the bill when the waiter had deposited his tray on a small table. "Did you fight?" Skip asked the waiter.

"No, sir. Not really. They put the older people in the second-class dining room, sir, and assigned four of us to guard them. I was one of those."

"Did you have a gun?"

"Not at first, sir. A kitchen knife. We got guns after, sir."

"Can you shoot?"

"No, sir."

"Neither can I." Skip added a tip to the check, and the waiter went out.

As the door closed, Miles said, "I heard you killed quite a few of them, sir." He had not opened his beer.

"Yes, but I burned a lot of ammunition, and they were so tightly packed that when I missed one I hit another. I'll try to do better next time, if there's a next time."

Skip sat, and twisted the top from his bottle. "You know Chelle, I know. Do you like her?"

"I'm not trying to move in on you, sir."

"I didn't think you were. I just wondered what you thought of her."

"Everybody likes her, sir."

"Do you?"

"Yes, sir." Miles paused. "She's good-looking, and sharp as hell. She's got that air of command, too. You know what I mean? She's a leader. She knows it, and you know it as soon as she shows up. I don't know how many decorations she's got, but Private Bonham called around, he said, and he says the eagle and maple leaf, silver. If she stays in, they'll pin bars on her. You bet your ass, sir."

"She's not staying in," Skip said. "Or I don't think she is."

"I don't blame her, sir."

"I ought to add that I don't want her to. She has a problem, a serious one, and I'm trying to help her with it. I'm a great deal older than she is, as I feel certain you realize."

"A little older, sir. Just a little bit. I guess you two contracted before she went up."

"Correct. I can't be a young man for her again. I can help her, though, and that's what I'm trying to do. Are you contracted?"

"No, sir." Miles's face went blank.

"Have you ever been?"

"No, sir. We— Can I explain, sir? You won't believe me, but it's the truth."

"If it's true, I'll believe you."

"There was this girl in high school. We . . . You know."

"You fell in love."

"Yes, sir. That's it exactly. We said we were going to contract. I believed it, and I think she did, too."

"Continue, please, Corporal. Let's have the whole story." Skip sounded as sympathetic as he ever had to a defense witness during a murder trial, and that was very sympathetic indeed.

"Only she went off to college, sir. We said we'd call and e-mail and all that. You know?"

Skip nodded. "I certainly do."

"Only I didn't have the money to call very often, and I'm not very good about writing anything. After a while, well, I enlisted and she stopped calling. It—it didn't bother me back then. It wasn't a big thing. This next is the part you won't believe, sir."

"Try me," Skip said.

"She was on the planet, on the world they sent me to. She was an officer, sir."

"Really?"

"Yes, sir. She'd studied physics in college, and gotten really high up. There was a weapon we had there. She couldn't say what it was, but it was something one of her teachers had come up with. He was old and hadn't wanted to go, but he told the Army they ought to take Jane. He said they ought to make her an officer and all that so she could take care of his weapon, and they did it. After I'd been at that base about a week, we—well, we saw each other. I can't tell you how that was, sir. I haven't got the words."

"I think I understand."

"We said we wanted to get together to talk about old times, and that was all it was. Only we knew better, both of us. We'd go to the officers' club. I was an enlisted man, but nobody said anything. They could see how it was, and they just smiled and went back to their card game or whatever. We said we were going to contract, and we meant it. We were going to do everything right. You could get model contracts on one of the computers she worked on. Then . . ."

"Something happened," Skip said.

"She got killed." Miles cleared his throat. "I was out on the periphery then, sir. There were outposts, and that was where I was when the missile hit. It was just a little one, not one of the big ones like you fire into space, but it . . . It killed Janie—killed her, and a hell of a lot of other people."

"One question, please." Skip paused. "I know this must be painful."

"Go ahead, sir. It's not going to get any worse."

"Was Janie's last name Sims?"

"Yes, sir. It was. How'd you know, sir?"

"Chelle told me. You were on Johanna."

"Yes, sir. I'm not supposed to tell anybody that, but you know already."

"So was Chelle. She was hurt pretty badly there, perhaps by the same missile, although I don't know that." Skip returned his glass to the tray and rose to pace the floor. "Before we knew about Sergeant Kent-Jermyn's group, Chelle gave Captain Kain her word that she wouldn't go down into the hold. Her word's usually good. Better than mine, I think. Achille—do you know Achille?"

Miles nodded. "The little guy with no hands? Yes, sir."

"He'll have hands again when we get back home. I'm going to get him replacements. I owe him, and I like to pay my debts."

For a few moments Skip paced, swinging along with the pronounced roll of the ship and collecting his thoughts. "You know that Chelle assembled a force of her own and went down to rescue you. They were defeated, just as the group you were in were. A good many of them were killed and the rest were captured, including Chelle."

Miles nodded again. "It's called defeat in detail, sir. It's what happens when you break up and let the enemy fight you piece by piece."

"Thank you. I didn't know that. You did, but you went down with Kent-Jermyn anyway."

"Yes, sir. A raiding party of a few men can get a lot done sometimes. You and the skipper didn't know the setup down there, for one thing. We found out."

"I think I understand." Skip sipped his beer and set it back down. "What I started out to say was that Achille came with a list of the captives. The hijackers had gotten all of you to write down your names."

"Yes, sir, except for the ones who were hurt too bad to write. We wrote theirs for them."

"I see. I believe that was before Angel Mendoza escaped?"

"Yes, sir. We wouldn't have put down his name if he hadn't been there."

"I see." For a few seconds, Skip paced in silence. "I've been assuming that he had a similar list. And of course he may have—he could have written such a list himself."

"Yes, sir."

"I think he did. When we found Chelle, she told me she needed a psychiatrist. She was joking, I'm sure; but many a truth is told in jest. As we took her up to J Deck, I asked what she'd meant by it; and she told me that when she'd read your names she felt compelled to get you men back, and that her compulsion to do it overrode every other consideration."

"I don't think I've got this yet, sir."

"I think I do," Skip said, "and right now that's what matters. It involves Jane Sims and a note Chelle wrote once. It may also involve my secretary in some way, and I admit I don't understand that yet. Perhaps I never will, but . . ." He smiled. "But we may get to the bottom of it today, Corporal Miles. I dare hope so."

"Then so do I, sir."

"Good! I want to take you to the infirmary to talk to Chelle. I want you to tell her about Jane Sims, in much more detail than you told me. And I want you to tell her how Jane Sims died. Did you see her body?"

"Yes, sir. Not for long, because the medics grabbed it and froze it. They use them for organ replacements, sir. Then the parts they can't use—whatever's chewed up too bad—get shipped home in a sealed coffin. People here don't seem to understand that, but that's how it is."

"I see. Do you happen to know whether Jane Sims's family has received such a coffin?"

"No, sir. I don't, and I'd like to."

Skip nodded, mostly to himself. "I have a man in Boswash, which is where I live, who'll look into things like that for me. I'll have him find out, and I'll tell you what he learns."

"Thank you, sir!"

"In return, I'd like you to talk to Chelle. Tell her what you've told me about Jane Sims, and about seeing her body. Describe it. Give her as much detail as you can remember."

"I will, sir."

Skip took a deep breath. "It may work, and it's certainly worth trying; I'll be indebted to you whether it works or not. A moment ago I said I liked to pay my debts. Are you going to stay in the Army?"

Miles nodded. "I'll have to, sir. It's damned hard to get a civilian job, sir. That's what everybody says. I qualify for a pension—they say I've got twenty years' service—but for a corporal that's not much."

"Suppose you could get a civilian job, a good one?"

"Then I'd put in for a discharge, sir. I'd have the salary, whatever it was, and my pension, too. I'd be set."

"Do this for me, and I'll get you one."

Miles swallowed the last drop of his beer, and paused as though afraid to speak. At last he said, "Really, sir?"

"Yes. I've got connections. Let's go see Chelle."

Someone was shouting in the infirmary, his hoarse voice audible far down the corridor: *"Hey! Hey! Anybody! Come here!"*

The middle-aged woman who had sat at the desk when Skip and Susan had come to see Chelle was dead, her body slumped across the desk, her white cotton blouse bullet-torn and scarlet with her blood. Chelle's bed was empty, her pillow on the floor, her sheets tangled.

The man in the big room next to hers stopped shouting as they came through its door. "Don! What the hell's going on?"

"That's what we want to know, sir," Don said; Skip felt that he spoke for both of them.

Five minutes later, they found Dr. Prescott's body behind his desk in his consulting room.

Hours later, Skip told the captain, "He had been dragged there. He'd heard them shoot his nurse and had come out of his office. The gunman shot him three times and dragged him back inside. I don't know why."

"We'll find him," Captain Kain promised.

"Will we? We've spent three hours looking without finding him." Skip took a long swallow of a vodka-and-tonic he felt sure he should not have asked for. "Can he get off the ship?"

"No."

Skip raised an eyebrow. "Just like that?"

"Yes, just like that. You're going to suggest that he could escape in a lifeboat."

"Couldn't he?"

"No. It takes two people to launch one, one at each davit—two able-bodied men with strong arms. If they were going to ride in the boat themselves, they'd have to jump into the sea after they had it down. That's how it would be done if we were sinking. Do you want to hear more?"

Skip nodded.

"Very well. That wouldn't be possible if it's only one man. He could threaten Ms. Blue with death and force her to help, agreed. He could also force her to jump before he did. But you say she has a broken arm. I doubt that the strongest man in my crew could operate one of those davits without two sound arms. No doubt Ms. Blue is strong for a woman, but with her right arm broken? There's not a chance."

"Suppose—"

"That there are more than one. Exactly. That's the chance we cannot take. Here's another, one you may not have thought of. Suppose he's got a great deal of money. He finds a couple of my sailors and offers them . . . Oh, ten thousand noras to let down a lifeboat for him. Some of my men wouldn't take it, I know. Others might. I've got patrols on the Boat Deck watching the boats for just that reason."

"An inflatable raft," Skip suggested. "He forces her to jump, jumps in after her, and inflates his raft. She'd have to climb aboard or drown."

"Normally, we have only one lookout, a man who looks forward. Now I've stationed a man aft to watch for that, or a suicide attempt." The captain sighed. "For a raft or dinghy of some kind, or a body overboard."

"You think he might kill her."

"Of course I do. Who is he? Why does he want her?"

"I don't know."

"Then we can't even begin to guess——"

The captain was interrupted by his phone. When he hung up, he told Skip, "That was Dr. Ueda. She's a passenger, but she's agreed to fill in for Dr. Prescott until we reach port. There are a lot of wounded in the infirmary, and she's found women with medical backgrounds to help her take care of them."

"I hadn't even thought of that," Skip said.

"Naturally not. But it was my duty to find somebody, and I did. While we were searching she's been looking at bodies, Dr. Prescott's and Nurse Eagan's, and those poor girls who used to work for Virginia." The captain paused. "If I weren't so damned tired I could probably think of their names."

"Amelia was one," Skip told him. "The other was Polly, I think. Or Paula. I don't remember the last names."

"Amelia Nelson, I believe, and Polly Lutz. They were both killed by the explosion. No bullets."

"I'd assumed that."

"You were right," the captain said, "but now we know. Eagan was shot once through the heart. Prescott was shot three times." The captain paused.

"You've got something." Putting aside his drink, Skip leaned forward. "What is it?"

"I do. Or rather, Dr. Ueda does and I don't know what it means. Prescott was shot once in the abdomen and twice in the chest. The bullets in his chest probably came from the gun that killed Nurse Eagan. Dr. Ueda can't be sure of that, but she says the wounds look the same. The third bullet is from another gun."

When Skip said nothing, the captain added, "It's about the same size, or she thinks it is. Everything else is different. It didn't expand, and the metal doesn't look the same. She weighed them, and that third bullet is quite a bit heavier. The bullet that killed Eagan looks like the ones from Prescott's chest."

"There are two of them. Two shooters."

"That's how it looks. Did Ms. Blue have a gun?"

Skip nodded. "She did when I came to see her. Yes."

"Could she have been one of the killers?"

"Of course not." Skip made it as positive as he could.

"Why not?" The captain smiled to take the sting out of his question.

"Chelle isn't a criminal, just to start with. I've talked to people who believe that the Army turns its soldiers into heartless killers, but I'm in the business of defending people accused of crime and I know how low the crime rate is among returned veterans."

"It doesn't bother you, defending criminals?"

"I'm not finished yet, and in fact I've hardly begun. I'll get to that in a moment. Second, Chelle was badly hurt. She'd be killing the people who were trying to help her."

Skip raised three fingers. "And third, she didn't have a ghost of a motive. The real killers had a clear one: they wanted Chelle."

"Why?"

"I could guess, but I'm not going to. It would only be a guess, and I prefer to deal with facts. Fourth, Chelle is right-handed and her right arm is broken. She said your doctor put in a plate and held it in place with screws driven into the bone. She could hold her gun when I handed it to her. But could she have shot it? I'd like your honest opinion."

"Yes," the captain said. "With her left hand."

"Possibly, but notice how unlikely it is. Fifth, from what I saw at the scene, the nurse was standing behind her desk when she was shot in the chest. If Chelle had left her room and shot her— Just a minute."

Skip's mobile phone was vibrating. He took it out and flipped it open.

Susan appeared in its small screen. *"'Hell hath no fury like a woman scorned.' Do you remember saying that, Mr. Grison? You quoted it during the Zayas trial."*

"Correct."

"I'm going to disprove it." Susan's smile was bitter. *"We've got your precious Chelle. She's a mess, but . . ."*

Skip said, "Please don't hurt her."

"But I feel sorry for her, and for you, too." Susan paused for so long a time that he feared she would hang up. *"I still love you. Does that surprise you?"*

"Yes. Yes, it does. I still love you, too, Susan. I love you and I'm terribly sorry I hurt you."

"I love you, but I love him more and we're going to kill her." The words brought the ghost of a smile. *"It will be fast, I promise. And soon. He's promised me that."*

"Who is he, Susan?"

"But I'm going to let you talk to her first. Just for a few minutes, because I'm not sure when he's coming back. I think you should have a chance to say good-bye." Susan's face disappeared from the tiny screen.

Chelle's replaced it. *"Don? Is this Don?"*

There was a knock at the door, which Skip ignored. "I'm afraid not. I'm S. W. Grison, Don's attorney. How can I help you?"

"I want to tell Don how much I love him. I—I'm going away again. Going away for good. That's what they say. Please let me speak to him."

The captain had risen and admitted Rick Johnson.

"He's not here, I'm afraid, but I'll find him and send him to you at once. Where are you?"

"In Jerry's room." Chelle turned to speak to someone out of frame. *"This is Jerry's room, isn't it?"*

Susan's face replaced Chelle's. *"Did you say goodbye? I hope so."*

The screen went black as Johnson whispered, "Something up?"

Skip snapped his phone shut. "We need the number of Sergeant Kent-Jermyn's cabin. That's where Chelle is."

"Half a minute." The captain turned to his computer. "Thank God his name's not Smith."

REFLECTION 12

Women and Men

Defending criminals doesn't bother me in the slightest, and I ought to have told the captain that. Criminality depends upon circumstances much more often than not. "I know you to be a man of the most scrupulous honor, one who cannot be tempted to a shameful or dishonest act, save by money." I read that somewhere.

It's not me. If defending criminals is somehow dishonest, why, I can be tempted by nothing at all. I often take pro bono cases.

Nor is it Susan. I would be amazed to learn that the man using her has tempted her with money. Or jewelry, or any such thing. With the offer of a contract? Perhaps, but I would bet against it and give odds. Susan has found a new Mr. Grison, a Mr. Grison who has not betrayed her yet. How I wish that I might find a new Mr. Grison!

Don Miles will never find a new Jane. He will find another girl, and why not? He's levelheaded, decent, and quite smart. Get him a good job—and I will—and he'll be able to pick and choose. But not another Jane. For him there can never be another Jane Sims.

Just as there can never be another Chelle Sea Blue for me. We hurried to the elevator, and now we wait. In the elevator we will wait again. And I know that I must save Chelle if I can, and that I'll lose her—and very soon—whether I save her or not. I long to be the white knight riding to her rescue, Sir Galahad in spotless armor, astride a white stallion. I'll save her from the bastard who's got her; and after that, for a night or two, possibly three, I'll be Sir Galahad.

No longer than three, I'm sure.

What is it women look for in a man? Don's wanting his Jane back, I understand easily. But why did Jane want her Don all over again? Was it the shared background? They'd been schoolmates after all.

Or was it just that Don was someone she could rely upon? There could not have been many such men, for her. She would've had to look for spies everywhere, just as we—but here's the elevator.

13

JERRY'S ROOM

The captain inserted his master cabin card and twisted the knob. With his submachine gun off-safe, Skip kicked the door open and burst into the room. Rick Johnson was at his heels, gun drawn.

A pretty brunet looked up from her book and screamed. Skip froze. Johnson pushed past him, flung the bathroom door open, and stepped in.

"Please," Skip said. "Please. It's all right."

The brunet screamed again.

Over Skip's shoulder, the captain asked, "Are these men bothering you, ma'am?"

"I . . . You're searchers."

"We are," the captain said. "We're sorry we disturbed you. Both these men will apologize, I'm sure."

"I do," Skip said. "Profoundly. I'm very sorry."

Johnson shook his head. "Not until I've looked in the closet." He did, and apologized.

The brunet smiled weakly, although she seemed on the point of tears. "I knew the ship was being searched. I . . . I guess I just never thought they'd search here."

"We'll leave at once," the captain told her.

"Almost at once." Skip sat down on the bed, with his submachine gun across his lap. "Please let me introduce myself. My name's Skip Grison."

"I know that," the brunet said. "I'm Nan Olivera."

"You know our captain? Captain Kain?"

"I know who he is."

The captain cleared his throat. "I don't get to see as much of the passengers in this class as I would like, Ms. Olivera. You're here with Sergeant Kent-Jermyn?"

She nodded. "We're contracted. I—well, I know that Mr. Grison is contracted with Mastergunner Blue, the woman they're searching for. I don't think I've said I forgive him yet, but I do. I know Gerald would look for me until he was too tired to stand up."

She turned back to Skip. "You are, you know. You ought to see yourself."

He shrugged. "Nothing a few hours' sleep won't fix. You spoke of the sergeant a moment ago. You called him Gerald?"

"Yes. That's his name."

"I know it is. Don't you call him Jerry sometimes? I thought people did."

"Oh, no! He hates it. I've got—sometimes I use a pet name, only never in public. I won't tell you what it is."

"Not even if it might help us find Chelle? Find Mastergunner Blue? Because it might. You could whisper it, if you like."

The brunet's mouth opened, then closed again.

"I'll go," the captain said. "I'm sure Mr. Johnson will, too."

Johnson nodded.

"Will you promise never to tell anybody? All three of you? It's supposed to be something private between Gerald and me."

Johnson said, "I promise."

Captain Kain added, "We all do."

"All right. It's Pickle. That's what his mother called him when he was little, only she'd never tell me why. But I've called him that ever since, when . . . You know. When we're in bed and like that."

"I see. There was a party—"

He was interrupted by a familiar voice. "Hello! May I come in?"

The brunet stood up. "Aren't you Mastergunner Blue's mother? That's what somebody said."

"Yes, indeed!" Vanessa's smile would have charmed a queen. "I remember you from the party, Nan. You were the prettiest girl there."

"Oh, I wasn't! But come in, please. I'm surprised you remember me at all. We only met for a minute or two."

"I could never forget you," Vanessa declared. She took Skip's hand. "I said I had to talk to you, remember? It was during that meeting. I've been waiting for you to call, but you didn't, so I went looking for you. Raimundo told me you'd gone in here—Raimundo's the steward on this deck, and very nice."

"I'm sure he is. That party you mentioned a moment ago—the one at which you met Ms. Olivera. Was that the one you arranged for the soldiers?"

"Yes, of course. It was a very nice party, if I do say so myself."

"Who issued the invitations?"

"Polly did. Polly Lutz."

"She decided who to invite?"

"No," Vanessa said, "I did that."

The brunet smiled. "Thank you for inviting us. We had a super time. I want to apologize for not searching for your daughter, but Gerald didn't want me to. He said there were plenty of searchers, and it could end in another gunfight." She paused for a deep breath. "So I stayed in here. I'm sorry now that I did."

Vanessa kissed her cheek. "Don't you worry. We'll find her."

Skip had been dialing Susan. Having been informed that her phone was out of service, he flipped his own shut. "I apologize to everyone here. This has been a mess, and I made it. Virginia has an urgent matter to discuss, and I put it on the back burner for this. I made Rick and Captain Kain look like fools and I can only hope they'll forgive me for it. I am the fool, not they. We broke in on Ms. Olivera—"

"Call me Nan, please."

"We broke in on Nan and terrified her, and I regret it more than I can say."

The captain cleared his throat. "This cruise has been disastrous, and it's my fault. The hijackers caught me flatfooted, something that won't happen again if I live to be a thousand."

Skip said, "There will be lawsuits, none of which will involve me. For your company's sake, you should be careful about what you say."

Johnson grinned. "I didn't hear a thing."

Vanessa added, "Hear what?"

"I won't sue anybody," Nan Olivera said. "I don't think Gerald will, either."

Captain Kain smiled. "You know, I've been neglecting my duties. I'm afraid I've let the hijacking push my day-to-day job out of my mind. We have some empty staterooms in first class, and we normally upgrade a few second-class passengers to fill those. Would you like to upgrade, Nan? You'd have a sauna and a veranda—and a lot more room, of course."

"I'd love it! I'm sure Gerald would, too."

"I'll see to it, and send your steward to help you move. He'll have your new cabin card, and it will get you into the first-class dining room."

Skip motioned to Vanessa, and they left together.

"Where shall we talk?" she whispered.

"Out on deck, if that's agreeable to you." He sighed. "I've a touch of claustrophobia. It rarely bothers me, but with so many people in that tiny cabin . . ."

"We could go to your stateroom. Out on your veranda?"

"No." Skip had started up the stairs. "People on the neighboring verandas could overhear us, and we couldn't see them listening."

The sun was bright and warm, the sea sparkling like sapphire, and the big ship heeling to a whistling wind. Skip found them seats in the shade, well away from any listeners.

"You said you told Polly whom to invite. This was a party for soldiers on leave?"

"For anyone who'd been in service." Although her careful coiffeur was whipping in the wind, Vanessa smiled. "Did you see our announcement? It was in the *Bulletin*."

"I suppose I did. I didn't pay much attention to it."

"The computer's got a register of passengers, and the soldiers on leave are listed under their military titles—their honorifics, or whatever you call it. Private so-and-so. Chelle was Mastergunner Chelle Sea Blue. Like that."

Skip nodded.

"So those were easy to find. I had Amelia contact a few and get the names of some who'd been discharged, and I put that announcement in, and after that I listed everybody and had Polly send invitations. Amelia watched the door, and each of them could bring a guest. Just one. Only some who'd seen my announcement or been told about it just dropped by. If they could show they'd been in the service, Amelia let them in."

"Do you remember the names you gave Polly?"

"All of them?" Vanessa shook her head.

"Some of them."

"Yes, certainly. Quite a lot, actually."

"I'm looking for a man called Jerry. Was there anyone?"

"Ah! I see. Is this to get Chelle back?"

"Yes. Please help if you can."

"But you won't tell me what's going on for fear I'll be hurt."

Skip had put on his sunglasses and was studying small white clouds that rode the west wind; he muttered, "That's close enough."

"I'd like to get closer. Why?" Vanessa's hand found his. "Don't you trust me, Skip? After all we've been through?" It was a firm little hand, and it held his tightly.

"I do, but I don't trust Reanimation. If they get you, they'll have your mind on their computer. I don't know how deeply they'll look into it, but they may find memories they can use to damage Chelle. Or to damage me. We'll be trying to get you back, and they'll twist our arms, if they can, to make us stop. Do you recall inviting anyone called Jerry?"

"Jerry? Jerry . . . I don't think so. There was Gerald Kent-Jermyn, of course. We were just talking to his wife."

"Contracta," Skip said.

"Whatever. She sounded just like a wife. He won't do?"

"No. We've eliminated him. Jerome?"

Vanessa's eyebrows went up. "I thought you said Jerry."

"Men named Jerome are often called Jerry, informally."

"I didn't know that. What about G-E-R-R-Y? I've known women with that name, and it's pronounced like Jerry."

"I don't think it's a woman, but I heard the name on the phone, so it could be that. Or Geri with an I. Were there any?"

Vanessa shook her head. "Not that I know of."

"Jeremy? Gerard?"

"I don't think so. John and James. Alan and Robert. There were lots of those."

"Don Miles."

She nodded. "Yes, I remember him. And Joe. There were several Joes. Josephs. Several Josephs and one Jake. But I can't help you with Jerry, I'm afraid, if it isn't Gerald Kent-Jermyn. I have something to tell you, though, and I wish you'd let me get it out. It's important, and I'm about to burst."

"There was someone at that party called Jerry," Skip insisted.

"If you say so, then I'm sure there was. But I don't know about him, and Amelia's dead. She was at the party much more than I was." Vanessa snapped her fingers. "Why don't you ask Nan? She was there. Or her husband."

"I will."

"Now please don't tell me why you have to know. Not until I tell you. Do you remember the restaurant? I saw the people eating, and the woman saw me?"

Skip nodded.

"Afterward I was stabbed. Not long afterward, either. Just a few minutes. Did I describe the woman to you?"

"Yes. Round-faced, heavy, nice-looking, light brown hair."

"There's a woman on this ship. The first time I saw her I knew I'd seen her before, but I couldn't place her. She's more of a blonde now, but that's easy and it could be the sun. Then we had that meeting. You had me take off my little gun so everybody could see my arm. Remember?"

"I do." Skip was staring. "There was only one other woman in that room."

"Does she work for you? I got that impression."

"She did. She was my secretary. You're saying that Susan—Susan Clerkin, who worked for me for years—belonged to a suicide ring."

Vanessa shook her head, earrings bouncing. "I'm not. I don't know that. I'm just saying that the woman who was with you in that meeting is the one who saw me in Simone's. She is. Could she have planted the bomb that killed Polly and Amelia?"

"Yes."

"Just like that, Skip? Your secretary?"

Skip did not speak.

"My God, you look awful. Does it really hurt that much?"

"I hurt her very badly, Vanessa. I wounded her far more deeply than I realized at the time, and now she's getting her own back with interest. She called me. That was when I was talking to the captain, after a couple of hundred of us had spent hours searching the ship for Chelle." Skip paused, remembering. "She told me she had Chelle, and to prove it she let Chelle talk to me for a few seconds."

Vanessa waited, large brown eyes wide, crimson mouth poised to moan.

"Chelle said they were in Jerry's cabin. By that time I thought I knew who 'Jerry' was. I told the captain, and he came with us. You walked in on that."

"So I could tell you what I just did."

"I wish you'd told me earlier," Skip said. "She was there. We could have held her."

"Well, I couldn't tell you without telling the others, could I? Not unless you'd been willing to go into a corner with me and whisper, and you wouldn't have done that. You know you wouldn't."

"I suppose you're right." Skip closed his eyes. "Did I say that Susan had Chelle? I mean a moment ago."

"You certainly did."

"Then I misled you. Susan said 'we.' 'We have Chelle.' She talked about a man, apparently a lover."

"That would be Jerry. I see."

"Would it? That's what I thought. I wish I weren't so tired. It's hard to think straight when you're tired."

"You need coffee. I can try to find you some if you like."

He opened his eyes. "I need sleep, but I have to find Chelle, and find her quickly."

"She said Jerry's room?"

"Yes. Just that. Nothing more."

"Then she expected you to know who Jerry was."

"Correct. When she came back from that party, she mentioned a man called Jerry. So that's the man, or I think it is. If she thought about it at all, she must have thought that it would be easy for me identify the Jerry she knew."

"I can go through the list for you." Vanessa sounded thoughtful. "My terminal's gone, but I can find another. Richard would let me use his, I'm sure. There are bound to be more Geralds, perhaps some of those other names, too."

Skip took off his sunglasses to rub his eyes. "The thing is, we've searched the ship. All the cabins. Even the crew's quarters. They may have killed her already and disposed of the body. Only I don't dare let myself assume that. What if they haven't?"

"Well, I don't believe it. Let's get back to that little blonde who was at your meeting. You said she was your secretary?"

Resuming his sunglasses, Skip nodded.

"And it sounded as if the man with her was her lover?"

"She didn't say so, only that she loved him. But yes, it did."

"Only you think she was in a suicide ring."

"Correct."

"Well, she hasn't committed suicide. I can promise you that. If there's one kind of woman in the whole world who won't kill herself, it's a woman with a new lover. You're fretting because you didn't find Chelle. Did you find your secretary?"

Skip shook his head.

"You had the others looking for her? As well as Chelle?"

"Yes, certainly."

"Then Chelle isn't dead, and they're still together. It's just that nobody looked in the right place. She said she was in this Jerry's cabin?"

"Let me think. Yes. She said Jerry's room. 'We're in Jerry's room.'"

"That might not be a cabin at all. We've an artist on board. Her name's Cynthia Van Houten, and she's teaching sketching and oil painting to anybody who wants to learn. She got half off on her ticket for that."

"Are you sure this is germane?"

"I think so. She's got a studio on D Deck, and just about everybody calls it Cynthia's room. Suppose we go around the ship asking people where Jerry's room is? If Chelle knew, other people are bound to know, too."

They stopped an elderly man with a corncob pipe who had come up on deck to smoke. When Skip explained, the elderly man said, "Who's Jerry?"

"Just someone I ran into a few days ago." Skip paused, trying to place the man. "Young, nice-looking. We'd like to find his room. Do you know where it is?"

"'Fraid not."

Ramón, the C Deck steward, knew no one of that name. Hoping against hope, Skip selected Susan's number yet again. It was still out of service.

The muscular woman standing in the door of the spa said that there had been a woman called Jeri on the previous cruise. "Real nice lady, only she gone now."

Skip said, "That won't help, I'm afraid."

"This important, Ms. Healy?"

Vanessa nodded. "Very important."

"You wait jus' one minute an' I'll help. I got to lock my place up."

She returned a moment later. "Don't anybody want no massage now anyhow, an' three's better'n two."

"Let me have your number," Skip said. "I've already got Virginia's. We can search a lot faster if we split up. I'll call you both if I find something; you call Virginia and me if you do. Ask for Jerry's room. That's all we know."

They separated, Vanessa going up to B Deck and the muscular woman to the crew's quarters, forward on E Deck. Skip began knocking on doors.

"Yes?" The woman's face was innocent of makeup and smeared with cream. Her hair was in curlers.

"I'm sorry to disturb you," Skip said, "but this is important."

"I was getting ready for bed." The woman paused. "You should go to bed, too. You're that man who goes around with the captain, aren't you?"

Skip nodded. "I'm trying to find Mastergunner Chelle Blue. I don't suppose you've seen her within the past few hours?"

"Not since yesterday, I think."

"She told me she would be in Jerry's room. Just that—Jerry's room. Do you have any idea where that would be?"

"No. Not here. I have son-in-law named Jerry back home. Should I call him?"

"I don't think that will be necessary," Skip said, and thanked her.

The knocking at the doors of the next three cabins evoked no response. The fourth was opened by a boy. In response to Skip's question he said, "I'm Jerry, and this is my room, right here."

No words came.

"See, my folks don't want me in with them because I drive Dad nuts, and I don't want to be in with them anyhow because Mom drives *me* nuts, so I get my own room. Brass, right?"

"Very brass." Skip had recovered himself.

"Only this game's kinda itchy, and there's never anything on tele."

Wondering what an itchy game was like, Skip nodded.

"So I'm gonna sit around the pool, and maybe swim if it's not too crowded."

"Could we go into your cabin for a minute? Please? You'd be doing me a great favor."

"Mom says not to let anybody in." The boy shrugged. "Only you look okay, so I guess so." He stepped aside.

"Thank you, Jerry. I don't think Chelle's in here, but I've got to look. I really must."

There was no one in the lavatory, no one out on the veranda, and no one in the closet.

Jerry said, "Who's Chelle? Is that Mastergunner Blue? I saw her once, and Steve says her first name's Chelle. Is she hot or what?"

Skip nodded.

"You think she might be hiding in my room? Wait'll I tell Steve!"

"I was hoping she was hidden in your room," Skip said. His phone vibrated as he spoke; he took it out and flipped it open.

"This Trinity, Mr. Grison. I found that man got no hands. You know? He say you know him."

"Achille," Skip said.

"Got big ol' hooks. He say he know where that Jerry's room is, and he take us there."

"Did he say what deck it was on?"

There was a murmur of speech too faint for Skip to understand. Then: *"This Achille, mon. Is on bottom, mon. Bottom deck, you know?"*

"M Deck?"

"You know cheap bar? We meet you there, you buy drink, I show you."

"The tourist-class bar?"

"Is so, mon. Meet there. I take you Jerry."

Skip sighed. "All right."

As he shut his phone, Jerry said, "Did somebody find Mastergunner Blue?"

"I don't think so. I think I'm going to find a wild goose. The tourist bar is aft, isn't it?"

"Sure. I'll show you."

REFLECTION 13

Sleep

When we need to be at our best, we're always far from it. I could sleep now for twelve hours straight, or I feel I could, and rise refreshed. Instead, I walk through half the ship with a loaded submachine gun slantwise across my back and a pistol shoved into my belt. Both are much too heavy, and I much too tired. Would Chelle do this for me?

I would like to think so, and perhaps she would. God only knows what she did on Johanna. She did much worse, in all probability. . . .

Which is my cue to whine that she was younger.

As she still is. Much, much younger than I, and she sleeps on her side, always turned away. It's clearly a defensive posture, but does she know it? On her back sometimes when she has had a few; she snores then, snoring so soft that it is almost purring. I sleep on my belly, a good reason for staying in shape, for not gaining another kilo. Does the ship have a handball court? I don't even know.

I could walk around and around the Main Deck. A lot of people do that, but I have walked now until my feet are blistered and feel that they must burst through my shoes. Through canvas shoes I bought for comfort, visualizing much shopping on this island and that, see the fort, built in 1615 by the Spanish. "There are a hundred and fifty-three steps so perhaps the old people should wait here while the rest of us go up." Me climbing the stairs to show Susan that I was still young, Susan climbing behind me to show that she was still loyal. Once Susan would have combed this ship for me, I know. She'd have combed it 'til she dropped, and I may drop soon.

Would I do this if Chelle and I were the same age? Yes, and if anything more willingly. Chelle has still the fire of youth, a fire I would control if I could. That's wrong, perhaps. Wrong but right. Wrong but true.

Correct.

Why is it my dreams are never the dreams I would like? Other men have good dreams, or so they tell me. Dreams of success. Of flying without a plane, of flying like a bird or flying like a balloon. (But it is never the fat ones who fly like balloons. Am I the only one to notice?)

I dream of prisons, of windowless concrete walls and being locked in boxes. Prisons in which I never sleep and never eat, or drink, or defecate. Dreams of driving down doubtful roads that narrow and narrow, of driving a car as big as a bus across a footbridge that falls to bits behind me.

Of getting out of the car in a wilderness to shout at someone on the farther side of a gorge, someone who turns away with no sign of having heard. Soon I give up—and do not try the car door, knowing that the car cannot cross the gorge and that I have locked myself out.

In the future, I may dream of walking through this endless ship, of painted corridors that rock and pitch and lead only to more corridors, silent corridors lined with locked doors.

Once I dreamed of Chelle, dreamed that she was leaving me, going to the stars to fight a war from which she would never return, and I was old.

No dream, that last. I am. Fifty will be at my doorstep only too soon. Chet is what? Eighty-something. I have never hoped that Chet would die; now I hope that he will live. If Chet achieves one hundred, why Skip might, too. At one hundred, no one will care if I remain abed, or how long I sleep.

14

~~~

NO YOU DON'T!

A long walk to the nearest stair was succeeded by a weary descent to E Deck and an even longer walk aft, a walk that took Skip and Jerry through the tourist-class casino and almost to the tourist-class dining room. By the time they reached the tourist-class bar, the ship was pitching hard enough to force them to hold the railings.

Trinity and Achille were sitting at a table in the bar, Trinity with a glass before her and Achille with none. Trinity waved them over. "He say he know, Mr. Grison. Say he know Jerry and know where is Jerry's room, too. We buy him a drink, an' he show us. Only I didn't buy him none. I don't think we ought to 'til Ms. Healy come. I call her after I call you. She say she come right away. What you bring this li'l boy for?"

"He knew where this bar was," Skip explained, "and I didn't. At least, I wasn't sure."

Jerry stopped staring at Achille's hooks. "I'd have followed you anyhow."

"Yes. I thought you would, and I might as well make use of you."

Achille asked, "You buy drink, mon?"

Skip nodded, and signaled the barman. "What do you want, Achille?"

"Drink rum, mon."

"A rum, please. Whatever kind you have. It might be best if there were a straw as well."

The barman nodded. "I'm on it. What about you? I could get the kid a Coke or something."

"Coffee," Skip told him, "if you're got it. What would you like, Jerry?"

Trinity looked startled. "This Jerry?"

"This is another Jerry."

"Pepsi," Jerry said. "Is that okay?"

Vanessa arrived soon after the drinks, bracing herself against the pitching of the ship and moving cautiously from one handhold to another. "Shouldn't we be going?"

"I doubt it." Skip stirred his surging coffee as he spoke. "I don't have a lot of confidence in this, to tell you the truth. Have you found anything?"

She shook her head.

"Then this is all we have, this room Achille knows about on M Deck. If it doesn't pan out—and I don't believe it will—what are we going to do?"

In the silence that followed, Skip flipped open his mobile phone and selected Chelle's number. Her phone was off; so was Susan's.

"We need to talk to everyone who was at that party," Vanessa said.

"I concur. Unless you can get us a list, we'll have to talk to those we can find. If each of them names everyone else he can think of we *may* get something. I said *may*." He drew in air and let it out. "We can ask about Jerry's room at the same time."

Achille grunted, bent over his shot glass, closed his mouth around it, and raised his head. The boy called Jerry watched him, fascinated, as he swallowed, lowered his head again, and spat out the shot glass.

"Did you see that!" Jerry's eyes were wide.

"I did," Vanessa told him. "I wish I hadn't."

"You don't got to do this you say, mon." Achille rose. "I take you now."

M Deck, reachable by freight elevator, smelled of hot oil and smoke, and housed the storage batteries that hoarded the electrical energy created by the *Rani*'s wind-driven generators. Achille led the little group along a straight central corridor that seemed to reach beyond the ship, a corridor blocked at one point by what Skip decided was most likely a disassembled heat exchanger. Even here, well below the waterline, they could hear the crash of thunder.

"You see big door, mon? Door there, this side. You see him?"

As Skip was about to reply, the big door opened and a middle-aged man stepped out; he wore coveralls and carried a tool kit.

Skip waved to him. "Just a moment, please. We need to talk to you."

He stopped, but shook his head. "You can't schedule a job through me, sir. You'll have to book it through the engineering office."

"We don't want to schedule anything," Skip explained, "but I have to ask you a few questions."

"Something go wrong with the hooks? I can probably fix 'em in a minute or two, but you ought to leave them with me and get a work order."

"They're fine." Skip held out his hand. "My name's Skip—Skip Grison. Are you Jerry?"

The man grinned. "No, sir. My name's Gary." He accepted Skip's hand and shook it. "I'm Gary Oberdorf."

Vanessa asked, "Is there a man named Jerry who works with you, Mr. Oberdorf?"

Skip began, "This is Gary—"

"We've already met." Vanessa smiled. "He fixed a filing-cabinet drawer for me. Now it seems like a long time ago."

"Nobody," Oberdorf said. "There's only four of us, ma'am. That's Eddie Qualter, Walt Weber, Ray Upjohn, and me. Listen, I'd like to talk to you folks, but I've got to change the lock on Lieutenant Brice's door."

"We'll walk with you," Skip told him. "What's the matter with Lieutenant Brice's lock? Did someone break in?"

"No, sir. It's just that he's lost one card. The officers get two, just like passengers. Only he lost one, and anybody who finds it could go into his stateroom and take everything he's got."

"I see." Skip nodded to himself. "Brice is in the infirmary, isn't he? Isn't he the officer who was shot?"

"Yes, sir. He was in the Navy, and I guess they get training there with pistols and so on. Only he had some bad luck."

"A former serviceman." Skip nodded again. "I don't suppose you know his first name?"

"No, sir. No, I don't."

"Virginia?"

She shook her head.

"You got that li'l fold-away phone," Trinity remarked. "I got me one, too." She displayed it, flipped it open, and pressed keys. "Silvia, honey, this Trinity. You got that Lieutenant Brice where you workin' now? I got a lady asking 'bout his first name. You know what 'tis?"

A moment later she thanked the woman she had called Silvia and closed her phone. "His name Gerard," she told Vanessa.

Skip touched his lips before turning to Oberdorf. "Do you know how he happened to lose his cabin card?"

"I haven't talked to him, sir." He pressed the worn button that summoned the elevator. "But I know a lot of people lose things in the infirmary. They've got those lockers in there, and they hang the patients' clothes in them. Only they don't lock. Visitors come in and go out all the time. I got my foot broke once, and they put me in there for a couple of days before we made port, so I know how it is."

"Chelle had a private room," Skip said.

"Is that a lady? They've got two rooms like that for women, because it's nearly all men. So they get those and don't hear the nasty words. Not that they don't know them already, if you ask me."

The freight elevator arrived. They went into it, and Oberdorf pressed a button for the signal deck.

"I don't understand this at all," Vanessa whispered.

"Later," Skip told her, and turned to Oberdorf. "Will you have to open the door to change the lock?"

"Sure. That's the only way you can get those locks out, sir. You open the door, take off both knobs, and slip the lock out the side. That lets you get at the little keyboard. When you've got it, you can wipe the old code and stick in your new card. Press a couple of buttons and your new card opens the lock."

"I see."

"Hotels and so on use a different system, mostly. They can send a wireless signal that will change the code. Only a hell of a lot of people can send them now, and read them, too. Ours is more secure."

"You've got to have a card?"

"Yes, sir. Or a master. Got to be able to open that lock before you can change the lock. Only a hell of a lot of passengers just walk off with their cards at the end of the cruise, sir. We try to get them to turn them in." He shrugged.

"But they don't."

"Right. About half don't. So one of the things we've got to do when we refit is recode those locks. Generally it takes one man four days to do them all. After the last cruise it took Walt and Ray three."

Skip had to brace himself against the side of the elevator.

"She pitchin' now," Trinity remarked. "This wind behind her. Don't nobody like it."

Vanessa said, "It must make us sail faster, though."

"No, ma'am. Off to the side and jus' a little bitty bit back is what they want. That's the fastest, and don't pitch much. Don't roll much neither."

"Are we gonna sink?" Jerry clearly hoped they would.

"Not us, honey. We been through lots worse than what this is."

The elevator doors slid open. The ship's motion seemed more pronounced here, the thunder almost deafening. Oberdorf ambled down the corridor, compensating for the pitching floor without apparent effort.

Skip hung back. "There might be shooting." He kept his voice down. "I'll take the lead. Try your best not to shoot me in the back."

"How 'bout this li'l boy?"

"Keep him away from the doorway."

As they neared the door, Oberdorf slid a master cabin card into the lock, pushed the door open, and froze.

"Come in." To Skip, still a dozen steps away, it sounded like an old man's voice.

"Come in. We must talk to you."

Oberdorf raised his hands, and Skip drew his gun.

When consciousness returned, he could not remember firing or being shot. Nor did he, for a minute and more, know where he was. He knew only that his head felt ready to split.

His questing fingers found a broad strip of tape.

Someone's shoes were rather too near his eyes. They were white and nearly new, wing-tip shoes with pointed toes and a sprinkling of vent holes. He studied them, and could not have said for how long. Having marooned him, time had not yet returned for him.

White shoes, and the crutch-tipped end of a blackthorn walking stick.

Voices droned overhead: A man's voice, quick and clipped, youthful and energetic. Another man's, quietly humorous and overprecise. A woman's, dark, frustrated, and angry. Another woman's, mocking and almost too proper. A third, tremulous with . . . fear? Anger? A boy's.

Then a new woman's, violent, profane, and lovely beyond every other voice in the world.

Skip sat up. The man seated in front of him had overlong white hair, a wide white mustache, and a neatly trimmed white beard, the beard shaped like the blade of a spade. Blue eyes swam behind thick lenses.

"Skip!" It was she, and in a moment she was on her knees beside him, her sound arm embracing him and her immobilized right arm trying to. She kissed him and kissed him again, and he was too stunned to respond. Thunder roared outside, lightning flashed beyond the glass doors, and he longed, suddenly and painfully, to make love to her in the midst of such a storm. They had never done it, and it seemed likely that they never would.

"I told you we shouldn't have untied her." Rick Johnson needed no handhold to brace himself against the pitching of the ship.

"Quite the contrary," the older man replied. "The wisdom of my course is being made apparent to you. You are too stiff-necked to see it, which is a real pity."

On Skip's left, Oberdorf said, "They're going to kill us."

"These amateurs?" Chelle broke off another kiss to snarl it.

"I'm no amateur," Johnson told her.

"It seems unlikely." At that moment, Skip felt that he would sell his soul for two acetaminophen tablets and a glass of water. "It seems much more probable that some accommodation can be reached."

"I'm going to k-kill you, Mr. Grison." Susan's face was tearstained. "Mr. White says I can. That I can be the w-w-one if we decide to."

"Do you really hate me that much?"

"No! Don't you see?" Her voice shook; so did the hand that gripped her short-barreled revolver. "I'll k-kill you because I l-love you. It ought to be somebody like me, somebody who l-l-loves you."

"I would rather it were nobody at all."

The boy, Jerry, moaned. "I just wanna go home." His face was less tearstained than Susan's, but the stains were there.

"You're going to kill me," Skip told Susan. "Who's going to kill this kid?"

Chelle said, "Oh, for God's sake! Shut your fuckin' mouth."

"It's a serious question." Skip's attention had never left Susan. "It deserves a serious answer. Because you're going to have to kill him. He knows who you are and where you are, and I imagine he's got some idea of what you're doing. So if you three are going to kill us, you'll find he's one of us."

Silence, save for Jerry's sobs.

At last Johnson said, "You think you can get us to swear you to silence and let you go."

"I don't," Skip told him, "but I'd like to propose a rational plan that will end this mess without bloodshed. I know the information you wanted from Chelle—I don't mean that I have it. I don't. But I know what it was. Have you got it?"

Johnson nodded. "I've got it, and I won't forget it. I don't forget."

"Good. That makes everything much easier. We're what? Ten days out of Boswash?"

The white-bearded man said, "Closer than that. Less than a week."

Johnson jogged Susan's elbow. "Keep your gun on them, darling. Keep it on your boss. He's dangerous."

"Less than a week," Skip said. Privately, he was trying to place the white-bearded man. "That's fine. It makes everything easier. There are six of us. You can take hostages. I'd think you'd want two at least, and I'll volunteer to be one of them. Give us your word that you'll release your hostages unharmed as soon as you get clear of the ship. If the rest talk, you'll kill the hostages."

"Absurd!" The white-bearded man was fumbling in a coat pocket.

"Hell, yes!" Johnson turned to face him. "For once I agree with you. We've got to kill them, and we've got to do it now, while we've got the storm to cover the noise."

"It will last for hours. Before they die, we need to find out how they found us." His corncob pipe clenched between his teeth, the white-bearded man rose, gripping the edge of Lieutenant Gerard Brice's desk. "I questioned the others, Mr. Grison. They told me they didn't know, that you were the one. So how did you do it? I speak as an unwilling admirer."

Vanessa said, "I have some questions for you, too. May I ask them?"

"Later." The white-bearded man waved the interruption aside. "Later, madam, or never."

Every few seconds the floor heaved beneath them; Susan muttered, "I think I'm going to be sick."

The blackthorn pointed at Skip like the barrel of a pistol. "How, Mr. Grison? How, precisely, did you find us?"

"By good luck, mostly. Achille's a friend of mine. Do you know him?"

The white-bearded man shook his head. It seemed to Skip, as it had earlier on deck, that there was something familiar about him.

"He has no hands. When the hijackers captured him, they took his hooks. Mr. Oberdorf here made him new ones, sharp hooks that he can fight with; they have spikes for stabbing. You may have seen him."

"No."

Skip shrugged. "Rick and Susan have, I know. Anyway, Achille's a friend, so when I had volunteers searching the ship for Chelle, he was one of them. He called me and said he thought Mr. Oberdorf might know where Chelle was."

Oberdorf interrupted, "I didn't, and I have no idea why anybody'd say something like that."

Skip nodded. "I imagine Achille had been impressed by your knowledge of this ship. It may have been no more than that."

He turned back to the white-bearded man, who was still erect, still grasping the edge of the desk to keep from falling. "It didn't sound like much, but we had no other leads. Trinity here and Chelle's mother had been searching with me, and we decided we ought to follow this one up."

"Admirable." The blackthorn was laid across the arms of the chair.

"So we trooped down to M Deck, meeting Mr. Oberdorf on his way up here. He told us he had no idea where Chelle was and didn't have time to talk. Lieutenant Brice had lost the card to his stateroom; the lock would have to be reprogrammed so he could give Brice a new card." Skip smiled. "After that I had an idea, whether Mr. Oberdorf did or not."

"Elucidate."

Johnson snapped, "He's grinning. Can't you see he's about to put something over?"

"I'm not," Skip told him. "It's just that your boss seems—"

"He's not my boss!"

"Reasonable. And if he's reasonable, he won't kill us. Or let you do it."

"I refuse to be diverted," the white-bearded man said, "just as your explanation becomes interesting. Continue, please."

"You see, we hadn't searched the officers' staterooms. The officers were in and out of them several times a day, and an absent officer would have been noticed immediately; so there seemed no point in looking there. But Lieutenant Brice was in the infirmary, and now his card was missing. Someone had taken Chelle out of the infirmary. It seemed entirely possible that the people who had taken her had taken Brice's card, too. Mr. Oberdorf told us he would have to open the door to reprogram the lock, so we tagged along. After that, well, I seem to have been shot in the head; but you'll have to tell me about that—I can't tell you."

Chelle said, "Dammit!" and her embrace tightened.

"The cry of a guilty conscience," Johnson murmured.

"You were shot," the white-bearded man explained, "by Mr. Johnson here. You can hardly blame him for it, since you were shooting at him at the time. You missed. He did not. At first, we thought you dead. When we realized you were not, Ms. Clerkin here put that tape over your wound to stop the bleeding."

"She's soft," Johnson said. "I'm soft on her, but she's soft on everybody."

"I suppose she is." For a moment, the white-bearded man struggled to regain his balance. "I let her because you were making a dreadful mess.

Though no physician, I can offer an opinion concerning your wound. Do you wish to hear it?"

"Yes," Skip said. "Very much."

"I believe Mr. Johnson's bullet struck your skull and was deflected by it. It appears to have traveled about three and one half inches between skull and scalp before exiting. You are fortunate to be alive."

"He won't be lucky much longer," Johnson said.

The white-bearded man shrugged. "Who is to say the living are luckiest?"

Chelle took her arm from Skip's shoulders and lifted his hand from her left leg. "I'm not going to let this go on. Skip loves me and he lied for me. I love him, and I'm not going to let him."

"Indeed?"

"Right. Mom threw a little party for us vets, and I went. I could've brought Skip, but I didn't. I went alone and met Jerry Brice there. We made out, and Skip caught us at it."

The white mustache twitched. "My, my!"

"Yeah. He caught us, and Jerry beat it—grabbed his clothes and ran. He left his shoes, but they were black and I shoved them under the bed. They were on my side, which was damned lucky."

"Chelle, darling, don't you—"

"Shut up!" She turned to Skip. "They're going to kill us, and I don't want to die with this on my chest. I don't give a fuck who else knows, but you've got to. It'll hurt you and I'm sorry, but I'm going to die clean. I met Jerry again the next day, and he gave me a card to this room. I stuck it in my pocket thinking maybe I'd use it sometime and maybe I wouldn't."

Skip nodded.

"When these motherfuckers came in and shot the medics, they grabbed me and my clothes. They went through my clothes before they made me put them on, and they found that card. This was in the theater on D Deck, backstage. They figured nobody was going to put on a show after the hijacking, but Jerry's room looked even better. If it seemed like he was going to get out of the aid station, they'd shoot him again."

"You have a conscience," the white-bearded man said. "I have none—they're damnably inconvenient—yet I admire yours. May I, too, set the record straight?"

Johnson spun around. "All right, keep talking if that's how you want it. While you're talking, I'll be shooting. And guess where I'll—"

His final word was lost in a clap of thunder.

"You shut your own mouth!" Trinity was on her feet. "He older than you! Smarter, too!"

Johnson shouted in return, his gun in her face. She caught his wrist, jerked the gun to her left, and closed with him.

"You're shaking like a leaf," the white-bearded man told Susan. "Give me that." With one smooth motion, he took her revolver, raised it to eye level, and shot Rick Johnson in the back.

REFLECTION 14

Much Later, While Watching the Atlantic

Why should storms provoke violence? Why must our moods reflect the weather? We leave the winter cities and travel to warm southern lands because winter exhausts us. We have huddled in the brightly lit apartments for too long; we know the night waits outside, and feel it even when our drapes hide us. We want warmth and a natural breeze. Most of all, we want sunlight.

Would Rick Johnson have been shot without the storm? I don't believe he would, because he wouldn't have been so anxious to kill us without it. Had he not been so anxious to kill us, his life might have been spared, at that time at least.

Might have been, but would it really have been? He said he had Chelle's secret, which was once Jane Sims's. Susan says she does not have it, and I believe her. Should I believe Rick as well?

To what degree was Rick really Rick? How much of the man who went from West Point to Johanna was left? What did the Os take away, and what did they leave behind? Does anyone, any wise man or woman, any supercomputer concealed beneath a mountain, really understand the Os? We do not even understand ourselves. The proper study of mankind is man, they say: *nosce te ipsum*. But what do the Os say?

Did Susan know what was coming when she surrendered her gun? I have not dared to ask her and will not so dare. I have brought her near to suicide already. I must not—and will not—do that again.

The suicide ring must be destroyed and destroyed utterly, not only for Virginia's sake but for Susan's. Virginia might be protected; what measures could protect Susan from herself?

What of the shooter? What of Charles? Did he plan from the beginning to kill Rick? Did he fear that we, with the Os's model before us, would do as they did?

I would have. *Silent leges enim inter arma*. In order that Earth survive, our rulers would gladly render Earth not worth saving.

Was he unarmed? He's surely working for somebody, but for whom?

And why?

15

FORMAL NIGHT

The flash and bark of Susan's revolver were lost in the blue fire that roared from Rick Johnson's back, blinding and gone. As it vanished, he collapsed like a marionette whose strings had been cut.

The white-bearded man puffed away an invisible wisp of smoke from the muzzle, his mustache twitching. Susan shrieked and wailed. Chelle and Vanessa scrambled to help Trinity, who had fallen.

Skip went to Rick Johnson, wrestling Johnson's gun from a hand that death had locked around the grip.

"You won't need that," the white-bearded man told him. "But if it makes you feel better, you may keep it."

Susan gasped, "I'm going to be sick," and stumbled away; a moment later Lieutenant Brice's bathroom door clicked behind her.

Trinity moaned and writhed. Her face was burned, her hair scorched and smoking. Skip and Oberdorf got her to her feet and walked her to the elevator, preceded by Chelle and Jerry, who had pushed the button before they got there.

No one spoke as the elevator descended save Jerry, who said, "Wow!" His voice soft and almost reverent. A moment later he got out on C Deck.

Achille was waiting for them when the elevator doors opened on J Deck. "You have bad day, mon."

"I want to talk to you later," Skip said. "Chelle, we move pretty slowly. Will you go to the infirmary and tell them we're coming?"

She nodded and hurried away.

"That's quite a woman," Oberdorf said.

"Too much woman for me, I'm afraid, but I'm very proud of her."

Trinity coughed, retched, and spat.

"Left my tools up there. I'll have to go back for 'em."

"I'll go with you," Skip told him. "I don't think you'll need me, but I need to talk to that old man. To Chelle, too."

"What about this guy I made new hooks for?"

"Him, too. He was with us when we went up to the signal deck, but gone when I recovered consciousness. I want to ask him about it. Before I do, I'd like to get something for my headache. Will you wait?"

Oberdorf nodded.

After treating Trinity, Dr. Ueda provided two white tablets, stitches, and a transfusion.

When Skip, Chelle, and Gary Oberdorf returned to the signal deck, there was a seaman with a holstered pistol guarding Lieutenant Gerard Brice's door. Seeing Skip, he touched his forehead and stood aside. Oberdorf's toolbox remained where he had left it. Rick Johnson was the sole occupant of the stateroom, and Rick Johnson had been blown in two.

"He looked so human," Chelle said.

"He was a cyborg." Skip was on his knees examining him. "If we had weighed him we would have known something was wrong."

"Or if we'd made him take off his clothes."

"Right." Skip rose. "As it was, your mother noticed that he wore a wool jacket in this tropical heat without perspiring. She told me, but I didn't pay much attention to it. I should have."

"They did things to me. Hypnotized me or something."

"Correct," Skip said.

. . .

When he woke, that "correct" was the last thing he remembered saying. Someone had taken him back to the stateroom he shared with Chelle, removed his clothes, and put him to bed. An Oriental woman, small and no longer young, had leaned over him, perhaps, and given him an injection. Certainly he had been made to swallow pills.

He sat up; and Chelle, who had been shooting energy thieves on his laptop, said, "How are you feeling?"

"Not bad." He considered. "I don't think I ought to stand yet."

"I'll get your cane," Chelle said. "Do you know where it is? I haven't seen it around."

He shook his head. "We were searching and searching, and I was very tired. I may have left it someplace."

"Then I'll buy you one. It may not be a nice one like your old one—I don't think they'll have those on the ship. But there's a drugstore place, and they might have aluminum canes."

"I don't want one," Skip said.

"It's whether you need one, soldier. If you need one I'll get you one, only I doubt—" Her phone played and she cursed.

A moment later she said, "It's for you. I turned yours off, so Mother called me."

He accepted her phone. "Virginia?"

"Vanessa please, Skip. I'm very happy being Vanessa just now."

He tried to think of something gracious to say.

"We wish to invite you and our lovely Chelle to dinner tonight. Chelle already knows, this is merely the formal invitation. It would have been nice to have cards printed, but—you know. You'll come, won't you? We'll be terribly disappointed if you don't."

"I'm a little disoriented right now, Vanessa. I need to find my feet."

"Roast lamb, Skip. Nothing facilitates orientation like roast lamb with mint jelly. I'll see to it."

Chelle whispered, "Say yes."

"I . . . We'll come of course. It's very kind of you. If I sound strange, I just woke up. I seem to have slept for hours."

"*You regained consciousness,*" Vanessa told him. "*Do you remember what day it was when that horrible cyborg shot you? What day of the week?*"

"Yes. Wednesday. Wednesday evening, I believe."

"*Wednesday night. This is Saturday, Skip. It's, um, eleven thirty-one. There were . . . complications. Chelle knows more about all that than I do, and she'll tell you everything, I'm sure. Will you come to dinner? Please? We've been so worried!*"

"Certainly. We'll be delighted. I think I already said that."

"*You did. I just wanted to make sure. It's Formal Night. Isn't that just marvelous? We get a Formal Night before we make port. Richard wants to show everybody that things are finally back to normal, even if he does have to cut the cruise short. You won't mention Richard tonight? Promise? Nothing about Richard and me?*"

"Promise," Skip said. "May I ask how you knew I was no longer in a coma?"

"*I didn't, really. I talked to Chelle about an hour ago—inviting her, you know—and she told me you were beginning to stir. She suggested I call back in an hour because you might be well enough for dinner tonight. The first-class dining room? Twenty hundred? Would that be convenient?*"

"Yes, fine."

"*Charles desires to explain, Skip, and I've told him he ought to retain you as his attorney. I think he may face criminal charges, even though it was just a cyborg he killed. Richard isn't confining him, which I think truly noble of him. Don't you?*"

"Yes. Yes, indeed."

"*It's all settled then. Just the four of us, and we'll have a nice talk. Twenty hundred. Dinner jacket. You do have a dinner jacket, don't you, Skip? If you don't, I can—*"

"I do." Skip said. A moment later he hung up.

"We'll have a wonderful time," Chelle told him. "Family! There's nothing quite like family."

"A great deal seems to have happened while I was ill."

"Not really. Things got back to normal, that's all." Chelle went to him and kissed his forehead. "Everything was fixed, and you were the one who fixed it. We've still got the hijackers locked up and we've got wounded on board, but—"

"Including you."

"Sure, only my arm's mending nicely, so Dr. Ueda let me go. She let you go, too. . . ."

"Because I was healing nicely?"

Chelle shook her head. "She didn't say this, but I think it was really because she couldn't do anything more for you. She said you might need brain surgery—that isn't what she called it, but that's what she meant."

"I hope you're joking."

"And she wasn't qualified. She's a pediatrician. Do you really want to hear all this?"

"Absolutely."

"Aren't you hungry? You can't have eaten since Wednesday. I could order something."

"No. Tell me."

"You had a blood clot on your brain. That's what put you in the coma. She gave you some stuff she said might dissolve it, and I guess it did. Only if it didn't you'd need a brain surgeon."

"According to a pediatrician."

"Right. Only she seemed to know what she was talking about. She told me about a patient of hers. He fell off a swing."

"And tonight I'm going to dinner. Who's Charles?"

"Smokin' shit! Don't tell me she's found a new guy! Wait a minute." Chelle's phone had played again, and she flipped it open. "Hello. What is it? That's right, he's fully conscious, sitting up and talking. He's doing great." She grinned at Skip. "Okay. As soon as I can get there. Bye."

"Who was that?"

Chelle rose. "Nothing important. Now listen. You're supposed to get an intravenous feeding, only they haven't been in here yet. They're terribly shorthanded. So order yourself something to eat. And eat it."

"Chelle—"

"Gotta see a man about a mine. I'll be back soon." She breezed out.

Tentatively, he swung his feet over the edge of the bed. For a moment, it seemed that the ship was pitching as it had in the storm, but the moment passed. He felt a little light-headed, his two-cocktails-at-lunch feeling; otherwise, things were quite normal. He shaved, and well before he had finished discovered that he was ravenous. First-class dining would open for lunch at twelve thirty, assuming that "Richard" had really returned the ship to normal.

He showered, and decided he would go down to lunch alone if Chelle had not returned. He could leave her a note.

His gun was beneath the clothing that someone (almost certainly Chelle) had heaped on a chair. It reminded him of his submachine gun. It was under the bed. He—they—would be permitted to take no weapons ashore with them. Chelle would certainly try to smuggle her gun out, and would presumably be arrested for it.

Well, she knew a good lawyer. Selecting her mobile phone brought a tune from the upper right-hand drawer of the bureau.

After dressing, he called the second-class bar. The barman knew Chelle and swore she had not been in that day. The first-class bar in that case.

"This is Chick, Mr. Grison. What can I do for you?"

"I'm trying to find Chelle. Mastergunner Chelle Blue. Do you know her?"

"Sure, Mr. Grison. She was in here with Mr. Tooley. They had a drink and talked, you know. The little table in the corner. They left, oh, maybe five minutes ago."

Mick Tooley's phone was out of service. Skip called his building instead and spoke with his manager.

When that call was over, he put on sunglasses and left the bedroom for the veranda, finding the rolling gray-green water of the Atlantic even more conducive to thought than the blue Caribbean had been. "Charles" White (whoever that was) might be prosecuted and Vanessa wanted him retained. Might he himself be prosecuted? He found, oddly enough, that he hoped he would be—and could not explain the hope even to himself. Guilt about Susan? It seemed possible, though the thought woke no shock of recognition. Where was Susan, anyway? Had somebody killed her? If so, who?

How many people had he defended whose sole crime was resisting criminals? A hundred, perhaps? Not so many as that, but the almighty law—which would defend no one but politicians—hated those who defended themselves. His guns, most of all his submachine gun, would be flourished to persuade a jury that he was a menace.

What about Chelle's gun? With her mother still in danger, she would insist on keeping it. . . .

There was another veranda beneath his own, the veranda to which Lieutenant Jerry Brice had dropped when he had vaulted over this rail. Beyond that, E Deck. He might—or might not—succeed in throwing his pistol into the Atlantic from here. An athlete might have thrown the submachine gun too. He most certainly could not.

He pushed his pistol into his waistband, where it would be concealed by his untucked shirt. Everyone who had a pistol had been carrying it everywhere when he had been shot, most openly. Was it still like that? Formal Night implied that it was not. His laundry bag, plus a few soiled shirts and shorts, concealed the submachine gun.

It was much harder than he had expected to let that submachine gun drop into the Atlantic, but he did it. After vacillating for a minute and more, he returned his pistol to his waistband. There was plenty of time, after all.

The barmaid in the tourist-class bar knew Achille but had not seen him that day. "We open at eleven," she said. "We get maybe half a dozen people then. Mostly they have a quick shot or maybe a double, then they're gone. You want somethin'?"

Skip shook his head.

"I don't think that guy with spikes drinks unless somebody else is buying." She hesitated. "He did yesterday. Showed me his cabin card. It was him all right, only the name wasn't what everybody calls him. You know?"

Skip nodded. "I don't suppose you remember the cabin number?"

"Hell, no. But the computer will have it. All I got to do is search yesterday's charges for a straight shot of white rum." She touched buttons, scrolled something, and touched more buttons. "Two forty-four E."

Skip put a five-nora bill into the big brandy glass on the bar. "If you see Achille—that's the man with hooks and spikes—I'd like you to call me. I'd appreciate it." He scribbled his mobile phone number on his business card and gave it to her.

"Hey! Skip Grison! You were big when everybody was fightin' the hijackers. I guess that's how you got that bandage on your head."

"No," Skip told her, "I was shot by a friend."

No one answered the door of 244E. Where was Achille, and why hadn't he been in Brice's stateroom? Where was Susan? For that matter, where was Chelle? You found a thread, Skip reminded himself. You found a thread, any thread, and you pulled.

Out on deck, he called the offices of Burton, Grison, and Ibarra; prompted, he entered his new secretary's number.

"You have Dianne Field."

"This is Skip Grison. I'm still on the *Rani* but I should be back in the office soon, and I need a little inside information. I think you'll probably have it."

"Yes, sir, Mr. Grison. If I don't know I'll try to find out."

"Has Mick Tooley contracted?"

"No, sir. The girls talk about him all the time."

"I didn't think so. Living with somebody?"

"Not anymore, sir. It was some girl from the Sixth District Courthouse, but she got ticked when he went down south to try to get you off that ship, sir. He wanted her to go with him, but she wouldn't so they split. I don't remember her name, but Edna knows it. Want me to find out?"

"No." Skip paused to think. "No, I don't, Dianne. But if you happen to hear it, make a mental note. You never know."

"I understand, sir. You sure don't."

On the signal deck, Skip was stopped by an officer. "Sorry, sir. No passengers on this deck."

Skip sighed. "It's like that again?"

"Yes, sir. I'm afraid it is."

"I'm a friend of Captain Kain's. I hesitate to bother him, but I will if I have to. I'm looking for Lieutenant Brice. Is he out of the infirmary?"

"Yes, sir. He's returned to duty now." The officer hesitated. "Or anyway, we say he is. He's still taking it pretty easy. Doctor's orders."

"Is he on the bridge?"

The officer shook his head. He was a very young man, Skip decided. Probably not as old as Chelle.

"Then he might be in his stateroom?"

The officer shrugged.

"Let me knock on his door. If he admits me, I'll be his guest. You know and I know that you ship's officers entertain guests from time to time. If he's not there, or will not admit me, I'll leave without a fuss."

"I'm afraid I can't do that, sir."

Skip's shoulders rose and fell. "In that case, you get the fuss, Lieutenant . . . ?"

"King, sir. Tom King."

Reflecting that he needed to add his new secretary to his list of contacts, Skip dialed the number.

"You have Dianne Field."

"This is Skip Grison again. I'm still on the cruise ship. It's the *Rani,* Canaveral Cruises."

"Yes, sir. I know."

"Perhaps you also know that I was shot on Wednesday. Shot in the head." Covertly, Skip watched Lieutenant King's face.

"No, sir. Nobody told me that."

"Then I'm telling you now. I was unconscious as a result of my wound until today, and I believe my faculties may be permanently impaired. The wound I suffered resulted from the negligence of the Canaveral—"

Lieutenant King broke in. "Just a moment, sir!"

"Cruise Line. We'll ask twenty-five mil. Write a memo summarizing this call and get Bud Young on it. Tell him to call me when he needs more detail, the captain's name and so forth. Have him get the paperwork ready. We'll file as soon as I get back."

"Yes, sir! Right away, sir!"

"Fine. Get on it." Skip hung up and turned back to Lieutenant King. "Now you. I was shot in Lieutenant Brice's stateroom. Perhaps you know that. I want access to that stateroom and to Brice, and I want it now. If I don't get it, that will go into my suit, too."

Lieutenant King backed away. "I need to talk to the captain."

"You certainly do." Skip went to the door of Brice's cabin and knocked. When Brice opened, Skip said, "You need to talk to me, and I'd like to talk to you. If we talk, I may not file a suit for alienation of affection; but if we don't, I most certainly will. May I come in?"

Brice nodded, still blocking the doorway. "You've been wounded, too, I see. Hit on the head?"

"Yes, by a bullet. I was standing right where you're standing now. I don't like threatening you, but I want to come in, have a look around, and ask a few questions."

Brice stood aside. "Come in and sit down, sir."

Skip did, taking the only armchair.

Gingerly, Brice lowered himself to the sofa. "Fire away."

"First—you must know there was a shooting in here."

"Right." Brice's grin was small but real. "You guys left a mess."

"I'm sure we did. Do you know who was involved?"

"No, I don't. Only I think a blonde I saw at the infirmary was. I don't know her name, but I saw her brought in before I left."

Skip nodded. "Short and a little plump? About thirty-five?"

"That's her. From the look of my stateroom, she'd done a lot of bleeding."

"Some of that was mine." Skip drew a deep breath. "I passed out twice, Lieutenant; but I think the woman you saw must have been my secretary, Susan Clerkin. I ought to go down and see her."

"I'm sorry she got hurt, sir."

"So am I. Where was the blood?"

"On the rug in this room, and in the bathroom. The bathroom was a mess."

"You cleaned it up?"

Brice shook his head. "I got our steward on it, and he brought in some maids."

"What was found in the room? Besides the blood?"

"You'd like to make your suit stronger. I'm not going to help you with it."

"No. I'm trying to find out what happened and why. A man named Rick Johnson was killed in here."

"I didn't know him. Listen, I don't want a drink—I'll be on duty in a couple of hours. But if you'd like something . . . ?"

"Thank you. A sandwich and a glass of iced coffee."

"I'll join you. What kind of sandwich?"

"Any kind," Skip said.

Brice picked up the telephone and ordered.

"I'm Chelle's contracto. You know that."

"Right." Brice's eyes were guarded, his nod almost imperceptible.

"When I came into our bedroom not so long ago, you were in bed with her. You grabbed your clothes and dashed out, vaulting over the rail of our veranda. I don't know what you did after that, and to be honest I don't care."

"Then let's not talk about it."

"Earlier that evening, you had given Chelle a card for this stateroom. That's the important point. Do you deny it?"

"I don't, sir. I don't, but you've got it wrong. Can I tell you the whole thing from my end?"

Skip nodded. "I wish you would."

"Fine. There was a party for vets. I came off duty and decided to put on civvies, drop in, and see if there was anybody I knew. There was, and he bought me a drink. That meant I had to buy him one, so I hung around and talked. Somebody introduced me to Chelle, and she and I hit it off. Maybe it was just because I'm taller than she is. There aren't a lot of guys who are."

"Including me," Skip said.

"I didn't mean it like that. Well, anyway, she said it was getting too noisy, how about going to her stateroom? I jumped at it. I didn't know she was contracted then. I hadn't asked and she didn't tell me. Do you want to hear what we did in bed? There wasn't anything very freaky."

"I think it would be better if I didn't know."

"I've got it, sir." Brice pushed his chair back; the distance might have been three centimeters. "It would hit you hard. I can see that."

"Go on, please."

"I just wanted to say she was good—"

Skip's phone vibrated. He answered it with alacrity.

"Mr. Grison? This is Lana. Remember me? The bar on E Deck?" The tiny screen showed him a tired blonde.

"Yes. Certainly."

"If you're still lookin' for the guy with the hooks, he just came in. He's with three other guys."

"Can you talk to him privately?"

"Sure. I'll just get him to come over to the bar for a minute. They're at a table."

"Then tell him I was looking for him. Tell him I want information and I may have a job for him."

"Got it. Will do."

Skip hung up. "When will we make port? Your professional opinion."

"If the weather cooperates, it could be as early as tomorrow." Brice paused. "The old man's anxious to get there, and I don't blame him. We've got forty-three hijackers locked up, some on K Deck and some in the hold. If we can't do it tomorrow, probably Monday. It could be later, but I doubt it."

"Thanks. You must have known that Chelle and I were contracted, since you ran when I came in."

"I didn't," Brice said. "Would I have gone up to your stateroom if I had? I don't know. Probably I would have."

Skip nodded.

"She said she had a boyfriend. Okay, but those doors lock every time they close, and I thought she meant some guy who didn't have a card. You came in after that. I figured you'd take a punch at me, and I knew that if I got mixed up in a fight—that kind of fight—I could kiss my job goodbye. So I beat it."

For a moment, Brice hesitated. "I've done that sort of thing before, sir, only it wasn't your Chelle. This was another passenger on the last cruise."

"Are you saying you didn't give Chelle your cabin card?"

"No, sir. I did, but it was the next day. I ran into her—I was out on deck where they'd fouled a halyard, and she came over to watch. So we talked for a minute or two, and I slipped her my spare card. Some girls really go for that, sir. They like being up here with an officer."

"Mostly tourist-class girls, I would imagine."

Brice shook his head. "I try to stay away from those."

"You must know who was in this room when the shooting occurred."

"No, sir. I was still in the infirmary."

"Someone must have told you," Skip insisted.

"No, sir. Nobody did, and I haven't asked. I still feel pretty rocky. Weak, you know. That's been on my mind a lot more than what happened up here."

"I could name almost everyone who was in here when I regained consciousness, although I'm more interested in someone who wasn't. Most of all, I'm interested in the one person I didn't already know. If you can tell me who he is, I'll be grateful. Extremely grateful."

Brice shook his head. "I don't know who any of them were, sir, except for you. You said you were here, that you were shot in here."

"I was. This man is elderly. His hair is white. He wears glasses. He has a white mustache and a pointed beard long enough to cover the knot in his tie. They're neatly trimmed. He's thin, and a good ten centimeters taller than most men—about your height or a trifle more. He walks with a blackthorn stick and smokes a corncob."

"How sure are you about all this, sir?"

"Certain. I talked with him, although not for long. I realized how tall he was when he stood up."

"I don't know him. I can't think of anybody remotely like that, not even somebody I saw on tele. He was well dressed? You said something about a necktie."

Skip nodded. "Seersucker suit. Blue stripes, I think. Soft white shirt. Navy-blue tie with a red figure. I couldn't tell what the figure was, but it was probably some kind of animal. White wing-tip shoes, well polished."

Brice grinned. "Socks?"

"White. His watch looked expensive, but I didn't recognize the make. No rings. This isn't helping you, and you're not helping me. Let me try another question. Do you know anyone currently on this ship named White?"

Brice paused to think, his fingers drumming the arm of the couch. "No, sir. No, I don't. I knew a White in the Naval Academy, sir. Bob White. I couldn't tell you where he is now."

There was a knock at the door. *"Steward."* Brice rose to admit a short, dark man with a tray.

When the coffee and sandwiches had been apportioned, Skip said, "Someone called the man I described Mr. White. If—"

"I thought you said you didn't know his name."

"I don't." Skip took a bite of his sandwich, chewed, and rediscovered that he was ravenously hungry. "I heard him called that. It may not be his real name. If I were made to bet, I'd bet that it isn't."

Another bite of toast, turkey, and bacon gave Brice time in which to speak if he wanted it. He did not.

"I watched the people Mick Tooley brought get off Soriano's boat," Skip said. "I saw Soriano's men, too. This man wasn't in either group. Therefore 'Mr. White' is a crewman or a passenger. Would you know him if he were in the crew?"

"Absolutely. From what you say, he'd be the oldest crew member by far."

"Then he's a passenger. I'm not sure the purser's office tells me the truth. Will you call for me, and let me listen in?"

Brice moved to the bed to use his computer. Settled there, he selected a number and touched the screen to turn up the volume.

"Purser's office."

"This is Lieutenant Brice. I'm looking for a male passenger named White—Mr. White. How many have we got?"

"Just a moment, sir."

Brice waited.

"None, sir."

"No passengers named White?" Brice looked at Skip inquiringly.

"Try Blue," Skip told him.

Brice nodded and told the purser's mate, "How about Blue? Mr. Blue. Anything like that."

"*I'll check, sir.*"

Brice waited again.

"*We've got one, sir. Mastergunner Chelle Sea Blue, sir. Stateroom Twenty-three C.*"

Brice glanced at Skip, who said, "Hang up."

"Thanks," Brice told the purser's mate, and did.

Skip rose and began to pace.

"Sorry I haven't been of more help, sir." Brice rose, too.

"So am I. I want you to promise me that if anything turns up related to that shooting, or you learn anything you think might be of value to me, you'll let me know."

"Will you promise not to take me to court?"

"Yes. I will. I do."

"Then I'll help you all I can." Brice returned to his sandwich and iced coffee.

"Good." Skip smiled, and wondered how long it had been since he had smiled last. "I need more favors. Will you question your steward for me? Find out if he knows anything?"

"Sure."

"Good. I'm going to go down to the infirmary to talk to Susan." As he opened the door, Skip turned. "One more thing. Tonight's Formal Night in first class."

"I know." Brice sighed. "Full-dress uniform, with decorations."

"Come by our table. I don't know which one it will be. You'll have to find us."

Brice nodded.

"Supposedly, this 'Mr. White' will be there. Have a look at him. Did I give you my card?"

"No. Maybe you could give me your phone number, too."

REFLECTION 15

———————— ⌇⌇ ————————

Summum Jus Summa Injuria

To be admitted to the bar is to be admitted to that area in the courtroom that is closed to everyone save the judge, the attorneys, and the witnesses. In times past, those ambitious to become attorneys attended court in order to familiarize themselves with the law, sitting as near as possible in order to hear better. When they were believed to have learned enough to practice, they were allowed to pass the bar that prevented spectators from intruding upon the workings of the court.

I passed the bar long ago, and have appeared in court more than a thousand times; yet I am not permitted to have even a small penknife on my person. I might (as the law supposes) produce that fearsome weapon, mount to the bench in a dazzling leap, and employ it to slice open His Honor's gizzard. This in a city in which ten thousand dojos teach their students how to kill with their bare hands.

The bailiff is armed by law and custom, and everyone knows it. What far fewer know is that most judges have guns concealed by their robes. The police, who do know it, and who know too that it is a violation of the law, wink at it. If in an instant I were to become violently insane, I might slaughter one or two persons with my deadly penknife. The judge (judges assure us) will not yield to insanity, since judges never do.

I have known judges who thought themselves God; it would seem that they were right. I was in court when another ridiculed a woman because she was pregnant. A judge once ruled that fleeing from the police gave the police reasonable cause to arrest, question, search, and lock up the terrified boy who fled. Who wouldn't flee from the police, if he (or she) thought he could escape?

There's a common thread running through all this, or so it seems to me. It is giving in to fear, the surrender that used to be named cowardice. The boy was afraid of the police for good reason; but the police were afraid of him, simply because he feared them. The judge who ridiculed the pregnant woman had at last found someone he felt certain could never harm him, a victim who could not strike back under any circumstances. The judge who thinks himself God has found a fantasy that makes him safe, God being beyond the range of human weapons.

The judges who bring their pistols to court fear even disarmed men and women, knowing in their hearts that some of their decisions should get them lynched.

16

TABLE FOR FOUR

Susan was in a private room more cramped than Chelle's. She smiled wanly when Skip came in. "I've been wondering when you'd get around to me."

There was no chair, only a white-enameled stool. Skip sat. "I learned that you were in here about one hour ago, perhaps less." When Susan said nothing, he added, "I was unconscious until eleven this morning."

"We've all got to sleep. They keep shooting me full of dope."

"Considering that you shot Dr. Prescott, I'd call it very kind of them."

Susan was silent for half a minute or more, seemingly studying beige walls without portholes. At last she said, "You know about that?"

"It was obvious. There were three of you in there holding Chelle. The old man had no gun—he took yours to shoot Rick. Two guns had been used to kill Dr. Prescott. One had also been used to kill his nurse. Do I have to go on?"

"No." The wan smile returned. "You've made one mistake already. Maybe you'd better stop."

"You didn't shoot Dr. Prescott?"

"I did it. I was supposed to kill him, and Rick was supposed to kill the nurse. I loved him, loved Rick. Or thought I did, and thought he loved me."

Skip shrugged. "Perhaps he did."

"He was a m-machine."

"He was a cyborg, part human and part machine. They do it with accident victims when there aren't enough limbs and organs available. I've met a few. Possibly they're capable of love, or some are. I wouldn't know."

"I thought you knew everything."

"A moment ago, you said I'd made a mistake already. Aren't you contradicting yourself?"

"I suppose." Her voice was weak. "Why did you come to see me?"

"There were three reasons, and it's going to take me a while to go through all three. What was my mistake?"

The wan smile flickered again. "Give me the first reason and I'll tell you."

Skip smiled in return. "I'll give you the first two—there would be no point in separating them. I care about you, Susan. I care about you, but I've treated you badly. I know that. I owe you damages. *Damnum absque injuria* is damage still. Is there anything at all I can do for you? Anything I can get you?"

Her head moved from side to side, five degrees one way and five the other.

"Then I'll go on to the second. We'll make port soon, and it could be as soon as tomorrow. An officer I spoke to thought it would be possible with fair winds and good luck. When we do, you'll probably—probably, not certainly—be arrested. If you talk, you may be charged with murder."

"Or even if I don't talk."

"Correct. Who killed the nurse?"

"Rick did." Susan shut her eyes. When she opened them again she said, "He'd wanted me to. I said I didn't think I could shoot another woman, so we traded. I shot the doctor. Then Rick shot him when he didn't die right away."

"Shot him twice."

Susan's eyes closed again. "Several times. I don't know how many."

"I'll defend you, if you want me to, without fee. If you'd like to engage me, we need to get that settled right now. As things stand, it will be hard for me to withhold information from the police. On some matters it will be nearly impossible. Make me your attorney and it will get much easier. Once we're ashore, I'll resign the case and assign someone else to handle the trial."

"I'd rather have you." She was groping for his hand.

Skip made sure that she did not find it. "I'll be a witness for the defense, so that's out. Do you want me to represent you? Now?"

"Yes. Of course."

"Then that's settled. I'll deal with the police to the best of my ability. You must insist upon having your attorney—Mick Tooley or me—present before you'll talk to them. I can see you're badly hurt, and that will make it difficult."

Susan's eyes closed. "Difficult is my specialty."

"Fine. I'll enlist Dr. Ueda if I can. She would be of enormous assistance to us."

Susan did not speak.

"I think I know what happened to you. Do you want to tell me?"

"I thought he loved me. . . ." Susan's voice hardly rose above a whisper.

"Perhaps he did. He was not simply a machine."

"He used me."

"So did I." Skip's voice was as soft as hers.

"Don't go. Please don't go."

"I'll have to leave soon, but I'm not leaving now. Who is the old man who shot Rick?"

"I don't know. Why did he shoot Rick?"

"That's one of the things I'm trying to find out. You called him Mr. White, and said Mr. White had said you could be the one to kill me."

Susan nodded.

"Who is he?"

"He was Rick's boss. . . ." Her voice faded away.

"Is he a passenger on this ship?"

"Rick did what he said to do. Except when he didn't. Rick called him Mr. White, so that was what I called him. Can't you see that none of this matters, Skip?"

He bent nearer her. "What does? What matters, Susan? Tell me."

"Love."

"Love made you cut your arms."

"I— Yes. Yes, it did that. You'd been talking about cutting wrists. . . ."
Skip waited.

"You showed us that woman's arm. Made her show it."

He nodded. "I suppose I did."

"So I thought that might work for me. Did you know I'd tried to kill
myself before?"

He shrugged. "You didn't tell me, but I guessed it. You were in a suicide
ring. I found that out shortly after you came on board."

He paused, expecting her to ask how he knew, and ready to refuse that
information. She did not.

"You planted the bomb. It killed two young women."

Susan shook her head.

"You didn't plant it?"

"We didn't want to kill them. Just Edith Eckhart."

"She's effectively dead now," Skip said. "You don't have to worry about
her anymore."

"She's here. . . . Another name."

From the doorway, Dr. Ueda said, "You're tiring her. Please leave immediately."

"I've got one more question," Skip told Dr. Ueda. "After that, I'll have
a few for you. It will be to your advantage to answer them, believe me."

"Are you threatening me?"

"Hardly. We've got a mess here, and the sooner we straighten it out and
see that the right people go to jail—if anyone does—the better it will be for
all of us."

He turned back to Susan. "Answer this, and I'll go. You said *we* didn't
want to kill them. By *we*, did you mean the ring? Or someone here?"

"Rick. Rick helped me and I helped him. Then she was with you. I
didn't think I could do it so he said it was all right, he'd set it off. He'd send
a signal. Only he's dead now, isn't he? Isn't Rick dead?"

Skip rose. "Yes. That was why you tried to cut your wrists."

"I nearly won." Susan's voice was louder that he had expected, and firmer. "There was a glass in the bathroom." Her voice rose again. "I was brave!"

"You're brave enough to live," Skip told her, and kissed her forehead.

When they were seated in the tiny book-lined office that had become Dr. Ueda's, she asked, "Are you trying to put that poor girl in prison?"

"No. I'm an attorney, Doctor."

"I know. A famous one."

"Did you also know that your patient—you called her 'that poor girl'—is my secretary?"

Folklore, Skip reflected, insisted that Orientals never showed emotion. Dr. Ueda's surprise was evident, although less than obvious. Another myth discredited.

"She is. Naturally, my firm will defend her. As I told her, I'll be a witness for the defense; so I can't be her trial attorney. Even so, I want to lay the groundwork now. Are you aware that she planted the bomb that killed two young women on this ship?"

Slowly, Dr. Ueda shook her head. "I didn't know that, either."

"She did. She admitted it to me in there, and I feel certain she'll admit it to others—to the police, as soon as we dock. It means we can't simply try to convince a jury that she isn't guilty. That would be unethical, and unwise as well. We'll have to plead her deranged mental and emotional state. If we succeed—as I think we will—she may get the treatment she needs. If we fail . . ." Skip shrugged.

"Lethal injection."

"Correct. We'll need a deposition from you. If the prosecution doesn't challenge your deposition, we won't have to call you as a witness. I'm not asking for that deposition now. You'll need time to think, and you may want to consult your own attorney. When you've had time for both, I'll send somebody to depose you."

"She tried to kill herself." Dr. Ueda hesitated. "Tried hard. She had slashed her arms—both arms—with broken glass."

Skip nodded. "Do you need someone to blame for that? Blame me."

"You dumped her?"

"Yes. I terminated our relationship. I didn't think of it as dumping her at the time, but perhaps she did."

To his surprise, Dr. Ueda smiled. "We like to dump men, not the other way around. We think men can take it. Men are tough. I've dumped three."

Skip nodded.

"We say you're just little boys inside. It isn't true, but we say it. Then we like to think that rejection can't hurt you—that rejection won't hurt little boys." She sighed. "Haruki was— You don't want to hear about my personal life."

"I'll listen, if you want me to."

"I don't. I was thinking about your secretary. About my patient."

"Susan. Her name's Susan Clerkin."

"Did she begin as a clerk? Filing? All that sort of thing?"

"I don't know. I suppose so."

"She probably changed her last name, hoping the new name would help her get a job. I don't suppose you know her original name?"

Skip shook his head. "It had never even occurred to me that she might have changed it."

"It's hard for women to find work. It has been since before I was born."

"Hard for men, too."

"Not as hard as it is for women. There are always more women, and there are fewer women in the Army."

"I suppose you're right."

Dr. Ueda smiled. "You've left the script, Mr. Grison. You're supposed to say fewer women enlist."

Skip smiled, too. "Sorry."

"It's when I win. I prove that more women enlist than men. Almost twice as many women flunk out during training. What is it?"

"Nothing."

"I hurt you without meaning to, and I'm very sorry. Let me change the subject. I went to medical school here, thinking that when I graduated I'd go back to Japan and practice there. They wouldn't take me—our government wouldn't. They told me to become a nurse. They needed nurses, or that's what they said. I came back instead."

"Are you afraid you'll be deported if you give us a favorable deposition?"

Dr. Ueda sighed. "I've been an NAU citizen for years. Even if I wasn't, I wouldn't give you—or anyone else—a favorable or unfavorable deposition. I'm going to make a true one, the truth as I see it or as nearly true as I can get it."

"That's all I ask," Skip told her.

"You said she's killed two young women on this ship. Who were they?"

"Their names? Amelia and Polly. I don't recall their last names." Skip fell silent, remembering. "I talked to one of them once. First on the phone, then in her office—in the social director's office. They worked for her."

"Virginia? I met her, oh, a few days ago. Before the hijacking. That seems like a long time ago now."

"Correct. Virginia Healy. Amelia and Polly were her assistants. Susan wanted to kill Virginia, but Virginia wasn't there when the bomb went off. The assistants were. Now I wish I knew which one I talked to."

"You're contracted with a girl named Chelle. Chelle Blue."

"Correct."

"A moment ago, you indicated that you and my patient had been, ah . . ."

"Together. Yes. For nine years."

"Did she think you left her for Virginia?"

Skip sighed. "I see what you're getting at. No, I left Susan for Chelle. I . . . Chelle and I contracted just out of college. She had gotten her bachelor's and joined the Army, and I had completed law school. When she came back from outsystem duty, I went to meet her. I thought she might want to void our contract."

"She didn't?" Dr. Ueda looked uncomfortable.

"No. And I certainly didn't. She had divorced her parents before she went in. She hated her mother, or said she did. I thought it would be the same thing for me. We would terminate our contract by mutual agreement, and I'd contract with Susan."

"You wanted that?"

Skip shook his head. "I wanted Chelle. She is all I've ever wanted, re-ally. I was overjoyed when she didn't want to terminate our contract." He paused. "I think—no, I know—that Susan had already joined a suicide ring by then."

"Oh you gods!"

"Correct. Virginia is the senior member. It's the others' duty to kill her, and Susan came to do it." Skip rose. "That was why those two young women died. Which was what you wanted to know. Have you heard enough?"

"She joined the ring before you dumped her?"

"Correct."

"Why?"

"I don't know, and I'd like to. I could offer three or four guesses, but they would be of no value to you or anyone. Guesses rarely are. If you find out, will you tell me?"

"That will depend on what the reason is," Dr. Ueda said.

The first-class dining salon was a paradise of gold and ivory three decks high, with opulent balconies for A and B Decks. "We're to meet another couple," Skip explained. "An elderly man with a beard, and your social director. Have they come already?" He was stiff and sweating in dinner jacket, formal shirt, and black tie.

The headwaiter awarded him a superior smile. "I really wouldn't know, sir. Their reservation would be under the name of . . . ?"

Chelle said, "Blue."

"Healy," Skip announced firmly. "It should be in the name of your so-cial director, Virginia Healy."

"Blue," the headwaiter said. He was looking at his screen. "Table for four. Follow me, please."

Table seventeen was near an open window and well away from the kitchen, the piano, and the center of the room. At present, it was unoccu-pied. Skip held Chelle's chair (outpointing the headwaiter) before taking a seat himself. "I thought this was your mother's party."

"It is. She must've made the reservation in my name."

"You said 'Blue.'"

"Right. She told me that." Chelle looked thoughtful. "Maybe it's be-cause she works here. Maybe employees can't make them."

It seemed best to change the subject. "How is your arm?"

"Lots better. I know what you're worried about, and we can. Just as long as you don't grab my arm, we should be fine."

"I wasn't thinking of that," Skip said.

"Uh huh."

He changed the subject. "I passed out, didn't I? I fainted. We were in that stateroom on A Deck—in Jerry Brice's stateroom where Rick John-son had been shot—and I must have lost consciousness. Did I fall down?"

Chelle nodded.

"But you were conscious. You saw and heard whatever went on after-ward."

"Sure."

"What did? Will you tell me about it? Please?"

"Sure, but there isn't a lot to tell. With two good arms I could've picked you up and helped carry you back to the doctor, but with one arm busted there was no way. I phoned, and she sent up two guys with a stretcher. They carried you back down to the infirmary, and I went with them. The doctor checked you over, said you needed a CAT scan, and kept you there overnight. They can't do CAT scans here."

Skip nodded.

"Next day she called and said there wasn't anything she could do there that couldn't be done in our room. I got Joe and Angel to carry you, and Achille and I went down with them. The doctor told me how to take care of you and promised people would come around." Chelle paused. "They have, sometimes. We thought—I think everybody thought—you'd still be out when we docked."

"I'm trying to remember who was present when I lost consciousness for the second time. Was your mother there?"

"No. I think it was just that mechanic and me. There was nobody in the cabin when we got there."

"Where was your mother?"

"I don't know." Chelle shrugged. "Does it matter?"

A waiter asked whether they were ready to order. Skip explained that they were waiting for another couple, and Chelle ordered a bottle of champagne.

"The man with the beard shot Rick Johnson," Skip said when the waiter had gone.

"Right." Chelle nodded. "He grabbed the woman's gun. I told the captain about it."

"Rick blew when he was shot. He was a cyborg."

"I remember you saying something about that. I guess the bullet hit his reactor or whatever."

"Not necessarily, but that's not to the point. The flash burned Trinity. She fell down, and you and Virginia went to help her."

Chelle nodded again.

"She's a big woman, and you couldn't get her on her feet. Gary Oberdorf and I got her up with your help and walked her to the elevator. I believe I can name all the people who were on that elevator with us. Correct me if I'm wrong."

"Your memory's probably better than mine," Chelle said. "Who do you think?"

"Gary Oberdorf, Jerry, and Trinity herself."

"You're right. I'd forgotten the kid, but he was there."

"Who wasn't there?" Skip's forefinger doodled on the immaculate table cloth.

"Everybody else in the world. What the fuck is that supposed to mean?"

"Who wasn't on the elevator whom you would expect to be there?"

There was a long silence. The champagne arrived, Skip sampled it and nodded, and the waiter poured a glass for each of them. Chelle sipped hers twice before she spoke. "Mother. Mother wasn't there."

Skip nodded.

"When Rick blew up, he was damn near in Trinity's face. She got burned. Her clothes were on fire a little bit. Remember?"

"No," Skip said. "I'd forgotten that."

"They were, smoking and a little flame. Mother and I had to slap them out. So Trinity was hurt pretty bad, and we were worried about her." Chelle hesitated. "Trinity was on that elevator going to the doctor."

"So were you. On the elevator, I mean."

"Yeah, I was. I'm her daughter and those spies had been holding me. Did you know they were spies?"

"I guessed it."

"Good for you. Someday you're going to have to tell me how. But they'd been holding me, her daughter, and she'd been helping you look for me. Is that right? Or were you helping her?"

"I enlisted her help."

"So why wasn't she with me? And Trinity? Why wasn't she there with us?"

"Because she didn't want to be, obviously."

Chelle put down her glass. "You're going to have to explain that. I think somebody grabbed her."

Skip sighed. "And I think that's rubbish. Shall we quarrel?"

"No. I'd win, but what good would that do? Why wasn't she grabbed?"

"Who was in that room with you before we came? Name them."

"I don't know the blonde's name. Maybe somebody told me once, but I've forgotten."

"Susan."

"Okay, she was there. Rick, of course, and the guy with the white whiskers."

"Now it's my turn. When our party started up to A Deck, it consisted of Achille, Oberdorf, Jerry, your mother, and me. Rick shot me as soon as the door opened. Achille was gone when I recovered consciousness. Do you know anything about that?"

"I don't think I even saw him."

"Then I have another question, one I think you can answer. Why is this a table for four?"

"The captain?"

Skip shook his head. "Your mother talked to me on your phone in our stateroom. Remember? She asked me, quite specifically, not to mention the captain during dinner."

"You're kidding!"

"No. I named the people who came with me. When the stateroom door opened, who was in there? I remember nothing after that, but you had been in there for some time. Who were they?"

"Susan. I said that."

Skip nodded.

"Plus Rick, the old man, and me."

"That was what I had assumed; all four of you were present when I returned to consciousness. When we left to take Trinity to the doctor, Jerry and Gary Oberdorf went with us. Rick was dead. Susan was in the lavatory slicing her arms with broken glass."

Chelle winced.

"Exactly. But who could have grabbed your mother? Only the old man, and even then she would have had to linger. I think he must have said something that made her remain behind. Something I didn't hear."

"I didn't either. I wasn't paying attention to them. What was it?"

"I think I know," Skip said, "but we may be able to ask them in a minute or two. Or we may learn it without asking." He nodded slightly in the direction of the couple threading their way through the tables toward them, and stood up.

REFLECTION 16

Couples

Here they come, he tall and very straight despite his age, she a full head shorter in the highest of high heels. Her arm's through his; she is in possession. In her free hand, a tiny bag bright with synthetic gems, a little gold bag that speaks loud for her, telling the world she won't have to pay, that a handkerchief, a lipstick, and a mirror are all she'll need tonight.

There's a bond between them stronger than Vanessa's frail arm, or stronger (as I should say) than the arm that she has been loaned by the woman named Edith Eckhart. In this world, it is the invisible things that are strongest.

What forges that bond?

Not intercourse, though it is tempting to say it is. It forms, sometimes, between couples who have not so much as kissed, and once formed is stronger than steel, a bond that cannot be broken, though it can rust away.

There was, God knows, such a bond between Susan and me. I doubt that there was a person in our office who failed to sense it. I was Skip—when I was alone. Alone, she was Susan. Put us in the same room, be it as big as a banquet hall, and we became SkipandSusan.

Sometimes SusanandSkip. I should not forget that because it is as true as a human thought can be. In that infirmary room we were SusanandSkip, though Dr. Ueda was not there long enough to sense it—or I don't think she did.

Look! Here in the air between us, Dr. Ueda. That is the bond, still bright, though others are brighter. Not yet red with rust, though it is rusting. It had begun to rust last year, in fact.

And now I know, or think I know, why Susan joined the suicide ring.

Can I have meant more than life to her? It seems incredible, but without me what did she have? No daughter and no son, because I never gave her any.

Virginia waves, and Chelle waves back. Do they sense the bond between Chelle and me?

Is there any bond there to sense?

17

***

THE DOUBLE AGENT

Vanessa waved. "We're late, and it's all my fault. I was silly as a girl, trying on dresses and shoes. I wanted to wear this, but my shoes didn't match. Charles took them away from me—why are you staring, Chelle dear?"

"I—I didn't recognize Charlie. All the time we were in that room . . ."

The white-bearded man pulled out a chair for Vanessa. "It's the beard, of course. The beard and the simple fact that you haven't seen me for almost three years that have been nearer twenty-three for me." He sat. "I'm a great deal older, even if you're not. A great deal older and a good deal thinner."

Vanessa said, "I wanted to make it a big surprise, darling, but Charles thought it might be unpleasant and fall ever so flat. So we didn't."

The white-bearded man said, "Is it unpleasant, honey? You divorced me, so I'm no longer your father. Will you accept me as a friend of your mother's?"

"She isn't. I divorced her, too. You—you're just a couple I know now. You're her date."

The white mustache twitched.

"I'm trying to get used to that, I guess. I—I've been calling her Mother, and she was waiting for me when I came dirtside. Her and Skip. We—we're contracted, Skip and me. But . . ."

"But she was there," the white-bearded man prompted. "She was there waiting for you."

"Yeah. She was and we hugged and all that. I . . . Oh, dammit! I was glad to see her. It was wonderful."

Vanessa smiled at Skip. "You see? I know I was a nuisance."

"To whom I was rude," Skip said. "I apologize." He turned to the white-bearded man. "You were with your daughter when she was captured. Captured on your order?"

"I was not, and she was not." The white-bearded man picked up his menu. "I was in the room with her after she was captured, but I did not order her capture. Will this cross-examination survive the arrival of our food?"

"It isn't a cross-examination," Skip said. "I'm just curious. Rick Johnson was plainly a spy. Do you know who he was spying for?"

"Certainly. The Os. I suppose you'll need to prove that in court if I'm put on trial. The roast beef's good here—"

"I haven't said I'll take your case."

Vanessa surprised everyone by asking, "What about the hijackers, Charles? Can you tell us who they were working for?"

"With certainty?" The white-bearded man shook his head. "The EU, probably, but I'm not sure of it. I was about to say that the roast beef's good. My doctor tells me I've got to eat fish, but I tried the roast beef last night and found it delicious."

Chelle said, "Have you had the yam and macadamia crusted red snapper?"

The white-bearded man appeared to study her over the top of his menu. "No, I haven't, honey. I might try it tonight, though."

"You two were contracted. You and Mother." Chelle glanced at Skip.

The white-bearded man's nod was barely perceptible.

"Yes, we were," Vanessa put in.

"Only you broke up, didn't you?"

The white-bearded man glanced at Vanessa. "That was none of my doing. Ask your mother."

Vanessa smiled. "He means your biological mother, Chelle darling. The woman who carried you in her womb. He's aware that you and I are divorced." She turned the smile on Skip. "That was none of *my* doing, Counselor. She sicced the Army's lawyers on me."

Chelle said, "You voided your contract with Charlie, though."

"I did. We're still married, however."

Chelle looked puzzled.

"It's religious, darling. Not law. They separated the two, oh, a long time ago. If I'd divorced Charles, we'd no longer be married. But it seemed like such a bother. Just voiding our contract cost a lot."

The white-bearded man muttered, "You hoped I'd do it."

"I did not!"

A waiter arrived to take their orders. Vanessa asked for roast lamb, and the white-bearded man for filet mignon. Chelle said, "What are you having, Skip?"

"A hard time imagining what went on in Jerry Brice's room."

"Shouldn't we talk about it in private?"

"The part that you mean, yes. The part that I mean, no."

The waiter cleared his throat.

Chelle asked him, "What's good tonight?"

"I'd try the filet of sole, ma'am."

"Fine. I'll have that. Rice pilaf and spinach. Tossed salad, vinegar and oil."

The waiter wrote.

Skip told him, "Lamb and mint jelly."

When the waiter had gone, the white-bearded man said, "What puzzles you, young man? I feel quite certain I can put all your doubts to rest."

"A great many things. And thank you for that 'young man.'"

"My pleasure. You may not credit my answers, of course. You're of a skeptical turn of mind."

"We'll see. I believe you implied that you were not there at the time Chelle was brought in."

"He wasn't," Chelle said, "and I was scared to death. Then he came in, and he was probably hoping I'd recognize him, but I didn't."

"That you would recognize me," the white-bearded man told her, "and keep your knowledge to yourself."

"I didn't recognize you either, Charles," Vanessa said.

"Now you will demand that I establish my identity," the white-bearded man told Skip. "Let's get that out of the way at once. I cannot."

"You're asking me to take you on faith?"

"No, sir. On the testimony of my wife and my former daughter. Do you recall the Old College Inn? You and I had dinner there one evening."

Chelle said, "I was there, too, Charlie. You told us about firing Marcia."

"Indeed you were." The white-bearded man nodded. "I talked about it for Skip's sake, though. You'll never have a secretary, honey. Or if you do, it will be some kind of dodge. The blonde was Skip's secretary."

"The one with the wheelgun? Not anymore. Skip fired her."

Skip cleared his throat. "I think I'd better set the record straight, Chelle. I didn't fire her, she quit. Now she's my secretary again, because I hired her back." He turned to the white-bearded man. "You told us Marcia had been doing a poor job. That was why you let her go."

The white-bearded man nodded.

"Susan was an excellent secretary. I was stunned when she resigned. And I'd be delighted to have her back in my office, although that wasn't the reason I rehired her."

"What was?" Chelle asked.

"She'll be charged when we reach port, probably with first-degree murder. I intend to defend her pro bono—to have Mick or whoever do it, nominally. It's liable to be an expensive undertaking, one that may drag on for the better part of a year. If she's no longer an employee, there will be questions. Chet Burton's not active in the firm these days, but he keeps an eye on things. Ibarra's junior to me, but he's just as much a partner as I am. If Susan's still working for us, that could be the difference. We try to take care of our own."

Chelle nodded. "She was lost. I could see that even when she was holding a gun on me."

Vanessa reached across the table to touch her hand. "You mustn't sympathize with them, Chelle darling. It's an emotional trap."

"Well, she was. She was loyal to Rick, but she hated what they were doing."

Skip spoke to the white-bearded man. "You came in after they had taken Chelle from the infirmary. Why?"

He chuckled. "Because I wanted to see Chelle, that's all. I'd heard she was on board." He paused, blinking. "She divorced me. You know that. It had been a long time for me, but only a couple of years for her. Frankly, I thought she might hang up on me if I phoned your stateroom, or slam the door in my face if I went there. Then I found out she'd been hurt by the hijackers." The white-bearded man paused. "You fought them, Mr. Grison. I heard about that, too."

Skip nodded.

"I didn't. I offered my services and was herded into the second-class dining room with the women and children, and the other old men. I've never been a soldier. Neither have you, I dare say."

"Correct."

"You're old when your dreams become regrets. Remember that. In time you'll learn how true it is."

Chelle said, "You must have known I was in there."

"I did. Your Mr. Grison told me, though he seems to have forgotten it. Did they feed you?"

Chelle nodded. "I'd been asleep. They made me go to sleep some way. When I woke up there was food. Not much, but some. Rolls and a little butter, and a bowl of cold soup. Crackers. I ate it all."

Skip said, "Is this to the point?"

"Absolutely. You wanted to know how I knew Chelle was in there. I phoned the infirmary, but nobody answered. So I asked Refugio—he's my steward—to find her for me. He asked somebody else, and that person said that she was up in Signal Three. I didn't ask how he knew. I simply assumed he'd asked a waiter who'd delivered food there."

Skip shook his head. "A moment ago, you said I told you."

"I did, and both are quite true. When I heard she was in Signal Three, I assumed she had been discharged by the infirmary and was being welcomed back to the glorious world of health by a dear friend. Had I been right, you would have been enraged, Mr. Grison. You were terrified instead. My dear wife, who failed to recognize me, was clearly very worried.

I'd met Lieutenant Jerry Brice, and knew he had been wounded. If he and Chelle were romping between the sheets, both of them had recovered from their wounds with astounding speed. It seemed clear something was amiss, so I went up."

Skip nodded. "Go on, please."

"There isn't much more to tell. I walked in on them—your secretary opened the door for me. I saw Chelle with her hands tied and pushed your secretary aside. The man she called Rick wanted to know what I was up to, and pointed a gun at me. After a little fencing, I told him I'd been sent by headquarters. He said he wasn't supposed to signal, so I said that's right. Don't."

Chelle said, "You kept telling them not to kill me. I remember that."

"Of course I did." The white-bearded man turned back to Skip. "They were using deeptrance on her. I told him it would be foolish to shoot her. Somebody might hear the shot, and after he shot her we would have to dispose of the body. All he had to do was to put her back under and tell her to forget the whole thing. Deeptrance suggestions last for weeks. Sometimes for a hundred-day, but always for two weeks or more. They use it to cure addicts."

Skip nodded. "I'm surprised you know."

"I read a lot. Any more questions?"

"Yes, several."

The white-bearded man poured himself a fresh glass of champagne. "Fire away."

Skip began, "Do you really expect us to believe—"

He was interrupted by the arrival of two waiters. The junior, who carried a tray and a folding table, handed each salad to the senior, who placed it before the appropriate diner.

Vanessa said, "I have a question of my own, Charles. If Skip gets so many, surely I ought to get one. Or two. Possibly two. Are you still in business? And if you are, can you tell us what business you're in?"

The white mustache twitched. "Shall I anticipate the rest? It will be my pleasure. Am I making a lot of money? And—oh, yes—how much have I got now?"

"I would never be so rude!"

The white-bearded man winked at Skip. "You see how it is, Counselor. I have wished for a wife much younger than myself, a comfort to my old age. Our Divine Master, whose exquisite sense of fun provides Him and us with so much entertainment, has granted my wish. Here aboard the *Rani*, I find my wife, a lovely lady to whom I'm already wed, and lo and behold! She is—miraculously—much, much younger than I. The angels harp louder than ever in order that we not hear His chuckles."

"I was thinking of contracting," Vanessa said. She struck a pensive pose, endeavoring to look thoughtful. "You *are* going to ask me to contract again, aren't you, Charles darling?"

The white-bearded man turned to Chelle. "You must have questions, too."

"Thanks." She nodded. "You didn't buy a ticket on this cruise just because I was here. Was it Mother?"

"It was neither of you. I'm an old man, much older than any of you, and certainly much, much older than you are. My wife voided our contract long ago, and even longer ago my only child divorced me. As old men so often are, I'm alone in the world. On a cruise, I hoped to make a few friends, and possibly even one special friend, someone who might eventually become more than a friend to me."

Vanessa said, "As you have."

The white-bearded man ignored it. "You may laugh at an old man clinging to romantic dreams, honey. I know it's foolish and am not offended. We cling to those dreams the way we do because we have so little left. You'll never understand that, nor will my beloved wife. Mr. Grison may. He will, in fact, if he lives long enough."

"I understand already," Skip said. "Are you retired? Completely?"

The white-bearded man nodded. "I've been retired for some years."

"Rick Johnson shot me when the door of that stateroom opened. Did you shoot at me, too?"

"No. You are wondering whether I might have fired the shot that wounded you. I, in place of poor Rick. I did not. I can't vouch for your secretary, but I don't believe she fired. If Chelle and I had been armed we would've shot Rick and your secretary before you came. We weren't."

Chelle's left hand found Skip's knee and tightened around it.

"Before Chelle and I dressed for dinner," Skip said slowly, "I questioned Susan in the infirmary."

"She'll recover, I hope."

"I'm sure she will. I made one simple statement to her, and she said I had made one mistake already. Would you like to hear the statement?"

Vanessa laid her salad fork aside. "I would. Do you remember?"

"I said that there had been three people in Brice's stateroom holding Chelle, Mr. Blue."

"Please call me Charles."

"Thank you. After that I said you had no gun, proved by your taking Susan's to shoot Rick. Shortly after I made those statements, Susan told me that I'd made one mistake already."

"As do I," the white-bearded man said. "I was only feigning assistance, while I tried to free Chelle. No doubt your secretary observed it."

Skip shook his head. "I don't think that was it. For one thing, you're too good an actor. Chelle says you were trying to free her, and I believe you were; but I don't believe that was what Susan meant. Didn't you say a moment ago that you had no gun? That you were unarmed?"

"Indeed I did."

"If you'd had a gun, you could have shot Rick Johnson without taking Susan's revolver. But if you had done that, there would be a good chance Susan would shoot you."

The white bearded-man's mustache twitched. "Or that I would have had to shoot Susan as well. All this is merely hypothetical, you understand."

"I do. Here's another. Let's say, hypothetically, that you have a gun. You might have to throw it over the side before we reach port. I, hypothetically again, might be able to get it past customs. I would return it to you later, of course. You may wish to consider that."

"If I had a gun, I certainly would."

Chelle said, "We're on your side, Charlie, Skip and me both. You went in there to save my life. It makes you one of the good guys."

"I'd like to think so, honey. I'm not sure Mr. Grison agrees."

Vanessa looked up. "Good evening, Captain Kain! Would you care to join us?"

"Only for a moment." The captain took a chair from an empty table, positioning it at the corner between Chelle and the white-bearded man. "We'll be taking a pilot aboard tomorrow, if the wind holds." He cleared his throat. "The forecast says it will, and I'll be busy. Very busy."

Vanessa said, "All of us understand that, I'm sure."

"Good. I wanted to say goodbye. To Mr. Grison here, particularly. We, well—there was a time when he watched my back and I watched his." The captain held out his hand.

Skip accepted it, and the two men shook hands across the table. Neither smiled.

"I'd like to ask you a few questions," the captain continued. "If you don't feel you can answer, just say so. I'll understand. If you send me a bill later, I'll pay it if I can."

"That will depend on the questions," Skip told him.

"I'll start with the worst one. If the answer's bad, there won't be any more. You folks are waiting for your food?"

Vanessa said, "Please don't tell us that was the worst question."

"No, I . . . Well, never mind."

Chelle muttered, "Shut up, Mother."

"Your firm saved us, Mr. Grison. Mick Tooley is a subordinate of yours? That's what he says."

"He's a junior member of my firm. I'm a partner, the managing partner."

"He came to save us. He enlisted mercenaries and volunteers, chartered a boat, and so on. The result was another battle. People died, and there was damage to the vessel. It's conceivable that the line will sue your firm over his actions."

"For saving you?" The white-bearded man sounded amused.

"Conceivable, I said. The lawyers aren't seamen, and if they advise it . . ." The captain shrugged.

"They'd lose," Skip told him. "I can't guarantee it, but that's my professional opinion. I wouldn't take their case."

"If they do," the captain continued, "you'll certainly counter-sue. Am I right?"

"Probably. I'd want to sleep on it and have my people research similar cases. But we probably would."

The captain nodded, his long, sun-tanned face worried. "If you accuse me of negligence and make those accusations credible, my career will be effectively over. I hope you realize that."

"I hadn't thought that far," Skip said.

"It will be. A ship's officer has to get his master's ticket to make decent money. I got mine six years ago."

Vanessa said, "You're contracted, aren't you? Someone told me that. Children?"

The captain nodded, his face expressionless. "Three."

"I envy you," Skip said. "Shall I put this to rest? Now? I believe I can."

The captain nodded again.

"If your company decides to sue us, you'll be deposed. At some point, as the case proceeds, we will read your deposition. How hard we are on you will depend, largely though not entirely, on how hard you are on us."

"I won't be hard on you at all. I'll say you saved us, which is the truth."

"In which case, it's your company you have to worry about, not us."

The captain rose. "If they blame me, they can't go on blaming you. Or not as much."

"Correct. Furthermore, they will be blaming their own agent. The chance that they'll do it is minute. They may threaten to fire you, however. Threaten, I said. If they are foolish enough to do it, you'll have grounds for a suit of your own. Your attorneys would show that your professional reputation has been damaged beyond repair by your company's negligence and subsequent actions. They would ask compensatory and punitive damages. Twenty or thirty million, I would think."

Chelle murmured, "I smell blood in the water."

Skip shook his head. "It probably won't happen—they'd be fools to do it. If they do, however, almost any attorney would take your case on contingency. Do you know any good lawyers?"

"I know one very good one," the captain told him, and left as the waiter's assistant began collecting the salad plates.

"That was my boss," Vanessa told the white-bearded man. "He's a bit too straitlaced for his own good, but it's terribly easy to do much, much worse." Her tone was merely conversational.

As the waiter himself distributed their entrées, Skip waved to Mick Tooley. "Over here. Were you looking for us?"

"For your beautiful contracta, sir." Tooley grinned. "For a few days she was giving me daily bulletins on your progress—on your lack of it, far too often. I'm going to miss her."

Chelle smiled in return, an amazingly warm smile that Skip found he associated with swirling leaves—brown, red, and gold—and young men in sweaters throwing footballs. "I'm not gonna disappear into some dress designer's salon forever, Mick. I bet there's a company Christmas party."

"Until then," Tooley told her, "and if you'll come, I'll bring the doughnuts."

Skip gestured toward the chair that the captain had vacated. "Sit down. We don't want to lose you so soon."

Vanessa said, "Really now! We can't eat in front of him while he has nothing."

"Please go right ahead," Tooley told her.

Skip put a half his entrée on his bread plate and set it before Tooley. "I'm sure there must be other attorneys on the ship, but most will be corporate. Very probably you and I are the only ones with backgrounds in criminal law."

Tooley nodded. "As far as I know."

"The gentleman to your right shot and killed a cyborg called Rick Johnson. He was one of your volunteers, wasn't he?"

"Rick? He was the best of them, my right-hand man."

"He was also a spy. The gentleman next to you says for the Os."

The white-bearded man said, "That was what I gathered from a remark of his. It's not iron-clad."

Tooley said, "Do you remember the remark? It could be important."

"Not precisely." The white-bearded man paused. "It was something about his superior not understanding humans."

"When the captain was here," Skip told the white-bearded man, "he got me thinking about the actions, and the failures to act, that might be brought up in court. One of them was his failure to confine you. He must know that you killed Rick Johnson; Chelle says she told him."

Chelle said, "He does. He also knows that Rick had kidnapped me and killed the doctor and his nurse. Mick saved this ship and everybody on it, but it was my dad who saved me."

"Your ex-dad," the white-bearded man muttered.

"Yeah. I divorced you. Don't rub it in."

Tooley stood up. "I didn't mean to interrupt your dinner. Skip and I will see each other in the office, but I wanted to say goodbye to you and now I have. You've got one hell of a woman there, Skip."

He nodded and smiled. "I know."

When Tooley had gone, Vanessa said, "There was something odd about that."

"He's a friend," Chelle told her. "He just wanted to say goodbye."

"He wanted something else, Chelle darling, and he got it. I'd love to know what it was."

"He wasn't even looking for us, Mother. Skip waved him over."

"He was, but he hadn't seen us. That was why Skip waved."

"How the hell do you know that?"

"We social directors know these things." Vanessa smiled down from a height of years. "We must, and I do. I don't suppose you've ever given a party. I've given . . . Oh, twenty."

"Fifty," the white-bearded man muttered.

"You're counting small gatherings, Charles."

Chelle's good hand struck the table hard enough to make the plates jump. "Don't look so damn smug!"

"I wasn't, darling. Just because I've got my man and you're losing yours? No indeed! I looked sympathetic."

A handsome young man too informally dressed for Formal Night was approaching their table. Chelle turned, and as she did, her expression became one that Skip had never seen before. Her eyes were larger and seemed, somehow, darker; her mouth was tremulous. "D-Don? You're Don, aren't you?"

He nodded.

Chelle rose, taller than he. "You knew I was in here. How did you know, Don?"

"I loved you, sweet thing. You're gone and I can't see you again 'til it's all over. I needed to tell you."

Chelle made a soft little sound that might have meant anything or nothing.

Vanessa gasped.

And Chelle said, "Listen, we gotta keep in touch, all of us. You tell Joe and the sarge. Tell everybody."

There was a soft sigh—perhaps from Don.

Chelle turned. "Hey, Skip, what's our address?"

He gave it.

"What's the apartment number? I forgot."

"Penthouse," he said. "Just tell them to write penthouse."

She stared at him.

"We were renegotiating the penthouse lease. Before we left I told the manager to terminate the negotiations, that we'd move in when we got home."

Don borrowed a pen and a used envelope from the white-bearded man and began scribbling rapidly.

"I don't know about e-mail or any of that shit yet," Chelle told him. "Only I'll give you my phone number if you'll hand over that pen."

"Thanks!" Don said. "I'll be calling you."

"Sure." When he had gone, Chelle sat down and took a sip of wine and a bite of fish. "You know, I donno why the fuck I stood up when he came. He's not an officer."

The white-bearded man told her, "All of us have forces within us, honey. Energies unseen by our conscious minds."

"Isn't he just amazing?" Vanessa looked from Skip to Chelle—then back to Skip, seeking confirmation. "Why did I void our contract, Charles? I've forgotten."

"I treated you shamefully, showering you with money, then stealing it back when you were out shopping. When I stole the money other men had given you—"

"Why you big liar! No wonder I voided it!"

"And now you know." The white-bearded man winked at Skip. "Which is what you wanted."

"What I want to know," Skip said, "is why you booked under an assumed name."

"Did I?" The white-bearded man looked puzzled. "Really? I have forgotten."

"I got a ship's officer to call the purser's office for me. He asked whether there were any passengers named Blue. The purser's office, which would surely know, said there was one and only one. That was Mastergunner Chelle Sea Blue. No other Blues."

"I see."

"I'd like to see, too," Skip said. "What name did you book under?"

"It hardly matters, does it? I could explain how I came to use my friend's reservation, but you wouldn't believe me—or at least you would ask confirmation, which I could not provide beyond a phone call."

"You would give me your friend's number?"

"Of course I will." The white-bearded man smiled. "His name as well."

"I'd like them both. Will you lend me that pen?"

He did, and Skip's wallet provided a scrap of paper.

"The number is two, one, two, nine . . ." The white bearded man paused.

"I've got it."

"Three, three, four, one, one, seven, seven, two, two. My friend is Cole Baum. Coleman A. Baum, if you wish to be precise."

Skip wrote.

"I have a phone, if you'd like to borrow it."

Skip shook his head. "I have one, too, and I'd like to eat before my food gets cold."

"You should trust Charles," Vanessa said.

"I'll begin as soon as Charles trusts me."

Although Skip was returning the paper to his wallet, he saw the white mustache twitch.

REFLECTION 17

Looking Over the Rail

Down there, four decks below me, five tugs prepare to bring us up to the wharf. They are long and rather narrow craft with fifty oars a side. One hundred and one men in each tug, including the tug's captain. Five hundred and five men, five hundred of whom are certainly making the Union Employment Administration wage—forty-three noras a week, enough to support a couple with one child (no more than one child) in subsidized housing, if both parents work.

Forty-three noras a week keeps these strong men busy and tired, too tired to riot. Too tired to steal, at least in theory. Our seamen mock them, although it seems good-natured. What is it the seamen get? The captain told me. Seventy noras a week, so one thousand per hundred-day. With a thousand noras every hundred-day, plus food and a bed, they have a right to mock.

I wonder how much he makes? He looked grim at dinner last night, though a part of that may have been the thought of losing Virginia.

That dinner . . . It will haunt me for a long time, I'm afraid—our last dinner on the *Rani*. We'll be going ashore in what? An hour? More like two, I imagine. We may get lunch before we go ashore.

But that dinner . . . What was it Mick wanted? He got it, Virginia said, whatever it was. Whatever information or confirmation he was after.

One possibility is that he wanted to find out whether I blamed him for bringing Rick. Another, and this one's my favorite, is that he wanted to see how complete my recovery was. Certainly he seemed happy when he left. And then there's the real reason, about which he was quite wrong.

Hooked up now, a suggestive phrase. The *Rani* moves slowly through the water, sidewise. The gulls wheel and shriek, the rowers strain at their oars, and we move—how fast? Two hundred meters per hour, perhaps. Certainly no more than that.

So much to think about, and so little to reason with. Coal is black and Mr. Blue was Mr. White. Chelle Sea Blue—Shell Sea Blue. He likes to play games with colors. He's playing a deep game now, and I may be better off not knowing what it is. Someone had talked to Don while I was unconscious. Was it Charles? More probably, it was Chelle herself.

Someone paging me. She wants to go to lunch. She doesn't want me to see her naked. Was it the same with Jerry? Is it the same with Mick?

18

NOT THE END

Formal Night over, Chelle dropped into a chair as soon as the door of their stateroom closed. "Sit down. I've got to talk to you."

"Not yet," Skip said. "I want to get out of this outfit."

"Are you trying to tell me you talk better in your underwear?"

"I talk better in anything. I'd talk better in a diving suit."

"You can't unfasten that fake bow tie, can you?"

"Yes, I can; but I can't see what I'm doing, so it may take a while."

She rose, and in another second his tie was gone. "Now the collar stud."

"Who the hell invented these clothes?"

"You really want to know?" She was grinning. "You won't like it."

"Lawyers?"

"Huh uh." The collar stud gone, Chelle stepped away. "Guys who wore them every day, like Lord This-'n'-that who always dressed for dinner. Band leaders and headwaiters. Guys like that."

Taking out one last shirt stud, Skip grunted.

"While you're doing that, how about unzipping me?"

A tug at the keeper at the back of Chelle's neck opened the graceful blue gown she had chosen to match her eyes. It fell around her feet, and she stepped out of it, a blue chemise half concealing a blue bra and blue panties. "Think you're going to get an eyeful? This is as far as I go until the lights are out."

"Fine."

She picked up her gown and hung it in the closet they shared, then returned to her chair, plainly waiting for him to speak. Silently, he stuffed his shirt, damp with sweat, into his dirty clothes bag.

She snorted. "You're waiting for me to make the first move, damn you."

"Or not. As you wish." He was stepping out of his trousers.

"Okay, I will. Did you believe Charlie?"

"Hardly a word of it. Do you believe he was Charlie? Is that man in actual fact your biological father?"

"Yeah. You don't think so?"

"I wasn't sure. Are you?"

"Hell, yes. Can I prove it? No. But that's him."

"Did you tell him about the College Inn? Firing his secretary?"

"Of course not. I never saw him until he came in with Mom tonight. You were there. If I'd told him, you'd have heard it."

"You saw him when you were being held in Lieutenant Brice's stateroom."

"Yeah. You're right, I did. Only I didn't know who he was then. He was just a nice old guy who was talking them out of shooting me." Chelle's deep sigh was followed by a wistful smile. "I loved him then. I could've kissed him, mustache and all. But I didn't know it was Charlie."

"They gave you deeptrance. I don't suppose you know what you told them."

"While I was under? All I know is they didn't get what they wanted. They put me under four times, I think it was, and every time I came to, Rick was madder."

"In that case, you might have told the man with the beard about dinner at the Old College Inn."

"I suppose, if he'd asked the right questions."

"I admit is isn't likely," Skip said. He leaned back in his chair. "It's possible, however. He could also have planted the suggestion that you would recognize him as your father the first time you saw him with your mother. I'll admit that neither of those are very plausible."

"I'll say! That's Charlie. A lot older, but still Charlie. Did you buy that story about his just happening to go into the cabin looking for me?"

"Certainly not." Skip paused. "He lied about having met Jerry Brice and half a dozen other things."

Chelle nodded. "He said all he had to do was say he'd been sent by headquarters, and they bought it. It was damn hard not to laugh in his face."

"Hard but wise."

"Yeah. He came to save me, just like you did. Only he pulled it off."

Skip nodded. "You don't know how he established his bona fides?"

"I'm pretty sure I was under when he came in, but I know somebody who does."

"Who might," Skip said. "So do I, and I want to talk to her."

"Will she tell you the truth?"

He shrugged. "Susan won't lie to me intentionally. But she may not have understood what was said or what sort of ID was shown. She may have been busy doing something, most probably because Rick Johnson saw to it that she was."

"Do you really think there would be papers? Something like a service card?"

Skip shrugged again. "Almost certainly not, but there may have been something else. A ring, a coin, a button. Maybe a gesture. A secret handshake sounds absurd, I know; but it might be good for just that reason. Or the repeated use of some particular phrase. Or something else—there's always the chance it was something else."

Chelle grinned. "You said 'something else' twice. I bet you thought I wouldn't catch it."

"I said it three times. Seriously now, it might be good for us to know what the ID was; but I doubt that we can get it from Susan because I doubt that she has it. I hoped you did."

Chelle shook her head. "Do you really, seriously think Charlie might be spying for the Os?"

"You knew him far better than I did, and your memories of him will be far more recent. Do you?"

"You want to give me time to think about it?"

"No. Off the top of your head. Would he do it?"

Chelle looked thoughtful. "For enough money, yes, he might. But he'd double-cross them as soon as he found out how to make double-crossing pay. You want more?"

"Absolutely."

"Charlie's loyal to Charlie. If God pays off on total no-slacking loyalty to a cause, there's a gold throne in heaven just waiting for Charlie. If he doesn't kill goats in front of his own picture, it's because he's never found goats good enough."

"He tried to save your life."

"Wrong. He saved it. It kind of worries me, because he figured he'd get something out of it and I don't know what. I've got a dozen guesses when what I need's one good one."

"He sees you as a detached part of himself. All right if I have the first shower?"

"No way. You'll be all nice and clean and smell good, and I won't take one at all. So me first. Do you think that's really it? I'm part of him? In his mind, I mean?"

"Biologically you are. You've got a bunch of his genes, and he certainly knows that. Would Virginia be as quick to take him back if she didn't know he'd saved you?"

Chelle rose. "I think so. It's money, not me. He's rich, or she thinks he is, or anyway she thinks he might be. She's poor now, and she doesn't like it. I'll try to leave you a dry towel."

There would be no one in Zygmunt's office this late, but there would be an answering machine. Skip selected *Zman* from his contacts list. "This is Skip Grison. Here's a phone number." He read the number the white-bearded man had supplied. "Find out who's answering that number and what they're doing. It's supposed to belong to somebody named Coleman Baum." He spelled it. "See if he's real."

He leaned back, conscious that he was very tired, and conscious, too, that he sometimes made bad decisions when he was tired. Something hard tapped the door softly. He stood, went to the peephole, and opened the door to admit Achille.

"You want see me, mon?"

"Sit down." Skip motioned toward the other chair. "Chelle's taking a shower, and that ought to give us all the time we need. We'll make port tomorrow. Will you go ashore?"

Achille shrugged. "Got to, mon. They don't let me on the ship no more."

"You could hide on board so that they would never find you. We both know that. Are you going to?"

"What you want, mon?"

"I want you to bring something in for me. There'll be money in it for you."

Achille thrust out his lower lip. "I'm going, mon. What you want?"

Skip unlocked his bag, rummaged through his dirty laundry, and produced the pistol he had wrested from Rick Johnson's dead hand. "You could sell this in the city for a good price."

Lips pursed, Achille nodded.

"I think I know about what you could get for it, but I'd like to hear your guess."

Achille leaned closer to inspect the pistol. At last he shrugged. "I ask five thous'. You give it to me, mon? I split."

"You'd ask five. What would you settle for?"

The spike that had replaced Achille's right hand scratched his chin. "For four thous', I think."

"What about thirty-five hundred?"

"You sell for this? Sell to me?"

Skip shook his head.

"Then I don' sell for him too."

"All right, here's my offer. This gun's mine. If you can get it ashore and deliver it to me, at my office, I'll give you three thousand noras. If you don't deliver it, you'll have turned a good friend into an enemy. I'll see to it that you're picked up and deported. Say no deal and walk away, if you won't bring it to me. That way, we're still friends."

Achille hesitated. "Cash. Must be cash, mon, or I don' bring."

"Three thousand noras in cash. Furthermore, if you're caught trying to bring it in, I'll defend you; but only if you say nothing about me to anyone."

Achille nodded. "I don' never talk, mon."

"I may have another gun for you before we dock. If so, I expect the same deal. You'll get three thousand more when you deliver it to me. Six thousand in all."

"I need him soon, mon. Where your office?"

Skip gave him a business card, tucking it into his shirt pocket.

When Achille had gone and Chelle remained in the bathroom, Skip telephoned the bridge. "Is Captain Kain there?"

"Who's calling?"

"Skip Grison."

"I'll see, sir."

A moment later the captain was on the line. *"What's up, Skip?"*

"You dropped by our table at dinner. Virginia was there with an elderly man. Virginia Healy."

"Yes."

"I need information about the elderly man, and I'm hoping you've got some. Who is he?"

"His name? I think it's Coleman Baum. He's a first-class passenger."

"Didn't he shoot somebody? I think I heard that."

"When we were fighting the hijackers? I doubt it. He's too old."

"Later. I've been told he shot one of Mick Tooley's volunteers, a man named Rick Johnson."

"I'll call you back," the captain said, and hung up.

Skip went out onto the veranda and sat down, staring at the sea.

He was still there when Chelle joined him.

"Beautiful, isn't it? Beautiful and immoral."

"I would have said amoral. What have you got on under that robe?"

"Nothing you can see until we're in the cabin with the doors locked and the lights out."

He smiled. "In that case—"

"Not yet. I want to talk. Women want to talk. Have you noticed?"

"No." Skip shook his head.

"Liar! Everybody has. Did I ever tell you how I got to be a mastergunner?"

"I'm not a liar, I'm a lawyer. Tell me how you got to be a mastergunner."

"I'll bet I've told you before, but it's an excuse to talk."

"You haven't." He felt a surge of genuine curiosity. "How did you do it, Chelle?"

"Women make better shots than men. Wait, let me explain. There are men who shoot as well as any woman, a few men who shoot as well as anybody ever can. But men always think they know everything already. They'll keep doing the same thing the instructor has told them twenty times not to do. Like this one student we had, Corporal Nesse. He could make a good fast shot and good slow shot. He could take his time and squeeze off four-hundred-meter groups about as good as you could get with a machine rest."

Skip nodded, feeling it was expected of him.

"Only nothing in between. Put a target at the seventy-meter line drifting off to one side, and he'd shoot like it was ten meters. They sent him to sniper. Buck sergeant is all you get there."

"What about you?" Skip asked.

"I noticed that all the other women wanted to sit down with the instructors and vent. The instructors didn't have time for that. They had a lot to do. So I didn't do it. Anytime I wanted to vent, I vented to somebody else. When I had something to say to an instructor, I said it and got the hell out. It meant I got special attention, because I didn't take up any more time than they needed to give me."

"I want to give you as much time as you want to take," Skip said.

"I know. I appreciate it and I don't want to abuse it, but what I'm trying to say is pretty tough to get out. I cheated on you with Jerry."

Skip shrugged.

"You know about that. Right back there, in the same bed you and I sleep in."

"Correct."

"You also know that he gave me a card for his cabin on the signal deck. You probably think I went up there and we did it again there, only I didn't. The only time I've been in that cabin was when Rick and what's-her-name . . ."

"Susan."

"Right. When they took me there." Chelle's hand found Skip's and held it tightly while she stared out to sea for a minute and more. "I've cheated on you with somebody else, too."

"I know," he said.

"You do?"

He nodded.

"You know who?"

"Yes," he said. "If you want to talk about it, we can. If you don't, we don't have to."

"I'm sorry. You—you were in a coma, and it just happened."

"I understand," he said.

"Then I wanted to tell him we were finished and there would be no more. Only it happened again." For a moment she was quiet. "I know how that must sound. Why aren't you mad?"

It was a good question, and he tried to think of a good answer. "Because I love you so much. I'm angry at Mick, but I owe him a great deal." Skip paused. "I would have said I'd never be able to repay him, but maybe I have. If I act as if I don't know and let him go on thinking that I don't know, maybe it will be paying what I owe."

"I'm money? A kind of money?"

He shook his head.

"Would you have asked me to do it? Because he wanted me, as a way to pay him back?"

"Of course not." Skip sighed. "I'm creating this after the fact. You don't have to tell me that. I could pull the rug out from under him. Destroy his career. I don't want to do it. I could void our contract and get a couple of clients to break your legs. I don't want to do that either."

"But you've thought of it."

He nodded.

"Didn't it ever strike you that I might kill your clients?"

"Yes. That's why I'm offering to get your gun ashore for you. So that you can kill anybody who tried to do it, whether I sent them or not."

"You're serious."

He nodded. "I love you so much that I might do just about anything. I'm not saying that's good or noble or divine. It isn't. It's just how I feel."

When Chelle did not speak, he added, "I can't trust myself."

"Or me."

He shrugged.

"My gun's going to get smuggled in, only I'll do it, not you. If you were doing it, you might be caught. You'd be disbarred."

"I won't be caught."

"Right. If I'm caught, I'll have you outside trying to keep me out of jail—and trying to get me released if I'm convicted."

"I wish you wouldn't."

"Would you rather I dropped it over the side?"

"Yes. Absolutely."

"Then I'll think about it. Maybe I'll do it. If Charlie's spying for the Os, why'd he shoot Rick?"

"To save your life. You're his daughter, whether you've divorced him or not. Rick wanted to kill you and had a pretty good reason for it."

"Think of another reason."

Skip shrugged. "Why should I? I've given you my explanation, and there's nothing wrong with it."

"There's a bunch wrong with it. I heard Charlie arguing, and he said that if they killed me somebody might hear the shot, and even if nobody did, they'd have to get rid of my body somehow, throw it over the side or whatever. Even if they got away with that, people would start looking for me."

"We were looking for you already."

"I know. The thing is, it would be the same thing if he killed Rick. Somebody would hear, they'd find the body, and if they didn't somebody would come looking for him."

"Ipso facto, you're wrong. By your reasoning Charlie should be locked up right now. He's not."

"Wrong!" Chelle's smile was triumphant. "Rick was a spy. Why lock up Charlie for shooting a spy?"

"Was he? Prove it."

"They must have found something showing that he was."

Skip nodded. "Photo ID issued by the Os. That could be it. Or a code book, maybe. Do they speak English?"

"You're making fun of me."

"No, indeed. I'm making fun of your suggestion."

"I could've told them he was a spy." Chelle sounded stubborn.

"And I'm sure they would have believed you. Did you?"

"All right," Chelle said, "you explain. Why's Charlie still loose?"

"After Rick blew up, you and I took that big woman—"

"Trinity. She's a masseuse."

"Thank you. Gary Oberdorf and young Jerry went with us. Charlie and Virginia stayed behind."

"You said that he told her something that made her wait. This was back before dinner. It was probably just who he was. That would have stopped her dead."

"After which," Skip said, "they probably went down to the first-class bar for a friendly drink."

"Stop trying to be funny."

"All right, I will. Rick blew up on the signal deck. Those staterooms belong to the ship's officers, and the bridge is at the end of the corridor. The explosion sounded loud to us because we were in the same room, but it would have been muffled by walls and distance for the officers on the bridge. Even so, the captain would have sent someone to investigate as soon as someone could be spared. Where you there when he arrived?"

"What are you getting at?"

"That someone would probably have found them there; she would certainly have had a few questions for him, and he would have had a few more for her. The officer would have asked them what happened. You know them both a great deal better than I do. What would they have said?"

Chelle looked thoughtful.

"Basically, they would have had four choices. First, they could have said they didn't know, that they had heard the explosion and come to investigate."

Chelle nodded. "That sounds good."

"It could sound better. Charles Blue is a first-class passenger, so his stateroom must be on A Deck, B Deck, or C Deck. The elevators won't run if the distance is less than four floors. Would he, an elderly man, be one of the first to arrive?"

"I suppose not."

"Virginia's even worse. Her cabin's on J Deck. If she were there, she wouldn't have heard the explosion, or would have heard a sound so faint that it could've been anything. So she just happened to be on A Deck talking to Charlie when they heard the explosion and ran up the stairs to check it out together. They could tell that story and stick to it, but they'd certainly come under suspicion."

"And there's what's-her-name."

"Susan. Correct."

"Second choice. Admit that they had been present but say the shot had been fired by someone else. That someone would almost certainly be Susan."

"We saw it. You and I both did. So did Trinity."

"And Jerry, and Gary Oberdorf. It couldn't possibly have worked, in other words. Too many witnesses."

Chelle nodded. "What's the third choice?"

"Say nothing at all. Stand mute. If they had done that, you would have been questioned. Were you?"

Chelle nodded.

"Did you say Charlie did it?"

"Hell, no. I didn't know who he was. I told them this nice old guy had been trying to save my life, and he'd shot the guy who kidnapped me."

"At which point the nice old guy would have been locked up until we made port and the whole mess could be turned over to the police."

"Which didn't happen."

"Correct."

"But if he said he did it, wouldn't they lock him up anyway?"

"Not if he had a get-out-of-jail card. Kiss me, and I'll explain."

It was a lengthy kiss, during which his hand slipped into her robe.

Followed by more kisses.

REFLECTION 18

What Happened—and Might Happen

I have not yet explained it to Chelle, but it seems to me that there is only one explanation and that it is a fairly obvious one. Charles Blue is a double agent. He could not simply have told Captain Kain he was, he had to be the real thing. Captain Kain would then radio South Boswash, trying to be circumspect. (Or so one hopes.)

God only knows who he talked to there, but he was clearly told to keep hands off and mind his own business; and that is what he did.

Was Charles Blue armed? Yes, certainly. Susan saw his gun, or at least saw a telltale bulge in his clothes. By taking her gun and shooting Rick, he wiped out his more dangerous opponent and disarmed the less dangerous one. Furthermore he positioned himself to blame Susan, should that become necessary. He may well tell the Os that she killed Rick.

If he does not, how will he explain his actions? He may find it difficult—but he may not. Rick refused his orders, and that alone could be enough. If it is not, he will point out that Rick was anxious to kill Chelle; with Chelle dead, all chance of resurrecting the knowledge Jane Sims took to the grave would be lost. Better to lose Rick, who had botched his assignment, than Chelle, who may still harbor information of great value. I don't think Charles Blue will have much trouble with the Os; he may well be commended.

Note that all this assumes that Rick did not get that information—that he was so eager to kill Chelle that he was willing to lie about it, to me at least. That was almost certainly the case; he had clearly continued to question her after Charles Blue arrived, which he would not have done if he had what he needed already. He would, in fact, have killed her as soon as he had it.

If Rick believed that Charles Blue was a fellow agent—as he unquestionably did—would Rick not have feared Charles Blue's report? Charles Blue would report that he had tried to preserve the life of the woman who carried the information they sought (information that could surely be obtained by a brain scan), but that Rick had panicked, defied his order, and killed her. Rick must have foreseen that difficulty before I regained consciousness. Once he had foreseen it, his course would have been plain: kill Charles Blue and report that Charles Blue had killed Chelle. He would have one more body to dispose of—six bodies instead five would be no great increase.

What about the authorities here, Charles Blue's human employers? Chelle cannot know anything that they do not already know. They financed the research, and Jane Sims willingly became an Army officer; so they have it. Even if they didn't have it before debriefing Chelle (but they did) they certainly learned anything she may have known at that time. After learning it they would certainly have wiped it.

Their reasons for classifying her as mentally and emotionally unstable are quite plain; she shelters a secondary personality. Since its cause is organic, mere psychiatric treatment will not benefit her. Surgery might cure her—but it might kill her, too, and it would be fiendishly expensive. Better to let her go, which is what they did.

Would it have been better to take Rick alive? Almost certainly not. Who knows what may be learned from his wreckage? If he had been captured, he would very likely have killed himself in way that would have destroyed all the information of interest. Provision for that would be an elementary precaution. As things stand, the NAU still has Chelle for bait. If another Os agent bites, so much the better. She will be in danger, clearly. But her father and his NAU employers will do their level best to keep her alive and sane. The fishermen have found a fine lure. They will want to keep it.

But do I?

19

BACK TO BOSWASH

The building manager met Skip and Chelle in the little lobby beyond the dedicated elevator. "I hope you'll like it, sir," he said. "We didn't have a lot of time."

"It's whether Chelle will like it." Skip glanced at her; she smiled but did not speak.

"Everything's on approval, you understand—all the furniture as well as the pictures. Ms. Moretti charges a base fee for her work, but the furniture and pictures can be returned for full credit. That's individual pieces or everything. It's strictly up to you."

Chelle said, "I'm sure I'll like it."

And Skip, "Let's see it."

"It's terribly—ah—plain." The building manager looked apprehensive. "Simple, you know. Made by Navajos, mostly. The same sort of furniture they built for the first missionaries hundreds of years ago. Functional and sturdy."

"I like that chair." Chelle pointed. "And the settle with the serape over it. Isn't that what you call it? A settle?"

Skip shrugged.

The building manager said, "I'm sure you're right, contracta."

Skip held out his hand for their cards, received two, and opened the door.

Chelle followed him in, shutting it behind her. "This is the penthouse? You said that. Very posh!"

"I hope you'll enjoy it." Skip was looking at the snow-covered roof garden through a Changeglass window that stretched from floor to ceiling.

She joined him. "You know, you tell me a lot, but you don't tell me everything."

"It would bore you to tears. It would bore me just reciting it all, for that matter. I answer your questions as honestly as I can, whenever I can."

"There was no tele on Johanna, maybe I told you." She sounded thoughtful, and almost dreamy. "No tele, but we got to watch telefilms now and then. Long shows made for tele, that had run for an hour every night for a week back on Earth."

"I know what they are."

"After six weeks on line, you went back to a rest camp for a week. You could shower every day if you wanted to, and sleep and sleep with nobody to wake you up. Most of us slept 'til lunch."

Waiting, he nodded.

"There'd be a telefilm as soon as it got dark. Hot dogs and nachos and all that, just like at home. Popcorn. Everybody missed junk food. You didn't have to go, but everybody did."

"Comedies?"

"Sometimes, only we laughed more at the war stuff, the propaganda ones." Chelle fell silent, remembering, pensive and beautiful.

"Go on."

"Only twice they had . . . I don't know what you would call them. They were really lovely and terribly ugly, and the people in them were interesting. Only nothing was ever settled. Nothing in them really made sense."

"Art shows," Skip said.

"I guess. Only after the second one, it came to me. They were real life—it was what our lives are like. It sure as hell was what mine had been like."

The lights flickered.

"I'd left the place where everybody tried to dominate me to come to a place where the Os were doing their level fucking best to kill me, and if

I could fight way out here and live, why couldn't I fight back there? Why go so many light-years away?"

"You're back now." He handed her one of the cards.

"Right. They made me go back." Chelle dropped into a comfortable-looking, rather mannish chair, laying the card he had given her on its broad, flat arm. "When I saw that kind, I wanted to shove the director into a corner and swear to God I'd kill him unless he explained everything. I'll shoot you in the fuckin' head—that's what I'd say."

"I've been shot in the head already," Skip pointed out.

"Yeah." Chelle looked disgusted. "You're way out in front as usual. But you're the director."

"Far from it. I don't even know who runs the show."

"Just for now you are. I just appointed you. When we were living in your place down on whatever floor it is—I mean before we got on that cruise boat—you called this building your building. When you said it, I thought you meant you lived here."

He grinned. "I do."

"Sure. Only it really is your building. You own it, right?"

"There are legal complications, incorporation and so on, but yes. I do."

"There was somebody else living here then?"

Skip nodded.

"Only you kicked him out. That's what you told me you were going to do on the boat."

"I did not. We bought out his lease, that's all. It had less than a year to run, and we were negotiating a new one. We dropped the negotiations and offered him a profit on his remaining time. He took it."

"Who's 'we'?"

"The man you just met. He manages the building for me. I told him what I wanted, and he called me when he had a deal. I told him to take it, clean and fix everything, and line up a decent decorator, meaning not one of the crazy ones, to pick out furniture."

"Your decorator will have gotten a kickback from the guy who sold him the furniture."

"Her. Of course she will. What would you have done?"

"Picked it out myself while we lived in your old place, I guess."

"I see. Do you know a lot about furniture?"

Chelle shook her head. "I like this. How did you know?"

"I didn't. She did. Am I finished as director?"

"Hell, no! You've hardly started. You said Charlie was a double agent."

"I didn't." Skip sighed and leaned against a small but sturdy table, suddenly weary. "I said he had a get-out-of-jail card of some kind. That if he hadn't had one Captain Kain would have locked him up, that he must have told the captain to contact the Civil Intelligence Bureau or some such place. That Captain Kain had, and had been told to release him. You wanted to know how he could have gotten such a thing, and I said that he might be a double agent. That was one possibility and it seemed the most likely."

"But you don't know?"

"No." Skip shook his head. "You're quite correct. I don't know."

"Here's another one. Mother said that you said Rick couldn't have been the one who stabbed her. So who did?"

"Rick, almost certainly."

"You were lying?" Chelle sounded incredulous. "It could have gotten her killed."

"I wasn't lying. I didn't know he was the one. I still don't, although I think it quite probable. When I said what I did, and when I outlined the evidence in his favor, I was trying to show him I didn't suspect him."

Chelle was looking at a desert landscape, and Skip paused to admire her profile. "Do you want the honest truth?"

She nodded.

"All right. I was trying to persuade myself. I liked him and he had gone down into the hold to rescue you. I didn't want it to be him. So I said he wouldn't have had to use a steak knife because he had a license for a gun, and all the rest of that folderol."

"Well, he wouldn't have, would he?"

"If he had his gun on him—if he carried it when he had no reason to think he would need it. But he probably didn't—most people don't."

Chelle nodded reluctantly.

"Just for the sake of argument, let's say he did. A gun attracts a lot more attention than a knife. Guns have serial numbers, too. If he had left it at the scene—"

"He wouldn't. Nobody would."

"Then if he came under suspicion and was searched, it would be found on him."

"It would have been anyway, but the cops wouldn't care. He had a license, and she'd been stabbed. You're saying he was in the suicide ring?"

Skip nodded. "Absolutely. Has it occurred to you that he may not have wanted to kill Virginia?"

"Vannessa. Are you serious?"

"Certainly. She was the senior member."

"Which meant the others were supposed to kill her."

"Correct, and Rick was a member. Suppose he didn't want to die."

"Well, I thought . . ."

"Rick was a spy. Entrée to a group like that could be useful to a spy; it would give him access to a selection of unbalanced people, pathetic individuals who could be easily manipulated by a clever operator."

"Like your secretary."

"Exactly. Rick had taken her to lunch, hoping to learn something about me that would lead him to you, and thus to whatever may remain of Jane Sims."

"You know about her."

"I do."

"I—well, I guess I didn't want you to think I was crazy."

"You're not," Skip said, "and I know it. You came out of an explosion alive, but with a lot of damage. Some of that was brain damage, and the brain tissue you lost was replaced with a transplant from Jane Sims, who had been too badly hurt to live. They would have had brain scans, of course; presumably they uploaded those into somebody else who may go looking for Don Miles. Can we get back to Rick and Susan, or are we through with that?"

"I still don't think you're making a lot of sense. I mean about not killing Mother. Are you saying he stabbed her just for fun?"

"Not at all. For show. He needed to show Susan that he was a good member of the ring, but he didn't want Virginia to die. She was their senior member, after all. Nobody would die until she did."

"Including him."

"Correct. Also including Susan, who seemed certain to be useful to him. He was trying to get his hands on you, and he didn't know—either because Susan hadn't told him, or because Susan herself didn't know—that we had booked on the *Rani*."

"I see." Chelle nodded. "We did that ourselves, online."

"Exactly. From that point on, we can guess pretty easily what they did, and my guess is that Susan did most of it. The news would've told her that Virginia survived. She must have gotten her address from the hospital; quite possibly she had my researcher do it for her. When they got to the apartment, they found it empty, no woman and no clothing. They searched it because Susan hoped to find something that would tell them where she had gone, but they found nothing."

"I've got a another question," Chelle said. "Who planted the bomb?"

"Susan, of course, acting on Rick's orders; and I'll get to that in a moment. Susan quit a few days after we sailed. It must have been a blow to his plans, but she still knew everyone in our office. Somebody told her our ship had been hijacked, and that Mick was recruiting people to rescue us. Rick and Susan joined. They would surely have done that separately; Rick was much too cagey to have them come in together. When they were on Soriano's boat they would have pretended they were strangers who had just met."

"They acted like that on our boat, too."

"Correct. Finding Virginia on the *Rani* must have been a shock, to Rick particularly. But he wanted to get his hands on you, and wanted Susan to help him with it. To get her, he needed to prove that he was a loyal member of the suicide ring. He proved it by having her plant his bomb in the social director's office—a bomb he detonated by broadcasting a signal when he knew Virginia wasn't in there."

Chelle raised a graceful eyebrow. "Why'd he bring a bomb?"

"I don't know, and I don't know that he did. Perhaps the hijackers had one. Rick was down in the hold, too. He may have found a small bomb and decided it might be useful. Or he may have brought one—in imminent danger of capture, he could threaten to kill himself and hostages. He may merely have thought that a device that would permit him to kill while he was elsewhere was apt to be valuable."

"Okay if I ask why you're not sitting down?"

"I was hoping we'd take a look around. Living room, dining room . . . You know."

"Bedroom."

"Yes. There, too."

"Okay, we will. Only we're in the living room now, so all you've got to do is turn your head."

He smiled. "I'd rather look at you. Besides, this is the reception room. It's where our guests take off their coats and our housemaids hang them up. The living room is where the party is, there and perhaps in the family room and the entertainment center."

"No lounge?"

"And the lounge. I forgot."

"The kids will be in the nursery, I suppose."

"Yes. Or the entertainment center."

Chelle nodded to herself. "You want kids?"

"Yes, if you do. Do you?"

"I don't know." She paused, staring out a window. "What about our round-the-world cruise?"

"We'll take it, but not until next year. They don't want you to leave the country."

"I remember. Did you leave your gun on the ship?"

"No. No to both." The colorful sofa was wide, deep, and comfortable. "Are you asking about my pistol or the submachine gun?"

"Either one, I guess—I'd forgotten about the subgun. Don't tell me you tried to bring in that."

"I did not. I threw it over the side, but I kept my pistol."

"The pistol didn't get you busted."

"Correct."

"Have you got it?"

"Not yet. Achille was supposed to take it ashore for me."

Slowly, Chelle nodded. "If anybody could sneak it off the boat, he could."

Watching her, Skip decided that her inquiry was far from idle. He said, "He'll have to sneak himself off. I thought that if he could do it, he could bring my gun—or both our guns—easily enough. Did you get your own gun ashore?"

"Huh uh. I gave it to Charlie. He said he could do it. No problem."

"No doubt he was right."

"Only I don't know where to contact him." Chelle paused. "Do you know where he is?"

Skip shook his head.

"Do you know anybody who would know?"

"Certainly. So do you."

"Give me a minute. . . ." Chelle looked thoughtful. "I got it! Mother."

"Excellent."

The lights flickered again.

"You know where she is?"

"No. I haven't the least idea, and I'm not at all eager to find out." Skip rose and opened a door. "What do I have to do to get you to look at our living room? From what I can see of it, it's really quite beautiful."

"Answer my questions, that's all. I want to know where my mother is. My biological mother. Let's not get into the divorce thing."

Skip said, "I think we ought to call her Virginia Healy."

"That was on the boat."

"Yes. On the *Rani*—and here, too, if you'll take my advice. There's a company called Reanimation Incorporated. Have you heard of it?"

Chelle shook her head.

"I thought not. It probably didn't exist when you went into space."

"Reanimation—you're saying they bring the dead back to life."

"In a way, they do. Anytime anybody enters a hospital for a serious operation, he or she is given a brain scan. When things go wrong, the patient sometimes becomes brain-dead."

"That's dead." Chelle looked decidedly uncomfortable, stretching her long legs out before her and drawing them up again. "If you're brain-dead, you're dead."

Skip shook his head. "Legally, a person is not dead until he—or she—cannot be restored to life."

"Bullshit!"

"Not at all. You have life insurance. I know you do, because all soldiers get it."

"You're right, I do. You're my beneficiary. What the hell does that have to do with anything?"

"Let's say that you were taken to a hospital—the reason doesn't matter. While you were there your heart stopped. That triggered an alarm, and a therapy 'bot kept you breathing and shocked your heart into beating again. Let's also say that I, your beneficiary, knowing what had occurred, then tried to claim your death benefit. No court would award it to me."

"I see. Because I'd been dead, but I was alive now."

"Exactly. Brain death means that thought has ceased. The patient is no longer conscious and will never return to consciousness spontaneously."

"Never wake up. I've got it."

Skip shook his head. "Thought doesn't stop in sleep, it's just that its character changes. Dreams are the most obvious example, but there are others. When a patient is brain-dead, no thought processes are occurring. None at all. There are medical techniques, however, that will sometimes return the brain to normal activity."

Chelle fidgeted. "Are we still talking about my mother?"

"In a way, yes. I was explaining why the brain is scanned. When a previously dead brain is returned to activity, a great deal can be lost. Some memories are always gone, I'm told. Certain skills may be lost as well."

"Like, I might forget how to shoot?"

"Exactly. A brain scan permits the physician to remedy that. The revived brain is wiped clean—all its information is nulled. The scan is uploaded in place of it."

"Do you know," Chelle muttered, "I'm sorry we started talking about this."

"I'm not. It's something I knew I'd have to tell you sooner or later, and

278 ⌒ GENE WOLFE

I want to get out of the way." Skip paused as if to study the off-white walls, the brightly patterned hangings, and the dark, stolid wood. "This was going to be our new home, Chelle. About thirty seconds ago, I realized that it won't be. You and I, as a couple, will never live here."

She straightened up. "What the fuck are you saying?"

"That I've always been a man who relied on reason, on logic, and on precedent; but there is a higher knowing, and sometimes it comes to me. You wanted to know where your biological mother is."

"Yes! I do!" Chelle's hands clenched. "I do, and you'd better tell me."

"Very well. I will. Your biological mother is dead. She died, if I remember correctly, about five years after your leaving Earth. Presumably she is buried somewhere, though she may have been cremated. It shouldn't be hard to find out."

Chelle stared without speaking.

"You'd divorced her before you left; thus you weren't notified."

"What the fuck are you talking about?"

"What Reanimation does is really pretty simple. It uploads a dead person's last brain scan into the brain of a living volunteer."

"That—my mother . . . ? That's what she is?"

"No, that is what Virginia Healy is. The package is costly. I paid to have it done because I wanted to make you happy; I hope you'll take that into consideration."

"But she isn't really my mother?" Chelle looked incredulous.

"That's a question for philosophers. She hasn't lied to you about it, and you need to understand that. She believes that she is your mother, and in fact she's as sure she's Vanessa Hennessey as you are that you're Chelle Sea Blue. Vanessa Hennessey's memories are there, and so is her personality. The genetic heritage isn't. Nor are the fingerprints. She couldn't pass a retinal scan."

"You want me to call her Virginia Healy."

Skip nodded. "I suggest it."

"Do you know what her name was before all this?"

"I do, but it would be nonsensical for anyone to use that name for her now. She wouldn't even recognize it. Mentally, although not physically, she really is Vanessa Hennessey. Or at least, a very close approximation."

"And you are a complete and total bastard!"

"For trying—"

"Shut up! Just shut up!" Chelle was on her feet and raging. "I know everything you're going to say, you sneaky son of a bitch! Shooting me full of dope would have made me happy, too, and by God it would have been cleaner!"

The lights went out. Skip closed his eyes—but heard the door slam.

Later, after he had stacked Chelle's luggage out by the elevator, he called his building manager. "I need the locks changed. Change them, and bring me up the new key-card."

"Just one card, sir?"

"Yes, just one." Skip hung up.

His next call got an answering machine.

His third, the call after that, was to his office. "This is Skip Grison, Boris. I gave the Z man a little job a few days ago. He was to check out a name I'd been given and find out whether there was any such person. I've called his office several times since, but there's nobody there."

"I see . . ."

"I don't want you to start the same investigation, so I'm not going to give you that name. All I want is for you to look around for the Z man. He had a secretary, didn't he? And a Girl Friday? Some kind of assistant?"

"Yes, sir. Yes, he did. Chrissie was the secretary. I think the other girl was Wendy something."

There was a pause.

"Wendy Kaya. She was a criminology major just out of UCTI, but he said she was smarter than a good many people who'd been in the business for twenty years."

"Find Zygmunt if you can." Skip's fingers drummed the table. "Find those girls. The second should be better but either one of them. Get the story and get back to me."

"Yes, sir." Boris paused. "There's a man here who wants to see you.

I know you told Dianne not to bother you today, but since you're on the phone now, I thought I'd tell you. He . . . well, he doesn't have hands, for one thing. He says he's a friend of yours, but he won't even give his name."

"I understand. I know him, and he is. Tell him to wait. Say I'll be there in an hour and I'll see him first. Is he carrying anything?"

"Yes, sir. An old lunch bucket. I suppose it's in case he gets hungry."

Skip smiled. "No doubt you're right. Tell him I'll be there."

After picking up his new card at the manager's office, Skip went to the bank and left with three thousand noras in his briefcase. When he reached the offices of Burton, Grison, and Ibarra, Achille was lounging in the waiting room, his left hook through the handle of a battered black lunch box. Skip nodded, motioned to him, and led him into a small conference room.

"I bring what you give me, mon. I give him back. You got the money?"

"Right here."

"You show him, I show you."

"Fair enough." Skip opened his briefcase and produced packets of bills. "Three thousand was the price we agreed on. These are fifties. There are twenty banded together in each stack, so each stack is a thousand noras. If you want to count them, go ahead."

"I look at, mon." Achille's right hook drew a packet to him. His left held it down while his right tore the paper band.

"Some are new, some aren't. The bank didn't have sixty used fifties."

Achille nodded—mostly, as it seemed, to himself. "Look good, mon. Look real good." Picking up the lunch box, he put it on Skip's desk. "You look, too. I don' cheat you, mon."

Opened, the lunch box revealed a soiled red rag. Skip took it out.

His gun, the sleek gray pistol he had wrenched from Rick Johnson's dead hand, lay upon an even dirtier rag that had once been white. Skip picked the gun up, took out the magazine, and pulled back the slide far enough to see that there was a round in the chamber.

"I don' shoot him, mon. I don' do nothin' to him. He is like you give him to me."

"It's good to see it again."

"I got more. Open like before."

Skip did.

"That man got shot? You got his gun. I got his bullets."

Skip lifted the dirty white rag, finding it heavy and tightly knotted.

"I don' want him to make no noise," Achille explained.

"I understand. How much for the ammunition?"

Achille shook his head. "You say friends? I can be good friend, too."

Skip felt cartridges through the rag and set it down. "I understand. You've earned that money. Take it."

Achille did, inserting the still-banded packets in his pockets dexterously, before he pushed the other bills into a loose stack.

"Want some help with those?"

"I do it, mon. I drop, I get back." He held the stack down with the side of his left hook and folded it over with his right, held it between both hooks, and bit the fold. One hook pulled his filthy shirt out; he bent his head and dropped the bills into it

"You're amazing, Achille."

"Got to be, mon. You know what I do now? Get new hands, the best. They got good here."

Skip nodded.

"I clean up, first. You think I like be dirty? I don', only I been long time. On ship I get shower. Got soap in bottle. I pour on my head, rub with arms, only I don' wash clothes. Need woman for wash. New clothes now an' get room."

Skip smiled. "And after that?"

"New hands, the best. Go somewhere, not here. Only I need paper for police. You know?"

"Indeed I do. Wait a minute." Skip clicked an icon, scrolled, wrote on a pad, and tore off the sheet. "Can you read this?"

Achille glanced at the sheet. "Sure, mon. Miguel Fonseca."

"Correct. He may be able to help you. Tell him I sent you."

"I got it, mon. What cost?"

Skip considered. "It should be under two hundred. He'll ask a lot more if he knows how much you have."

"You say him?"

"No. Of course not."

"I don' neither, mon." Achille rose, grinning. "I got hands, know what I do here? I hold gun, you give me noras, an' I run."

"Would you really do that? I don't believe you."

Achille shrugged. "Maybe. I don' know. *Merci pour votre aide*, mon. Get new hands, papers, go new place. Go Cayenne, maybe. You know Cayenne?"

Skip shook his head.

"I don' neither. Maybe nice place for me. Only I don' see you no more." Achille held out his spiked hook.

Skip rose and shook it. "It's possible we'll meet again. I doubt it, but you never know."

"Is so, mon."

A minute or more after Achille had gone, Skip sat down. For a still longer time, he stared at nothing, sitting quietly with both hands flat upon the polished surface of his desk.

At last he picked up one of the compact telephones there. "Dianne, there's a legal arm down at the south end of the city that represents all the armed services; I think it may be called the Judge Advocate's Department. I want to talk to somebody there, a receptionist if I have to, or a liaison with the civilian justice establishment, if they have one."

He was silent for a few seconds, listening.

"Yes, whatever you can get. I don't know who I should be talking to, but I've got to start somewhere." He hung up.

Another telephone chimed at once, and he answered it. Boris's long, worried face filled the tiny screen. "I've been looking for Stanley Zygmunt, Christine Vergara, and Wendy Kaya, sir."

Skip nodded. "What have you got?"

"Stanley Zygmunt is dead, sir. That was why I called. His body turned up this morning. As of now, I haven't been able to find out where it was or how he died. Or even what condition it was in. They're being very close-mouthed about the whole thing."

"I see."

"The women seem to be missing, sir. Both of them. The police have them listed as missing persons." Boris cleared his throat. "There's no investigation of missing persons, sir. I'm sure you know. They just wait for something to show up on the computer."

"Correct. Discontinue your inquiry—I don't want to lose you."

For a moment Boris was quiet; then he said, "Thank you, sir."

"You're welcome." Skip hung up.

REFLECTION 19

Cobblestones

Someone once said that to destroy a man one need only bring his work to naught. I would say instead that to destroy a man the Fates need only grant his wish. For me—

What of Chelle? She went into space, saying that when she returned she would have a rich contracto and I a young and beautiful contracta. Chelle hasn't been destroyed, nor would I wish her to be. As for me . . . Well, I wished more deeply. For Chelle on Johanna or Gehenna or wherever it was, there can only have been the wish to live. That wish, and that wish alone, if not always at least on many days. She will have wanted life and natural sleep, and no death, no pain.

She very nearly died. Without Jane Sims, she would have died, perhaps; she can't have thought a lot about Earth and a rich contracto. I dreamed of Chelle for hours, almost every day. Granted one wish, I would have wished for what I got, Chelle stepping out of the shuttle, Chelle in my arms.

Yes, even though she did not know me.

I knew then what I had known earlier, although I was loath to admit it. I knew I'd have to win her again, win her a second time; and I told myself that as I had won her once I would win her again, and that I'd begin my second courtship with enormous advantages I had lacked for the first: wealth, position, and a contract already in force.

They have not availed. Should I give up? To give up would be to welcome death, to agree to it, to surrender to it. I will not. My wish has never
changed. "If wishes were cobblestones there would be no grass." Cobblestones could not hurt more.

I never welcomed death on the *Rani*. Some hid and some cowered, and I
understood both all too well. The courtroom had given me so much practice, putting on a brave face for clients I knew would perish, pressing each
argument with every fact I could lay hand to—and every sophistry. With
conviction, above all. Conviction is the seed of passion, and before nine
juries in ten passion will carry the day. How often have I won cases I knew
were lost?

Ellen Woodward had a rifle that might have served some soldier fifty
years ago, Connell a pistol Ellen had to explain to him, and Auciello a
kitchen knife. I told all three to follow me and I kept my game face, though
my heart pounded and my bowels had turned to slop. They followed. Ellen's
bullet took their leader in the face as he aimed at me, and we won.

I won't surrender now. Third time's the charm, they say. Once more,
just once more, and I win. *Omnia vincit amor.*

20

'TIL THEN

Winter had ended, spring had forgotten the city, and the heat had come. A lanky young woman with mismatched hands sweated beside two open windows, under a sodden sheet.

There was a street carnival, and it was already very late. She dodged a man with the pale face of an absentminded angel; he was juggling too many things to count, balls of silver and gold, painted eggs, a black-and-white kitten, a little brown rabbit that looked dead. The crowd jostled her and she jostled back, glad she was on skates when they had none.

A fire-eater lit his torch with a great puff of orange flame; and the rockets came in as if it had been a signal, rockets that flew without a sound, the explosions throwing stones and bodies high into the air. No one in the crowd paid the least attention. She tried to hit the dirt, to fall facedown and take what shelter she could from the cobblestone street; but the crowd pressed her too tightly, the big, fat, frowning, moon-faced man shoving her aside.

"Where's Mick?" She had intended a demand and voiced a plea. An exploding rocket shook the ground and somehow harmed her head. "Where's Mick? I know you know. Please tell me! I've got to find Mick."

The moon-faced man seemed not to hear her and pushed past again, his expression intent and inscrutable.

"Mick! Skip! Skip!"

Someone had opened a cage of white doves, a cage that must have held thousands. They fluttered above the crowd, which fired on them.

"Don! Donny! Where are you, Donny? Where have you gone?"

Something was shaking her shoulders. She trembled, her teeth chattering, as a wounded dove spattered her feet with blood.

"Wake up, Chelle."

Her face was wet. She blinked.

"That's better. I'm right here, darling. Don't be afraid."

He lifted her, sat beside her, and put his arm around her. "What were you dreaming about?"

She wiped away tears with the edge of the sheet, and for a moment failed to recognize him.

"You were talking in your sleep. Then you started crying, and I thought I'd better wake you up."

"I've got a headache." Pressing her temples eased the pain, but only a little.

"Sure, darling," Mick Tooley said. He left, and returned moments later with white tablets and a tinkling glass. Chelle swallowed the tablets without protest and sipped from the glass. Soda water.

"Drink it all," Tooley said, "that's what you need."

She nodded. "Shouldn't you be at the office?"

He glanced at his watch. "I will be in twenty minutes."

"About that job . . ."

He shook his head. "I can't, and I wouldn't if I could. How would it look? He's a senior partner, and he'll be in the office two or three times a week."

"If I could earn some money—"

"We'd get a better place and get out of his building. Right. And I'll find you a job, and we will. Only not at Burton, Grison, and Ibarra. That's out."

"How was I last night?"

"Fine. You were fine." He kissed her forehead. "Now listen up. You drink all of that, then lie back down and go back to sleep if you can. Let those pills work. You'll wake up again around ten, and I'll call you if we can go out to lunch together."

She nodded, and found that nodding hurt. "You can't say for sure?"

He shook his head. "It'll depend on how things go at the office. Every day is different. I told you."

She sipped the soda until the door closed behind him, then held the glass up to the light, which hurt almost as much as nodding. There was no color, but he might have put vodka in it, or gin.

Hoping for vodka, she finished it and carried it out to the kitchen. There would be more soda somewhere, and vodka, too.

Dishes in the cabinet and dirty dishes in the sink. Ice in the little refrigerator, but no vodka and no soda. Come on! It's just a fucking two-room apartment.

There was vodka in the other room, next to the tele—vodka, but no soda. She poured what was left in the bottle over the ice in her glass, and carried the bottle back to the kitchen; there she ran it through the disposer, where it crashed, clicked, and growled.

No soda. She sipped the neat vodka. It burned her throat, and she turned the tap. There was pressure for a change, but the water smelled like sewage.

She threw the whole mess down the drain.

Army water on Johanna had smelled like chlorine; but once she had found a little trickling creek there, and the water had been cold and clean and good, better than any bottled water.

The screen buzzed. Automatically, she blacked the camera and flicked on the picture. Buckhurst's face appeared in the screen, big, black, and scowling. "Ms. Blue? Is this you?"

"Yes," she said, "but I'm not going to turn the camera on. You got me out of bed."

"Sorry, Ms. Blue. Mr. Tooley, he done gone, so I think you be up, too. Man here say he got a package for you. Say you don't know him, only you know the man sent him. I say what his name, only he won't tell. His name Smeedy. He show me his card. Got his name on it an' say he a musician."

"Did he say what was in the package?"

"No, ma'am. Say he don't know."

"Put him on, please."

Buckhurst turned away, and a familiar face appeared on the screen. "I'd like to come up, Ms. Blue. All I have to do is hand you this." The package that he presented for her inspection could easily have been a shoebox wrapped in brown paper. "I'm told it belongs to you."

"I was up late last night," she told him, "and I'm sure I must look like hell. It's twenty-nine eighty-nine, and the door'll be open. Come in and sit down. I'll be in the bathroom splashing stinking water and combing my hair. Make yourself at home. I'll be out in ten minutes."

Softly: "I can just leave your package and go, honey."

"Don't you dare!" Raising her voice, she added, "Let him in, Buckhurst. He's okay."

She had carried a bottle of cologne into the bathroom, and smelled like a flower garden when she came out. He was sitting in Tooley's big vinyl-covered chair, with the package on his lap.

She smiled. "Hello, Charlie."

"No thanks?" His eyes—the bright blue eyes she had inherited—twinkled. "I risked prison for you. I deserve a kiss."

"You didn't. But you'll get one anyway." She bent, and her lips brushed his.

"Since I'm no longer your father, I can ask you for a date."

She straightened up. "You can, and I might go. Is it a good show?"

"How about a picnic?"

"You're serious?"

"Entirely serious, honey."

"I'd offer you a drink if it wasn't so early. Would you like me to make coffee?"

He shook his head. "We need to talk to you, honey."

"We?"

"I thought I'd bring my wife."

She sat on the couch, one long leg drawn up. "You two think I'm getting fat."

He shook his head again.

"Do you know about her? That's not really Vanessa."

"Depends on what you mean by really."

"Well, I am getting fat. Fat and soft. See, I know all about it, so Mother doesn't have to make those cream-cheese-and-watercress sandwiches."

He said nothing.

"Fat and soft, and I've been drinking too much. I know that, too. What else is there?"

"Now it's my turn to change the subject. Do you want to open this box? Check it over?"

"No, I don't. How much is she costing you? How much a hundred-day, or how much a year? However you're paying."

He grinned, displaying teeth more regular than she remembered. "Your mother ought to have taught you that it's impolite to ask how much things cost."

She started to say, *I don't consider her a thing*, when she realized she did. She substituted, "There are times when I've got to make exceptions. How much, and when will you get tired of paying?"

"She's cost me quite a bit so far. Dresses and shoes and jewelry, none of them cheap."

"That wasn't what I meant, and you know it."

"Then nothing." He was no longer grinning. "You're asking about Re-animation?"

She nodded.

"Nothing. That file is closed, and Reanimation gets to stay in business. They were greatly relieved."

"I don't even know whose body it was. Skip knew, but he wouldn't tell me."

"That was probably wise."

"So you're not going to tell me either?"

"At the picnic, perhaps. It will be up to my wife. What would you do if you knew the name?"

"Damned if I know. Find her family, I guess, and tell them what happened."

"They think she's dead, and they're right. She was suicidal, honey. That's why she did it, why she went to work for Reanimation. This is what she was hoping for."

Chelle rose and went into the bathroom. When she came out, her eyes were dry once more and the lean, white-haired man who was no longer her father had gone.

She had gotten dressed slowly, thinking of breakfast. As a civilian, she had always hated going into restaurants alone. Now she was a civilian again. She could make her own breakfast—SoySunRise, milk, and coffee or tea—or go out.

Find a restaurant and go into it alone.

The street was filled with sunshine and clogged with patient trucks, hulking yellow buses, gliding bicycles, and hunchbacked cars. She flipped a mental coin and turned to her left, a slender, hard-faced blonde taller than most men. After two blocks of shops, she was about to stop someone and ask about a good place to eat when she saw the cheerful red-and-white sign: Carrera's Café. The café was plainly open and serving, though not now (Chelle glanced at her watch) terribly busy. She went in and took a booth.

She had finished ordering by the time the lost woman came in. The lost woman looked at her and looked again; Chelle looked back and—after a second or two—waved. "Sit down."

"I . . . Really, I wouldn't want to intrude."

"You're not." Chelle kept her voice low. "There's nobody seating people, and you don't want to sit alone. So you sit here with me. Solves both problems."

The lost woman nodded gratefully. "My name's Martha Ott."

"Pleased to meet you, Martha," Chelle said, and held out her hand.

The lost woman accepted it doubtfully, held it a moment, and released it.

"What would you like for breakfast? I'm having ham and pancakes."

"Oh, I've already eaten breakfast." The lost woman tittered. "That was hours ago! I just—just wanted a place . . ."

"Where you could sit down," Chelle added helpfully.

"Y-yes. And have some tea."

"And toast? I like toast myself, when I'm not having pancakes."

"Oh! So do I, ever so much! Cinnamon toast."

Chelle waved at a waitress. "Martha wants tea and cinnamon toast. Put it on my bill."

"I don't know about the cinnamon toast," the waitress told her. "It's not on the menu."

Chelle leveled a finger at her. "Any jerk can make cinnamon toast—it takes about five seconds. You tell your fucking cook we want cinnamon toast, and we want it fast. Now get going!"

The lost woman tittered and the waitress scampered.

"You and me," Chelle said, "are going to help each other out. You're going to tell me your troubles, and I'm going to sympathize with you. Then I'm going to tell you mine, and you're going to sympathize with me. By that time we ought to be through eating, and we'll both feel a whole lot better."

"Do you know," the lost woman said, "you remind me of somebody I went to school with. That's why I was looking at you."

Chelle grinned. "She was shot up, too, I guess."

"Shot up?"

"You ought to see my scars."

"She—she wasn't shot. She was captain of the fencing team. Just wonderful at sports, you know. I wasn't, and I envied her, oh, terribly!"

"Maybe she envied you, too."

The lost woman cocked her head thoughtfully. "I, well, I really don't think she did."

Chelle's phone played. Telling the lost woman to wait a moment she answered it. "I'm in this place right now. Why don't you join us when you can get away?"

She listened for half a minute, then said, "Carrera's. Carrera's Café. It seems to be pretty cheap and pretty good."

She listened again. "Okay. Love you! Bye."

As she shut her phone, the lost woman said, "Your contracto?"

"Not yet. Just a boyfriend. He's been trying to find me a job, and he's got something he wants to talk about."

The lost woman looked stricken. "I suppose I ought to leave."

"Hell, no. I want you to meet him. Besides it'll be a while before he shows up, and I need somebody to talk to. What's troubling you?"

"I—I'm lost, that's the main thing. . . ."

"Where are you trying to get to?"

"I know where I am, it's just that I don't know what to do."

While Chelle was nodding sympathetically and sipping her coffee, the waitress arrived with tea, ham, pancakes, and a cruet of syrup. "The cook won't make you cinnamon toast," the waitress told them. "He says it's not on the menu, so he won't cook it."

Chelle rose. "I'll talk to him."

Another waitress, emerging with a tray from an arch at the back of the café, betrayed the location of the kitchen. A sweating fat man was flipping burgers there while a much smaller man with the furtive manner of the oppressed loaded a dishwasher.

Chelle approached the fat man. "What's your name?"

"Who wants to know?"

"I was hoping we could be polite about this." Chelle stepped nearer and her voice hardened. "That's what I was hoping, but I can play it any way you want, buster. I can have you down on that floor yelling for mercy in less time than it takes a rat to shit."

"Lady . . ."

"Shut the fuck up!" Chelle's left hand gripped her blouse and tore it. "I'll have you down there, and I'll start screaming. I'll say you tried to bite my tits, and by God I'll have you locked up in an hour. I'll sign every complaint the cops shove at me, understand? And I'll cry my eyes out at your trial, and you'll do ten fuckin' years easy. Get the picture?"

The cook looked as if he were about to spit, threw his arms up in a gesture that sent his spatula flying, and fell at her feet.

"That was just a sample." She bent over him, almost whispering. "Make us cinnamon toast, buster. Make it good, and make a lot of it, or I start yelling. Only I mess you up a whole lot more first."

He groaned.

"Which is it? Cinnamon toast or jail?"

Grinning, Chelle returned to her booth.

"Goodness!" The lost woman's eyes were wide. "What happened to you?"

"My shirt?" Chelle glanced down at the tear. "Oh, the cook did that. It doesn't matter."

"I think I've got a pin . . ." The lost woman snapped open her purse.

"It's okay." Chelle cut a piece of ham and forked it into her mouth. "Tell me about being lost."

The lost woman did, and at some length, while finding a small safety pin and pinning Chelle's blouse to her own satisfaction.

"Your kids don't need you anymore and your contracto never did," Chelle summed up for her as a heaped platter of cinnamon toast arrived. "You need to be needed. Maybe we all do. That's it, isn't it?"

"I . . . Well, I just feel so helpless. And I feel like I ought to die."

"Do you know about the soldiers in the hospitals?"

The lost woman shook her head.

"If the docs can patch you up in a hundred-day or so, they keep you up there, on whatever crazy planet it is. But the long-term cases get shipped back here. Some of them won't be well for years. Some won't ever be, not unless the doctors figure out something new."

The lost woman's nod was hesitant and small, but it was unmistakably a nod.

"You said you had two boys. What're their names?"

"Jack and Jeff . . . That's what we call them, I mean. Their real names are Jeffrey and—"

"Doesn't matter. Jack's older?"

The lost woman nodded, positively this time. "By two years. We spaced them like that."

"Okay, let's suppose Jack went into space. Say that he enlisted at twenty. Jeff was eighteen. Jack's off fighting for a couple of years, his time. When he comes back, it's been more than twenty. His folks are dead, and his kid brother's pushing forty and lives in the EU. Get the picture? Jack's in some hospital hooked to a bunch of machines, and nobody gives a damn. You're your Jack's mother. How about if you go to some of those hospitals and be my Jack's mother? I'm not going to tell you you'll get your reward in heaven or any of that shit, because I don't know. But one day pretty soon you'll get your reward from my Jack's eyes."

Chelle paused, and sighed. "I spent a hundred-day plus in a hospital once, and believe me you will."

For a time that seemed stretched, the lost woman was silent, nibbling while she watched Chelle eat. At last she smiled. "I . . . Well, I'm not a forceful woman, but I'm going to do it. I spend hours and hours shopping. Just shopping for nothing, really. Or watching tele. Vic can't object, but if he does I'm going to do it anyway."

"Good for you!"

They had nearly finished eating when Mick Tooley came in. He grinned and said, "Hi, Chelle! Who's your friend?"

Chelle slid over to make room for him. "Martha, this is Mick." Her right eyelid drooped. "He's the wonderful boyfriend I was telling you about."

Tooley produced a card and handed it across the table. "You hang on to this, Martha. Call me anytime you need somebody kept out of jail."

"He's a lawyer," Chelle explained.

"A good one. What's with all the cinnamon toast?"

Chelle said, "The cook made it for us."

The lost woman nodded. "She made him do it." After a glance at Tooley's card the lost woman added, "I asked for cinnamon toast, Mr. Tooley, and she's a very kind person."

296 ∿ GENE WOLFE

"I know," Tooley said.

"I didn't even have to pull my gun." Chelle took a piece of cinnamon toast. "We'll call this the appetizer before our early lunch."

"It looks like you just finished breakfast. You sure you want lunch?"

"I'll order something light, like a roast pig with an apple in its mouth. You know. Have you got me a job?"

"I think so. They want to talk to you first, but you're a natural and I've got the screwdriver." Tooley demonstrated, tightening an imaginary screw. "We used to use the Zygmunt agency, a little shop over on a hundred and fifty-first, only Zygmunt's dead and it looks like they've closed. So we're looking at some others."

"He's talking about private investigators," Chelle told the lost woman. "Lawyers use them all the time."

"Right. This outfit, Confidential Security Research, would love to have our business. I've told them they ought to staff up a little for us, and I've made an appointment for you."

"Honestly, Mick, I'd like to get this job because somebody wants me."

The lost woman said, "You are."

Tooley looked startled, then nodded. "That's right. And they'll want you, too, once they get to know you. You'll see."

"I hope so." Chelle's coffee cup was empty; she pushed it away.

"And another thing," announced the lost woman, who no longer looked even a little bit lost. "I've been thinking and thinking, and I've finally re-membered the name of that girl I went to school with. Her name was Shelly. Shelly something with a B. Shelly Blaine or something like that."

"Was she nice?" Chelle asked.

The no longer lost woman slid to the end of her seat and stood. "Very nice. Good at games, you know, and she could run like the wind. But a really nice girl. Now I've got to go. It was wonderful talking to you, but if I'm going to see Jack I've got to get started."

"Who was she?" Tooley asked when she had gone.

"A girl I went to school with, only her name was Martha Watson then. She used to help me with my math."

"Are you sure you're up to eating lunch?"

"I told you, a wild boar's head with an apple in its mouth. Those things take a long time to cook."

Tooley took a bite of cinnamon toast. "This is good."

"You're hungry. I bet you didn't eat breakfast this morning. I'll eat the toast and I might steal your food, too. Now order something."

Tooley did. The café was beginning to fill, harried office workers with an hour for lunch and no time to look at the menu. The waitress who had taken Tooley's order brought Chelle more coffee.

Not long after that, an Army officer came in. Chelle, who had to repress the impulse to stand and salute, needed a full six seconds to recognize him. Tooley, who did not, took even longer.

By which time Skip had reached their booth. "Glad I found you," he told Chelle. "I was going to call you after I got some lunch."

"You joined." For an instant Chelle's voice faltered. "You're JAG, by God!"

Tooley said, "What's that?"

"He's in the Judge Advocate General's Department." Chelle pointed. "See? Crossed gavels on his lapels."

"Nobody knew where you were, Skip." Tooley seemed on the point of stammering.

"Luis did, he just wasn't talking. I asked him not to, in case I washed out."

Chelle said, "You're a major, so you didn't."

"Correct. I didn't. They call it officers' school. Do you know about it?"

Chelle nodded.

Tooley said, "I don't. What is it?"

"Easier than I expected, for one thing. Basically, it's a three-week crash course in how to be an officer. How to salute and return salutes, how to wear the uniform, the moral code expected of an officer and so forth. Say that some kid just out of law school wants to join. He looks good, he's physically fit, and they need him. They send him to officers' school, and he's commissioned as a second lieutenant when he finishes it."

"You're not a second lieutenant," Tooley said. "Major sounds pretty important."

Skip shrugged. "I've been practicing law for over twenty years, and I've made something of a reputation, so that's one thing. Another is that my field is criminal law, which is basically what military law is. Disobeying an officer's direct order is a crime, punishable by death or such lesser penalty as the court may decree, *et hoc genus omne*. But is Private Doe guilty of it? Were there mitigating circumstances? It's all pretty familiar." Skip paused. "Another thing was that I was asking to go into space."

Despite the noise surrounding them, Chelle's gasp was audible.

Skip grinned. "They don't hear much of that. Most of those new lieutenants want to stay right here, so there was that. Still another thing was that a second lieutenant my age would look silly."

Chelle said, "You're going up there." It was not a question.

"I am. I'd been holding out for a captaincy, telling them I wouldn't enlist without it. General Le Tourneur called me in. He's the Judge Advocate General, the Armed Service's top attorney. We must have talked for an hour or more, but main things were that he was going to make me a major, and as soon as I was actually out there I would be promoted again, jumping a grade to full colonel."

"You were going to call me." Chelle's voice quavered. "You said that."

"I was. I wanted to tell you where I was going, and why." Skip paused again, waiting for a question; but none came. "I can't tell you what planet they plan to send me to. That would be secret even if I knew it, and I don't. The why . . ." He shrugged. "I suppose it's obvious enough."

"I'd like you to say it just the same."

"All right. I want us to be about the same age. It won't be exact, I know; but we'll be a lot closer than we are now. My hair will be a little grayer and a little thinner. You'll be a middle-aged woman. If you want me, I'll be yours for the asking. If you don't . . ." He shrugged. "I'll try to find something else to live for."

Tooley said, "What about the firm? You'll be creating one hell of a vacancy."

"Ibarra can run things in my absence, and do it about as well as I could." Skip was brusque. "As for me, I'm a senior partner, and I'll remain a senior partner. There are hardnosed statutes protecting the rights of men and women who go into the armed services. If you don't know about them, I advise you to bone up on them."

He turned back to Chelle. "A court will void our contract if you try hard enough. Mick can tell you all about that. You may have contracted with him or someone else by the time I'm sent home. I realize that. If you haven't—well, you know. Now it's goodbye until then."

"Not before I kiss you. Get out of the way, Mick."

Tooley slid to the end of the seat and stood, and Chelle slid as he had, rose, and embraced Skip. "I can't make a kiss last twenty years," she told him, "but I'm going to try."

It was in fact a long, long kiss. When it was over, Skip turned and left the café.

Chelle followed him and stood on the sidewalk watching him—his bright blue dress uniform made him stand out—and heard not a word when her heart poured from her lips. "I didn't want to tell you, but now you can't hear me. And they'll be after me, whoever it was that hired Ortiz and his gang. You wondered why they wanted you? Why they sent Achille for you, to bring you back to them? It was because they wanted me, and you should have seen what they did to me when they had me, trying so hard to drag out Jane Sims and everything she knew."

A woman like a small, gray mouse touched Chelle's arm. "You're talking to yourself, darling. Did you know it? Talking out loud?"

"Bad, mad Chelle!" She nodded, smiling. "I'm psycho, that's why the Army doesn't want me anymore. Only I was really talking to somebody, to that major in dress blues. See him? He's crossing the street now."

"Yes. Yes, I do, darling. He can't hear you."

"That's the good thing about it." Chelle's smile was still there. "If he could hear me, he'd come back and we'd be miserable all over again."

She turned away from the mousy woman. "They think I've got part of Jane Sims's brain, Skip. That's the EU, because I think it was them, and the Os, because they sent poor Rick. Only I don't. All I've really got is her left arm up to the shoulder, only I feel her in me sometimes just the same, so I'm psycho and the Army won't take me back."

He had vanished among hundreds of other pedestrians. She stood beside the mousy woman for a moment longer, and another moment after that, before she turned away and began to walk.

REFLECTION 20

Walking

The fat man who kept pushing past me was God, and Charlie. Or was Charlie, who was God. When you're a little kid, you think your father is God. That's wrong, but maybe I went too far the other way. Where the hell's Charlie now? I have to tell him I want to go on his picnic.

Most of all I want to get out of this city, get away from the dirt and cold and these gray-faced people. I'm turning into one of them, and I'd rather be dead.

Maybe you go to the dream-world when you're dead, maybe that's what death feels like. Tell me, Jane? Can you hear me? You're dead, so what's it like? Do you see the white pigeons, white pigeons falling from the sky, all speckled over with their own blood? People are so damned cruel.

I didn't run out on Skip because he tried to make me happy, I ran out because he thought that horrible thing he did would make me happy and after that I knew I could never trust him anymore, that when he gave me something there might be dead kids behind it, might be anything behind it, any kind of murder.

I killed Mort Pununto. I know I did. They were all saying afterward that they hadn't aimed at him, that they'd made sure they missed. I'd aimed for the middle of his chest, and what I aim at, by God I hit.

So I looked in the truck where they'd put his body, and there he was,

Master Sergeant Pununto, the best damn noncom I ever saw. And he didn't look one fuckin' bit like he was asleep. He looked dead and he was dead, and there was my bullet hole in the middle of his chest three buttons down and no other bullet holes at all. And I knew then why they had put me on the firing squad.

Goodbye, Mort! Sometimes I see you in my dreams. I guess I always will.

You and Skip.

Is the Army a kind of death? Or is death a kind of enlistment? If it is, we all enlist, even if we don't want to.

We're sick of this life. Was I sick of winning the fencing tournament, sick of being the star pitcher on the softball team? No, sick of being out of college and in a world where I couldn't do any of that, sick of living with Skip in a studio apartment. Sick of waiting for him to come home so I'd have somebody to bitch at. We weren't going to last a year, and I knew it.

So I joined, and then he wanted to contract and I said sure, darling, you wait for me.

The Army seemed so damned glamorous then. And damn it, up there it was glamorous! We were us. That was the big thing. We were us, and we could tell an officer to fuck off if we wanted to, because what was he going to do? Lock us up where the Os couldn't get at us? Some fucking punishment! Not that we did it a lot. Our officers were fighters, or most of them were.

So was Mort Pununto and I killed him.

He enlisted. He was sick of whatever it was he'd been living in the EU, so he signed up for a job he must have known would get him killed within a year or two. He signed up for death.

Skip's a fighter, too. I was surprised, on the boat. Skip with a subgun, jumping the rail with the gun in one hand; we used to call them rattle-snakes, those little short-barreled subguns.

I should've known. How many battles in court, risking disbarment, risking everything to set some scumbag free? Then blam! He came back to our stinking studio and he's signed on with Chet Burton. God knows I didn't know much, but I knew who Chet Burton was, the guy the celebrities went to when it was win or die and blood on the knife in their car.

So he was higher than Johanna, so I rained on his parade. But he was always a fighter.

Old and tired, in the penthouse he'd fixed up for me. Around the world next year, only no next year. So long, buddy. So long, Skip. The way I am now, you're better off without me.

I'm going on Charlie's picnic, out of the smoke and the dirt, away from Mick and the bottles behind the bar, and the all the gray faces. I'm going away, and I'm not coming back.

They'll tell me when you do, and I'll be there.

CHARACTERS

Note: The most important persons are listed here, with a few of lesser importance. Listings are by the name most often employed in the text. Thus SKIP Webster Grison will be found under "S," and Captain Richard KAIN under "K."

ACHILLE   A beggar lacking hands.

BORIS   The chief researcher at Burton, Grison, and Ibarra.

BRICE, Lt. Gerard   Second mate of the *Rani*.

CHARLES C. Blue   CHELLE's biological father.

CHELLE Sea Blue   SKIP's college sweetheart and contracta. Note that her first name is pronounced "Shell."

DIANNE Field   SUSAN Clerkin's assistant.

DON Miles, Cpl.   A soldier on leave.

FEUER   A vice president of Reanimation, Inc.

JANE Sims   A physicist.

JOHNSON, Rick   One of Mick TOOLEY's volunteers.

KAIN, Capt. Richard   Master of the *Rani*.

KENT-JERMYN, Sgt. Gerald   A soldier on leave.

NAN Olivera   Sgt. KENT-JERMYN's contracta.

OBERDORF, Gary   A mechanic on the *Rani*.

SKIP Webster Grison   The managing partner at the law firm of Burton, Grison, and Ibarra.

SORIANO   The soldier of fortune employed by Mick TOOLEY to retake the *Rani*.

SUSAN Clerkin   SKIP's confidential secretary.

TOOLEY, Mick   A young attorney at Burton, Grison, and Ibarra.

TRINITY   The masseuse on the *Rani*.

UEDA, Dr.   The pediatrician who becomes the *Rani*'s doctor.

VANESSA Hennessey   The woman who meets CHELLE when she returns to Earth. Aboard the *Rani* she is known as VIRGINIA Healy.

ZYGMUNT   A private investigator often called "the Z man."